Strivers Row

During the 1920s and 1930s, around the time of the Harlem Renaissance, more than a quarter of a million African-Americans settled in Harlem, creating what was described at the time as "a cosmopolitan Negro capital which exert[ed] an influence over Negroes everywhere."

Nowhere was this more evident than on West 138th and 139th Streets between Adam Clayton Powell and Frederick Douglass Boulevards, two blocks that came to be known as Strivers Row. These blocks attracted many of Harlem's African-American doctors, lawyers, and entertainers, among them Eubie Blake, Noble Sissle, and W. C. Handy, who were themselves striving to achieve America's middle-class dream.

With its mission of publishing quality African-American literature, Strivers Row emulates those "strivers," capturing that same spirit of hope, creativity, and promise.

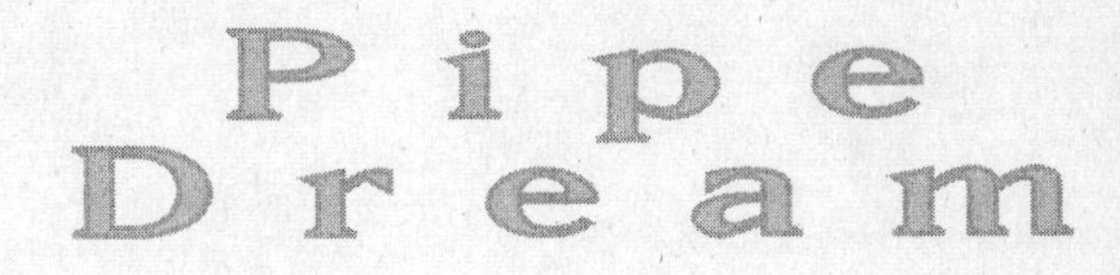
Pipe
Dream

Villard/Strivers Row
New York

Pipe Dream

Solomon Jones

a novel

 Published in the United States by Strivers Row, an imprint of Villard Books, a division of Random House, Inc., New York, and simultaneously in Canada by Random House of Canada Limited, Toronto.

Library of Congress Cataloging-in-Publication Data

Jones, Solomon

Pipe dream: a novel / Solomon Jones.

p. cm.

ISBN 0-375-75660-4 (trade pbk.)

1. Police—Pennsylvania—Philadelphia—Fiction. 2. Philadelphia (Pa.)—Fiction. 3. Narcotic addicts—Fiction. 4. Crack (Drug)—Fiction. 5. Politicians—Fiction. I. Title.

PS3560.O5386 P56 2001

813′.6—dc21 00-068049

Villard Books website address: www.villard.com

Printed in the United States of America

98765432

First Edition

Book design by Mercedes Everett

For my wife, LaVeta, who stepped into my world and made it beautiful. And for my brother, Brian. I love you.

Acknowledgments

First, I must thank my Lord and Savior Jesus Christ, without whom none of this would be possible. My deepest gratitude to my inspiration, my lover, my wife, LaVeta, who believed in my work and edited the later drafts so wonderfully. Thanks to my parents, Solomon and Carolyn Jones, and my grandmother Lula Richards, for never giving up on me. Thanks to my aunt Juanita Bryant, who came out to the corner to pray for me. Thanks to my daughter, Adrianne, just for being. I love you. My undying gratitude to Susan Jacobs, who walked into a shelter and gave me a second chance at life. Thanks to Ben Jacobs for his wise counsel on the publishing industry. Thanks to Barnett Wright and Arlene Morgan, my mentors. Thanks to Vanesse Lloyd-Sgambati, whose recommendation opened doors. Thanks to Kristi Zea and Dick Dilsheimer, who shared their wisdom and contacts so unselfishly. Thanks to Manie Barron, who believed in this work. Thanks to the *Philadelphia Weekly* for publishing the first excerpt. Thanks to Victoria Sanders and Angela Cheng, my agents. Thanks to Melody Guy, my editor. Thanks to Avis Davenport, who read the very first draft. Thanks to the streets that taught me the hard truths contained in these pages. And thanks to you, my readers. You are the mirror that reflects the essence of each story I tell.

Pipe Dream

Prologue

Black sat handcuffed to a table in the prison's visiting room, waiting for his court-appointed lawyer to come for his final visit before the trial. The visits were a formality, really. They both knew it. The lawyer was always polite about it, though. Black had to respect that.

But that didn't change the reality. The man who was tethered to the table was poor and he was black. Which meant that he would probably be found guilty of first-degree murder and sentenced to death in the shooting of city councilman Johnny Podres. Statistics dictated it.

Still, they had to go through with the routine. The lawyer would come in and ask about what happened that night. Black would refuse to talk. The lawyer would assure him that he knew he was innocent. Black would remain silent. This would go on for an hour or so, and then the lawyer would leave.

That was the normal routine. Today, it was going to be different. Black had finally seen enough and read enough to piece together exactly what happened and why, thanks to the yearlong media coverage of the Podres murder. The only missing piece was his own. And he was just about ready to fit it into the puzzle.

The buzzer rang, the lock on the door clicked, and the guard escorted the lawyer into the room.

"Hello, Samuel," the lawyer said.

Black didn't respond. It was strange to hear someone use his given name. For as long as he could remember, people had always called him Black, because his skin was like a layer of liquid chocolate. The name fit. At least it used to. But here, behind the walls that had been his home for the last year, nothing fit. Not his name, not his past, not even the truth. Which was why he'd refused to speak before. Something inside him had told him that the truth wouldn't matter.

"You know we go to trial in two days," the lawyer said, breaking into his thoughts. "And I've got to tell you, I won't be able to provide an effective defense without your cooperation. Now, I can step down and let the court find you another lawyer. Or I can stay on and do the best I can with whatever you give me. It's up to you."

"I'm ready to talk," Black said, interrupting the lawyer's standard speech.

The lawyer cocked his head to one side. "What did you say?"

"I said I'm ready to tell you what happened."

The lawyer fumbled around in his briefcase, took out a tape recorder, and placed it on the table, then took out a notepad and pencil. "Okay," he said, visibly flustered. "I guess the first question I should ask you is this: Did you kill Johnny Podres?"

"No questions. I just want you to turn on the tape recorder. You have more than one tape, right?"

"Yes, but I—"

"Good. Just turn on the tape recorder. You got any smokes?"

The lawyer turned on the tape recorder, handed his client a cigarette, and lit it for him. Black drew hard, squinting as the smoke rushed into his lungs.

"Where do you want to start?" the lawyer said, lighting a cigarette of his own.

"I guess there's only one place to start—at Broad and Erie."

Chapter 1

The priest pulled up outside the church, put his car in park, and walked inside, glancing backward to see that he had locked the doors, as was his practice. Black and Leroy knew his habits, like they knew everyone else's habits, because they watched. And watching paid off when it came to breaking into cars.

Of course, watching paid off with houses, too. But they tried to stay out of houses, because you could get caught in a house with nowhere to run. And there's nothing quite like being distracted from the task of rummaging through someone's bedroom drawers by the sensation of cold steel pressed against the back of your neck.

Cars aren't quite that risky. People walk away from their cars and leave all kinds of things inside. Once, they watched a man walk into one of the clubs on Broad and Erie with two women—right after he'd opened his trunk and put their fur coats inside. Another time they watched someone leave a case of CDs sitting on the front seat of his car as he went inside the barbecue place to order half a slab of pork ribs. They even profited from auto accidents. Like the time a woman crashed her car into a pole in front of the chicken place and left it there with a brand-new JVC system inside—complete with equalizer, subwoofers, CD changer, and amplifier.

Unattended cars often meant money. But on Sunday nights, when everything was half speed, there weren't any unattended cars with anything inside, which meant that there was only the flat-tire thing. And Black knew that Leroy was intent on doing the flat-tire thing that night.

"I gotta get p-paid," Leroy said, talking quickly and with a slight stutter as he looked over his shoulder.

"You just did him two days ago," Black said, knowing that Leroy wasn't one to listen to reason. "Just wait for somebody else."

"Man, I'm not waitin' for nobody else."

Black smiled, knowing that Leroy seldom waited for anything, especially when he wanted to get high.

And that night, like every other night, Leroy wanted to get high. Black knew that Leroy wouldn't do anything else until he had hustled up enough money to get a hit. He also knew that after the first hit, they would both be off to the races.

Leroy had just smoked two treys—three-dollar caps—so it was just a matter of time before he slashed the priest's tire. Black knew this because he knew Leroy. He even knew how Leroy would go about it.

First, Leroy would take about thirty seconds to convince himself that slashing the priest's tire would work, even if he knew in his heart that it wouldn't. Second, he would poke a hole in the tire and wait for the priest to come out of the church. Then he would walk by, see the priest struggling with the flat, and offer to help him change it. If everything went right, the priest would pay him and Leroy would run up to Pop Squaly's and buy five caps. If Black stayed close by, Leroy would probably give him one.

"He ain't gon' know," Leroy said. "How he gon' know?"

He said this more to convince himself than to convince Black. He probably knew that Black thought he was stupid to do the same thing to the same person less than a week after the last time he did it. Black started to tell him as much, but thought better of it.

"All right," Black said evenly. "I'll be over there."

He walked across Broad Street and watched as Leroy poked the hole in the priest's tire. All Black could do was laugh, because he knew it wouldn't work. But Black didn't have anything else to do, so he stood over by the barbecue place, waiting, like Leroy, for the priest to come out of the church.

He didn't have to wait for long.

The priest came out and looked at his tire, then Leroy came out from behind Lee's Chicken and walked by like he was just passing through. Black couldn't help smiling because, even from across the street, he could tell that Leroy was trying to look like a straight-up Good Samaritan.

His smile broadened as he watched Leroy walk up to the priest, follow his gaze to the flat tire, and throw his hands up in the air as if to say, "Not again!" Like he was really sympathizing with him.

The priest didn't react so dramatically. In fact, Black could tell that the priest saw right through Leroy's little game. But Leroy couldn't see that. He probably thought the priest was just disappointed that he'd gotten another flat tire so quickly. And the priest let him go right on thinking that.

After Leroy went through his little act, the priest gestured toward the tire and told him to go ahead and change it. But the priest's face was flushed with anger. He was trying to act like he was grateful that Leroy had come along, though he probably was just trying to figure out what to do next. While Leroy examined the tire, waiting for the priest to get his tire iron out of his trunk, Black eased back into the shadow of a trash-filled doorway and watched through the darkness as Leroy's master plan unraveled.

The priest told Leroy to wait, then went back inside the church. To Black's amazement, Leroy waited.

If the priest had done that to Black, he would have known, no matter how much he wanted another cap, that the man was going back inside the church to call the police, because Black got paranoid when he took a hit. Leroy wasn't like that, though. He took a hit and thought he was John Gotti. He would do things in broad daylight and get away with them because, in his mind, he was invincible. Sometimes Black thought he was, too. This wasn't one of those times. This was one of those times Black wanted to grab Leroy by the neck and make him stop. But by the time he made up his mind to go across the street and do that, it was too late.

Just as the priest came out and made his way down the church steps, the cops rolled up on Leroy. When Black saw them, he crept back farther into the trash-strewn hallway, because he and Leroy had done so much dirt together that Black was used to getting arrested every time Leroy was.

As Black watched, the two white cops and the white priest gathered around Leroy, gesturing toward the tire. Images of Rodney King popped into Black's mind. And then the images vanished. After all, five or six cops on a dark road beating a big man like Rodney was a far cry from two cops and a priest beating a piper near Broad and Erie, one of the busiest intersections in North Philly. It just wasn't going to happen. The cops beating a piper in a squad car or at the station was a different thing altogether. But from what Black could see, Leroy wasn't going to make it to the squad car, let alone the station.

While the priest stood by with his arms folded, Leroy made placating gestures as if to say: I was just walking by and I wanted to help.

The cops were looking at him like: Yeah, right, nigger. You could almost hear them saying it. In a few minutes, though, they got tired of listening to him and told him to walk. His mouth, which had been going a hundred miles a minute, abruptly stopped moving. He stuffed his hands into his pockets and walked briskly across the street. When the cops got into their car—thankful, no doubt, that they wouldn't have to do any paperwork, since the priest wasn't pressing any charges—Black came out of the doorway and met Leroy in front of the barbecue place.

"Told you it wouldn't work, didn't I?" Black said, grinning. "What'd they say?"

"Th-they was like, 'Why did you slit this g-guy's tires?' " he said, stuttering as he always did whenever he got nervous or high. "I told them he didn't see me do it, and I was just trying to help the man out."

"Looked like you was beggin' for your life to me."

"Shut up, Black."

Black grinned even more broadly. "What you gettin' ready to do now?" he said.

"I'm goin' in the house. What about you?"

"You know that hole in the floor of this abandoned house over here—the one that goes to the vent with all the electric wires for the club they fixin' up?"

Leroy nodded.

"I'm goin' up in there," Black said, locking eyes with Leroy.

Leroy looked back at him questioningly, because they both

knew what that meant. They had considered breaking into the club once before, but they didn't want to fry in the vent. Black knew Leroy was thinking of the wires and had already concluded that the vent was a waste of time.

"You down?" Black said, knowing the answer as well as Leroy before he even spoke it.

"Naw, man, I almost got popped one time already. I'm gon' run it on in."

Translation: "I have something else in mind and you're not included. There is no way in hell you're going to be able to get through all that wiring to get into that club. If there were a remote possibility of your succeeding, I would go with you. As it stands, there is not. Good luck."

Leroy couldn't have known that he was dead wrong. And Black figured it wasn't his job to tell him. So Black turned toward the dark doorway he'd just exited, climbed over the wrought-iron fence that was held closed by a flimsy chain and lock, and walked toward the stairway that led up to the hole in the floor and the wiring to the club.

Black was either going to get paid or get fried. Not that it mattered. He was so strung out he figured he might as well be dead anyway. If he'd known what was going on in the house, though, he might have gone with Leroy. Then again, maybe he wouldn't have.

"You gotta give up half a cap, and you gotta use one match," Pookie told the suited-down Puerto Rican she had lured into the house. "I don't want you burnin' up my screens."

They were sitting in the living room of the abandoned house on Park Avenue where everyone went to smoke. On the news, it would have been called a crack house. To them, it was just "the house." So when Leroy said to Black that he was on his way to the house, Black knew that he was going there. Leroy probably thought he could catch somebody in there smoking and maybe get a hit. Apparently, some other people had gotten that idea before he did.

The Puerto Rican was going to be the source of everyone's high that night. He must have had it like that. He was wearing wingtip shoes, an Armani suit, a tailored shirt, and a silk tie. But there was something more to him—an air of authority. He looked to be about fifty, graying at the temples, with the hard lines around his eyes that come with a high-pressure career. Along with the executive air, though, there was a sort of somber defeat. Everyone there could see it. They could smell it. They knew that if this man had not felt defeated, there was no way in hell he would be in a crack house on Park Avenue. He just didn't belong there, and everyone knew it.

The Puerto Rican looked around the room to see if anyone had heard the girl hollering at him. Then he looked at his watch and saw that it was 11:42 P.M. Satisfied that the other people in the room were occupied with the caps he had handed out five minutes before, he turned his attention back to the girl.

"Okay," he said. "One match."

He reached for the straight shooter, a small hollow glass cylinder filled on one end with a rolled-up piece of a copper scouring pad. But she looked at him and pulled it back.

"Don't be reachin' over here," she said, her voice rising. "Where's the cap?"

He didn't even notice that the price had gone from a half a cap to a whole cap. And he didn't care. He just gave it to her. And everyone in the house looked at him as if they were measuring him up, waiting for him to take another hit.

Guys like him came through the house every once in a while. New Jacks, trying to get a blow job for a cap. Guys who had never smoked crack before. If a trick could convince them to take a hit, and they liked it, these guys would spend every last dime and give up the title to their car just to keep smoking. Most of the time, they would never even get the blow job, because by the time most men smoke four or five caps, they can't get it up anyway. But it feels like they might be able to, because crack stimulates the same part of the brain that sex does. Tricks, being the astute medical experts that they are, know this, and use this knowledge to their advantage. That's why they call them tricks. The trick is, the man spends all of his money for something they never give, and they end up telling him what to do, smoking up most of the dope, and maybe setting him up in the process.

"Can I get the straight?" Johnny Podres said, loosening his tie and glancing around the room at the hardened gray faces that seemed to lurk in every corner.

"Just wait a minute," Pookie said.

"Okay," he said. "Calm down."

Podres was beginning to think it hadn't been such a good idea to come to this place. The girl was making him look like a fool. But he needed another hit like the first one, when he'd put two caps in the straight and lit it with two matches, pulling the smoke slowly into his lungs and holding it there for what seemed like an eternity. Just one more like that and he could leave.

Pookie struck two matches and held them so close to the end of the glass tube that it cracked. "See what you made me do?" she said.

She gave him the straight shooter. He tried to put two caps in, but Pookie stopped him.

"What you doin', man?" she said.

"I'm trying to get a hit," he said, feeling like the room was closing in on him.

"You put one cap up in there and you hit it one time, with

one match, then you pass it," she said, as Butter got up slowly from the couch on the other side of the dim room and crept toward the mantelpiece.

Butter was what you might call the houseman. At least he was this week. The truth was, the house didn't belong to anybody. It was an abandoned house that people came to to smoke crack. But every once in a while, somebody would clean the place up, maybe bring in some extra candles, and call himself the houseman. Everybody who came in to smoke had to pay the houseman either one dollar or a hit. This week, Butter was the houseman. And Podres was the victim.

"What you coming over here for, man?" Podres said. "I gave you your hit."

"I'm just making sure we got enough light up in here," Butter said as he put another candle on the mantelpiece. "You know I gotta look out for the house. Everything's cool, though. Go 'head and smoke."

Butter smiled, revealing a mouthful of yellowed teeth stuffed haphazardly between sunken cheeks.

Somehow, Podres wasn't reassured. Holding a match halfway between the straight shooter and his lap, Podres watched as Butter placed the new candle on the mantel. Then he felt something slithering down the cushion of his chair. It was a mouse, but to him it felt like someone's hand. He thought about the four sixty-dollar bundles everyone knew he'd bought from Pop Squaly, and the five thousand dollars he was hiding in his sock. Then he looked at the way everyone was looking at him, and the slithering mouse felt even more like someone's hand. He noticed that everyone was closer to him than they'd been only two minutes ago. Then he saw Butter's mouth moving, saying something he couldn't quite make out. Johnny Podres was from the Badlands, and he knew a setup when he saw one.

"Yo," a voice called out from the back door. "It's Leroy."

As footsteps approached the living room, Podres decided that he had to get out of there. He reached into his suit jacket, turned around, and pointed a nine-millimeter at the chair cushion, dropping the straight shooter to the floor with a clatter that broke the silence in the room. After that, all hell broke loose.

Pookie screamed and threw herself to the floor. Rock, who had been sitting silently in a chair in the corner, dived at Podres. Butter blew out the candle and kicked Podres in the back, knocking him over the chair and into a small pile of trash in the hallway. The gun fell to the floor, slid across the room, and went off with a flash in the corner opposite Rock's chair.

"I don't wanna die," Pookie whimpered, as she crawled toward the back door.

"Shut up, bitch," Butter said quickly.

When Podres heard Butter's voice, he got to his feet and swung in that direction, catching Butter with a left hook. Butter fell into Rock, who had grabbed the gun. The impact caused Rock to pull the trigger. The shot went straight up in the air, hitting the ceiling. Three tricks and their customers came running downstairs screaming. Then Podres lunged at Rock and tried to take the gun.

Podres almost had the gun when Butter, thinking Rock was Podres, punched Rock in the neck, knocking him backward. Rock stood in front of Podres and aimed at what he hoped was the man's head. There was a gunshot, then another, and what had been an all-out struggle just seconds before became deadly stillness. The bullet hole in Podres's temple caused him to slide to the floor. Then everything stopped.

Butter thought he saw a hand with a heavy gold link bracelet pull back the curtain and dart toward the shed kitchen. But the hand was white, and Butter knew that the white boys only came through on Fridays. So he shook the image from his mind and whispered through the darkness to Rock.

"You all right?"

"Shut up and get the money," Rock said. "Hurry up!"

Rock reached into the dead man's pockets and pulled out the bundles he had bought. Butter, still numb but recovering quickly, reached into another pocket and pulled out a wallet. He had started to open it when he heard sirens approaching from about a mile away.

"Five-o," Butter said.

Rock finished searching Podres's pockets and started toward the stairs. "Get his car keys so we can roll. Pookie, which car was he drivin'?"

For half a minute, Pookie didn't respond.

"Pookie!" Rock said loudly.

"I don't wanna die," Pookie managed to mumble through a shock-induced haze of tears from the far corner of the room.

"Bitch, I'll make sure you die if you don't hurry up and tell me what car these keys go to. Get up! Now!"

Rock slapped Pookie hard and dragged her from the corner. Then he picked her up and carried her upstairs to a bedroom whose window was opposite the bedroom of the abandoned house next door. Butter was not far behind.

"Dig this here," Rock said, holding Pookie's face in his hands. "You can either jump over there or you can wait for five-o. And I know you ain't tryin' to go to jail. Them dykes up there would have your little scrawny ass for breakfast, lunch, and dinner."

After a moment's hesitation, Pookie jumped across the alley to the other bedroom window. Rock and Butter followed. Downstairs, in the deafening silence that followed the melee, Leroy, who had been coming through the back door when the shooting started, fished out the five thousand dollars Podres had been hiding in his sock. Then he climbed the stairs to the second floor and ran along the rooftops to the end of the block before disappearing into the night.

Officer James D'Ambrosio pulled up at the back of the house about one minute after Pookie, Butter, and Rock had gone out the front of the house next door.

"2512 on location," he said into the radio that sat perched on his shoulder like some bizarre mechanical parrot.

"Okay, 2512," the radio squawked back. "Use caution. We're getting numerous calls from that location reporting gunshots."

"2512 okay."

"Tell him to wait for backup," a crusty old man's voice yelled over the static-filled radio.

"2512 okay," D'Ambrosio said, thanking God that his sergeant had sense enough not to send his officers into these places alone.

D'Ambrosio's philosophy was simple: Criminals don't care about anything, but pipers care about even less than that. He had survived many a hairy situation by remembering that simple philosophy.

"You're damned right I'm waiting for backup," D'Ambrosio mumbled to himself, then chuckled. "This ain't *COPS* in North Philly."

The radio started clicking. Everyone in the district had heard what D'Ambrosio said and they were pushing their "talk" buttons.

"You're hanging up, Jim," somebody said, informing him that his radio was stuck in the talk mode.

D'Ambrosio pulled out his talk button just as a wagon with two female officers arrived. The sergeant pulled up, and the four of them drew their weapons.

The sergeant went in first, with the two officers from the wagon following closely. D'Ambrosio brought up the rear. They moved slowly, half expecting someone to rush at them from the dining room or living room. The front of the house had been cinder-blocked and cemented as part of a campaign to close down drug houses, which meant that the back way was the only way out. So when they didn't see anyone in the rooms that had been the shed kitchen, kitchen, and dining room, they approached the curtain that sectioned off the living room from the dining room.

The sergeant indicated that the officers from the wagon should cover the hallway. He pointed toward the curtain and signaled to D'Ambrosio. Then he pointed his gun at the corner that would be exposed when D'Ambrosio pulled back the curtain.

"Now!" the sergeant said in a stage whisper. When the curtain was drawn, the four officers trained their guns on a person who lay in the corner, bathed in the haunting glow of their flashlights. When they saw that he had been shot, they tensed, knowing the shooter could still be in the house.

One of them went over to check for a pulse. As she did so, the radio squawked. Two more cars had arrived at the house.

"25A, have 2520 take the front of this property," the sergeant said into the radio. "Have 25 Tom 2 take the back. We have a founded job here. One male down, no flash on any suspects. Send rescue to this location and inform 25 Command that—"

"25 Command en route," the lieutenant said before the sergeant could finish the sentence.

Two officers came in the back door, flashlights blazing. The sergeant signaled for them to turn their radio volume down.

Then he signaled for D'Ambrosio to come with him to check upstairs. He pointed to the basement door and signaled for the female officers to check the cellar. He signaled for the guys from 25 Tom 2 to stay at the back door in case anyone decided to run.

The officers fanned out, creeping up and down darkened staircases to conduct a room-by-room search of the upstairs and the basement. But it became apparent fairly quickly that the house was empty. After the space under the basement steps, there was no place left to hide. Someone might have hidden behind the hot-water heater, but that had disappeared over a year ago along with the copper plumbing. The doors had been taken—sold to carpenters and junkyards—so there were no closets to speak of. There was no furniture other than the tattered love seat and couch in the living room. And the tub and toilet were filled to the rim with human waste. Not even someone in Podres's condition could have stood the stench, so that was out, too.

By the time the search was halfway through, Fire Rescue 1 had arrived. Tom 2 radioed upstairs to the sergeant, who told him to keep rescue out until the house had been thoroughly searched. Two minutes later, after looking out over the rooftops that extended beyond the front and rear windows on the second floor of the row houses on Park Avenue, the sergeant radioed downstairs to allow rescue to enter the house.

The officers who had conducted the search came back to the living room and watched the guys from rescue declare Podres a 5292—the code assigned to dead bodies.

"25A, call Homicide, we've got a crime scene here," the sergeant said over the air. "And hold Tom 2 out on the scene on a detail."

After the dispatcher answered, the sergeant started mumbling to himself.

"When are these suit-and-tie guys gonna start believin' what they see on the news about crack?" he said as he took in the image of congealed blood and gray matter sticking to the wall where the bullet had exited Podres's head.

"Sergeant, I think you'd better come take a look at this guy," one of the fire rescue workers said. "I think he's a—"

"Oh shit," D'Ambrosio said. "That's Johnny Podres."

"The guy who runs the what d'ya call it?" the sergeant said.

"Yup. The city councilman who runs the Police Civilian Review Board," one of the female officers from the wagon said.

"25 Command," the sergeant said wearily into the radio, "please expedite."

"25 Command on location," the lieutenant said into his radio as he stepped up on the landing that led to the shed kitchen.

Everyone drew in their breath as the lieutenant strode into the living room of the house. When he saw the figure everyone's flashlights were trained on, Lieutenant John Flynn put his head in his hand and said to the sergeant, "Call the captain at home. He'll probably want to notify the commissioner, maybe even the mayor. They're going to want to know about this one before the press gets a hold of it."

What the lieutenant didn't say was that Podres—the man whose anticorruption record was supposed to take him straight to the mayor's office—could not have died in a crack house.

Chapter 2

When Black reached the top of the stairs in the abandoned house next to the club, he already knew where to go because he'd been there a few times and had taken some old chandeliers that looked like brass antiques. Needless to say, they were worthless, like most of the stuff in abandoned houses.

Still, the run-down ghost houses were as much a part of the dope game as straight shooters and caps. A piper could go into an abandoned house and strip it, selling the pipes and fixtures to salvage shops and collectors. Or he could pirate some electricity, clean the place up, and turn it into a smokehouse.

But this place was next door to a storefront church on the corner of Germantown Avenue and Broad Street, so the options were fairly limited. At most, a piper could break in at night and maybe smoke two or three caps by himself. But even that was impossible most of the time, because there were workmen in the club next door at all hours of the night working to refurbish it.

They weren't there that night, though. Black had watched them leave and lock up the place an hour earlier.

He walked across the dark room and set to work ripping some of the rotting planks from around the hole in the floor until he could get a better view of the inside of the club. There was some sort of backup generator powering lights that ran along the wall, and that helped him to see what was actually in there—power tools, rolls of insulation, and boxes of ceramic tile. It wasn't much, but knowing he could get at least a couple hundred dollars for that stuff was incentive enough to risk being electrocuted. He didn't care.

After listening for a few minutes to make sure no one was inside, Black lowered himself into the hole feet-first and nestled carefully between the wires. He moved slowly, making sure he didn't jerk any of the wires loose, and it took what seemed like forever just to move about three feet toward the opening in the vent.

As Black lay prone between the wires, trying to avoid jerking a wire out of some unseen power source, his mind wandered to the son he'd left behind after his wife divorced him. If he was electrocuted, would they come to the funeral? Would the baby know him if his ex-wife bothered to bring him? Would death erase the guilt of being a bad father and a worse husband? Would anyone even find him there, stuck in a vent to an unfinished club?

After a few minutes, and after seriously considering going back, Black made his way to the end of the vent, pushed his feet through the opening, then hung by his fingertips and dropped down onto the bar.

"There must be more than this in here," he said to himself after surveying the array of power tools that were spread out on the floor.

Hopping down off of the bar, he walked to the back of the club and into the deejay booth. He glanced to his left and noticed that there was a microwave oven and a small television on a shelf next to a back door. On his right, there were some cheap imitation-African made-in-Taiwan prints that probably would be hung on the walls when they finished the place. In the corner, next to the prints, was what looked like some new bathroom equipment. Scattered along another wall were boxes of nails and screws.

He left those things and walked toward the basement stairs, where a bright light reflected off the cellar wall. He went down the rickety steps, quickly searched through some boxes, and found that there was nothing there but some rusting deejay equipment.

The heat was stifling; there were two big, rusting oil tanks against the wall, and cobwebs, graffiti, and reddish-brown dust covered everything. It felt like his lungs were getting dirty just breathing it.

He was getting ready to go upstairs and collect the microwave and power tools when he heard a car pull up outside. There was something familiar about the sound of the car, but he couldn't place it.

Before he figured out where he'd heard it before, Black heard voices outside, then keys jangled in the door. The deadbolt slid back, and the only other sound in the building besides the noise of someone entering the club was the double thud of his pulse. He looked around quickly, searching for a place to hide, then walked around to the back of one of the oil tanks and sat down in a mound of dust.

As the car drove away, the driver yelled that he'd be back in five minutes. Black knew that he could sit perfectly still for five minutes, but sitting still wasn't his main worry. He was starting to breathe in more of that dust. And the more he breathed, the more he felt like coughing. Black couldn't risk that.

He started looking around for some kind of weapon—a rock, a pipe, anything that would give him enough time to get out of there if the man spotted him.

Black listened as the man began to whistle a Spanish tune. He heard the man's rubber-soled construction boots pace back and forth across the floor. When the whistling and the walking stopped, he heard the man grunt, as if he were fat and having trouble bending down.

Behind the oil tank, Black suddenly began to feel very hot. It was as if the dust were closing in on him, daring him to cough. His throat began to itch, then his nose. Streams of sweat began to make their way down the sides of his face, meeting at his chin and dripping down into his lap. His heartbeat, already furious, began to vibrate through his body like the sound of a bass drum. He clasped his hands around his nose and mouth, shut his eyes tight against the swirling dust, pulled his elbows in to his sides, and then sneezed.

For a full minute, there was nothing. The footsteps stopped, the whistling stopped, the grunting stopped. Black's heart, he could have sworn, stopped. The man was listening. He had to be. He was wondering where the sound had come from, or if he had heard a sound at all. He was looking around him for signs that he was not alone. He was deciding if he should call his workmates, if he should call the police, or if he should be the police. Then, just as suddenly as everything had stopped, he started to whistle again.

Black let out a long breath, then breathed in deeply, a mistake. As the man began to walk toward the basement steps, Black could feel his throat and nose begin to itch again. He was trying to will the itch away, praying for it to disappear, when he heard the man's foot pound against the first basement step. The step creaked under his weight, and there was a pause between that step and the next one as he stopped to steady himself on the rickety wooden stairs.

Black covered his nose and mouth, feeling like his heart was going to squeeze out from beneath his eardrums. He sneezed twice and breathed short shallow breaths, praying that the heavy footfalls on the squeaky steps had covered the noise. As the man came to the final step, Black tried to breathe normally.

The man took several steps toward the oil tank. Black tightened his hands into fists, then sat on his haunches and watched as the man's shadow crept under the oil tank and blackened the wall behind him. The man stood there for a moment while Black sat coiled tight as a spring. Then the man turned and began to rummage through the boxes on the floor, swearing to himself as he realized that whatever he was looking for was nowhere to be found.

All at once, the man stopped moving, as if he was trying to think of another place to search. He came and stood in front of the oil tank again, filling the room with a stillness that Black could have reached out and touched. At that moment, the man must have decided to look behind the oil tank.

As he started to walk slowly around to the side of the tank, Black prepared to spring. The rusting, graffiti-scarred hunk of metal that stood between them seemed to shrink beneath the man's lengthening shadow. Then the familiar rumble of a car engine broke the silence.

The driver banged on the basement window.

"Okay, okay, I'll be right there," the man said, his deep voice matching the size of his gargantuan shadow.

He turned to look at the oil tank once more, and disappeared up the basement stairs.

After the man left, Black did not move for the next five minutes. It took that long for his heart to descend from the top of his throat down into his chest.

But it didn't take nearly that long for Butter, Rock, and Pookie to get away from the house.

When Pookie pointed to Podres's late-model Mercury Marquis, Butter and Rock both knew something wasn't right.

"What's this, a cop car?" Butter said.

"Dude was a cop?" Rock said, backing away. "Y'all must be tryin' to get popped."

"He wasn't no cop," Pookie said, as they approached the car. "He said he was some kinda—"

"Just get in the car," Butter said. "We can talk about it later."

"No, let's get a hack," Rock said. "If they see three pipin'-ass niggers rollin' in a brand-new black Mercury in the middle of the night, they gon' know somethin' wrong."

"Just keep walkin'," Pookie said, stressing each word. "And don't look back. The rollers just pulled up by the house."

Butter and Rock both hesitated, almost imperceptibly, then rounded the corner of Park and Erie, hoping that the police car that had just pulled up in front of the house wouldn't approach them. When the guys at the hack stand saw them walking toward Broad Street, they started to yell, hoping to get a five- or six-dollar fare so they could take the money and go cop some dope.

"Taxi hack, hack cab!" a piped-out man in a piped-out gray Granada screamed at them across Erie Avenue.

Pookie started toward him. Butter and Rock followed, thinking that a gray Granada was inconspicuous enough for their purposes.

Another man, this one in a late-model Oldsmobile with a twisted grill, yelled out, "Taxi hack, taxi hack, take you there and bring you back, faster than SEPTA, cheaper than a cab, taxi hack."

"Yo, Rock, c-come here, man," a familiar voice said to them in a quick stutter.

They all turned, relieved to see someone they knew, and walked back toward the dull-brown Impala with no hubcaps.

When they got in, Butter grinned a ghastly yellow-toothed smile and said, "Where you get a ride from?"

"That's the last thing you need to be worried about right now," Leroy said as he pulled away from Germantown Avenue and drove across Broad Street. "The last thing."

"So what you sayin', man?" Butter asked, his grin disappearing. "You know somethin' I don't know?"

Leroy, sensing that he had slipped up, said quickly, "You need to be worryin' about where you tryin' to go."

"We should go to the Crescent Moon," Pookie said. "I'm tryin' to lay back and take a bath before I take my blast."

"I can't go to West Philly," Rock said. "They lookin' for me out there."

"For what?" Butter said.

"I snatched a pack off this young boy out 52nd Street."

"You swear you a gangster, don't you?"

"I ain't say all that," Rock said. "I just gotta get mine."

"All right, well, get mine and break me off some o' them caps you got."

"Don't worry 'bout that, I got you," Rock said, while he passed ten caps apiece to Rock and Pookie. "You worry 'bout gettin' that cash outta that wallet and throwin' the rest of that shit outta here."

"Shakedown, breakdown," Leroy said, smiling.

Rock passed five caps to Leroy.

"That's a down payment," Rock said with authority. Then, as

if he were trying to confirm that he was in charge, he added, "Now, shut your dumb ass up."

Leroy glanced in the rearview mirror, wondering if Rock and Butter still had the gun.

"Dig this here, man," Leroy said as he pulled the car over at 21st and Erie, about two blocks from the 39th Police District. "You think I don't know where you got all that dope? I was comin' up in the house when everything jumped off. I know wussup."

Rock glanced at Butter to see his reaction, but Butter seemed oblivious to the fact that there was now a witness to Podres's murder. He just sat completely still, wearing a blank stare. Pookie, on the other hand, seemed to hang on Leroy's every word.

"You can play that hard role on Butter and them, but that don't move me," Leroy said matter-of-factly. "Now, you can either get out and tell five-o how that Puerto Rican got slumped, or you can throw that gun and all that I.D. down the sewer before we all get popped."

With that, everything stopped, until Pookie tore her gaze away from Leroy and looked expectantly at Rock.

Rock glanced at Pookie and then turned his murderous stare on Leroy. Then he pulled the gun from his groin and chambered a round with an ominous double click.

"I'll splatter your brain against that windshield. Now, shut up and drive."

Leroy glanced leisurely at Rock, bent down, emptied two caps into his straight shooter, lit two matches, and pulled the smoke into his lungs. He held the smoke in for half a minute, then released it slowly through his nostrils, filling the car with the sickeningly sweet smell of burning crack. He turned around, his eyes the size of half-dollars, and stared at Rock.

"Do it," Leroy said, reaching for the barrel of the gun and placing it gingerly against his own forehead. "Do it now, while they still lookin' for you from the last body."

He paused and pressed the gun more firmly against his forehead.

"I just hope you know how you goin' somewhere in a car with blood all inside the windows and a gun with at least two bodies on it."

Rock stared back at Leroy and decided to kill him. But as his finger began to tighten around the trigger, a police car rode slowly down Erie Avenue from Hunting Park. He lowered the gun, allowing the police car to pass, and eased his grip on the trigger. Then he glanced away from Leroy.

"Man, you know I was just bullshittin'," he said, grinning nervously. "Let's get outta here."

Leroy stared at Rock for a second longer. Then he turned around, put the car in drive, and pulled off slowly, his jaw moving from side to side, as it always did when he took a hit. There was silence as everyone took in what had just occurred.

Butter thought that it might be a good time to change the subject. All the gunplay was blowing his high. And in this, his first moment of clarity since the shooting, the thought of the white hand pulling back the curtain came roaring back to him in Technicolor. He could even see the heavy gold bracelet dangling from the wrist.

"Yo, Rock," he said suddenly. "You see a white boy come in the house tonight?"

"No, I ain't see no white boy tonight," Rock said, his voice a little harder because Leroy had embarrassed him. "You know them white boys don't come through after Friday. What, that shit got you hallucinatin' again?"

"I don't know," Butter said, but the image stayed in his mind as he handed Podres's I.D. to Rock. "Throw this out the window on your side."

"All right," Rock said, already feeling his authority slipping away. "Pull over by this sewer, Leroy."

Leroy pulled over. Rock got out, stood with his back to the car, and threw the I.D. and the gun holster into the sewer. But he stuck the gun back into his underwear.

Rock, like everyone else in the car, knew that Leroy had just taken his heart—humiliated him in front of a woman. He couldn't leave a slight like that unanswered. Not ever. So, while he realized that it would have been stupid to kill Leroy at that moment and in that place, Rock knew that when his chance came, he'd take it. He was one of the big boys now. He was a killer. And in his mind, he couldn't allow anyone or anything to return him to the status of a mere piper.

"Come on," Pookie said, interrupting Rock's thoughts.

"Shut up, Pookie," Rock said as he opened the back door and got in the car.

Satisfied that Rock had thrown the gun and the I.D. into the sewer, Leroy pulled off, just as the police car that had passed them a moment before turned on its dome lights and made a U-turn.

When Leroy looked in his rearview mirror and saw that the cop was following him, he floored it.

Officer Harry Flannagan, a rookie assigned to the 39th District, had lucked out and been assigned to work steady last out, the midnight to eight A.M. shift that was coveted by most officers because it allowed for a somewhat regular life. That's if being a constant target for bad guys with better guns can be viewed as regular.

He learned during his first two months of duty that the things that happened on last out—burglaries, murders, and the like—weren't discovered until the morning shift. And that shift, he learned, was manned by pissed-off guys who had to rotate every two weeks between eight to four and four to midnight. They weren't like him, guys who slept on one schedule and saw their wives regularly. More often than not, the day-shift guys were the type of cops who would sooner bust somebody's head than give them a ticket.

Flannagan, on the other hand, was the type of guy who loved people. He distributed more warnings than tickets, and he generally gave people a break whenever he could. So when he passed three guys and a girl in a car that was parked on the side of the street, he figured they were just having some fun. And when he looked in his rearview mirror and saw a guy get out of the car and throw some stuff down the sewer, he wasn't immediately suspicious. But he took a second look when he saw the guy coming back to the car trying to stuff something in his waistband. And when Harry Flannagan had to take a second look, he knew it was always for a good reason.

Flannagan hung a U-turn and picked up his handset to call for backup just as a message went out over the police radio for East and Northwest divisions.

"Cars, stand by," a dispatcher said. "Committed at Park Avenue and Pike Street within the last five minutes, a founded shooting. Suspects may have fled from Broad and Erie in a vehicle. No flash. All units use extreme caution when . . ."

In the middle of the message, the car Flannagan was trying to stop suddenly darted toward Hunting Park Avenue. Flannagan couldn't wait for the dispatcher to drone on anymore.

"3910, priority!" Flannagan screamed into his handset to

make it known that he had an emergency. "I'm in pursuit of a brown Impala, Pennsylvania license tag Tom Edward X-ray Andy Nathan, west on Erie from 21st."

"3910 is in pursuit of a brown Impala, license tag, TEXAN, west on Erie from 2-1," the dispatcher repeated. "3910, occupants?"

"Three black males, one black female, wanted for investigation at this time," Flannagan said loudly.

"What's your location?"

"West on Hunting Park from 2-7."

"39A, put me in, I'm at 2-6 and Hunting Park," the sergeant said, joining the chase.

"396, put me in, I'm at 2-8 and Pike, approaching Hunting Park."

"3910, I'm going north on Henry from Hunting Park."

The brown Impala turned at Roberts Avenue, and Flannagan skidded around the corner in pursuit.

"East on Roberts from Henry," Flannagan screamed into the radio as a popping sound erupted in the background. "3910!"

The radio hissed for half a beat.

"Shots fired!" Flannagan said loudly as the radio began to hiss and crackle again.

"3910, your location!" the dispatcher said. "3910!"

"3910, they're . . ." There was another popping noise, then a loud crashing sound in the radio, followed by a tortured scream and an abrupt end to the transmission.

"Cars, stand by," the dispatcher said, flicking the switches that would allow her transmission to go out over every division. "Henry and Roberts, assist the officer, police by radio. Henry and Roberts, assist the officer, police by radio!"

Every car within ten miles of 3910's last location, except the ones that were still at the house at Park and Pike, started toward

Henry and Roberts. It seemed like a hundred sirens went off at once.

Leroy knew what the sirens meant. Every cop in Philadelphia would be looking for them now. They would know what they were driving and how many people were in the car, all because Rock had shot at that cop and made him crash.

In his rearview mirror, Leroy could still see the flames from the police car shooting ominously toward the sky. If the cop hadn't made it out of the car, he was either dead or so burnt up he would wish for death. Leroy knew what that meant, too. If he didn't get that gun from Rock before he killed somebody else, and if he didn't figure out a way to get out of Philadelphia before first light, they'd all be dead by daybreak.

Cop killers don't live long in Philadelphia.

Chapter 3

When Black was sure that the men weren't coming back, he crept out the back door carrying a band saw, the microwave, a jigsaw, and a power drill. There was a chain-link fence topped with barbed wire that separated the backyard from the alley, so he had to put the stuff in a plastic trash can cushioned with wrinkled newspapers, hoist it over the fence, and hope the mud in the alley would soften the fall and keep the stuff from breaking. He climbed over the fence after it, then carried the can to the wooden gate at the end of the alley and hoisted it up and over again, this time hoping a little harder that it wouldn't break, since there was only a concrete sidewalk to cushion the fall. When it hit the ground, he picked up the can and set off for Tone's house, looking over his shoulder once or twice to make sure no one was watching him.

Tone, of course, was the dope man. With him, Black could sell the stuff for caps, get straight cash, or get half and half. That, and the fact that Tone had the best dope, made him option number one. Pop Squaly, the other dope man, would pay in caps, no cash, so he was option number two. Option three was Mr. Paulem. He would pay in straight cash, but he was cheap. He would try to get the microwave, the band saw, the jigsaw, and the power drill for thirty dollars. Paulem was definitely a last resort.

Having worked out his options, Black started toward Broad Street, heading for Tone's. He was counting up how much the stuff would be worth when he turned the corner of 15th and hit Butler Street. That's when he heard the sirens. There were dozens of them, twenty or thirty maybe, coming from every direction. For an instant he thought they might be coming for him, but he knew that if they were trying to catch a burglar, they would come maybe three or four cars deep, lights out and sirens off. There wouldn't be twenty cars. And they certainly wouldn't be coming from every direction. To be on the safe side, though, he carried the trash can to the curb, like it was garbage, and walked away from it. Anybody who hadn't seen him climb over the fence would have thought he was taking out the trash—he hoped.

After Black tucked the trash can safely behind a tree, he started walking toward Broad Street, trying hard not to look over his shoulder and get a clue as to what the hell was going on. Within five seconds a police car rolled past him, going the wrong way down Butler Street. A second later, another one flew up 15th Street toward Hunting Park, again in the wrong direction.

"Somethin' musta happened to a cop," he mused to himself, "'cause ain't no way in hell they rollin' like that for no nigger."

Satisfied that they weren't looking for him, Black went back to retrieve the trash can and walked quickly across Germantown Avenue to Broad Street, his mouth watering and his stomach flipping as he thought about that first hit. As he got closer to

Lee's Chicken, though, he noticed something odd, something that caused him to stop in his tracks. It was a rescue truck. And it was right in back of the house.

Black knew that no one would call rescue for a piper. If anything, other smokers would shoot through his pockets to see if he had any more dope or any more money. Then they would leave him for dead. And if the cops happened to roll up and he wasn't dead yet, they would do everything they could to finish the job. If they were nice, they might even lock him up. Or if they were really nice cops, they might take him to the hospital. But rescue?

Something big had happened in the house. That much was apparent. And Black wasn't trying to be around anything big. Cops tend to grab anybody and everybody when something big happens. He'd seen it too many times—guys who had never done anything remotely illegal doing life for someone else's crime. Black wasn't trying to go out like that. Which meant he'd have to catch Tone on the next go-round. Taking a left, he headed up to Pop Squaly's, mumbling, cursing, and trying unsuccessfully to convince himself that Pop Squaly's dope was just as good as Tone's.

"I need a blast," he said in a barely audible grumble.

A lady coming out of the bar looked at him and said, "Who you talkin' to?"

"Do it look like I'm talkin' to you?" he said, and readjusted the trash can, switching the weight of it from his left to his right side.

The lady, barely fazed, looked at him and resumed her drunken stumble from the bar next to the barbecue place to the bar up the street.

Black picked up the pace, walking quickly toward Pop Squaly's, and watched police cars, one after another, turning left on Hunting Park Avenue. Since they hadn't stopped, Black knew that he was safe for a while. As long as they were going to help one of their own, he could smoke fifty caps in the middle of Broad Street and the cops wouldn't care.

But in spite of his newfound feeling of security, something kept nagging at him, pulling at him like a pinched nerve run amok. The faster he walked, the more intense it became, until it was almost an actual pain pounding against his head. Then, as he dragged the trash can up Pop Squaly's steps, it hit him. Leroy. Could he have had something to do with what happened in the house?

It wasn't like they were friends or anything. People don't become friends out there. At most, they might become partners. And Leroy—stuttering-ass, crazy-ass Leroy—was one of the best partners Black had ever had.

You had to be one of the best to bring rescue to a crack house. That's why Black knew that Leroy had something to do with it. Trouble was, the same instinct that told Black that Leroy had gotten away with doing something in the house was telling him that Leroy wouldn't be getting away for long.

Leroy looked in the rearview mirror at the police car burning against the median that separated Roberts Avenue from the expressway off-ramp and tried to think of a way out. When he thought he'd figured something out, he spoke quickly.

"Pookie, when we get up to Wayne Avenue, get out the car and lay down in the street," he said.

"Nigger, you must be on ALPO," Pookie said, rolling her eyes and snapping her neck at the very thought.

"I said lay down in the street!" Leroy screamed.

"Ain't nobody givin' no orders up in here but me," Rock said, once again aiming the gun at Leroy's head. "Matter fact, just pull over."

"All right, I'll pull over," Leroy said, then made a hard left and slammed the accelerator to the floor as he came around the curve leading to Wayne Avenue.

The sudden turn caused Butter to slide across the backseat and bump into Rock, who sat stuck against the door, struggling against Butter's 130-pound frame. In the front seat, Leroy opened his door and crouched, waiting for a second before he jumped. Pookie followed suit, fighting desperately against the door handle before she finally got it open.

Rock, his eyes wide open, was yelling something no one could hear as Butter, his terror-stricken face flush against Rock's chest, pulled at the door handle. When Leroy and Pookie rolled from the vehicle, barely avoiding the stone curb that buttressed the asphalt street, the car barreled into the steps of a row house. The last thing Pookie saw before the car burst into flames was Rock's horrified expression as he pounded against the rear window. Neither Pookie nor Leroy saw Butter crawl from the other side and collapse a few feet away. And neither of them cared.

Leroy got up quickly, ignoring the flame-riddled car. He started toward Wayne Avenue, trying to walk normally in spite of the rapidly increasing swelling in his right knee. Pookie, her face scraped badly along the left side, tore her gaze away from the burning vehicle, got up from the oil-slicked asphalt, and jogged half a block to catch up with him.

"Pookie, go lay in the street," Leroy said. "That's the only way we gon' get outta here."

There was a gentleness in his voice that hadn't been there before. She looked at him to see where it had come from and their eyes met. They connected. But as quickly as the connection had appeared, it hid behind the reality of the moment. Yet somehow, Pookie knew in her heart that it was there.

Leroy walked to the curb and knelt behind a parked car. Pookie lay facedown in the street. She knew they only had about ten seconds before the police arrived. And she knew that Leroy was her best and only chance of getting out of this thing alive. So no matter how crazy he sounded, she was going to listen to him. And if they ever got out of this thing alive and got their lives together, she would follow him to something better. Because anything was better than this.

As soon as Pookie lay down, an elderly couple in a late-model Cadillac—church folk from the look of them—stopped. When the man started to get out of the car, Leroy walked up behind him, jammed a stick in his back, then directed him back to the car. Pookie, knowing full well that Leroy would just as soon leave her lying in the street as take her with him, got up and slid into the backseat behind him.

"Just d-d-drive, man, nice and slow, that same thing you do every Sunday—holdin' up traffic—just d-d-drive!" Leroy said.

"Okay, son. Calm down," the old man said, glancing at his wife. "Which way you—"

"Nigger, j-just drive!" Leroy said. "I'll tell you which way."

"All right, son," the man said, taking in Leroy's quick stutter and believing that he was just nervous and afraid enough to kill him and his wife. "The Lord—"

"This nigger don't understand English, do he, Pookie?" Leroy said, glancing at Pookie, then fixing his gaze on the old man. "Drive, man, the Lord ain't got nothin' to do with this here."

The man fell silent, just as two fire engines and a police car approached from the opposite direction, going toward the two car fires that burned within the next three blocks.

"And don't try to make no signals and signs to nobody,"

Leroy said, indicating the police car and fire trucks. " 'Cause I'll blow so many feathers off your woman's Sunday hat, you'll think it was a chicken coop up in here."

The man drove on as if he hadn't seen the police and fire engines. But when they had passed, he said, "Boy, why don't you just take the car? You can have it. Just let my wife go. I don't care what you do after that. Just please, let Mother Jones go."

"Mother Jones?" Leroy said. "You call your woman 'mother'? What y'all into, somethin' kinky, Pops? Probably be tearin' it up, don't you?"

Pookie grinned. Mother Jones patted her hair, turned toward the window, and tried hard to stifle a grin of her own. Pops, who didn't find Leroy the least bit amusing, pursed his lips and gripped the steering wheel tightly.

"Make a right on Germantown and make a right on Clarissa," Leroy said. "We gotta find Black."

"Black?" Pookie said, trying unsuccessfully to hide her exasperation.

"Yeah, Black," Leroy said. "He 'bout the only one I know smart enough to get us outta this."

Pops started to accelerate, causing everyone in the car to grab for something.

"Slow down, Pops," Leroy said. "We ain't tryin' to get no tickets."

The old man looked at Leroy in his rearview mirror, then eased his foot off the gas pedal.

"Now make this left on Hunting Park," Leroy said, taking in the dozens of police cars that were darting along Hunting Park Avenue, turning up and down the maze of one-way streets that ran along either side of one of North Philadelphia's major thoroughfares.

"Look at these nuts," Leroy said, talking more to himself than to anyone else.

He looked to his left and saw five or six officers with flashlights walking through the Simon Gratz High School football field. On his right, a K-9 cop in front of the Amoco station was getting out of a Jeep with a remarkably docile-looking German shepherd.

"Make a right on Broad Street," Leroy said, as the old woman turned her head slightly toward him.

"Turn around, Mother Jones," Leroy said quickly. "I can't let you live if you see my face."

Pops looked in the rearview mirror again.

"That's why Pops gon' get his ass out that mirror," Leroy said. "Ain't that right, Pops?"

The old man fixed his eyes on the road and nodded.

As the car turned onto Broad Street, Leroy began to scan both sides of the street. Except for two police cars and a bus going south on Broad from Rockland Street, there were maybe five or six cars going in either direction.

"Go in this Roy Rogers like you goin' through the drive-through, Pops," Leroy said, watching the approaching night-owl bus that he knew only stopped at subway stops after midnight.

The old man pulled into the parking lot.

When they entered the drive-through, Leroy said, "What time is it, Pops?"

"It's twelve-twenty."

"Black probably around Pop Squaly's by now," Leroy said to himself.

"Huh?" Pops said.

"Nothin'. Just pop the hood and give me the keys."

The old man handed over the keys. Leroy broke the lock

handles on all four doors and got out of the car, beckoning for Pookie to do the same. When she did, Leroy opened the old man's door and employed the power locks. Then he looked under the hood and disconnected the battery. With no electricity, the car was all but useless, and there was no way to disengage the locks.

"Catch that bus," Leroy said to Pookie as he bent down and pretended to tie his shoe.

She walked hesitantly toward the bus, thinking that Leroy was going to leave her.

"Go 'head, girl, ain't nobody gon' leave you," he said, sensing her hesitation.

Pookie looked back over her shoulder at him, wavering between the bus and the car, then fell in line with the other three people waiting at the corner of Broad and Hunting Park for the bus. One woman looked at her strangely, staring at the long red abrasion down the side of her face, but as quickly as Pookie had gained the woman's attention, she lost it. A skinny, dirty girl with a fresh scrape along the side of her face was nothing compared to the other sights and sounds of North Philly after dark.

"Fare, please," the bus driver said when Pookie climbed up the bus steps.

Pookie just looked at him.

"I'm only going to ask you for your fare one more time, miss," the driver said as he reached for the button that would change the flashing ORANGE LINE sign on the front of his bus to the HELP, CALL POLICE sign.

"Here's the fare," Leroy said, boarding the bus and handing the driver a fifty.

The driver looked at it, pocketed the money as if that sort of thing happened every day, and spoke into the microphone. "Erie next."

"I might want you to stop before we get to Erie," Leroy said. "I know it's against the rules and everything, but I'm lookin' for somebody, and he probably on one of these corners you pass on your way to Erie."

"Whatever you say, brother," the driver said, suddenly affable.

Leroy looked over at the corner of Broad and Jerome streets, hoping he would recognize one of the shadowy figures beneath the trees that lined the opposite side of the street. It was only the drug dealers, though, and a trick who waved at Leroy as he glanced out the window over the driver's shoulder.

At Lycoming Street, Leroy started to think of what he would do when he got to Erie Avenue. The police, he thought, would probably board the bus there, if not before, and he could only hope that no one would know that he had been in the house when the Puerto Rican was murdered. He was about to tell the driver to stop at Pike Street, when he glanced over the driver's shoulder and saw a figure turn the corner of Broad and Dell near the auto-parts place.

"Stop," Leroy said calmly.

"Right here?" the driver said as he slowed the bus and reached for the button to open the doors.

"Yeah, nigger, right here!" Leroy said, losing all pretense of politeness.

The driver opened his mouth as if to say something, but thought better of it and opened the doors without so much as a whisper.

When he and Pookie got off the bus, Leroy began to call out before the bus had even passed him, and the loud rumble of the engine muffled his voice.

"Black!" a voice called out as the bus on the other side of Broad Street pulled away, and Black knew before he even looked that it was Leroy.

Leroy called again, and Black stopped and turned.

When the bus passed and he saw the look on Leroy's and Pookie's faces, Black was reasonably certain of two things. Whatever had happened in the house wasn't over. And he was about to become a part of it.

Inside the house, detectives took measurements, fingerprints, and photographs. Lab technicians took blood samples from the floor and semen samples from the mattresses in the upstairs bedrooms. Uniformed officers stood guard at the front and back doors, keeping nonexistent onlookers outside the perimeter of yellow crime-scene tape on what had turned out to be an easy detail—so far.

Homicide lieutenant Jorge Ramirez, who had been busy organizing and overseeing the frenzy of activity, came back into the house for what seemed like the hundredth time and asked to speak with the 25th District four-to-midnight supervisor.

"That'd be me," Lieutenant John Flynn said as he strode from the living room to meet Ramirez.

"Okay, so what's up?" Ramirez asked.

"Well, the victim is a city councilman," Flynn said. "As if that wasn't bad enough, he's the head of the Police Civilian Review Board."

"I know," Ramirez said. "What I meant was—"

"And get this," Flynn added, rolling his eyes in the air. "He's a spick, to boot. The papers will have a field day with this one."

Flynn expected Ramirez to agree. After all, he looked Caucasian. With his dirty-blond hair and light brown eyes, it was a natural assumption. But a closer look revealed a dark, almost ruddy complexion and full, voluptuous lips. He could have been of Mediterranean descent, or he could have been Latino. As Ramirez looked at Flynn, unshaken by the overt racism that he'd always found to be present within the department, he realized that Flynn was trying to figure out which one he was.

"I forgot to introduce myself," Ramirez said. "I'm Lieutenant Jorge Ramirez, Homicide. And when I said, 'What's up?' I was referring to stuff like: Did your officers question any witnesses? Has any weapon been recovered? Have any suspects been identified? You know, police stuff.

"The political and racial overtones do not concern me," Ramirez added, looking Flynn straight in the eye. "I'd just like to know if anybody under your command has done anything other than roll out the yellow tape."

Flynn was flustered for a moment, but recovered quickly.

"No offense, Ramirez. But you know how you people get when something happens to a Latino. I was just saying that—"

"Well, well, well. If it ain't the Red Man himself!" Ramirez said, interrupting Flynn when he saw another detective from his squad. "Come to show us rookies how it's done?"

Detective Reds Hillman bristled at the reference to his age. Although Ramirez outranked him, no one could touch Hillman's experience. He had worked Homicide for almost twenty years and had seen a little bit of everything. In less than a year, he would retire. He'd promised himself that he would take it easy for the next few months, and no one was going to deny him that. Not even Ramirez.

"Give a kid a lieutenant's bar and he thinks he can start giving lip to his elders," Hillman said.

"You know I'm just messing with you, Reds," Ramirez said. "You don't write, you don't call. I was beginning to think you had something against your coworkers."

"Work, Ramirez. I'm a prisoner of my work," Hillman said, shaking his head in mock exhaustion. "You know how it is."

Ramirez didn't respond. He knew that Hillman was a prisoner. But he knew that he wasn't imprisoned by work. The walls to Hillman's prison were thicker than work. They were so impregnable that no one had gotten in for years. Mostly, people had stopped trying.

Sensing Ramirez's discomfort, Hillman changed the subject. "Speaking of work, how'd that Faison case ever turn out?"

"Conviction, felony murder, life without parole," Ramirez said. "The jury wouldn't go for the death penalty."

"Can't win 'em all."

"No kidding," Ramirez said wistfully. "So what've we got on this one?"

"Well, I've only been here for about fifteen minutes. From what I can gather, we haven't got any eyewitnesses, naturally, but we've got a list from Radio of the addresses where the calls came from. I wanted to save them for you, but I figured I'd be nice and call 'em back for you, since us little guys end up doing all the legwork anyway."

"Aren't you just the sweetest thing," Ramirez said, batting his eyes and blowing a kiss at Hillman.

Hillman ventured a sidelong glance at Ramirez, then looked at an investigator from the medical examiner's office and a crime-lab technician to make sure they hadn't seen Ramirez's little display.

"You're just a barrel of laughs tonight," Hillman said. "Marriage must be doing wonders for you."

Ramirez just smiled. He had been married for a year, and his wife had just had a baby boy a month before. His family and his career were everything to him, and it showed.

"Anyway," Hillman said, "the lady that lives two doors down—a Mrs. Green—says she heard a guy say, 'Yo, it's Leroy,' about five seconds before the gunshots."

Ramirez jotted down the name Leroy.

"Guess how long it takes to walk from the shed kitchen to here," Hillman said.

"Five seconds," Ramirez said. Then, almost as an afterthought, "So who's Leroy, a dealer?"

"Nope, he's a piper. Name's Leroy Johnson. Does cars, burglaries, never anything violent. Never even had a gun charge. That's why it doesn't figure that he'd do this."

"Maybe he got sick of fifty- and sixty-dollar hits," Ramirez said.

"Maybe he didn't do it."

"He's got a sheet, right?"

"Yeah, but there's a lot more to him than the sheet," Hillman said.

"Whatever. Let's get a general radio message out on Leroy, and any of his known associates who frequent this house."

"Done. I'll pay Mrs. Green a visit, too. And here's the list of the others who called."

Hillman handed over a list of names, addresses, and telephone numbers.

"Let's get the first wagon that comes in service to round up the girls on Old York Road," Ramirez said, looking over the list. "They probably know ten times more about this than we ever will."

"Good idea. If you want, I'll get a couple of guys to round up the dealers. Tell them a city councilman's been killed, start talking lethal injection. Somebody's bound to talk."

"How many dealers are we talking about here?" Ramirez said.

"Let's see," Hillman said, pausing to count on his fingers. "There's the guy on Butler Street and the guy on Broad Street, Tone and Pop Squaly. Then there's the girl up on Pike Street, Donna, the one that sells from the house."

"Damn, you know this neighborhood like the back of your hand, don't you, old man?"

"It's called experience."

"You gonna be able to get warrants for all of them?" Ramirez asked.

"For a city councilman? For this guy, I could get a quickie warrant to extradite the pope from Rome."

"Somehow, I still think our best chance is this Leroy guy," Ramirez said. "He was just too close not to have anything to do with it."

"Okay, you've got a point. But I know Leroy. I've watched him walk these streets for a long time. If it wasn't for crack, he'd probably be in business somewhere, doing something legitimate. He's got a head on his shoulders. I don't know too much about Black—the kid he hangs out with. But I hear he's pretty smart, too."

"Did you get Black on the GRM?" Ramirez said.

"Yeah, I got him on the GRM. Problem is, they didn't do it."

"Maybe not," Ramirez said. "But if Leroy and Black didn't do this thing, they damn sure know who did. And they're going to have to tell me something, because somebody's gotta take the fall for this one."

Chapter 4

"Wussup with you, man?" Black asked as Leroy finished limping across Broad Street with Pookie in tow. "And why you rollin' with her?"

"I ain't got time to explain, Black, but you know I'll break you off a little somethin' later on," Leroy said. "We just need someplace to chill for a little bit."

Black glanced at an uncharacteristically silent Pookie, who was wearing a fearful expression he'd never seen on her face, and then at Leroy, whose eyes were filled with a desperation that didn't quite fit him. For a second, he thought of leaving them, of walking away from whatever trouble they had fallen into. But they seemed to be reading his thoughts. Just as he thought of leaving, the fear and desperation he'd seen in their eyes seemed to turn to outright terror.

"All right," he said, hoping that whatever it was wasn't as serious as it looked. "Come on."

Beckoning for them to follow, Black walked down Dell

Street, a block that runs diagonally from McFerran to Broad. He tried not to look at the two or three parked cars on the opposite side of the street, but he couldn't help noticing that the passengers' heads in two of the cars were bobbing up and down—somebody was getting what they had paid for. When he passed the third car, watching crack smoke steam its windows and praying that the police car he'd just seen wouldn't circle back around, he stopped and rang the bell on a well-maintained two-story brick row house.

"Who is it?" a high-pitched female voice called out from behind the barred first-floor windows.

"Everett," he said.

"Just a minute," came the answer, followed by the soft padding of feet approaching the door.

"Don't say nothin'," Black said to Leroy and Pookie, just as his old classmate Clarisse Williams started to unlock the door.

"Hey, Ever . . ."

A smile quickly faded from her lips as she opened the door and saw three of them standing at her front door.

"I told you never to bring anyone to my home, Everett," she said, her eyes darting quickly to her left and then to her right, trying to see if her neighbors were looking out their windows.

Clarisse was so afraid that someone would learn that she, a registered nurse, was smoking crack, she just knew the world could see her every time she got ready to take a blast. She was, after all, the type of woman people watched. She was all soft curves and luminous chocolate-brown skin, with full lips and a rounded nose set beneath eyes that slanted over high cheekbones. Yet her beauty was overlapped with something else—a simmering attitude that gave hard edges to the curves and a dark tint to her chocolate glow.

"Good night, Everett," Clarisse said, trying to hide her paranoia behind a stern mask that was meant to tell Black that he was no longer welcome in her home.

But as she began to close the door, she took on a look that seemed to depict a struggle between two separate people—the one who was a principled, respectable, professional young woman, and the one who was smoking the pipe.

"I'll give you a bundle," Black said, reading her expression and taking a chance that the crack fiend would win the struggle.

The door stopped in midswing.

"A bundle?" she said.

He nodded.

Clarisse looked at Leroy and Pookie again, hesitated, then opened the door wide, motioning for them to go back to the dining room.

"Thank you," Leroy said, and limped through the living room, looking at the gray three-piece leather living room set and the big-screen television that sank down into thick burgundy pile carpeting.

"Thank you," Pookie said, her normally brash and arrogant voice barely audible as she tagged behind Leroy.

As Black tried to come in, Clarisse stopped him at the door and held out her hand. He looked at her, considered giving her half a bundle, then reached into his inside pocket and gave her one of the three and a half bundles Pop Squaly had paid him for the microwave, the drill, and the saws. As she looked to make sure there were twenty caps in the plastic baggy, she stepped aside and let him pass, closing and locking the door behind him.

"Don't sit down!" Clarisse yelled as she turned to walk through to her dining room, still counting the caps. But it was too late. Pookie was already sitting on one of the heavily cushioned beige chairs that surrounded the rosewood dining table.

"Look, Clarisse," Black said before she passed through the

portal that led to the dining room. "We won't be here long, I just—"

"You got that right," she said, cutting him off and making him feel small in a way that only a sister could. "You won't be here long. And . . ."

Her mouth dropped open as she stopped in the doorway and watched Leroy sit down, squirming in pain as he tried to adjust himself—the oil from his jeans rubbing off onto her beige chair covers.

"I know you're not rubbing oil in my chair," she said, and Leroy tried to jump up, but fell down when his swelled knee buckled under the full weight of his body.

Clarisse walked over to him—her scowl replaced by the concerned, gentle countenance of a nurse—and removed Leroy's hand from his knee. With her fingertips, she touched his knee on either side. When she did, Leroy winced.

"What happened to you?" Clarisse asked as Pookie walked over to Leroy and touched his forehead with a tenderness she had never displayed before.

"It's a long story," he said, dumping a cap into his straight shooter and holding out his hand with his thumb and forefinger extended. "Gimme two."

"Can't you wait a minute?" Clarisse said. "Your knee's as big as a basketball and you're saying gimme two. Let me wrap it and—"

"No, I can't wait," Leroy said, accepting two matches from Pookie. "The way it's goin' tonight, this might be the only medicine I get before—"

"Before what?" Black said, trying to get Leroy to shut up before he got them kicked out of the only safe place they could be for the next few hours. "Before we go get some more dope?"

As Leroy struck the matches and held them up to the end of

the metal piece of antenna that he had stashed in his sock along with the five thousand he'd taken from Podres, Black dumped two caps into one of the glass straight shooters he'd just bought and offered it to Clarisse.

She accepted it, Black handed her two matches, then dumped two more into another and lit two matches for himself. Pookie pulled out her own straight and lit up two of the caps that Rock had given her earlier, and for the next few minutes, they all pulled poison into their lungs.

Black had to force himself to sit still as he held in the smoke, because his ears began to ring. It sounded almost like sirens, and it could have been, but he had learned long ago not to let paranoia consume him or cause an outward change in his behavior. That could get you killed, he thought, as he released the smoke slowly through his nose and looked around at everyone else.

Pookie began to twitch in a way that was almost frightening as she blew out the smoke. Clarisse stood perfectly still for a moment, her eyes as big as tea saucers, then sat slowly down in the same chair Leroy had soiled just moments ago. Leroy's jaw began to move rhythmically from side to side, and his eyes were momentarily filled with the desperation Black had seen earlier. Then he relaxed and began to look slowly around the room, fixing his gaze on Black, then on Clarisse, and finally on Pookie.

As the momentary high gave way to the almost sexual sensation that followed, each of them lost themselves in private, crack-induced thoughts amid the slowly swirling cloud of acrid smoke. In the maze of streets that surrounded them, however, the news of what had happened in the house began to spread. And the net that the world was trying to throw around them was rapidly taking shape, being transmitted over police radios even as they smoked themselves into a schizophrenic stupor.

• • •

The dispatcher on J band—the police's main radio frequency—cursed herself for agreeing to stay over and work the four hours of overtime. As usual, they were shorthanded in the Radio Room, and she was needed. That, and the fact that she actually cared about the cops she had worked with every day for the past ten years, was what kept her going.

One of the few experienced people in Radio—a high-stress, high-turnover job—she was probably the only one the lieutenant would entrust with J band on a night when it seemed that all hell was breaking loose on the border of East and Northwest divisions. Not even one of the uniformed officers who occasionally worked the consoles could have handled the pressure of a high-speed chase across two or three divisions as well as she could, and everyone knew it. So they endured her barbs and watched her switch back and forth across the Radio Room, teasing any and every man who would dare think he could have her.

That was another thing that kept up her zeal for the job—the men. At fifty, her chances of finding another husband were slim, but if she didn't, it wouldn't be for lack of trying, and it wouldn't be because she didn't look good. With caramel skin that looked as if it would melt at the slightest touch, luxurious, thick hair cut to shoulder length, and a curvaceous figure that belied her chair-bound profession, she still attracted stares from men half her age. She was getting stares even now. But she was ignoring them. Her concern now was leaving. She'd had enough excitement for one night. With that thought in mind, she looked at her watch and immediately had a fit.

"It's only twelve-thirty?" she said, thinking that it seemed like she'd been there forever when she'd only done a half hour extra.

Half seriously, she sucked her teeth and made an announcement, ignoring the corporal who hung over her shoulder and the static-filled chatter of the commanders and detectives who occupied J band.

"I'm tellin' y'all, if I don't get some coffee right now, and I mean right this minute, I'm not responsible for what happens to these idiots on my radio," she said.

"I'm going to get us some now," one of the cops said as he passed his headset to another officer and started toward the hallway.

"And make mine black," she said. "You know I don't like nothin' too white."

"Not even me?" the cop asked sheepishly.

"Especially not you," she said with a devilish smile.

"Well, I guess I'll have to hope the jeweler takes refunds on three-carat diamond engagement rings. And here it is I thought there was a chance for you and me."

"Now, you know you ain't thought nothin' of the sort. You don't make enough money to keep me like I need to be kept."

"Not even with overtime?"

"Not with two jobs, a water ice stand, and double time on Sunday."

The cop laughed and went out into the hallway.

One of the sergeants hung up the phone at the supervisor's desk and ripped a sheet of paper from the printer. "We just got this GRM on the guys from the Park Avenue job."

"Okay," she said, taking the paper and glancing at it before broadcasting it over J, T, M, and all eight divisional bands.

"Cars stand by," she said, pausing for a half second before reading on. "GRM 92635. Wanted for investigation for a founded shooting at 3746 Park Avenue and an assault on a police officer at the Roberts Avenue off-ramp of the northbound Schuylkill Expressway on September 24, 1992, two males. Number one, Leroy Johnson, black male, thirty-four years, has black hair and brown eyes, is five feet eleven inches tall, one hundred sixty pounds, with a scar on his right forearm and a tattoo on his chest area that reads 30TH STREET NATION. He is dark-complexioned with a thin build and was last seen wearing jeans, red sneakers, and a black sweatshirt with the word FILA written across the chest. He has a thin beard and mustache and speaks with a slight stutter. Number two, Samuel Everett Jackson, black male, twenty-four years, has black hair and brown eyes, is five feet ten inches tall, one hundred fifty pounds. He is dark-complexioned with a thin build and wears a mustache and goatee. No further description. These males may have made their escape on foot from Roberts and Wayne Avenue, where they may have been involved in an auto accident at or about twelve-fifteen A.M., September twenty-fifth, 1992. They should be considered armed and dangerous. Please use caution. This is KGF 587, the correct time is now 12:35 A.M."

When she had finished reading the GRM, the dispatcher looked puzzled.

"A general radio message fifteen minutes after the last time somebody saw them?" she said. "Excuse me, not the last time somebody saw them. The last time somebody thought they may have been involved in an auto accident."

"Yeah, they're really trying to move on this one," the sergeant said.

"Yeah, I guess they are."

They both sat quietly for a moment, listening to the static-filled transmissions on the radio.

"It's a shame about that rookie," the dispatcher said seriously, remembering how he'd screamed over the air just before his car ran into the median. "Have they said anything about his condition?"

"He's over at Abbottsford Hospital with second- and third-degree burns on his arms. He'll live. But get this. One of the suspects from the car he was chasing is in Abbottsford, too. He hasn't regained consciousness since they brought him in, and it doesn't look good. Apparently the guy got burned pretty bad before he managed to crawl out of the car. If he wakes up, Homicide can question him to see what he knows. If not . . ."

The sergeant let the sentence hang in midair as the dispatcher sipped at her coffee and tried to suppress a shudder at the thought of being trapped in a fiery wreck.

"In the meantime," the sergeant said, breaking into her thoughts, "I'm getting it straight from the top that we have to read the GRM every five minutes."

"Why'd they move so fast on the GRM, anyway? Who'd these guys kill, the president?"

"Close." The sergeant lowered his voice to a whisper. "It was Podres."

"Podres?" she said loudly as the sergeant put his fingers to his lips in an effort to keep her quiet. "The head of the Police Civilian Review Board?"

"Yeah," the sergeant said, looking around the room self-consciously.

They were both quiet for a moment, probably going over the implications of a city councilman's murder happening on their watch. Every move made by the police, including the actions taken in the Radio Room, would be under the close scrutiny of the jackal-like Philadelphia press corps.

What the dispatcher and the sergeant both should have known is that the cat was already out of the bag. Half the people in the Radio Room—call takers and dispatchers alike—already knew. Some of their friends on the outside knew, too, and had probably tipped off the press. Which meant that the prey had been selected, the hunt was afoot, and the feast of the jackals was just about ready to begin.

Homicide lieutenant Jorge Ramirez was directing two of his detectives to begin door-to-door questioning of all the neighbors, when he saw a guy in a sweatshirt and a woman with a trench coat get out of a news van and start setting up in Lee's parking lot.

He motioned to a young detective, who dropped what he was doing and walked over to him.

"Has anybody called the captain?" Ramirez said.

"I left a message on his answering machine," the detective said. "He paged me a few minutes ago and said he'd be coming down with the commissioner."

"Good, because I don't want these reporters asking me about a whole lot of stuff they know I can't talk about. As a matter of fact, call Radio and have them try to get a hold of the girl from community relations. Sergeant Harris, I think her name is. Let her get out of bed and answer some questions."

"Sure, Lieutenant."

"You notified Podres's family, right?"

"Ten minutes ago."

"Good. As far as the press is concerned, the family hasn't been notified yet, okay?"

"Sure, Boss."

"I want to keep a lid on this thing for as long as possible. At least until tomorrow morning."

Ramirez turned to walk back inside the house, wondering how Leroy had disappeared so quickly. Mrs. Green, the woman from two doors away, said she saw Leroy go into the house just before the gunshots. That's how they'd lucked out and got a clothing description. The stuff on Leroy's partner, though, was pure speculation. No matter. Ramirez figured that the best way to flush out Leroy was through another piper. And since the guy in the hospital wasn't likely to wake up, he figured Black was the next best thing. After all, a piper would rat on his own mother for a three-dollar cap. He'd seen it happen.

"Detective," the trench-coat-bedecked reporter called out.

Ramirez turned around, wondering what had made her pick him from the crowd of officers who were walking in and out of the house.

"Yes?"

"Is it true that Councilman Johnny Podres was found shot to death inside that house about an hour ago?" she said.

"No comment."

"Detective," the reporter called out as her cameraman trained a bright light in Ramirez's face. "We have confirmed from several police sources that the victim, city councilman Johnny Podres, was shot to death in this house. Now, can you tell me if his family has at least been notified?"

A few people, older neighbors and kids who shouldn't have been out at that time of night, began to gather, drawn by the lure of the camera and lights.

"Look, lady," Ramirez said. "I don't know who your sources are, but, as you know, Ms. . . ."

He left a space for her to fill in her name.

"Miss," she said. "Miss Jeanette Deveraux. Don't you watch the news?"

"No. Too much blood and guts."

"Oh great," she said, holding down her microphone. "A detective who can't stand blood and guts."

Ramirez stifled a grin.

"You were saying?" she prodded.

"I was saying, Miss Deveraux, that we cannot comment on an ongoing investigation. We're withholding the identity of the victim until the family can be notified. Now, if you'll excuse me."

"Do you have any suspects?" she asked, rushing the question to keep him from walking away from her.

"You probably already know the answer to that," Ramirez said, knowing that all the news agencies monitored police transmissions with scanners.

"One more question," the reporter said before he could run back into the house. "Isn't 3746 Park Avenue a crack house?"

"One might call it that," Ramirez said, feeling like he'd already said too much.

"Yeah, it's a crack house!" someone from the crowd yelled.

"They know it's a crack house!" another voice shouted.

"If you were doing your job from the beginning, shutting down these houses, you wouldn't have to be here now!" an older woman said angrily.

The reporter looked at the woman. "What's your name, ma'am?"

"Eva Richards," she said.

"Can I talk to you when I finish talking to the detective?" Deveraux said.

"I don't talk to reporters," the woman said. "Especially about what goes on in these houses, because nobody's going to protect me when these dope fiends and murderers come back here. Nobody."

"Okay," the reporter said. "But if you change your mind—"

"I won't," the woman said, and moved back into the crowd.

The reporter turned back to Ramirez.

"Well, Detective . . . ," the reporter said, pausing to allow him to introduce himself.

"Ramirez. Lieutenant Ramirez."

"Lieutenant Ramirez," the reporter repeated. "What was Johnny Podres, the head of the Police Civilian Review Board, doing in a crack house?"

A murmur ran through the crowd as some of the neighbors learned the identity of the victim for the first time. Ramirez turned beet red. As far as this reporter knew, Podres's family hadn't even been notified. So why would she stand there and tell the world that the man was dead when his wife might still be at home waiting for him to come to bed?

Ramirez started to argue that point. He paused for a moment and opened his mouth to speak. But common sense got the better of him.

"No comment," he said, and disappeared into the house.

Jeanette Deveraux looked at her notes, breathed deeply, and turned to her cameraman.

"Okay, Mike, are they ready for the live shot?" she asked him.

"Yeah, Jeanette. Ready when you are."

"Okay, let's take it live."

He gave her a silent countdown, then pointed at her. Standing against a backdrop of barricades, yellow tape, police officers, and neighbors, Jeanette Deveraux contorted her face into that grave, concerned expression television reporters resort to with blood-and-guts stories. And then, as three more news vans and two cars pulled onto the block, she milked it for all it was worth.

"This is Jeanette Deveraux reporting live from the 3700 block of Park Avenue in North Philadelphia, where a Philadelphia city official has been found dead in this reputed crack house."

She turned and extended her hand toward the house, and the camera zoomed in as a child on a bike rode past and waved.

"The official's name is being withheld by police pending

family notification," she continued. "But several police sources, speaking on condition of anonymity, have said that the victim, shot once in the head, was a prominent member of city council."

She began to walk along the edge of the yellow tape, making her way toward Mrs. Richards, who had retreated to the wooden gate that separated the houses from the alleylike street that ran between the Lee's Chicken parking lot and the back of the Park Avenue houses.

"Police have begun the search for two male suspects who may still be in the area. The car they are believed to have escaped in was involved in a high-speed chase in which one occupant was killed and another was taken into custody and hospitalized in critical condition. A police officer was injured during that chase and is also hospitalized in serious condition."

She walked right up to Mrs. Richards, who turned too slowly to walk away. "Neighbors, including this woman, are fearful and outraged. How does it feel to know your public servants are being found in crack houses?"

"I told you," Mrs. Richards said. "I don't talk to no reporters about what goes on in these houses."

"Because of fear?" Jeanette Deveraux said.

"Because I don't," Mrs. Richards said as she walked away.

"This is Jeanette Deveraux, reporting live from North Philadelphia, a neighborhood besieged by fear."

Two men and a woman, all with perfect hair and trench coats, got out of the other news vans and scrambled to set up live reports from the back of the house. Two other men, armed with notepads and tape recorders, got out of cars that had pulled up along with the news vans and began to talk to the neighbors who were willing to talk.

As they did, another car pulled up. A man wearing a suit and a man pulling on the jacket to a police captain's uniform walked up to the barricades and flashed badges. Before they could make it into the house, the lights and cameras were upon them.

"Commissioner Nelson, Commissioner Nelson!" a reporter from Channel 3 yelled out in a voice too forceful for someone her size.

Commissioner Nelson turned around. "We will not have any comment on any aspect of this case until the family of the victim has been notified. Thank you."

"What about the officer who was injured chasing the suspects?" a reporter from the *Daily News* asked. "Will the suspects be charged in relation to that?"

"No comment," Nelson said, bending down to get under the yellow tape.

"Do you have any idea where the suspects might be hiding out?" a reporter from Channel 6 asked.

"No comment," Nelson said, walking briskly toward the back door.

"How could the suspects have walked away from a crash in which one of their companions was burned beyond recognition and another was critically injured?" Henry Moore, a freelance reporter, asked the retreating commissioner. "And how could they disappear in an area flooded with police officers?"

"No comment," he said over his shoulder as he walked into the house.

"Are you sure they were even in the car?" the reporter from Channel 3 asked.

But by the time that question was asked, the commissioner and the captain were inside the house.

"Don't tell me," the reporter said to herself. "No comment."

The commissioner was seeking out Ramirez, whom he had heard live on ABC on the car radio. When he found him, he gave it to him with both barrels.

"Lieutenant, may I speak to you privately?" Nelson said, looking weary and red-eyed, like he always did.

"Yes, sir," Ramirez said, bracing himself and walking with the commissioner to a corner of the living room.

"If I ever hear you say anything other than 'No comment' when the press asks you about an ongoing investigation, I will personally see to it that you get taken to the front," Nelson said, threatening the police equivalent of a court-martial. "Is that understood?"

"Yes, sir."

"And I will guarantee that I will make that experience so long, so drawn out, so frustrating, so painful, that you will not want your badge by the time it's over. I will see to it that Internal Affairs gets you for everything from wiping your ass the wrong way to jerking off in the shower. Is that understood?"

"Yes, sir."

"Good," Nelson said. "Now, why the hell haven't these guys been apprehended? What'd they do, disappear into thin air?"

"Well, sir, I think—"

"I don't care what you think, mister!" Nelson said. "Think about apprehending those suspects before we're all out of a job."

"Yes, sir."

"I want you to understand something, Ramirez," Nelson said. "I want you to understand that I think you're a hell of a detective. That's why I'm putting the entire East and Northwest divisions at your disposal for this investigation. But even though I think you could probably handle this thing yourself, myself and Captain Sheldon are going to personally supervise everything that goes on here.

"We're going back to headquarters to pick up a mobile communications unit," Nelson said, putting a fancy name on what amounted to a trailer with some electronic equipment inside.

"We're going to set it up right outside this house, you'll report directly to us with requests for any resources you need, and we'll find these guys within the next twenty-four hours. Because if we don't, if we're depicted in the press as a bunch of incompetents who were outsmarted by pipers . . ."

Nelson paused in an effort to calm himself.

"If we don't find them," Nelson said, "and I mean yesterday, then God help us all."

"Yes, sir."

As Ramirez watched the commissioner and the captain walk back to their car for the ride back to headquarters, he realized that he wasn't terribly eager to work with either of them. He had the feeling there would be too many chiefs and not enough Indians. He knew he could handle it, though. It wouldn't kill him. It was what he didn't know that could kill him.

Chapter 5

Clarisse broke out a six-pack, and they all had a cold one. It helped them to feel the high every time they took a hit, instead of smoking cap after cap and feeling nothing. But even with the beer, none of them felt the way they thought they should, because the first good hit of crack is often the last one. That's one of the reasons that people get strung out. They get caught up in the cycle of trying to get one more hit like the very first one. But they never do.

"You ain't got no forties up in here, Clarisse?" Leroy said, pushing his screen back to the other end of his straight to scrape the residue from the caps he'd smoked up to the top of the screens.

"No, I don't have any forties, Leroy," Clarisse said, shaking her head.

" 'Ain't got no,' " she said to herself, mocking him. "Somebody call the English police."

"I wish it was only the English police," Leroy said.

"What are you talking about?" Clarisse said.

Leroy looked at Black, who jumped in quickly.

"Why don't you ever push your straight, Clarisse?" he said, changing the subject and wishing that Leroy would stop saying stupid stuff.

"For what?" she said, going over to the radio and turning on KYW News Radio. "By the time I do all that, I could just get somebody to go and get me some more."

"Yeah, but you missin' the best part o' the hit," Black said. "Let me show you."

Black reached for the straight shooter he had given her.

"I don't think so," she said, pulling the glass tube away.

For a moment, Black was offended. But after he thought about it, he couldn't blame her for not trusting him. Crack isn't a social drug, like weed, where everybody can get high from a single joint. And it isn't like beer, where people drink it and get happy. No, crack is a lot different from anything else people use to get high. Very rarely is it fun to smoke. Usually, the high is scary, and the people who smoke it are worse than scary. So Black was almost relieved that Clarisse didn't give up her straight that easily. If she was going to keep smoking, she would have to be that way, because most of the people she would end up smoking with wouldn't care about her, about themselves, about anybody, or about anything.

Pipers are devious. They do all sorts of things to make sure that the person who's treating doesn't get high. That way, the person will keep buying more. The tricks range from poking a hole in the screens, so that the crack burns too quickly, to burning the screens so that the smoke doesn't come through. There are a million ways to get over, and Clarisse wasn't about to fall victim to any of them.

"Girl, gimme the straight and lemme show you somethin'," Black said, extending his hand for the straight shooter.

Hesitantly, she handed it to him, watching carefully to see that he didn't do anything extra. Keeping his hands in front of her so she could see what he was doing, Black pulled out a broken umbrella spoke with an empty cap attached to the end of it. With the jagged end, he scraped the thick brown residue off the side of her straight and shook it gently onto a bent piece of matchbook. When he had finished, there was an inch-high mound of flaky brown scrapings on the piece of cardboard.

"See that?" he said. "That mean your screen's too loose. You tighten 'em up with this."

He showed her the empty cap that he had forced onto the other end of the umbrella spoke.

"Okay," she said, watching with wide-eyed fascination, as if he were performing some kind of complex experiment.

Turning the straight until the end she had been smoking from was flat on the table, Black pushed the screen down until the empty cap crushed it against the tabletop, making it more compact, and thus tighter. Then he turned it over, pushed the screen down enough so she could dump one or two caps, and handed it to her.

"Hold this," he said, and emptied half a cap into the straight, then half the contents of the matchbook, then the other half of the cap on top.

Black lit two matches for her, held them to the end of the straight, and watched her pull the smoke into her lungs. There was a crackling sound, louder than that of a regular cap by itself, and a thick stream of cream-colored smoke shot through the glass tube.

Clarisse's entire face seemed to change as she pulled in the smoke, her eyes bulging and her hand shaking as she tried to hold the straight steady. Her body began to move in small twitching motions, and Black became afraid for her, thinking that her heart might give out, as he had heard other people's had done when the hit was too good. But she continued to pull in the smoke, then held it in, her entire face quivering, and handed him the straight shooter with a slightly trembling hand.

Black looked at her, then at Leroy and Pookie, who sat watching them, and he knew that this was the hit Clarisse had never gotten before, the ghost that she would chase until she'd reached the end of her road, either in needless death or in hopeless surrender to the crack demon.

Her eyes became wide, and her jaw became slack as she stood, watching Black in a way she never had. She glanced at Leroy and Pookie, her body involuntarily swaying in a circular motion. Then she looked down at the straight, and down at Black, and roughly slid her hand up and down his crotch.

He looked into her eyes, and then at the smoke swirling at the end of the straight. Then he shook out the two matches he had held for Clarisse, lit one match, and began to pull the remainder of the thick smoke into his lungs. Clarisse sat down in a chair directly in front of where he stood, sweating and breathing heavily, and began to unbutton her blouse, as if she were melting under the force of some incredible source of heat. Pookie and Leroy sat at either end of the table, watching her and moving closer to each other.

"You always wanted this, didn't you, Everett?" she asked through lips that were frozen in the mouth-numbing grin of a crack fiend, while she undid his pants and stared at the eerily silent Leroy and Pookie.

As Black pulled on the seemingly endless stream of smoke, Clarisse placed him in her mouth, pulling him down into a place where smoke and pleasure whirled around each other in a swirling play of light and sound. When he finished pulling in the smoke, he stood with his eyes closed and felt her hands caressing him while her lips and tongue ran up and down the length of him.

Black put down the straight, slowly released the smoke through his nostrils, and began to caress her breasts. She gasped and he fell to his knees, pulling her down from the chair, his hands exploring her, learning for themselves what his eyes already knew—that she was delicious.

Kneeling there, Black could feel her, could smell her, could taste her. He put her fingers in his mouth and sucked them, one at a time, then ran his hands along the inside of her thighs, touching her softly until her essence poured out beneath his touch. He licked her breasts, teasing and then sucking, whispering the things he had never felt good enough to say to her, running fingers through hair, hands over hips, lips over eyelids and shoulders and neck. And then he sat before her, beckoning for her to move closer, to respond.

Clarisse pulled her skirt around her hips and sat atop his thighs. Gently, he wrapped her legs around his back and thrust into her, searching her eyes for the Clarisse he knew he'd never find again. She locked her ankles behind him and rocked back and forth, her waters running down and through him like hot streams. He met her every motion with a motion of his own, still searching her eyes and hoping that the Clarisse he'd known was still there, still salvageable. She began to scream, to curse him, to love him, to hate him. And then, with a violent shudder, she climaxed, and Black knew that she was someone entirely different. The Clarisse he'd known before had died in the swirl of creamy smoke that drifted toward the ceiling, fading into nothingness, like a ghost.

Now all that remained for either of them was to watch and to wait for whatever was next. There was no turning back. So they sat, their juices running down between them, and watched Pookie give to Leroy what she had never given to anyone who had paid for it.

When Black turned around, Pookie was pulling in smoke, standing and slowly gyrating in a strangely erotic grind. Then she held her straight to Leroy's lips and let him pull the remainder of the smoke from the tube. While he inhaled the smoke, she dropped to her knees and released him from his clothing, caressing him slowly and gently, as if she wanted nothing more than to touch him. Then she began to roll him around on her tongue like candy. For a moment, he watched her. Then he rose from the chair, turned her around, threw her against the wall, and entered her.

Black laid Clarisse on the floor and was upon her, pushing into her as he braced her legs over his shoulders, penetrating her and reveling in the sound of her childlike squeals. Clarisse met his thrusts head-on, giving him all there was to give, while Leroy and Pookie gave their fear and their excitement and their relief to each other against the wall on the other side of the room.

Forever, it seemed, they continued, filling the room with screams and sweat and musky embraces, clawing and tearing at each other like animals, holding on to whatever they could salvage of the moment. And then, through the haze, Black heard someone call his name.

He stopped and turned to Leroy, who was stock still against the wall, listening. Clarisse stopped moving, sensing that something was wrong, and Pookie began to adjust her clothes. The same voice called Leroy's name, and Leroy looked at Black, then at the radio, and they all began to listen.

". . . and to recap the top story this hour, police are looking for two males in connection with a murder in a reputed North

Philadelphia crack house and an assault on a police officer," the voice was saying against a Teletype backdrop. "Although they have not released the name of the victim pending family notification, police have formally released the names of the suspects. They are Leroy Johnson, thirty-four, and Samuel Everett Jackson, known as 'Black,' twenty-four. Johnson is a dark-complexioned black male, five feet eleven inches tall, one hundred sixty pounds, with a scar on his right forearm and a tattoo on his chest that reads 30TH STREET NATION. He speaks with a slight stutter and was last seen wearing jeans and a sweatshirt with the word FILA written across the front. Jackson is a dark-complexioned black male, five feet ten inches tall, one hundred fifty pounds. No further description. They may have made their escape on foot from Roberts and Wayne at or around 12:15 A.M. They may be injured, and they should be considered armed and dangerous. If you spot either male, police are asking that you immediately call 911. KYW News time is 1:46. AccuWeather is next."

For a moment, they were all still. No one looked at anyone. No one moved. No one breathed. They simply stared into space, wondering if it was all part of the high.

Clarisse was the first to speak.

"Who did you kill, Everett?" she asked matter-of-factly.

"I don't know," Black said, pulling on his clothing and staring hard at Leroy. "Ask him. He should know."

"I'm asking you!" Clarisse shouted. "You, Everett. That's who I'm asking. The one I let into my home, the one I trusted!"

"Clarisse, I—"

"Clarisse, nothing!" she said, picking up her underwear. "Now, unless you plan to kill me next, I suggest you get out of my house."

"He ain't k-kill nobody," Leroy said, mumbling.

"What?" Clarisse said.

"I said, he ain't kill nobody," Leroy said.

"I don't care what he did," Clarisse said. "They're broadcasting your ass on KYW and—"

"He ain't kill nobody and I didn't either," Leroy said. "Now, I don't know how they got our descriptions and I don't know why they think Black was there, because he wasn't. But we ain't kill that dude."

"Well, how do you know it was a dude?" Clarisse said. "They didn't say it was a dude. It could've been a woman. As a matter of fact, I don't even know why I'm arguing with you. We can settle all this right now."

Clarisse picked up the phone. Pookie went over and snatched the phone cord from the wall.

"Bitch, you ain't settlin' nothin'," she said. "You might as well go 'head over there and sit down in one o' them chairs 'fore you get—"

Clarisse punched Pookie hard on the side of the head, knocking her into the doorway that separated the kitchen from the dining room.

"Bitch, don't you ever," Clarisse said, kicking her in the head.

"Dis—" she said with a punch to the ribs.

"Respect," with a kick to the midsection.

"Me," punching and kicking her in the face.

Pookie fell on her back, sliding across the kitchen floor, then recovered and kicked a charging Clarisse in the stomach, knocking her back into the dining room table. Clarisse lost her balance and fell hard into a table leg. The leg broke, and the table fell across Clarisse's arm, pinning her to the floor.

"Yeah, bitch, what?" Pookie said, getting up from the kitchen floor and preparing to pounce.

"Nah, y'all gon' stop this right now," Black said, grabbing and pushing Pookie away from Clarisse. "Leroy, get your girl, man."

"That ain't my girl, man."

"Yeah, that's what you think."

Black pulled Clarisse from beneath the heavy rosewood table.

"Go in the freezer and get some ice," he said to Pookie. "And put the rest o' your clothes on. We gotta get outta here."

Pookie looked at Leroy, who nodded, and then she went into the kitchen to get the ice.

"That ain't your girl?" Black asked facetiously.

"Look, man, I—"

"Look, nothin'!" he said, taking the ice pack from Pookie and placing it on Clarisse's arm. "I should be up in here kickin' your ass. You got my name all on the radio and I don't even know what's goin' on. You gon' have to tell me somethin', or I'm callin' 911 myself."

"Black, I—"

"I'll be just like this," Black said, picking up a mock phone. "Yeah, 25th District? This Black. Yeah, that's right, Black—the one y'all got on the radio."

Black paused for a minute, waiting for his make-believe cop to say something.

"Okay, I'll hold for the sergeant. I'm holdin' for the sergeant," Black said to Leroy in a stage whisper, placing his hand over the mock receiver.

"Yeah, Sergeant? Dig this here, Sarge, I ain't kill nobody, but here go the nigger right here. Lee-roy John-son. L-E-R . . ." He paused, as if he were listening.

"Oh, you know how to spell it? All right, well, I'm at 3934

Dell Street. And I'll hold him till you get here. Hurry up before he put his shirt on."

"Everett," Clarisse said. "This is not a joke."

"Yeah, but I gotta laugh to keep from cryin'," Black said. "I shoulda known by the way y'all looked when I seen y'all on Broad Street."

"Look, Black, I ain't kill nobody," Leroy said soberly. "Rock did it. I just walked up on dude and went up in his socks. And I found this."

Leroy reached into his sock and pulled out a wad of hundreds and fifties.

"I went out the front window on the second floor and ran across the roofs. Then I gave this hack two hundred ones to let me use his ride. I was gettin' ready to pull off when Pookie and Rock and Butter—"

"Look, man, save the details. Just tell 'em Rock did it. What, you gon' do life for that nigger?"

"Rock dead," Leroy said.

"He what?"

"I crashed the car up on Wayne Avenue. That's why they think we up there somewhere."

"What you mean *we*?" Black said, growing angry.

"Black, they know we roll together. They probably just assumed we was together again. Now, you can stand there till they walk up in here and lock us all up. Or you can help me get outta this."

Black looked at him, speechless, and began to understand the gravity of their situation.

"So what it's gon' be, nigger? 'Cause ain't neither one of us got time to be standin' up talkin' 'bout it."

"Why should I help you?" Black said. "Give me one good reason."

"I'll give you a thousand." Leroy peeled off ten hundreds.

Black looked at the money, then at Leroy, and the dope fiend inside told him that he could escape from Alcatraz for one thousand dollars.

"All right," he said after a lengthy silence. "Let's do this."

Chapter 6

After nearly two hours of gathering evidence, the police were ready to remove Podres's body from the house. Channels 3, 6, 10, 17, and 29 were carrying the crime scene live, with so-called experts providing commentary via satellite as to why a politician might be frequenting a crack house. Everything from the Marion Barry–like conspiracy theory to the undercover-investigation-gone-awry theory was being advanced. But no one really cared about any of that. They were just talking to buy time until the police walked out to the van with the zippered body bag.

When the television reporters saw the officers walking into the house with the bag, all the cameramen started positioning themselves to get the best shot. It didn't matter whether it was stated. Everyone knew that city councilman Johnny Podres was going to be carried out of that house, and the body-bag piece would be good for at least a week's worth of dramatic replays.

Ramirez knew that. And he was determined not to be a part

of it. So he tried to walk in unnoticed behind the officers with the body bag. Before he could take five steps, the reporters were on him.

"Lieutenant Ramirez!" Jeanette Deveraux shouted.

"No comment," he said, before she got a chance to ask a question.

"Lieutenant Ramirez!" the other reporters began to shout, creating an almost riotlike atmosphere of people yelling and cameramen jostling for position.

"No comment," he said as he worked his way through the crowd, trying hard not to give in to his desire to push somebody down.

When he got to the door, he leaned against the doorjamb for a minute to catch his breath. "Are they ready to bring the body out?" he said to the young detective who was helping him to keep the scene under control.

"Zippin' him up now," the detective said. "The family just called back, too. The wife and daughter said they'll meet you at the medical examiner's."

"Does the medical examiner know that I'll be sitting in on the autopsy?"

"I spoke with an autopsy technician a few minutes ago. They're waiting for you."

"Thanks."

As he prepared to walk out the door, Ramirez straightened his tie and ran his fingers through his hair. He hated attending autopsies almost as much as he hated meeting victims' families. Yet there he was, about to do both. He was still trying to convince himself that it would be worth the sacrifice, when Reds Hillman walked up behind him.

"You know, you're never going to figure this thing out like that," Hillman said.

Ramirez turned around to face him. "What do you mean?"

"You're going down to the medical examiner's to watch an autopsy, for God's sake. You're not a doctor. What the hell are you going to learn from an autopsy?"

"It's not like I'm going to be weighing organs," Ramirez said defensively. "I just want to be there when the medical examiner declares this thing a homicide so we can get all the warrants we need quickly."

"Lieutenant, you're going to have to excuse me for being so blunt, but screw the warrants. You wanna know where to find Leroy? Talk to the people he knows. He's got a friend who lives right around the corner here. If you want, I'll take you around there and we can have a little talk with him."

Ramirez hesitated. But as he watched the grizzled detective with the curly red hair and the smooth stroll make his way to the car, he couldn't help thinking that Hillman was the one person who could help him to sift through the facts to find the truth.

"Come on, Lieutenant, take a ride with me," Hillman said.

Ramirez waited half a beat, then walked out to the car just as the body was carried from the house. The reporters ignored Ramirez as they flocked toward the body bag, and the detectives rode the two blocks to Leroy's friend's house undisturbed.

When they arrived, a man with an easy smile answered the door.

"I was wondering how long it would take for you to get here, Reds," he said, opening the door and extending his hand to Hillman. "Come on in."

"John, this is Lieutenant Ramirez," Hillman said. "I know you probably heard by now . . ."

"I know. You're looking for Leroy. News travels fast around here."

"Me and John go way back," Hillman said to Ramirez. "I was

a beat cop in the 23rd when they used to gang war back in the seventies. I watched him and Leroy grow up."

"No offense, Reds, but I don't really have a lot of time to talk about the good old days."

Ramirez turned his attention to John. "I need to find your friend."

"Why?"

"You tell me. You said that news travels fast."

"If it's the same news I heard, I can tell you right now. Leroy didn't shoot anybody."

"How do you know that?" Ramirez said. "Were you there?"

"I know because I've known Leroy for more than twenty years. I'm probably the only friend he's got left. Everybody else is either dead or in jail."

"So when was the last time you saw him?" Ramirez said.

"Maybe a month ago. He used to come around sometimes when he was hungry and I'd get my wife to make him some chicken or something. But I think he's too proud to come around now. I hear he's looking real bad."

Ramirez's patience was wearing thin. "What can you tell us about him that we don't already know?"

"Look. I know you said you don't want to talk about the old days, but you've gotta understand who Leroy is before you start running around saying he shot somebody."

"Okay," Ramirez said, taking out a notepad. "Who is he?"

"First I gotta tell you where he came from," he said with a wistful smile. "Thirtieth and Columbia—Cecil B. Moore now. He came from a time when Philly was real crazy. Especially North Philly and West Philly. Everybody had a gang, and you couldn't even leave the block without worrying that you'd never make it home.

"You had the Valley, Redner Street, the Moroccos, Zulu Nation, Hoopes Street out in West Philly, Brick Yard and the Hollow up in Germantown. And you had 30th Street Nation down around 30th and Columbia.

"By the time I came along, everything was out of hand. It wasn't just chains and bats and car antennas anymore. It was zip guns and twelve-gauge shotguns and .38s. It was another dead body every day and brothers doing life in Graterford. It was babies growing up without daddies, and mommies ending up prostitutes, turning tricks for pimps who strung them out on heroin.

"It was like the same thing that's going on now, only it was less about the street dealers fighting over corners and money than it was about a people fighting for an identity. Whatever money was made from the heroin trade went to the Mafia boys in South Philly, so big-time drug dealers were almost nonexistent. You didn't see a lot of young boys riding in Benzes and BMWs like you do now. You saw maybe a couple of pimps and a couple of drug dealers driving Caddies around the neighborhood. The rest of us were just stuck, killing one another over worthless corners. You know, Martin was dead, Malcolm was dead, and every other day it seemed like another one of our boys was dead. After a while, it was like, you wanted to be dead yourself, because you just didn't care anymore."

Ramirez looked at him and tried to understand what all this had to do with Leroy.

"I used to sit up nights and wonder how I was going to get out of it," he said. "Sometimes I even thought about just blowing my own brains out so I wouldn't have to worry about somebody else doing it. It was that bad. You know, it was like, every other day there was a funeral. We would try to come in, just to view the body or whatever, and the boy's mom would be there like, screaming that we were the reason her baby was dead. After a while, it was hard to believe that we weren't the reason. At least it was for me.

"But knowing we were the reason that so many people were dying wasn't enough to stop the young boys from joining. Well, that's not really true, because looking back now, I guess they really didn't have any choice. You were either with us or you were against us. And if you lived in the neighborhood and you weren't in the gang, you were against us. The only ones we really let slide were the athletes—basketball players or whatever—and the drug addicts.

"Leroy couldn't play basketball. And he wasn't on dope. Not yet. He was just a young boy, thirteen years old. He lived right there on Oxford Street. I remember seeing him going to the store for his mother one day, and going through the roo the next day. Everybody had to hit him and kick him. That's what the roo was—like two lines of guys. And you had to go down the middle and let them beat you down to prove you were tough enough to join the gang. Can you imagine that? A little boy coming through a line of damn near grown men, taking all kinds of punches and kicks, just to be initiated into a gang that he might or might not live to say he'd been a member of.

"I'll never forget how he looked when he came out of that line. His eye was swelling, his bottom lip was split down the middle, and he was trying hard not to limp where someone had kicked him in the knee. But he was smiling the most incredible smile, as if he'd achieved everything he'd ever wanted in life.

"I don't think it really dawned on me right then that this was someone who really didn't belong there. I don't think I even cared. But the more he hung around, the more he came with us to the gang wars, the more he stood on the corner with us and drank Wild Irish Rose, the more it seemed like he was different from the rest of us. He never said much, because he had that stutter, and I guess he didn't really want to give anybody a reason to mess with him.

"But there were so many things about him that separated him from the rest of us. I mean, the boy just had heart. If we were outnumbered and we had to run back to the neighborhood, Leroy was always the last to go. He was the smallest one, but he would be the last one to go, covering the rear so the rest of us could get away. He would draw up plans like some kind of little general. Using abandoned houses as staging areas, setting up the gang wars so we had whoever we happened to be rumbling outflanked, using cars almost like foxholes, setting things up so that we attacked in waves instead of all at once. The boy was smart. I think the only reason he wasn't the leader was he was too small. But even that didn't stop him. He fought when he had to fight, took his lumps with the rest of us, got locked up when he had to. Didn't talk much, like I said. But the way he looked at you, it was like he could see everything you were thinking. It was like he had this sixth sense about everything that was going on around him. It was like he'd been here before.

"One time I asked him something right before we went out to fight the Valley. I said, 'Leroy, who's not going to make it back?' And when I said it, I was just joking, you know? But Leroy took it seriously. He acted like he didn't hear me. Then he looked at this boy named Porkchop and nodded his head."

He paused, trying to compose himself as the memory came flooding back to him.

"That night, Porkchop got shot in the chest with a twelve-gauge," he said, shaking his head. "The guy just ran up to him and shot him. And Porkchop slumped over a fire hydrant, like a rag doll."

His eyes lost their focus, like he was caught up in a trance.

"The way the blood was pouring out of his chest," he said in a soft monotone, "it looked like thc hydrant was leaking this bright red water. And Porkchop was bent over, trying to turn it off. It was almost like, if somebody would have come by with one of those wrenches, they could have stopped the leak and everything would've been all right."

Ramirez shifted uncomfortably.

"Everybody scattered. I remember I dropped the car antenna I had and ran toward 30th Street. We didn't want to leave him there, but he was dead already, and there was nothing else we could do. So we ran. We ran and we screamed and we tried hard not to cry. And then we bought some wine like that was going to make it go away.

"When we got back, I just looked at Leroy. I was almost kind of scared of him, to tell you the truth, because I thought he had some kind of crazy powers or something. I don't know, maybe that was the Wild Irish Rose talking. But I know I never looked at Leroy the same way after that. None of us really looked at ourselves the same way after that."

He stopped and gripped the bridge of his nose. Then he breathed in deeply and went on.

"On the day of the funeral," he said, "we all came to the church and stood in the back. The family didn't want us there, but we weren't bothering anybody, so it really didn't matter. Nobody said anything to us and we didn't say anything to them, either. Everything was fine. The preacher said his little piece about the gang wars and how we were in the final days. The choir got up and sang 'Amazing Grace.' The women cried, the children cried, the grandmother passed out, and the men all looked at us like it was our fault. Everything was going like it was supposed to go. As soon as the guys from the funeral home got up to close the casket, though, all hell broke loose.

"The guys from the Valley ran up in the church and flipped the casket over in the middle of the aisle. At first, we were like, frozen. And then—it was like somebody yelled, 'Action!' or something—it was just like we were out in the street. They tried to run back down the aisle, but they were trapped inside the church, stuck between us and the family. We kicked their behinds, and by the time they got out of the church, a lot of them were too hurt to even make it out of the neighborhood. The cops came and arrested some of them, but none of us got arrested, because we hid in a couple of abandoned houses across the street.

"When we came out, we caught one of them trying to stagger up the street. The rest of them had either run away or gotten arrested, so he was on his own. When he saw us, he tried to run, but we grabbed him and dragged him into one of the houses. Frank Nitty—that's what our leader called himself back then—told this dude to go and get some rope or some string or something to tie him up with. While we waited for the guy to come back with the rope, we beat that boy unconscious like three times. Every time he would pass out, we would make him wake up and knock him out again. By the time dude came back with the rope, the guy didn't even look like the same person anymore. His whole head was swollen.

"When we finished tying him up, Frank pulled a gun out of his waistband and gave it to Leroy. Then he told Leroy to kill the guy. I still remember the way he said it: 'Do it for Porkchop, 'cause Porkchop can't do it for hisself.'

"Leroy took the gun, cocked the hammer, and held it tightly in his right hand, aiming right at the boy's chest. Then Frank made everyone leave the room. The only ones who stayed were me and Leroy. My job was going to be to help drag the body to the window and throw it into the alley. And I would've done it, too, without the slightest reservation. But just as I was trying to brace myself for the blast, something strange happened. Leroy uncocked the hammer, handed Frank the gun, and told him he wasn't going to do it.

"I couldn't believe it. This little thirteen-year-old boy stood there and told Frank, knowing the consequences of what he was saying, that he could never just stand there and kill someone who wasn't trying to kill him. Leroy stood there and gave up what could have been his life, because Frank could have shot him right there for disobeying an order. He stood there and he did that because, even then, Leroy would do anything except take someone's life for nothing. He did it because he had something that I hadn't discovered in myself yet—the courage to stand up for what he believed in.

"Frank let Leroy walk out of there that day. But Leroy could never walk with his head up in the neighborhood again. Frank made him leave the gang the same way he came in; by going through the roo. We lined up in this little open space out in Fairmount Park. And then we made Leroy come through. Only it wasn't just about fists and feet that time. Oh no, when he came through that time, he wasn't supposed to come out alive. And he almost didn't. We beat that boy so bad that when we were finished, we ran away, thinking he was going to die in that lot. But he didn't. He got up and he walked away. And every time we saw him after that, we beat him down again.

"After a while, it was like he was immune to it. He would stand there and take it, day after day, time after time, like it didn't even hurt him anymore. But when you looked at him real close, you could see that he wasn't the same. The light in his eyes—the one he'd use to see into your soul—it died one day. And when the light died, he died. I guess he couldn't go on knowing that he didn't belong anymore. I guess it became too tempting to give up on life. So that's what he did.

"He started shooting heroin, and even though his body grew, you could see that his spirit was shrinking. He was withering away to nothing. The man he became was nowhere near the boy he had been. And everyone could see it. We started seeing him sitting on people's steps nodding, or walking up the street scratching the side of his face. His hands were as big as baseball mitts and his body started to look bloated. It got to the point where we didn't even bother him anymore. We just stood by and watched him killing himself.

"After I moved out of the neighborhood, I got into the church, went to school. I guess Leroy kept going in the opposite direction. When cocaine came out, he started using that. And I guess when crack came out, that was the next logical thing for him to do. Because when you're born to be a leader, and someone snatches all that away from you, sometimes you end up thinking that you don't have anything left to live for."

John shook his head sadly. Then he looked over at Ramirez.

"That's why I know Leroy couldn't have killed anybody," he said earnestly. "Because I know that the man cared too much about life to take it, even if it meant giving up his own."

When Ramirez and Hillman left the house and headed back to the crime scene, they weren't any closer to finding Leroy. But Leroy had become more than just words on a printout. He had become real to them. And Ramirez hated that.

He didn't want to know anything about a suspect's past that he couldn't read on a rap sheet. He saved his compassion for his family, for other cops, for people whose lives intersected with his own. But never for suspects. It was easier that way. He didn't have to feel.

Hillman had seen a thousand cops like that. Their every action was about detachment. But Hillman was going to make sure that Ramirez looked below the surface. He knew that there was more to North Philly than desolation. The people in the streets he patrolled were his family. Not other cops. Not his ex-wife. Not even his children. Perhaps that was why his life was in a shambles. He cared too much.

"What are you thinking so hard about, Reds?" Ramirez said.

Hillman started to tell the truth: that he was wondering how it felt to be detached, like Ramirez. But he just steered the conversation back around to the subject at hand.

"I was thinking about Leroy," Hillman said.

"What about him?"

"You heard what the man said. Leroy doesn't shoot people."

"Yeah, I heard him. But people change. Twenty years is a long time."

"Maybe, but doesn't this whole thing just seem a little odd to you?"

"Does what seem odd?"

"The commissioner and the captain wanting to be so close to the investigation. Focusing on one or two suspects without any real evidence."

"I do what I'm told, Reds," Ramirez said. "When the commissioner tells me to find somebody, I do it. I don't ask why. I get less grief that way."

The radio crackled to life. "Dan 25, meet two complainants at Northwest Detectives in reference to a carjacking at Roberts and Wayne Avenue. Please expedite. It may be related to the founded shooting on Park Avenue."

"Dan 25 received," Ramirez said, looking over at Hillman. "Hold me out on the scene at Park Avenue. Dan 50 will meet the complainants at Northwest."

"Okay, Dan 25."

Hillman smiled to himself and looked down at his lap. "You sure you want to send an old man to check that out?"

"Contact me if it turns out to be a solid lead," Ramirez said, ignoring Hillman's question as he got out of the car and walked back over to the house on Park Avenue.

Hillman was almost beginning to like Ramirez. He reminded Hillman of himself as a young detective. But as he shook his head and smiled at the young lieutenant's cocky attitude, Hillman couldn't help wondering about Leroy.

If he knew that he was wanted, he could probably elude the police for days without ever leaving the neighborhood.

But Hillman knew all too well that Leroy could never escape from his real enemy—himself. And that, more than anything, would be his weakness. That is, unless he had a lot of help.

Chapter 7

Clarisse looked at Black like he was crazy.

It wasn't as if he had asked her to kill herself or anything. But they needed her, and he didn't think the request was all that unreasonable.

"You want me to do what?" Clarisse asked in disbelief.

"I want you to let us hold your car," Black said. "And maybe some of your clothes, so we can make it out of the city."

Leroy and Pookie, fully dressed now, stood next to them in the dining room and listened, knowing they could only make matters worse if they interfered.

"Well, y'all might as well kill me now," Clarisse said. "Because there is no way I'm letting you and him and this bitch go anywhere in my new car."

"I got your bitch," Pookie said.

"Shut up, Pookie," Leroy said, and she immediately fell silent.

"Clarisse," Black said, pausing for a moment. "The only way we can get out of here is in a car. And we can only do that while it's still dark. Now, I know you think we killers, or whatever you think. But I ain't kill nobody, and neither did Leroy. Five-o ain't tryin' to hear that, though. You heard what they said, right? Two black males wanted for a shooting and an assault on a police officer.

"Assault on a police officer," he repeated, emphasizing each word. "You know what that mean to a cop? That mean shoot a nigger now, ask questions later. If we walk out that door, we won't live five minutes and you know it."

Clarisse looked at him hard and said, "So what."

"Oh, so what we did tonight ain't mean nothin' to you?"

"Nigger, please. You know just like I know that it didn't mean anything. And even if it did, you don't have a job or a place to live. Plus you're smoking. What can you do for me, Everett, or Black, or whatever your name is? So why don't you do me, and you, and all of us, a favor. Save the drama for your mama, 'cause I ain't tryin' to hear that shit."

"That's what they teach y'all in nursing school?" Black said. "How to cuss people out?"

"That's what they teach you in real life, Everett. How to survive."

"So what I got to do to get you to help us?"

"Nothing," she said. "Because I'm not going to help you."

"Look. Don't even let us hold the car. Just give us some coats and hats to put on over our clothes and drive us somewhere—anywhere. You can drop us off and drive yourself back home."

"You're going to ride around wearing women's coats and hats?" she said, stifling a grin.

"That's right. Not unless you got a better idea."

"And what about her?" she said, nodding toward Pookie.

"They ain't lookin' for her."

"They're not looking for her *yet,*" she said.

"They lookin' for two guys walkin'. Not four sisters in a ride. How they gon' recognize us if we shave and take showers and put on some of your clothes?"

"They probably wouldn't. Too bad I'm not going to let you shave and take showers and put on some of my clothes."

"I'll pay you," Leroy said.

"This isn't about money," Clarisse said, folding her arms and turning her head.

"Clarisse," Black said. "If we was killers you woulda been slumped by now. We woulda just took whatever we needed and left you up in here dead.

"Now, I like you. If things was just a little bit different, I could probably love you. But this here is life or death. And if you think I'm lettin' you stop me from gettin' outta here 'cause you don't wanna be involved, you wrong."

"No, Everett," she said. "You're wrong. I'm not involved. I've never been involved. I'll never be involved. I'm not the one who—"

"Shut up!" Black said, raising his voice for the first time. "You are involved. So stop tryin' to act like you so far above all this, 'cause you ain't. You smokin' just like I'm smokin'. And you want some more dope just like I want some more dope. So stop frontin' like you so shocked, 'cause you ain't no better than nobody in here. Now, take the money, girl, and don't make me do nothin' I don't wanna do. 'Cause I'll take your car, lock you in the trunk, and leave yo' ass out the airport till the dogs catch the scent."

For a moment, there was near silence. The only sound in the

room was the chatter of the radio and the hiss of Black's breathing. Everyone else, it seemed, was holding their breath. No one blinked, or shifted position, or spoke. Nothing, in fact, moved—until Pookie laughed.

Clarisse reacted before anyone could stop her. By the time Black looked up, her fist was flying past him in a blur, and Pookie's feet were leaving the floor. When he looked again, Pookie had banged into the far wall and was sliding down, her eyeballs rolled back in the sockets like marbles.

She crumpled to the floor in a heap, and Leroy rushed over to help her.

"How much money are you talking about?" Clarisse said, ignoring Pookie while she rubbed her knuckles and breathed heavily.

"Huh?" Leroy said, looking up from Pookie. "Oh, three hundred."

"Six hundred," she said.

"What?" Leroy said, acting as if she had asked for his right arm.

"I'll give her the other three," Black said. "Let's just get outta here."

"All right," Leroy said, looking at Pookie with glazed eyes.

"The shower's upstairs," Clarisse said. "There are new razors and toothbrushes in the bathroom cabinet, and some men's clothes in the closet in the master bedroom. They might be too big for you and Leroy, but you'll be wearing coats, so I guess it won't matter."

"What you doin' with men's clothes?" Black said.

"None of your business. And wake that bitch up. I don't allow any sleeping in here."

Leroy splashed water in Pookie's face while Black went upstairs to shower, stripping off his clothes as he climbed the stairs and hoping that Clarisse and Pookie could stop themselves from killing each other for the next five minutes or so.

"Throw your clothes in the trash can up there!" Clarisse yelled up the steps.

Black didn't respond. He was too busy hiding his thousand dollars between some towels and rummaging through the bathroom cabinet for a toothbrush. Finding one, he unwrapped it and hastily squirted toothpaste across its bristles before stepping into the shower.

"Everett?" Clarisse said, and he ignored her again as he turned on the water, watching the steam rise slowly against the glass shower doors as he scrubbed the toothbrush feverishly against his teeth.

Black could hear Leroy talking, and then the sound of someone coming upstairs, but it sounded like it was only one person, so he knew it wasn't five-o. Not that he cared. This was a shower, and nothing was going to stop him from getting it, because showers were special, particularly since he had begun living in the street.

Most of the time, he would just go into a McDonald's bathroom and wash up in the sink. Other times, he would spend the night at Ridge Avenue Shelter and shower there, or he'd go to 802—the place for the homeless on Broad Street—and sign the shower list. But a real shower in a real home? Black hadn't had one of those since his family had stopped letting him in the house. Maybe that's why he didn't hear Clarisse come in and slide the shower door back.

"Everett," she said, her mouth almost next to his ear.

Startled, he jumped and turned around to see her naked body draped in a cloud of steam.

"Don't be sneakin' up on me, Clarisse."

"How else would I get to see you in the shower?" she said, moving closer and stroking him gently as the water dripped down between them.

"Clarisse, we ain't got time for this."

"I know. I just wanted to ask you something."

"What?"

"I wanted to ask you if you meant what you said about loving me if things were different. I mean, how do you know you don't love me now?"

"How you know I ain't love you the first time I saw you? When you walked in Miss Shaw class in sixth grade wearin' that yellow sundress and those black Mary Janes."

She tried to respond, but Black put his fingers to her lips and kissed her. Then he lathered his washcloth and bathed her. When he finished, he quickly washed himself and stepped out of the shower.

"I gotta shave. Go get Pookie and Leroy and tell them to get in the shower. Then we can find us something nice to put on."

"How about a nice yellow sundress?" she said, smiling flirtatiously.

"Stop playin'. You got two sets of men's clothes in the closet?"

"Yes, I do."

"Shoes, too?"

"Yup."

"I guess we probably need some hats and sunglasses, too," Black said as an afterthought. "You got men's coats, too?"

"One. But I've got a trench coat that looks like it could belong to a man or a woman."

"We probably be better off wearin' all women's clothes anyway," he said. "Then they really won't recognize us."

"You might be right. I have a blue rayon skirt set that is definitely you, honey."

Clarisse chuckled as she walked out of the bathroom wrapped in a terry-cloth robe. When she went downstairs, though, the laughing stopped. Pookie was still unconscious—and going into convulsions.

"Oh my God," Clarisse said quietly. "Oh my God!" she said again, almost screaming.

Because the row house on one side of her home had been demolished, Clarisse only had one set of next-door neighbors. The Scotts, an elderly couple who had known Clarisse's parents, had watched Clarisse grow from a skinny little girl to a beautiful young woman, so they knew her better than anyone in the world. And since her parents' death in a car accident ten years before, the Scotts had tried to fill the void for her, gladly becoming more like family than neighbors.

They had taken on the role of surrogate grandparents. They had watched Clarisse graduate from high school, go on to nursing school, and struggle to become a registered nurse. They had encouraged her as she built a career and a life on the tail end of a tragedy that would have destroyed a lesser young woman. They had watched her socialize, and date, and laugh and cry. And now, they thought, they were watching her kill herself.

She was losing weight, disappearing before their very eyes. Her hours were becoming erratic, even for a nurse. She was speaking to them less and less. Truth be told, she was starting to avoid them. Even so, they convinced themselves that her strange behavior was due to the stress of a demanding nursing career. And for a while, that explanation worked for them. But when they noticed the young man who had started to visit her from time to time—the one they'd seen coming out of the drug house at Broad and Pike—they knew it was something more than stress.

But knowing Clarisse's problem and approaching her about it were two different things. They wanted to help her. They just didn't know how to begin. So, like so many families held captive by their loved ones' addictions, they ended up stuck between their desire to be there for Clarisse and their desire to distance themselves from the violence and depravity that had invaded their neighborhood along with crack.

It was only after much contemplation that they decided there was nothing they could do for Clarisse except to continue to pray for her and leave it in the hands of the Lord. That decision, they hoped, would allow them to sleep easier. And it did, until that night.

"Did you hear that?" Eldridge Scott turned over and asked his wife, Mildred.

"Hear what?" she said from beneath the covers.

"It sounded like a man said, 'Shut up!' real loud like."

"Eldridge, you know them boys always walking 'round here talkin' loud. Now, go to sleep."

"It sounded like it was next door," he said, reaching over and turning on the bedside lamp.

They both listened.

"You sure it was next door?" Mildred asked.

"Well, you know she be havin' that boy over there smokin' that stuff."

"You don't know that for sure."

"What else she doin' makin' all that noise five minutes to two?"

"Maybe she watchin' television. Don't she have one o' them big-screen televisions?"

"If she ain't sold it to the dope man yet."

"Eldridge," she said in an admonishing tone.

"Well, Mildred, you know what she doin' just like I do. Now, we already talked about that, so don't act like it's somethin' brand-new."

He paused for a moment, realizing, not for the first time, how much it hurt him to see Clarisse hurting herself.

"I love her as much as you do," he said finally. "But we got to face the truth."

They both fell silent, listening for the next sound, but they didn't hear anything. After a full five minutes, they began to breathe easier.

"Eldridge, can you turn off the light and go to sleep now?"

"I coulda swore somethin' was wrong over there," he said after listening a moment longer. "But I guess it was just the television."

"I tried to tell you that," Mildred said, clearly relieved.

But as Eldridge reached for the light, he heard a woman yell, "Oh my God!"

It sounded like Clarisse.

"That's the television, too?" Eldridge said, picking up the phone on the nightstand. "I'm callin' over there."

Mildred sat up in bed, hoping her husband would turn to her in a few minutes and tell her that everything was all right, that the sounds they heard were nothing.

"Fast busy signal. Phone must be off the hook."

"Eldridge," she said, biting her lip. "Call the police."

"You think I wasn't?" Eldridge said. Then he cleared the line and dialed 911.

"I think she may have a concussion," Clarisse said, "But she's . . ."

Pookie convulsed, her eyes opening wide in a look of pure terror. Clarisse took off her robe and covered Pookie with it, mumbling something about Pookie going into shock.

"Man, she ain't in shock," Black said. "She be shakin' all the time. Leroy, take her upstairs and put her in the shower with you."

"No, you can't move her," Clarisse said. "We have to keep her still and warm."

"We ain't got time for all that," Black said. "We gotta roll."

"We can't go anywhere until she's stabilized," Clarisse said, checking Pookie's pulse.

"Well, I guess we just gotta leave her."

"I-I ain't leavin' her," Leroy said. "And you ain't, either."

"What? We 'bout to get sent up for a body, and you talkin' 'bout we ain't leavin' her? Man, lemme tell you somethin'. When we on death row, strapped down, waitin' for some dude to give us a hot shot, she gon' be right here, down Broad and Erie, suckin' the next man's—"

"Don't say it, Black."

"Or else what?"

"Just don't."

"You's about a dumb-ass," Black said, shaking his head in disbelief. "But if you wanna roll like that, go 'head."

Leroy looked at Black expectantly, as if he thought he were going to walk out on them.

"Look, Leroy," he said, sighing heavily. "Go upstairs and shave, wash up, and be ready to leave in five minutes. I said I would get us outta this, so I'll do that, even if we gotta drag Pookie with us."

Leroy nodded and bent down to touch Pookie's forehead. Then he ran upstairs and turned on the water in the shower.

"You got her from here, right?" Black said to Clarisse. " 'Cause we gotta get outta here. You said the clothes in the upstairs bedroom?"

"Yes. And bring me something down, too."

Black went upstairs and started rummaging through her closets for the men's clothes. He found two suits, complete with ties and shoes. There was a rayon skirt set hanging near the suits, so he took that out for Clarisse and hoped the shoes he picked out for her were right. He picked out another skirt set for Pookie, and coats for everyone. He found two pairs of sunglasses in her bedroom drawer. And in the top of her closet, there were hats.

Once he'd gathered everything into a bundle, he walked back downstairs.

"Finish undressing her, Everett," Clarisse said without turning around. "And tell Leroy to put her in the shower. If we get stopped, I don't want anybody to smell like anything but perfume."

"All right," Black said, dressing quickly in a blue suit that was at least two sizes too big.

Clarisse began to dress in the skirt set he'd brought down for her, carefully watching Pookie as she began to come around.

"I think she's all right," Clarisse said as she put on her stockings.

Black cast an accusatory glance in Clarisse's direction.

"I wasn't trying to kill the girl, Everett," she said defensively. "But something about her just . . . I don't know."

"She probably remind you of yourself."

"Please," she said, as if he'd uttered the unthinkable.

"How you know she ain't never have no job and no house and all that?"

"I don't. But—"

"But nothin'. Keep smokin' crack, you ain't gon' have none, either."

"How can you tell me anything?" she said, her voice drenched with sarcasm. "Look at *you*."

"That's right. Look at me. Look real close, 'cause you gon' be lookin' just like me in a minute."

They finished dressing in silence. Black put the coats and hats on one of the dining room chairs, then undressed Pookie and carried her upstairs to the bathroom.

"I got her, man," Leroy said, taking her from his arms.

"Here, well, get this, too," Black said, handing him the gray suit and the other skirt set he'd taken from the closet. "And gimme the clothes you had on."

Leroy passed his old clothes through the bathroom door.

"Clarisse," Black said as they stood outside the bathroom door. "Let's take me and Leroy clothes and put 'em in a trash bag. We can dump 'em somewhere when we get from around here."

"Why don't you just leave them here and I'll get rid of them when I get back? It's not like anyone saw you come in here. And if they stop us and search the car with those clothes in a bag in the trunk . . ."

Black tapped on the bathroom door as he answered her. "If they stop us and find the dope and the money, we goin' up anyway. You wanna leave the dope and the cash, too?"

She just looked at him.

"Yeah, that's what I thought," he said as Leroy opened the bathroom door. "Leroy, we goin' downstairs."

"I'll be right down," he answered.

When Clarisse and Black got downstairs, he started straightening up the mess in the dining room, trying to leave the place in some semblance of order. He was funny that way. Even in the house on Park Avenue, when everyone else would be throwing stuff everywhere, Black would always be the one trying to keep the place neat.

"What are you doing?" Clarisse asked, clearly amused.

"What you should be doin'. I'm puttin' your house in order."

Leroy came downstairs dressed in the oversized gray suit with his tie undone. Pookie, groggy and bleary-eyed but dressed smartly in a skirt set that almost fit, followed him.

"Tie this for me, Black," Leroy said.

"Clarisse, go outside and start the car," Black said, reaching over and tying Leroy's tie in a half Windsor.

"Y'all got everything?" she asked.

Black nodded.

Leroy reached down and patted his sock. "Yeah, I got everything."

"Well, I don't," Clarisse said, holding out her hand.

Black reached into his inside pocket and gave her three hundred-dollar bills. Leroy peeled another three from the roll in his sock.

"All right?" Black said, reaching for one of the four trench coats and hats he'd brought down earlier. "Now let's get outta here."

"What's takin' them so long?" Eldridge Scott said to his wife as he picked up the phone to dial 911 for the third time.

"You know they take their time comin' down here," Mildred said. "You almost gotta tell 'em somebody been shot just to get a police car to ride down the block, let alone stop."

"Hello," Eldridge said as the call taker answered. "Yes I called earlier about a disturbance at 3934 Dell Street. Well, it sound like they shootin' over there now."

Mildred looked at him, surprised at the lie.

"I heard the shots less than a minute ago," he said, looking back at Mildred defiantly.

The call taker asked him another question.

"No, I don't have any description of the person with the gun, but I—"

The call taker interrupted him.

"Yes, I think the person's still there."

Again, there was a question.

"Look. Stop asking me all these damn questions and get somebody over here!"

After he'd slammed the receiver into the cradle, Mildred waited a few minutes before she said anything to him.

"Sweetie," she said as she reached for the remote control and clicked on the television, "I don't think that's going to make them come any faster."

"Time they finish askin' all them questions she could be dead. Suppose somebody really do have a gun over there? They could—"

"Eldridge," she said, reaching over and stroking the hair that framed the side of his head. "Calm down, honey. The only thing we can do is wait for them to come. Now, you called three times, so we might as well just see what's on the television, since we ain't goin' to sleep no time soon."

"I ain't studyin' no television," he said, turning over and pulling the blanket over his shoulders.

"Well, I'm gon' see what's on," Mildred said, turning up the volume on the television set.

"And this just in," the reporter was saying. Mildred looked closer, because he was standing in front of a house around the corner. "The two males who are wanted in connection with the shooting here on Park Avenue have been identified as Leroy Johnson, thirty-four, and Samuel Jackson, twenty-four."

As the reporter droned on, giving physical descriptions of the two men, their pictures, obviously taken from past police mug shots, flashed on the screen. Mildred tapped her husband on the shoulder.

"What is it, woman?" Eldridge said as Mildred struggled for words and tapped his shoulder again.

"What in the world is it?" Eldridge said, angrily jumping up.

Mildred pointed to the television, and his gaze followed her pointing finger to a picture of the man they'd seen visiting Clarisse's house.

"Eldridge," she said, finally finding her voice, "the boy done killed somebody."

"Dear God," he said, and picked up the phone to dial 911 again.

The call taker had only worked in the Radio Room for three months, and she hated it. Not only were there too many supervisors, but the people who called were rude, obnoxious, and most of the time liars. The pay was good, though, and once you got in with the city, you could switch to another department and make just as much money doing a less stressful job.

She always tried to think of that when she was stuck there, working overtime. Especially when somebody called with some crazy story just to get the police to come faster.

As the call popped on her screen, she looked at the time that was displayed in the corner of her monitor and saw that it was 2:10 A.M. Then she looked skyward and thanked God that she only had two hours to go.

"Police, dispatcher seven," she said.

"Miss," the elderly man on the other end of the line said. "The men they lookin' for from that shootin' over there on Park Avenue is in a house on Dell Street."

"What men, sir?" she asked, knowing full well what the man was talking about.

"Leroy Johnson and the other one. Whatever his name is—Samuel, Simon, somethin' or other."

"What's the address, sir?" she asked, making no attempt to hide her skepticism.

"3934 Dell Street."

"Didn't you just call a few minutes ago, sir?" she asked, looking on her monitor and recognizing the address.

"Yes, but I just saw the boy's picture on television, and he's in that house. Now, please send somebody out here before he—"

"Did you see the man go into the house?" she asked, determined to give him a hard time for hanging up earlier.

"No, I—"

"We'll send someone out, sir," she said, and entered the call as a disturbance, transmitting it back to the dispatchers without any indication that there were murder suspects in the house.

After she'd disconnected the call, cutting off Eldridge, another call immediately popped onto her monitor. It was the same address, but this time it was an old woman's voice.

"I'd like to speak to a supervisor, please," Mildred Scott said in her best business voice.

"Ma'am, if this is in reference to—"

"Miss, put your supervisor on the phone."

The call taker connected the call to her sergeant, who sat at the supervisor's desk in the call taker's room. Then she pushed her "unavailable" button so that she wouldn't have to answer any calls for the next few minutes.

The sergeant, after listening to the woman's complaint, looked over at the call taker angrily. Then he walked back to the dispatcher's console for East Division and told them to give the Dell Street job priority.

"We don't have anyone available to send there," the dispatcher on East told the sergeant, the exasperation evident in his voice. "One wagon's out on a prisoner run, the other's out transporting a 5292. Two supervisors, a wagon, a Tom unit, and a car are on the Park Avenue detail and—"

"I get the point," the sergeant said, and walked over to J band.

The dispatcher on the main radio band looked up expectantly and told the cars to stand by.

"See if you can get a detective to check this out," the sergeant said as he handed her a piece of paper with the job number.

"Okay," she said, then flipped back the switch to transmit to one of the Homicide units patrolling the 25th. "Dan 26, take 3934 Dell Street. A caller said your suspects are inside that location. Use caution, Dan 26. This is the fifth call from that location, but the first one saying the males are inside."

"Dan 26, okay," the detective answered, shrugging at his partner as he made a U-turn and started toward what they thought was the first of many prank calls they would get when people found out that a couple of pipers were giving Philadelphia's finest a run for their money.

Chapter 8

Reds Hillman headed straight to Northwest Detectives after he dropped Ramirez back at the crime scene. He was surprised when Ramirez sent him there to talk to the complainants who had run into Leroy. Usually, the young ones wanted him to stay out of the way. With his history, and with just over six months left before his retirement, some people in Homicide considered Hillman a liability. And he didn't blame them for seeing him that way.

The nights filled with sloe gin and dark memories had smeared his senses and left him as bitter as the tonic he sprayed into his poisonous elixir. In the eyes of his peers, he was someone to be pitied: a man whose yesterdays refused to stay in the past where they belonged.

Hillman had come up in North Philadelphia, in an era when the streets were clean and the people were white. He had pitched for a neighborhood baseball team, swum and played basketball at the Athletic Recreation Center, and studied at Thomas

Edison High School. After he graduated, he was drafted to fight in the Korean War.

It was there that Hillman came to know manhood. A Jewish boy from North Philly armed with a heavy rifle and too little training, he never let fear show through his actions. He always fought hard, even in the 1951 "meatgrinder" offensive, when outnumbered U.N. forces took heavy casualties at the hands of the Chinese.

On the first night of that battle, Hillman and a soldier named Smitty—the only man in his squad who had been willing to befriend a Jew—were separated from their unit during a firefight. The Chinese had them pinned down, and they both knew that they would never live through the night if they didn't make a break for it.

Hillman went first, running low and firing his rifle with abandon, dropping and rolling every ten feet in the face of enemy fire, then getting up and running again toward the security of friendly forces. They were about thirty feet from safety when Hillman dropped and rolled for the third time. Smitty ran in front of him. Hillman got up, fired his weapon, and wished as soon as he felt the rifle recoil against his shoulder that he could reach out and snatch the errant bullet from the air.

Hillman watched in horror as his friend's helmet shattered amidst a red and white star burst of flesh and bone, his arms spread wide as he dropped to the ground, motionless.

Hillman ran to him and picked him up, draping him over his shoulder and carrying him the remaining thirty feet, risking his own life as the Chinese let go a heavy volley of small-arms fire. But Hillman knew, even as he raced through the bullet-filled air, that Smitty was already dead.

They awarded Hillman the Silver Star for heroism in combat. But no one ever knew that it was Hillman's bullet that had killed his best friend. And Hillman never said anything.

After the war, Hillman came home to Philadelphia and joined the police department. He was assigned to the 23rd District, and he watched as North Philadelphia changed complexions. Taking advantage of the G.I. Bill, Hillman got married, bought a house in Northeast Philadelphia, and settled into his career.

That's when the nightmares began. At first, it was just the image of Smitty, his arms spread wide as he fell backward in the killing field. Then there was a recurring dream of Smitty's mangled face, the gaping exit wound opening and closing like a mouth trying to consume Hillman. But the one that broke him was a dream in which Smitty would stand before him, his face a bloody mass of destruction.

"Why did you kill me?" Smitty would ask.

Then Hillman would wake up in a panic.

By 1960, the dreams had caused Hillman to close himself off from everyone and everything that was important to him. He was afraid that if he allowed himself to care for anyone, he would destroy them. His wife took their two small children and left him. His friends drifted away from him. His commanders repeatedly tried to break through his shell. But it didn't matter what they did. No one could reach Hillman.

In 1962, Hillman made detective in North Central Division because, strange behavior notwithstanding, he was the best interrogator on the force. When Civil Service was instituted, he never took a test to try to attain higher rank. The only thing he wanted was to work Homicide, and in 1975, he was transferred there from North Central Detectives.

The nightmares continued. But they weren't as frightening

after he began his nightly ritual of sad songs, dim lights, and sloe gin. He almost looked forward to the dreams. They allowed him to visit Smitty, the young soldier whose friendship Hillman had won and lost on the faraway battlefields of Korea.

But dreams could not compare to his mistress. She comforted him with burlap truths dressed up as silky lies, and seduced him time and again with the magic of her touch. She had never questioned him, had never doubted him, had never abandoned him.

She was his career. And in six months, he would have to leave her. But before he turned his back on her forever, he would present her with one final gift.

Hillman was going to help find out what really happened to Johnny Podres. Because he owed it to the one thing in the world that he truly loved—his badge.

When Hillman walked in, a detective from Northwest pulled him aside and told him that the elderly couple had indeed been carjacked by Leroy and a woman. But the detective hadn't been able to get an accurate description of Leroy's accomplice.

"The man's name is Reverend Christopher Jones, and he's got a big church over in West Philly somewhere," the detective told Hillman, handing him a file and a borrowed book filled with mug shots from East Detectives. "These are all the girls we know to frequent the area where the shooting took place. The woman Leroy was with must have come from around there."

Hillman peeked through the window of the interrogation room and immediately recognized the man. He'd seen him around Erie Avenue and Old York Road about a dozen times in the past year.

"This shouldn't take long," Hillman said, walking into the room. "You're welcome to sit in."

The detective walked in behind Hillman as he extended his hand to Reverend Jones and introduced himself. "I'm Detective Hillman, Homicide. If you could just go through this photograph book, I'm sure we can have you out of here in no more than a half hour."

Reverend Jones had already been through a lot that night, having been carjacked, then held at the station for more than an hour. He was in no mood to talk.

"Look, Detective," the frustrated old man said. "I already told this gentleman that we didn't get a good look at the girl who was with that man Leroy. Now, unless you plan to arrest me and my wife, I suggest you call me in the morning."

The preacher reached for his coat and hat, which sat on a nearby chair. But Hillman wouldn't hear of it.

"I know you're probably very tired, sir. And I apologize for the inconvenience. But this isn't the same book you looked through the last time. This book shows all the young women we know who frequent that area. It'll only take a few minutes."

Reverend Jones sighed and looked at his watch. "Look, I'd really like to help. But all those girls really do look the same to me. And I've already pressed charges against the man, so why don't you just find him?"

Reverend Jones picked up his coat and hat and extended a hand to his wife as he got up to leave. "Come on, Mother Jones."

"Mrs. Jones," Hillman said, positioning himself between them and the door, "can you wait outside for a minute?"

"I'll wait right here, thank you," she said in a tone that bordered on haughty.

"Please, Mrs. Jones," Hillman said, smiling. "Your husband will be right with you."

She looked at him, then at her husband.

"Go ahead, honey," Reverend Jones said. "I'll be right out."

When Mrs. Jones closed the door behind her, Hillman walked over and locked it. Then he sat on the chair in front of the Reverend.

"I wanted us to have a little man-to-man talk," Hillman said, still smiling. "Seems like men don't do enough of that these days. Know what I mean, Detective?"

The detective who sat in the corner nodded his head in agreement, a sly grin playing on his lips.

"You know, Reverend," Hillman said, moving from the chair and sitting on the table in front of the preacher. "It sure strikes me as odd that a man of your stature would generalize that way about those women."

"Generalize how?"

"I mean, it's a shame that you would say they all look alike," he said, thumbing through the file and stopping at the description of Reverend Jones's vehicle. "Now, if I, as a white cop, was to say something like that about black people, whether they were pipers or not, you'd probably get up in the pulpit on Sunday and call it racism. Wouldn't you?"

"Well, I—"

"Especially if you knew that I knew those girls don't all look alike. Now, isn't that right?"

"I don't know what you're talking about, but I think you've wasted enough of my time," the preacher said, rising from his chair.

Hillman placed a hand on his shoulder, gently forcing him back into his seat.

"Get your hands off me!" the preacher said indignantly.

Hillman ignored him.

"You have a gray '92 Cadillac Fleetwood, don't you, Rev?" Hillman asked without waiting for an answer. "You don't mind if

I call you Rev, do you? Reverend's so cumbersome. Sort of ties up the tongue."

The preacher tried to say something, but Hillman cut him off.

"Anyway, Rev, I'm not really supposed to say anything to anyone outside the department about an ongoing investigation. But since you're a man of the cloth and everything, I guess I can trust you. You see, when I stopped over at East Detectives to pick up that picture book I've been asking you to look at, they gave me another book to go with it."

"Detective, I really don't have time—"

"Shut up, Rev," Hillman said calmly.

"I beg your pardon!" Reverend Jones said, attempting to stand.

The other detective walked over and again forced the preacher back into his seat.

"Where was I?" Hillman said, pausing. "Oh yeah, the picture book. You see, Rev, the guys over at East Detectives have been doing surveillance on the whores down on Old York Road, trying to figure out what kind of clientele they've been serving down there. Figured maybe it'd give us a leg up in the drug war. Cut off the demand by drying up the whores' cash flow. Know what I mean?"

"No, I don't know what you mean."

"Well, let me put it to you this way," Hillman said, speaking slowly and deliberately, like a teacher. "The girls buy most of the dope, because the guys can't afford it on what they make washing windows and stealing copper pipes. That stuff doesn't pay real well, you know what I mean?"

Reverend Jones glared at him, then turned his head.

"Anyway," Hillman said, "the girls make the most money,

and they get it from turning tricks. So as long as they can turn tricks, the demand for the dope stays sky-high. You following me?"

The preacher nodded slowly.

"A couple of months ago, some creative detectives over at East started taking pictures of the cars that came down there to trick. Figured they'd find out who the cars were registered to and feed the names to the *Daily News*. Let 'em run 'em on the front page. Of course the public would never know the police had given that information to the press, and . . ."

Reverend Jones began to look physically ill.

"You okay, Rev?" Hillman said.

The preacher nodded.

"You sure? 'Cause you don't look so good."

Jones nodded again and adjusted himself in his seat.

"Anyway, when this guy got killed over on Park Avenue tonight, one of the first things we did was round up the girls on Old York Road, because if anybody knows what happened over there in that house, they do. Know what I mean, Rev?"

Jones stared into space.

"It's not like I really care about what goes on over on Old York Road, because I work Homicide. And it turns out that those girls didn't know much anyway. But getting back to the picture-book thing. The funniest thing happened when I was looking at the surveillance photos on the way over here. It was like something straight out of *Unsolved Mysteries*, you know what I mean, Rev? I mean, there was this one car that kept turning up over and over again, in at least ten or twelve of the photos. I'm looking at this car in picture after picture and I'm thinking, this is really strange. Like, *Twilight Zone* strange. You ever watch *The Twilight Zone*, Rev?"

The preacher shook his head slowly, the color draining slowly from his face.

"You'll never guess what kind of car it was, Rev."

"What kind?" Jones said, his voice nearly inaudible.

"You're gonna love it, Rev," Hillman said, holding in a laugh as if he were delivering a punch line. "It was a gray Cadillac with—get this—a license plate of AVC-2392. Isn't that a scream?"

The preacher seemed to shrink measurably as he hung his head and placed his hands over his eyes. Still, Hillman pressed on.

"Do you know who that car's registered to, Rev?" he asked, the smile fading from his lips.

Jones sat absolutely still and said nothing.

"It's registered to Jones Memorial Apostolic Ministries."

The preacher drew back as if he'd been slapped.

"What do you do, Rev, lease it in the church's name and write off the expense at the end of the year? That's pretty shrewd. Now, if you wanna go down to Old York Road and get three-dollar blow jobs, that's your business. I just hope your congregation—and especially Mother Jones—doesn't find out. That'd be a shame."

Hillman paused, allowing the prospect of being found out to sink in.

"All I'm asking for is a little cooperation," the detective said, smiling again. "Look through the book, point out the girl, and press charges against her. Then you can go home and rest easy, because then we won't have to run your name in the *Daily News* along with the rest of the perverts who turn tricks on Old York Road. Okay?"

A defeated Reverend Jones looked up at Hillman. Then he looked at the detective who sat silently in the corner. And then, without another word, he picked up the book, thumbed carefully through it, and identified Pookie as the woman he'd seen with Leroy.

Hillman let the preacher go home after he'd pressed charges against Pookie. Then he called Ramirez and gave him Pookie's description, including her name—Patricia Oaks—and her nickname, which Reverend Jones had heard Leroy use while they were in the car.

"Did the complainant see which way they went?" Ramirez said after he'd written down the information.

"They were traveling south on Broad from Hunting Park about an hour and a half ago."

"Did he mention anything about Black?"

"He said that he heard Leroy say they had to find him."

"Anything else?"

"No, that's about it."

"Good job, Hillman," Ramirez said. "I'm going to call this in to Radio."

"What are you going to say about Black?" Hillman said before Ramirez could disconnect the call.

Ramirez didn't like his subordinates questioning him. But he deferred to Hillman's age and answered him anyway. "I'm going to include him in the description, just in case Leroy and Pookie found him."

"Even though Black wasn't with them when they were last seen?"

"If Leroy said they were going to try to find him, they must have known where to look," Ramirez said, the irritation showing through in his voice. "Which leads me to believe that Black was with Leroy when they left the house on Park Avenue, and that he told Leroy to meet him someplace."

"Why would he do that?" Hillman pressed. "You've gotta figure, Leroy and the girl were in the getaway car that crashed on Roberts, right? After the crash, somebody happens along and they borrow their car for a midnight spin down to Roy Rogers. Even if Leroy and Black killed Podres and split up to meet later at a certain place and time, you think Black would have waited around while Leroy and Pookie were crashing getaway cars and carjacking people?"

"I've seen stranger things," Ramirez said.

"So have I," Hillman conceded. "But I don't think this kid would be dumb enough to sit around and wait if he had been there when Podres was shot."

Ramirez was silent. He knew that Hillman had a point. But he also knew that drugs made people act irrationally. He'd seen it himself, in a time and place that he'd just as soon forget, but never could.

In the late sixties, Ramirez had watched his father, an immigrant from Puerto Rico, build a mom-and-pop gas station into a thriving auto-repair shop, convenience store, and service station.

His father took the profits from that business and bought his family a piece of the American dream. He moved them from a run-down row house at 11th and Cumberland to a single home in the exclusive Chestnut Hill area, sent his children to private school, lavished his wife with expensive jewelry, and bought two new cars. To Jorge Ramirez, he was a hero.

But by the time Jorge reached the fifth grade, he had begun to see a change in his father. The hands that had built the business from the ground up—strong hands that had always held his family together—became red and swollen. His manner became jumpy and he was always covered with a thin film of sweat.

One, then both, of the cars disappeared. Jorge and his three sisters were transferred to public school. When they were forced to give up the house and move back to a row house in North Philly, Jorge knew from the needles he found in the bathroom that his father was a drug addict.

The business was gone; the expensive jewelry was gone. The hope, Jorge knew, was gone. It had all been shot into his father's veins along with the methamphetamine that eventually caused him to die from an overdose.

So when Jorge Ramirez grew up, he promised himself that he would always treasure his family above anything else. And when he became a cop, got married, and had a child, he did everything he could to keep that promise.

He knew that Hillman could never understand that. No one could. But he also knew that Hillman could never truly know a drug addict. Just as Jorge had never truly known his father.

"Thank you for your input, Detective," Ramirez said after a long pause. "Since you're so convinced that Black wasn't there when this thing went down, do me a favor. Talk to his folks; anybody who might be able to give us something we don't already know about him. After that, if the kid in Abbottsford Hospital wakes up, interrogate him. In the meantime, I'm going to call this in to Radio."

It was Hillman's turn to remain silent. He knew that the mention of his rank meant Ramirez was going to do things his way. Not that it made that much of a difference. By the time Ramirez radioed in the information, the suspects were on the move again.

Clarisse's 1991 Honda Accord was parked directly in front of her door.

It wasn't like anybody messed with it, because Clarisse had a gun, and she'd used it once or twice when she heard her car alarm. Even so, she always breathed easier when she came outside and found it sitting where it was supposed to be, because you just never knew in North Philly.

"Where to?" Clarisse asked as her passengers got in the car.

"Off this block," Black said sarcastically. "Turn left when you get to Broad Street, and we'll figure it out from there."

"And turn on KYW," Leroy said from the backseat, obviously getting over the shock of finding himself a murder suspect.

She turned on the radio, and the KYW jingle played. The newscaster said something about the possibility of thunderstorms hitting the tristate area before morning. After that, he said something that no one expected to hear.

"And in our top story this hour, police are looking for two men—Leroy Johnson and Samuel Everett Jackson—in connection with the shooting of a city official in a reputed crack house. The men are also wanted for an assault on police after they allegedly engaged police in a shoot-out from a moving vehicle, injuring one officer. The suspects' vehicle later crashed, killing one occupant and critically wounding another. The wounded officer is in serious condition. The unidentified suspect, who has not regained consciousness, is in critical condition. . . . Police are withholding the names of the city official and the officer pending family notification, but several police sources have said the shooting victim was one of the most highly placed Hispanic officials in city government. . . ."

"Y'all shot a politician?" Black said, talking over the descriptions they'd heard earlier.

"Y'all ain't do nothin'," Leroy said angrily. "I keep tellin' you that, Black. Butter and Rock shot him."

"Yeah, and your girl the one probably set him up."

"I ain't tell 'em to kill him," Pookie said earnestly. "I just wanted the money."

"Whatever. I just hope you ain't touch nothin' in his car."

"Why?"

" 'Cause if you did, you gon' be on KYW, too."

They were all silent for a moment, thinking how much harder it would be if they were all wanted by the police.

"And I thought you said Butter and Rock was dead," Black said to Leroy, breaking the silence.

"I thought they was."

"So which one still alive?"

"I don't know. I can't see how either one of 'em made it outta that car."

"Yeah, well, you better hope whoever it is don't wake up. 'Cause the first thing they gon' do is cut a deal. And if they want him to say we did it, that's just what he gon' say."

Black glanced at Clarisse, who had started to look afraid for the first time. He thought how people are willing to do almost anything when they're high. Then he thought about the way people will do almost anything for something they think is love. He wondered what motivated Clarisse. Did she even know? Or was she just another confused individual who was floating in that tiny space where sanity peeks through emotion and asks the age-old question: What the hell are you doing?

"So where we goin'?" Leroy said.

"The last place they would expect us to be," Black said.

"Where?" Pookie asked skeptically.

"We ain't gotta get into all that," he said, turning to Clarisse. " 'Cause everybody don't need to know."

"No," Pookie said. "You ain't goin' into all that 'cause you don't know your damn self."

Black looked out the window, pretending to admire the scenery. Then he turned back to Pookie.

"I see that little catnap back at Clarisse crib did you some good. Got your mouth good as new."

Pookie flipped her middle finger and tossed her head sideways, folding her arms across her chest as she stared quietly out the window.

"Turn left when you get to Girard," Black said to Clarisse.

"Then what?" she asked nervously. "Do you even know where we're going? Because I don't know if . . ."

"You don't know what?" he said, his words sharp.

"I don't know if . . ." Clarisse let the words trail off again as her voice began to tremble. "Look, the truth is, I'm getting kind of scared. And I'm not sure I can do this."

"You drive until we tell you to stop," Leroy said. "You took the money, so drive."

"I'll give the money back."

"It's not about the money," Black said. "Ain't that what you said? Now, when you get to I-95, go north. I'll tell you what to do from there."

Clarisse looked over at Black. He looked back, and found himself staring into eyes that were lost somewhere between anger and fear.

"Who are you?" she asked, as if she'd just realized she didn't know.

"That's a stupid question," he said.

"No, really," she said, persisting. "Who are you? A few minutes ago, you tell me you could love me. No, let me get it right. You asked me if I could be sure you weren't in love with me. Isn't that right, Everett?"

He pointed at the red light they were approaching. "Stop."

Clarisse slammed on the brakes.

"Girl, I know you better slow down," Pookie said.

"I know you better shut up," Clarisse said, then turned her fury on Black.

"Look at me, Everett," she said, her words clipped and angry.

He ignored her.

"Look at me!" she screamed.

He pointed to the light, which had turned green. "Go."

Clarisse pounded the accelerator into the floor, and they all grasped at door handles and the dashboard, reaching out in panic like people who were about to drown. Black looked up and saw another car approaching from Clarisse's side. Clarisse saw it, too. But she barreled toward it anyway. She was smiling.

As the cars came closer to each other, Black could almost make out the terrified expressions of the other car's passengers. And he could definitely make out Clarisse's.

Black lunged for the steering wheel and Clarisse screamed—a battle cry of sorts. Then she hurled an elbow, barely missing his head as her face took on the grim expression of a person who has made peace with the inevitable. Black thought of how movies lie, making people believe that those moments slow down, when they actually flash by like so much lightning.

On impulse, he pushed his arms against the dashboard to brace himself. But then, with a sneer playing on her lips, Clarisse stood on the brakes and the car screamed to a halt about a half foot from the other car. When Black looked up, expecting to see death, there was only the horrible, tearful grimace of the little girl in the backseat of the other car and the hammering thump of his heartbeat.

Clarisse's chest heaved up and down, and the sound of her breathing filled the car. Leroy and Pookie slowly unfolded their arms from around their heads, no doubt expecting to see death also. When they didn't, Leroy began to look angry—almost disappointed. Pookie just looked pissed.

"This bitch crazy," Pookie said, fumbling with the lock to the back door. "So y'all can have all this here, okay? 'Cause I'm not gon' be walkin' away from a whole lotta these crashes and shit."

As Pookie continued to rave, the driver of the other car looked at them. He looked back at his little girl, pursed his lips as if to say something, thought better of it, and drove away. Black watched the man and wondered if the man had looked at them too closely.

"How you open this door?" Pookie yelled.

The only people outside were pipers, so Pookie's screams fell on deaf ears. The gas station on the corner was closed and the neighbors didn't bother to turn on their lights. Even the stray cats that rummaged through the trash can a few feet away barely looked twice. Two girls on the corner of Mascher Street gave a perfunctory glance, then went about their business.

"I don't know why y'all let this crazy bitch drive, anyway," Pookie said, still fumbling with the lock on the back door.

"Shut up, Pookie," Leroy said.

"No, you shut up. You went and got the money and broke everybody down but me. Now I'm supposed to sit here and take orders from you? Who the hell is you?"

Leroy gave Pookie a look that demanded silence. She complied. When she'd stopped trying to open her door, he stormed out of the car and went around to the driver's side. Then he opened Clarisse's door and stared down at her with a murderous patience that was frightening in its stillness. Black almost told her to drive away.

"Get out," Leroy said. "I'm drivin'."

"No," Black said, snatching the keys from the ignition. "I'm drivin'. You don't even know where we goin'."

"You don't know, either," Leroy said.

"So what you sayin'?" Black said, getting out of the car and walking around to the driver's side.

"What it sound like?"

Leroy glared at him, beads of sweat glistening on his forehead as his hands tightened into fists. Black returned his stare full on, his feet apart and his left leg thrust forward in a boxing stance. Clarisse and Pookie sat silently watching them. Black could feel their eyes, begging them to fight, or not to fight, to do anything but stand there.

For a moment, Black was frozen, wondering if he should be the first to swing. He could feel Clarisse willing him to look at her, but he dared not take his eyes off Leroy. He had seen people get seriously beat down for looking away. Still, he couldn't bring himself to do anything but stand there, preparing himself for whatever was going to happen.

As Black rolled his fingers into fists—with sweat rolling from his forehead to his chin—his gloved hand squeaked. And Leroy smiled.

Black looked down at the slim fingers of the ladies' leather gloves he was wearing. Then he looked over at Leroy.

"We out here tryin' to rumble in women's clothes," Leroy said, and burst out laughing.

Black tried to be serious, but when he looked at the pink trench coat and the wide-brimmed ladies' church hat Leroy was wearing, he began to laugh out loud, too.

"I know," Black said, focusing on the rhinestone-studded glasses Leroy wore under the brim of a black felt hat. " 'Cause them Catwoman glasses you wearin' got me trippin'."

"I know you ain't talkin' with your *Lady Sings the Blues* gloves on."

"They better than that *Josie and the Pussycats* trench."

Leroy looked soberly at Black, the laughter disappearing from his lips. "You want my arm to fall off?" he said, reaching toward him and doing a bad Billy Dee imitation.

They both laughed.

"Look, man," Black said. "I'll drive."

"Drive where?"

"To this little hotel I know. It's right behind the 7th District in the Northeast."

"The 7th Police District?" Leroy said.

"Yeah."

"Man, you crazy."

"We gon' have to be crazy to get outta this," Black said, pulling on his sunglasses and easing himself into the driver's seat as a police car approached from the opposite direction.

Their smiles immediately disappeared. Black thought of the money and the dope they were carrying, then imagined being arrested as a drug dealer.

"Everybody be calm," he said. "Nine times outta ten, he don't know us from a can o' spray paint."

Leroy walked around to the other side of the car and got in next to Pookie. Clarisse slid over into the front passenger seat. Black looked into the bright lights of the approaching car and fought the impulse to drive away.

"Have you ladies seen an auto accident out here?" the officer said, pulling his car parallel to theirs and speaking through the driver's side window. "Somebody called and said they heard a loud crash out here a few minutes ago."

They all shook their heads.

"It was supposed to have happened five minutes ago at this intersection," he said. "Are you sure you haven't heard anything?"

Again, they shook their heads. Black didn't turn around to look at Clarisse. But he hoped that she would follow suit. From what he could see, she was having second thoughts. Common sense was starting to tell her that what she was doing was wrong, and emotion was telling her that she was being used.

"Are you ladies having car trouble?" the cop asked.

"No," Clarisse said. "We were just trying to decide who should drive."

Black finally turned from the cop and looked over at her, trying to read something in her demeanor that would tell him what she was thinking. He didn't like what he saw. It looked like she was trying to decide whether to tell the cop who they were. She started to say something, but Black couldn't tell what she was saying or to whom she was speaking, because his imagination was in full swing.

He could imagine Clarisse screaming out for help, then throwing herself out the passenger-side door as the cop pulled his gun and shot through the driver's side window. He would miss, barely. Then Black would duck down and stomp hard on the gas, racing away as the cop hung a screeching U-turn, red and blue lights blazing in a cloud of blue-white smoke. That's as far as Black's imagination would go—probably because he knew in the back of his mind that if the police started to chase them, they wouldn't survive the ordeal.

"I didn't hear you, ma'am," the cop said.

Black looked up and prayed that the cop wasn't talking to him. He prayed that Clarisse wouldn't bring his imagination to life. Then he did what he'd always seen women do when they were uncomfortable. He smiled.

"I said, I was wondering if you could give us directions to . . ." Clarisse paused and looked at Black. "What was it, I-76? Yeah, that's what it was."

Black hoped the cop didn't notice his sigh of relief.

"We're trying to get out to my aunt's house in Valley Forge," Clarisse said. "We were just coming from a church revival and we're really too tired to drive all the way back to Pittsburgh."

"Yeah, that's a pretty long drive," the cop said. "But you're going the wrong way to get on I-76. You need to turn around and go straight out Girard to 34th Street. You'll pass the zoo on your left. Keep going to the next intersection. The signs will point to 76 West, and that'll take you out to Valley Forge."

"Thank you," Clarisse said, waving to him as he drove away.

Black made a U-turn, followed the cop until he turned off at 8th Street, and turned back around. No one spoke until they got down past Front Street and turned onto I-95.

"Well," Leroy said. "Pookie wasn't lyin' about you, Clarisse. You crazy as hell."

Leroy and Clarisse laughed. But Black was busy looking in the rearview mirror, waiting for the police to catch up with them.

Right before they pulled up at Clarisse's house, the detectives in unit Dan 26 saw a late-model Honda Accord swing onto Broad Street from Dell Street. The four women in the car looked like church ladies, so the detectives paid little attention to them. Their main concern was looking at the house and confirming that the call was a prank.

The first thing they noticed about the house was its condition. Compared to the others on the block, it was relatively well kept. In fact, it wouldn't have been out of place in a better neighborhood—one where crack wasn't the mainstay of the local economy. The detectives looked at each other, looked around at the two cars parked farther up the street, and moved closer to the house. At first glance, it looked like everyone inside was asleep. But when they looked again, they found that the vertical blinds that adorned the front window were partly open. The screen door was slightly ajar, too, which meant that someone had just left the house.

They both knew the blinds—and especially the door—couldn't have been left that way all night, because whoever lived there wouldn't have left them open and gone to sleep. The blinds would have been kept closed, lest someone look inside and attempt to break in. And the screen door would have been closed and locked to keep the pipers from stealing it off the hinges.

"Dan 26 on location," one of the detectives said as he stealthily approached the front window of 3934 Dell Street.

The radio crackled as the dispatcher mumbled a reply.

Cupping his hands as he looked in the window, the detective noticed something on the steps at the far end of the living room and motioned to his partner. "Take a look at this."

The partner sidled up and quickly peeked through the window. In the yellow streetlight glow that filtered between the openings in the vertical blinds, he could see an expensively appointed living room. There was an entertainment center with a big-screen television, leather furniture, deep-pile carpeting, and the outline of the doorway leading to the dining room. Everything appeared to be in order, except for the staircase that led from the living room to the second floor. On the fifth step from the bottom, there was a crumpled pair of pants, a worn pair of sneakers, and a sweatshirt with some letters on it.

"What'd they say that guy Leroy was wearing?" the partner asked as he backed away from the window.

"Jeans, a Fila sweatshirt, and red sneakers."

"I think we need to call Ramirez," he said. "Because he's not wearing that anymore."

Satisfied that he and his partner had seen the same thing, the detective removed his radio from his back pocket. "Dan 26 to Radio. Could we get some additional units and a supervisor at this location?"

"Okay, Dan 26," the dispatcher said, then raised Ramirez over the air.

"What do you have there, Dan 26?" Ramirez asked.

"Sir, I'd rather not say over the air."

"I'm en route."

Ramirez piled two other detectives into his car for the ride around the corner to Dell Street. On the way over, he called Radio on his cell phone to get the address of the person who'd made the Dell Street call.

When Ramirez pulled up and looked in Clarisse's window, he immediately connected the red sneakers on the steps with the description of Leroy. "Take either end of the alley," he told the detectives he'd brought from Park Avenue.

One disappeared around the near corner while the other jogged toward the far end of the block. Ramirez pulled out his radio and called J band.

"Dan 25 to Radio, get me two wagons at this location. Hold them out here on a detail."

"Okay, Dan 25," the dispatcher said, and called across the room to the dispatcher on East band to pull two wagons off Park Avenue and send them to Dell Street.

"I figure we've got two or three minutes before the newspeople get here," Ramirez said to the detectives from Dan 26. "I hope the wagons can keep them out of here until we can see what we've got."

Just then, a 25th District wagon and a 39th District wagon came over the air, announcing their arrival on the block.

Ramirez radioed in a command for the wagons to seal off both ends of the block.

Then he turned to the detectives again. "I'll give those guys I sent around back five seconds to secure the alley, then we'll knock on the door."

The detectives nodded.

Ramirez looked around at the empty side of the house, then

up into the second floor of the neighbors' house, where a light shone in the front window.

"Somebody's up late," he said to himself. Then he looked quickly at the vacant lot on the other side of Clarisse's house. "Did anybody check this lot over here?"

"Checked it while we were waiting for you," one of the detectives said. "Nada."

"Okay, let's hit it."

Ramirez directed the detectives to take up positions by the vacant lot and the Scotts' steps, respectively. They all drew their guns. Then Ramirez stood to one side of Clarisse's door and knocked. When there was no answer, he tried the doorknob.

It was locked, so Ramirez forced it open.

"You see them runnin' around the back?" Eldridge asked as he peeked behind the side of the window shade and saw white men running to the corners of the block.

"Eldridge, get in the bed."

"I just hope Clarisse don't get hurt foolin' with these people," he said, ignoring his wife.

"She won't, Eldridge, now get in the bed."

"You know what?" Eldridge said, still looking out the window and ignoring Mildred. "I don't even see Clarisse car out there no more."

Mildred, who was trying not to think that something might happen to Clarisse, bolted upright in bed. "You think she mighta left?"

"Well, you know ain't nobody steal it, 'cause that girl 'bout crazy out her mind with that gun."

"I know," Mildred said, getting up and joining her husband by the window. "I remember the last time somebody tried to take somethin' outta that car."

"Yeah, me, too," Eldridge said, wearing a toothless grin. "I bet they won't be tryin' to take nothin' else from outta there. She almost shot that boy hat off his head."

The couple peeked out in silence for a moment. Then Eldridge spoke.

"How she just come out and ride right by the police?"

"Same way we would. It ain't like they lookin' for her."

"Yeah, but they lookin' for that boy," Eldridge said, lifting the shade slightly to get a better look. "Black, or whatever his name is. And he was with her."

"You think he was with her. But you don't know that for sure."

They watched the three detectives who were in front of the house mill about for a half minute or so.

"Get back," Eldridge said, nearly knocking his wife down as he snapped the shade shut.

"What's wrong with you?"

"You ain't see that policeman lookin' up here?" he said, his voice filled with exasperation.

A second later, Eldridge lifted the shade and looked out again.

"I don't want them comin' over here askin' me 'bout nothin'," he said, slowly pulling the shade back into place. "And you know if they see us lookin', that's probably the first thing they'll do. Matter fact, turn off that light."

Mildred walked over and turned off the night-light. Then she walked back over to the window and looked out from the space between the bottom of the shade and the windowsill.

"Oh my God," she said, looking up at Eldridge. "They broke in the house."

Chapter 9

By the time they finished checking the house, Ramirez knew that he had been right to include Black in the description he'd called in to Radio after speaking with Hillman. All three suspects had been there with Clarisse, and they'd all left in a hurry.

There were signs that Clarisse had gone with them voluntarily, but that didn't rule out the possibility that she had been forcibly taken. In the absence of hard evidence and with time on the side of the fugitives, Ramirez decided not to call it a kidnapping until they could get more information.

"Secure the property," he said to the detectives after they'd determined that the suspects were gone. "I want to talk to the neighbors who made the call."

"Do you want to remove any evidence from the house?" one of the detectives asked.

"No," Ramirez said, closing the door behind him as they walked down the front steps and gathered on the sidewalk. "We can come back and get whatever we need later, after we get a warrant."

Ramirez watched television reporter Jeanette Deveraux jump out of a news van at the corner. She was yelling something that sounded like Ramirez's name.

"No comment," Ramirez mumbled to himself, turning his back on the reporter and looking up at the Scotts' bedroom windows.

Several news vans pulled up behind Deveraux's. Cameramen leaped out with lights trained on the house where the detectives stood, and neighbors began to look out from windows that had been tightly closed and shrouded in darkness only minutes before.

Squinting against the bright lights from the assorted news vans and the hum of neighbors' voices, Ramirez watched as several reporters tried to con their way past the barricades. The two officers from the wagon held them back.

"The neighbors must have fallen asleep in record time," Ramirez said as he surveyed the Scotts' darkened bedroom. "I just saw them looking out the window five minutes ago."

Ramirez spoke into his radio and had the two detectives posted in the alley come around to the front of Clarisse's house to stand guard. When they took up their stations, he pulled out his cell phone and called the Command Center to speak with Captain Sheldon.

He answered on the first ring.

"Sheldon here."

"I'm over on Dell Street," Ramirez said. "Looks like Leroy's been here."

"I heard you calling for wagons on J band. Do you have prisoners there?"

"No, sir. They were gone before we got here."

"I see," Sheldon said, clearly disappointed. "What is it, 3934 Dell Street?"

"Yes, sir."

"Whose house is it?"

"A woman named Clarisse Williams. She's a nurse."

It took a moment for Sheldon to respond.

"Did you find that out from the neighbors?" he asked.

"No."

"Was she at home?" Sheldon's words took on an edge.

"No."

"So you've been in the house," Sheldon said matter-of-factly. "With no warrant and with nobody at home."

"The door was open."

Sheldon sighed, and his breath made a sound that rattled over the phone like a wind through leafy trees. An illegal search wasn't something the detectives could just smooth over with those types of lies. Not this time. Because someone might look deeper into Podres's murder and discover the truth. Sheldon couldn't risk that.

"Have you ever heard the expression 'Shit rolls downhill'?" Sheldon asked smoothly.

"I've heard it once or twice."

"Well, son, let me put it to you this way. This is the most politically charged case we've handled since I've been assigned to Homicide. Nelson is feeling the heat from this thing, which means that the shit has begun to roll. Capisce?"

"Yes, sir."

"It's not going to stop with me. So if you don't want anything rolling down on you, don't lie to me. It's very important that we catch these suspects, without illegal searches or anything else that could come back to haunt us. Do you think you can do that, Lieutenant?"

"Yes, sir," Ramirez said, holding back the anger he felt welling up inside.

"Good. These suspects are the best chance we have for a conviction in this thing. And what I need from you is to do yourself and everyone involved in this investigation a tremendous favor. Don't screw it up."

Ramirez hesitated, and tried very hard to convince himself that Sheldon wasn't telling him to track down the suspects just because they'd be easy to convict.

"So what'd you find behind this open door?" Sheldon said after a long pause.

"It looks like Miss Williams likes a little crack now and then herself. There's enough empty caps in the trash can in the dining room to put the whole block in rehab."

"So?"

"There's more. Clarisse left her radio tuned to KYW, and they've been broadcasting these guys' names every five minutes for the last couple of hours. There's a smear of blood on the wall, and broken furniture in the dining room. We figure Clarisse heard their names on the radio and panicked. After that it gets kind of fuzzy. She might've been forced to go with them."

"I don't want a kidnapping charge on this thing," Sheldon said quickly. "I mean, we probably don't need to get the Feds involved in this case."

"It might not be a kidnapping," Ramirez said. "They straightened up in the dining room before they left, and I can't see her just sitting there while they cleaned up—or cleaning up herself—if she knew they were going to force her to go with them. There were semen stains on one of the dining room chairs and on one of the dining room walls, like they were doing the whole drug-sex thing. And somebody—or somebodies—took a shower before they left. Now, I'm not Sigmund Freud or anything. But I don't think kidnappers shower in the victim's house right after they've done the deed. Know what I mean?"

"So you think she helped them?" Sheldon said.

"I just don't think they forced her to do anything."

"I see."

"The only thing I'm wondering about is how they got out of here without anybody seeing them," Ramirez said.

"She must have a car."

"Well, we should know that in a few minutes, after we talk to the neighbors."

"Let's bet she does have a car," Sheldon said. "And let's bet they're all out for a little early-morning spin."

"Yes, sir."

"Call Radio as soon as you get a description of the vehicle," Sheldon added. "And as far as you going in the house, let's just keep that between us."

"Okay," Ramirez said hesitantly, even as he wondered if the people next door had seen them going in.

As he disconnected the call to Sheldon and joined the two detectives waiting for him on the Scotts' steps, he figured he'd find out soon enough.

Eldridge and Mildred Scott lay wide-eyed, staring at nothing. When the doorbell rang, they looked at each other, trying hard to pretend they hadn't heard it. It rang again and neither of them moved, except to burrow farther under the blankets.

Then the telephone rang.

"Hello?" Eldridge said.

"Mr. Scott, this is Lieutenant Jorge Ramirez, Homicide."

"Yes?"

"Sir, myself and some other detectives are down here at your front door. If you'd peek out your front window, we'd be glad to show you our badges."

"Son, I'm seventy-four years old. I can't see no badge from up here."

"Well, maybe you'd like to come down and we'll show you our badges through the front door. We'd just like to ask you a few questions."

"You from Homicide, right?"

"That's correct, sir."

"Well what questions you got for me? I ain't killed nobody."

"We know that, sir. If you'd just come to the door we—"

"Son, if the president of the United States came knockin' this time o' mornin', he'd have to slide a note under the door. So you know I'm not openin' it for you."

"Fair enough. I'll just ask you a few questions over the phone, if you don't mind."

"I guess that'd be all right," Eldridge said. "How'd you get my number anyway?"

"I got it from 911. We've got a system that tells us where every call comes from."

Before Eldridge could ask another question, Ramirez continued. "You called earlier about a disturbance at your neighbor's house and said there were some people there who we wanted to talk to. Well, Mr. Scott, we have reason to believe you were right. Now, I don't know what your relationship to your neighbor is, but if there's any more information you could give us, it would help."

"I want to ask a question first," Eldridge said. "Is Clarisse in any kind o' trouble?"

Ramirez figured from the tone of the question that Eldridge

Scott was worried about Clarisse. He wasn't just some nosy neighbor. So he told him what he always told concerned friends and family.

"No, she's not in trouble. But we need to find her before she does get into any kind of trouble or—God forbid—something happens to her."

He paused to give his words a chance to sink in.

"The people she's with are very dangerous," Ramirez added dramatically, hoping to frighten the old man into telling whatever he knew.

There was silence on the other end of the line, as if Eldridge were taking a moment to figure out what to say.

"What kind of information do you want?" Eldridge said cautiously.

"First of all, we want to know if you saw either of the men we're looking for go into the house."

"No."

"Did you hear them in the house?"

"I heard a man's voice say, 'Shut up!' And then I heard somethin' slam against Clarisse's dining room wall."

"Do you think the voice you heard belongs to one of the men we're looking for?"

"Yes, because I seen that boy Black goin' in there before. Clarisse must know him or somethin'."

"Did you see Black or anyone else leave Miss Williams's house?"

"No. But Clarisse's car was out there earlier and now it's gone."

"What kind of car does she have?"

"You askin' a whole lotta questions," Eldridge said. "You sure she ain't in no trouble?"

"We're trying to keep her from getting into trouble, Mr.

Scott," Ramirez said impatiently. "Now, please, what kind of car does she have? It's very important that we know."

Eldridge paused.

"Mr. Scott?" Ramirez prodded.

"She has a 1991 black Honda Accord," Eldridge said after a moment. "Her license plate says CWRN, for Clarisse Williams, registered nurse."

"A late-model black Honda Accord, license plate CWRN?" Ramirez repeated.

The detectives standing next to Ramirez—the ones who'd been the first to arrive at Clarisse's house—began to look confused. Then they looked as if they'd been struck by lightning.

"A late-model black Honda Accord?" one of them said as recognition swept across his face. "Isn't that the car . . ."

"That car rode right past us when we were on our way here," his partner said. "There were four ladies inside wearing big hats."

"If you remember anything else, or if you need to talk to me for any reason, call me, Mr. Scott," Ramirez said, quickly giving Scott his number when he heard them say that they'd seen the car.

"Which way was the car traveling?" Ramirez asked the detectives after disconnecting the call.

"South on Broad."

Ramirez reached into his pocket for his radio and called J band. "Dan 25 to Radio. I've got some flash on the suspects in the Park Avenue job."

"Dan 25 proceed," the dispatcher said.

Ramirez repeated the description of the car and its occupants over J band.

One of the detectives, still befuddled, said, "At least they *looked* like ladies."

• • •

The cop in car 611 was playing his usual cat-and-mouse game with the drug dealers on 6th Street. Every ten minutes, like clockwork, he'd ride slowly down the block and sit there. The drug dealers would walk away, never straying too far from the drugs they'd stashed when they'd seen his car. After five minutes, he'd cruise slowly away, and they'd complete the ritual by walking back to their corner.

This Sunday, like every Sunday, was slow. There was little more than the ritual to keep the officer occupied. Of course, there were a few disturbances here and there. But the closest thing to excitement was the search for the guys who'd killed the city councilman up on Park Avenue.

Homicide was broadcasting a blow-by-blow description of the search on J band, and car 611, along with the rest of the department and all of the Philadelphia press corps, was tuned in. From what he heard, the periodic updates on the descriptions of the guys who had supposedly shot the councilman sounded like hyped-up guesswork. But then, who was he to judge? The detectives from Homicide were supposed to be the experts. He was just a patrolman trying to keep the drug dealers off the corner. Not that he was complaining. Keeping drug dealers in check was important to him, even if everyone else in the department figured it was a lost cause.

Causes were his thing. He was the kind of man who wrote letters to the *Daily News* to correct the views of what he perceived to be the sickeningly liberal editorial department. He wanted abortion abolished, gun control loosened, and Bush reelected. He thought welfare was killing the people it was supposed to be helping and that crack was the scourge of the inner city. He knew that God was the only thing that could save Philadelphia from itself.

That's why, when he'd gone to check out the unfounded auto accident a few minutes earlier, he was glad to see the four ladies in the black Honda coming from a church revival. Attending revivals and spreading the good news was what everyone in North Philly should have been doing. Instead, too many of them were smoking crack and collecting welfare.

Still, there was something wrong about those women. The scenario just didn't seem right, no matter how many times he replayed it in his mind. He remembered getting a call about an auto accident at Mascher and Girard. He remembered riding up to them and asking if they'd seen an accident. That's when it had gotten weird.

Only the one in the passenger seat had spoken. The driver just sat there smiling and looking uncomfortable. The two women in the backseat sat absolutely still and looked at him as if they were praying for him to go away.

Under other circumstances, he'd have called for backup and checked the car. But the women looked like what they told him was true. They were coming from a revival. They were lost. They were tired. So he gave them directions to I-76 and left it at that. Still, there was something.

He was trying to put his finger on it—contemplating going to lunch so he could think about it over a hamburger—when he heard a detective come over the air with additional flash on the suspects from the Park Avenue job. He turned up his radio and listened.

". . . in connection with a founded shooting on the 3700 block of Park Avenue and an assault on a police officer on Roberts Avenue off-ramp of the northbound Roosevelt Expressway, two black males, Leroy Johnson and Samuel Everett Jackson . . ."

The cop tuned out the descriptions he'd heard five or six times in the last hour. He sipped his coffee and thought about taking another spin around 6th Street. But just as he began to turn the corner, he heard something that caused him to pull his car over and look at the radio in disbelief.

". . . last seen traveling south on Broad Street from Dell Street fifteen minutes ago in a 1991 Honda Accord painted black, license tag C—Charlie, W—William, R—Robert, N—Nelson. All four of the occupants are wearing wide-brimmed ladies' hats and ladies' trench coats. One or more of the occupants may be wearing sunglasses."

That's what had been strange about them, he thought. The driver and the one in the backseat were wearing sunglasses. And they weren't unattractive women, as he'd originally thought. They were men. And they were wanted for murder.

As he picked up his handset, not wanting to tell anyone that he'd seen them, talked to them, and let them ride away, the officer felt himself slipping into what could only be described as an embarrassment-induced state of shock. Still, he did what he had to do.

"611," he said, speaking over J band.

"611 proceed."

"I saw that vehicle ten minutes ago. It was occupied by four . . . people who fit that description. The driver and a passenger were wearing sunglasses."

The officer released his talk button and drew a deep breath. He knew what he was about to say was unforgivable. But there was no other way. He pressed his talk button again.

"I gave them directions to I-76 from Girard and Mascher," he said, wincing. "They said they were going to Valley Forge.

They were heading west on Girard from Second approximately ten minutes ago."

There was a cacophony of clicks as everyone on J band depressed their talk buttons repeatedly to show their displeasure at what they'd just heard.

"Dummy!" someone said between the clicks.

"Can't you tell a woman from a man?" someone else said.

There were more clicks and more anonymous comments. Someone gave a short rendition of "Sunglasses at Night" by Corey Hart.

"Six Command," his lieutenant finally said. "Have 611 take headquarters."

"611 okay," the officer said quickly, no doubt relieved that he wouldn't have to see another cop on the street for the twenty minutes or so it would take for him to get chewed out at headquarters.

If only the detectives from Homicide would find the suspects, he thought, no one else would have to endure the embarrassment of allowing them to slip away.

Reds Hillman heard Ramirez give out the flash information on J band, then listened as the 6th District cop confirmed the suspects' most recent location.

Hillman knew that they would need information in order to find them. So he went to the one person who could tell him all he needed to know.

When he arrived at Ruth Jackson's three-story house, Hillman saw two detectives staking out the property. One of them stepped out of the car and tried to wave him away as he walked up the steps. But Hillman had already rung the bell.

"Mrs. Jackson?" he said, holding up his badge when she lifted the blinds. "I'm here about Samuel."

Her face hardened at the mention of her son. "I used to

know a Samuel," she said, her melancholy voice drifting through the closed door. "But I don't know him anymore."

"Mrs. Jackson, please," Hillman said. "You might be the only person who can help your son now."

The blinds closed and Hillman stood on the steps, waiting for the thought of her son's plight to work its way through Ruth Jackson's mind. After what seemed like forever, he heard a series of clicks as she disengaged the locks.

"Come in," she said, stepping aside to allow Hillman to walk into her living room. "Would you like some coffee or something?"

"No, thank you," Hillman said, standing awkwardly in the middle of the floor.

As he looked around the sparsely furnished living room, Hillman could see that the Jackson home held a lifetime of memories. On the mantelpiece, there were two pictures: Black in a cap and gown at his high-school graduation, and an old wedding photo of Mrs. Jackson and her late husband.

The hardwood floors were swept and waxed to a shine, and the end tables were covered with framed snapshots from happier times. In one of them, a small boy hugged a puppy in front of a Christmas tree. In another, he rode on the broad shoulders of his father. In each of them, the laughter was almost audible.

Now the smiles were part of a long-forgotten past. All that remained was the pride of the woman who had helped to shape them. And nothing—not even the detective standing in her living room—could take that away from Ruth Jackson.

"Please," Mrs. Jackson said, pointing to a chair. "Sit down."

Hillman sat in the chair and watched as the woman walked to the opposite side of the room.

"Mrs. Jackson," he said soberly, "I'm going to cut to the chase. My name is Detective Reds Hillman. I'm here because we're looking for your son for murder."

"I know you're looking for him," she said, staring at Hillman's reflection in the mirror that stood over the mantelpiece. "I saw his picture on television and I see the detectives outside."

Hillman adjusted himself in his seat and asked the question that only Mrs. Jackson could answer.

"Do you believe that your son is capable of killing someone?"

Ruth Jackson turned from the mirror and sat down, twisting a handkerchief in her hands as she looked into the detective's eyes. Hillman returned her gaze, and he saw sadness and strength staring out at him as if they were alive.

"I knew a boy once," she said softly. "He was talkative, smart, curious. He wanted to know about everything in the world around him. And at the rate he was going, I was sure that he would find out all about it someday.

"Samuel wasn't like other children, Detective. And I'm not just saying that because he was my son. Other people noticed it, too."

Mrs. Jackson smiled fondly and walked back over to the mantelpiece, picking up the picture of her son and polishing it with her handkerchief before placing it back in its appointed space.

"When he was in kindergarten, his teacher told me that he had a way of letting you know he was there," she said, chuckling at the memory. "I guess that didn't change when he got older. He was just . . . special."

Hillman saw the strength in her eyes overtake the sadness. For a moment, she almost looked proud.

"When he was twelve, his father had a heart attack and died. I felt like I was going to fall apart. But Samuel stayed strong. It was like he knew something I didn't—like he knew everything was going to be all right. And seeing that gave me the strength I needed to go on.

"When he graduated from high school, he didn't even study and he had a B average. He went to college for a minute, but that bored him, so he got a job.

"I guess what I'm saying is, no matter what he did, no matter where he went, there was one thing about him that didn't change. He was smart—too smart. He could pick up on things faster than other people.

"Maybe that's why, when he started messing with that crack, he lost himself to it so quickly. He knew that he couldn't control it, so he gave up trying. He let it take over his life, and he lost everything because of it."

Mrs. Jackson looked at Reds Hillman, and her lips formed themselves into a wan smile.

"So, to answer your question, the Samuel Jackson I knew wouldn't have killed anyone. He couldn't have, because he had already killed himself."

The smile disappeared and was replaced by an almost tangible pain that poured out from her eyes like tears.

"My son is dead, Detective Hillman. And the only thing that keeps me going sometimes is my faith in God. I pray every night for my dead son. I pray because I know that only God can bring back the dead."

Reds Hillman sat for almost a full minute, staring down at the floor. Then he got up from the chair and walked toward the door.

"Thank you, Mrs. Jackson. If we hear anything about your son we'll be in touch."

"No," she said. "If God chooses to bring him back, he'll be in touch. Until then, if you want to know something about the man who's walking around masquerading as my son, know this: He's probably already one step ahead of you."

Chapter 10

As Black pulled up at the hotel entrance off the Woodhaven Road exit of I-95, Clarisse gave him a puzzled look but said nothing. And Pookie, who had been silent for most of the ride, seemed to strain forward, as if she were ready to bolt from the backseat. Only Leroy spoke.

"How we gon' stay in a hotel behind a damn police station?" Leroy said as they pulled into the parking lot.

"Same way you stay in any other hotel," Black said.

When no one said anything, he started giving orders. "They got a garage around back where the valets park the cars."

"The who?" Leroy said.

"Valets. Car parkers."

"Oh."

"Pookie, I want you to walk up to the valet in the lobby and tell him you parked your car in the garage and you checkin' out. If he ask you for your ticket, say you lost it. When he go the garage, ask the desk clerk if you can use the bathroom."

"For what?"

"So when he come back lookin' for you, you don't have to explain why you don't have no car in there. And you'll already be inside when Clarisse check in, so you can just come out and follow her and Leroy to the room."

"How you gon' get in?" Leroy asked.

"The elevator go straight from the garage to the hotel. After I park, I'll take it to the fifth floor. I want y'all to meet me there and we can all go to the room from there."

"How you know so much about this hotel?" Pookie said.

"I used to bring my hoes up here."

"Hoes?" Clarisse said, obviously offended.

"Yeah, hoes," Black said, looking at her as if she shouldn't expect women to be referred to any differently.

"You so damn ignorant," she said.

"Yeah, and I love you, too."

"Well, I don't love that plan," she said, looking at Black like he was crazy.

"What's wrong with it?"

"I know you don't expect me to check into a hotel with a man dressed up like RuPaul," she said, looking Leroy up and down.

Leroy and Black looked down at their outfits. Then they began to take off the trench coats, hats, and sunglasses to reveal the oversized suits they wore underneath.

"Keep on the glasses," Black said to Leroy.

"What about me?" Clarisse said.

"You can wear mine."

"Wear yours for what? They're looking for you, not me."

"Just in case. And when they ask you for a driver's license and a license tag, make up a tag number. Say you forgot your license—you left it in the car or whatever. If they say somethin', just make up a driver's license number. I think it's like eight numbers."

Black looked around to see that no one was approaching, then turned his attention to Pookie. "It's on you."

"How come I'm always the one kickin' shit off?" she said.

"Pookie . . . ," Leroy began.

"No, for real," she said. "Every time I turn around it's somethin' else. Lay down in the street, get on the bus. Y'all steady givin' orders and I still ain't seen no breakdown."

"You want a breakdown?" Leroy said. "Here."

He pulled out five hundred-dollar bills. When she reached for them, he pulled them back.

"When we get in the room," he said, placing the bills in the inside pocket of his suit jacket.

Pookie looked into his eyes, searching them to see if he was telling the truth. Then she got out of the car and began to walk toward the valet. She hesitated, looking around as if she might do something other than what she was supposed to do. But she must have decided that she had no choice, and began to walk toward the valet with purpose.

"Leroy," Black said as they all watched her go through her routine. "Don't trust her. I'm tellin' you."

Leroy tried to say something in her defense, but Black didn't give him a chance.

"She ain't been doin' nothin' but settin' niggers up since the day I met her. What, you think you different?"

When he didn't respond, Black looked in the rearview mirror and saw that Leroy knew he was right.

"Dig this here," Black said, tapping Clarisse on the arm. "Soon as she finish talkin' to the . . . No, matter fact, y'all go 'head in there now."

"You sure?" Clarisse said.

"Yeah. Make it look like y'all not with her."

Clarisse opened the door and got out. When Leroy got ready to follow, Black grabbed his arm. "Watch Pookie."

"I'm watchin' you," he said, and walked away from the car, looking back over his shoulder before continuing toward the hotel.

Black didn't answer him. The truth was, he had thought about driving away and leaving them there. But something wouldn't allow him to do it. It wasn't loyalty. It was something deeper than that, and something much more selfish. It was fear: the same fear that told him to tell Clarisse to give the desk clerk a phony name and a phony tag number; the same fear that told him he had to park the car off the street; the same fear that told him they hadn't gotten away as clean as they thought.

He watched as Leroy caught up with Clarisse and walked through the doors of the hotel. A minute or so later, the valet walked out of the vestibule leading toward the lobby and started toward the garage. Black shut off the headlights and tapped the gas, putting the car in neutral and allowing it to roll behind the hedges that lined the hotel driveway.

Black figured the parking attendant would use his electronic garage door opener to open the door, leaving him with a few seconds to shut off the engine and coast in behind him. If Black was lucky, the timer would be set at ten seconds, giving him enough time to wait until the attendant was well into the garage before following him inside. If he wasn't lucky, he'd know soon enough, when the garage door closed on the hood of the car.

Black hoped that having the engine and the lights off was enough to keep the valet from seeing him. If it didn't work out that way, he'd say that he thought garage parking was free. Then he'd park the car outside, because parking it legitimately meant going to the valet and filling out an information form with the tag number and his name. He couldn't do that. They'd already taken enough risks.

Watching from behind the shrubbery, Black saw the valet half jog to the garage to retrieve Pookie's nonexistent car. Black was sure the valet was about to open the door. But he suddenly stopped, felt his pockets, turned, and started back toward the hotel as if he'd forgotten something. Quickly, Black put the car in reverse and backed in behind the hedges. The engine revved slightly, causing the valet to stop for a moment and look toward the shrubs. Black leaned back in the seat and watched the valet watch him. It became obvious after a few minutes, however, that the valet couldn't see very well. He had to lean forward and strain to see past the bushes.

When he was satisfied that nothing was there, the valet walked to the hotel lobby, came back, opened the garage door with a remote control, then walked down the ramp that led to the garage. Black put the car in drive, drove toward the entrance, shifted into neutral, and killed the engine. Then Murphy's Law took over.

The door started to close. To make matters worse, the car was slowing down, like it might stop before it got to the door. Black knew he couldn't start it again, because the noise of the engine would be a dead giveaway. So he did what he was accustomed to doing whenever something like that happened. He shot up a prayer and hoped that the garage door wouldn't close before he got inside.

Just as he got ready to open the car door to get out and push, he saw another car's headlights pulling into the driveway of the hotel. From the car's outline, he thought it might have been a cop car. He could only hope, as he watched the car drive the winding path that led to the entrance of the hotel, that it wasn't.

Black looked from the garage to the rearview mirror, then back to the garage. In about three seconds, thc approaching car would disappear behind the shrubs. The garage door would close in about two.

He looked in the rearview mirror once again, saw the other car approaching the shrubbery, and decided to make a break for the garage. Half crawling out of the car, he pushed against the car door with one hand and maneuvered the steering wheel with the other. By doing so, he was able to gather enough momentum to make it past the garage door before it closed. When he got inside, he jumped back into the car and negotiated the curve that led to the far corner of the garage.

Hoping that the valet couldn't see the red glow from the brake lights, Black pulled into a space between a black BMW and another black Honda. Crouching, he got out of the car and crept toward the elevator on the other side of the garage. The valet came walking toward him, looking around like he was confused about something. From the look on his face, he was probably wondering if he'd looked in the right space for Pookie's nonexistent car.

Black knelt behind a red Cadillac and waited for the valet to walk by. When he did, Black crawled around the side of the car and scurried over to the elevator. He hit the up button and the light over the elevator door lit the number 5. After a long pause, the number 4 lit up. It took what seemed like forever for it to descend to the garage level. When it did, there was a loud chime. The valet looked, and started to walk toward the elevator. Black crawled on board, pushed 5, and hoped that the doors would close before the valet got there. They did. Barely. Black caught a glimpse of the valet's hand moving toward the "open door" button right before the elevator started up.

"What took you so long?" Leroy said when Black got off the elevator at the fifth floor.

"We can talk about all that when we get to the room. Where Clarisse and them?"

"They already went to the room. It's on the seventh floor."

"All right. Let's go."

Leroy pushed the up button and the other elevator came up from the parking garage. When the doors opened, Black found himself looking into the eyes of a very confused parking attendant. He looked from Leroy to Black and then back again. Then he paused to push a very thick pair of glasses back up on the bridge of his nose.

The three of them stood there and looked at one another across the elevator threshold. Leroy, who was unaware that the parking attendant had seen Black sneaking out of the garage, was the first to speak.

"You g-gettin' off?" he said to the valet with an impatient stutter.

"I, uh . . ." The parking attendant hesitated and looked at the knees of Black's pants, which were smudged with gray dust from the garage floor.

"Yeah, so like I was sayin' . . . ," Black said, looking at the attendant as he and Leroy got on the elevator. "Excuse me, brother, could you push twelve please?"

"Sure," the parking attendant said, pushing the button for the twelfth floor.

"Yeah, so anyway," Black continued, giving Leroy a look that begged him not to say anything. "She couldn't even wait until we got to the bed. She wanted to do it on the floor and I'm like, 'Damn, baby, can I at least take my pants off first?' But she just got on the floor and was like, 'Let's have it.' Straight freak. You see she got my pants all dirty. Man, I'm tellin' you . . ."

Black kept talking, and as the elevator reached the twelfth floor, he felt the tension ease considerably. The valet obviously believed he couldn't have been the person he saw sneaking out of the garage. Black even saw a smile creep over the valet's lips.

"All right, man," Black told him when they got off the elevator. "Have a good one."

"You, too."

When the doors closed behind them, Black steered Leroy around the corner and toward the stairs.

"Why you do that?" Leroy said.

"That was the valet. I think he mighta seen me sneakin' out the garage."

"That nigger be lucky if he can see his hand in front o' his face with them thick-ass glasses on," Leroy said.

Black nodded his agreement. "Nigger had on microscopes."

When they got to the seventh floor, Leroy led Black to the room and Clarisse answered the door.

"What took you so long?"

"Don't worry about what took us so long," Black said, rushing in and closing the door behind them. "Just don't come openin' doors like that no more if you don't know who it is. It woulda been the same thing if it was five-o."

"Well you weren't five-o. Now, where's my car?"

"It's in the garage. I parked it in the corner between a BMW and another black Honda."

"Well, give me my keys so I can get out of here. I have to be at work in three hours."

Black looked at her in disbelief.

"You said you just wanted me to take you somewhere outside the city," she said.

"Well, we ain't outside the city yet," he said.

"Is that my problem?"

"You talkin' 'bout don't trust Pookie," Leroy said. "You need to be worried 'bout *this* siditty-ass bitch."

Black glanced at Leroy, then looked at Clarisse with his mouth hanging open.

"Don't look at me like that, Everett. I've helped you as much as I could, and you know it."

"I know we gon' be stuck in this damn hotel if you leave," he said, thinking that they'd have to steal someone's car out of the garage.

"Look," she said, placing her hand on her hip. "When you wanted clothes, I gave you clothes. When you wanted a ride, I gave you that, too. When that cop pulled up on Girard Avenue, I helped you get out of that. Damn, what more do you want?"

"I want to get out of this thing alive."

"So do I. That's why I'm leaving."

"Clarisse," Black said as he moved closer and tried to put his hand against her face.

"Clarisse nothing," she said, pushing his hand away. "I really don't want to be caught up in this anymore, Everett. And you can call me a bitch or whatever you want to call me. I don't care. I just want to get back to real life. Now, hand me my keys so I can go."

Without another word, Black handed her the keys and turned on the radio. A commercial for a local car dealership ended with a man screaming something about deals as Clarisse gathered her pocketbook and coat.

"Well, while y'all handin' out stuff," Pookie said, "can I get mine? 'Cause I wanna go with her."

"You're not going anywhere with me. So you can get that out of your head right now."

"Why not?"

"Because I don't like you," Clarisse said, looking at Pookie like she would be stupid to think otherwise.

Leroy reached into his inside pocket and handed Pookie the five hundred dollars he'd placed there earlier.

Pookie stuffed the money into her bra. As Clarisse started toward the door, the broadcaster led off with the top story. Clarisse stopped in her tracks.

"Police are seeking a female in addition to the two males who are wanted in connection with yesterday's murder of city councilman Johnny Podres in a reputed North Philadelphia crack house," the broadcaster said in a deep resonating voice.

"Patricia Oaks, a twenty-two-year-old female, ninety pounds, five-two, light complexion, with brown hair and hazel eyes, is being sought by police along with Leroy Johnson and Samuel Jackson. Oaks has a scar on the side of her face and should be considered armed and dangerous.

"The threesome is believed to have escaped from the North Philadelphia area in a 1991 black Honda Accord with a Pennsylvania tag reading CWRN. The car is registered to a North Philadelphia nurse. Police are seeking the owner of the vehicle for questioning, but they have been unable to locate her, and they are withholding her name until they can gather more information as to her whereabouts.

"Anyone who can provide any information concerning Johnson, Jackson, Oaks, or the vehicle is being asked to call this number . . ."

They all looked at one another, speechless. Leroy finally spoke.

"Dig this here," he said calmly. "We can do it like we been doin' it, or we can do it the hard way. But ain't nobody leavin' till me and Black figure out where we goin' and how we gettin' there. 'Cause I can't have y'all doin' or sayin' nothin' to get us popped for somethin' we ain't do."

Black walked over and stood by the door.

Clarisse looked from Leroy to Black. Then she sat down on the bed and reached into her pocketbook for her straight shooter and a cap.

"Gimme two," she said.

Black walked over and handed her two matches. Clarisse sighed, took off her coat, and placed her pocketbook gingerly on the bed. As she emptied the cap into the straight shooter, Black watched her, and hoped that his decision to hide out in the hotel had bought them enough time to figure out what to do next.

Commissioner Nelson sat in the Command Center and rested his head in his hands. He knew that the suspects were hiding somewhere within the city limits. He could feel it. But because he had formed his strategy around the 6th District officer's assertion that the suspects were headed for I-76, he might never be able to prove it.

Shortly after the officer in car 611 had radioed in the suspects' last location and the direction he thought they would take, an expressway lieutenant contacted the Command Center and asked for permission to redeploy some of his units from I-95 to I-76. Commissioner Nelson approved the request, then had the districts that bordered I-76 assign cars to patrol the streets that ran parallel or perpendicular to the off-ramps.

An hour after he had approved the plan, Nelson knew something wasn't right. With no new leads on the whereabouts of the fugitives, with daybreak creeping over the city, and with the press preparing for a day of frenzied activity, it was clear that the lieutenant and the commissioner had guessed wrong.

The suspects had never gone anywhere near I-76. They were gone.

Nelson put down the coffee he had been nursing and got up to stretch. When he sat back down, the dispatcher on J band repeated the suspects' descriptions and Nelson sighed, because this meant that the suspects were still at large.

"It looks like we're going to have to get down in the trenches and start digging for these guys," Nelson said to Sheldon as the radio chatter died down.

"I've already got people digging, sir," Sheldon said. "Accident Investigations recovered what we believe to be the murder weapon from the car the suspects crashed on Roberts Avenue. We've brought in the dealers and prostitutes in the area, we've had detectives go door-to-door on Park Avenue, and we've got four extra teams on the streets in case these suspects decide to surface."

"It's not about what the suspects decide to do, Sheldon!" Nelson said, pounding the table in frustration. "We have to go out there and find them."

Sheldon licked his lips nervously and began to babble. "It's not like we're talking about rocket scientists, sir. These are drug addicts. They live their lives in a four-block radius—from the car they break into to the nearest dope man. Even if they did get outside the city, they'd have no idea where to go or what to do."

"That's your first mistake," Nelson said. "You never, under any circumstances, underestimate a suspect. I don't care if he is a drug addict. You got that?"

"Yes, sir. All I meant was . . . Well, I just meant to say that they'll turn up eventually."

"They're just not going to turn up tonight," Nelson mumbled.

Sheldon gave him a moment to calm down before he spoke

again. "I guess Jeanette Deveraux and the rest of them are going to have a field day with this thing if they don't turn up tonight."

"Yeah," Nelson said. "How's that sergeant from Community Relations handling the press, anyway?"

"I suppose she's doing all right, sir. She's been calling the news agencies with updates every couple of hours."

"And who's been approving these updates? I haven't seen any of them."

"Her captain has been helping her to coordinate the press releases."

"Call down there and let them know that no more updates go out without my prior approval."

"Yes, sir."

"Have any of the television stations broadcast Podres's name yet?"

"Yes, sir. In the last hour or so, they've all said that highly placed police sources confirmed that the Park Avenue shooting victim was Podres."

"Highly placed sources," Nelson said, massaging his temples and rubbing his eyes like he was waiting for Calgon to take him away. "Any ideas, Captain? I'm fresh out."

"Well, we know what they're driving," Sheldon said. "Do we have the helicopter in service?"

"It's been in service all night, but they haven't spotted the car."

"What about that helicopter that does the traffic reports for the radio stations?" Sheldon asked. "If we can get an officer on board that helicopter, we can have two choppers instead of one."

Nelson's face softened. "Good idea. Give them a call, Captain."

"I'll get right on it, sir."

"The only thing I'm concerned about now is whether that

young woman who's riding with them is all right," Nelson said, almost to himself.

"Ramirez says there were indications that she might have gone with them willingly."

"That would make her an accomplice," Nelson said.

"So what should I tell my men to do if they find them?" Sheldon asked.

"Tell them that Miss Williams might be a hostage," Nelson said, rubbing his chin thoughtfully. "We don't have anything concrete yet, though. There's no ransom note, and there haven't been any calls demanding money, so we're going to wait twenty-four hours before we call it a kidnapping. After that, we'll have to call in the FBI."

"The FBI?" Sheldon repeated.

"I don't want to have to call them in, either," Nelson said, sensing Sheldon's apprehension. "Believe me, I want this thing solved locally. The political implications of this department not being able to solve a major crime quickly and without federal assistance would be extremely damaging."

Sheldon was silent.

"We need to have that officer from the 6th look at some pictures, too," Nelson said, thinking out loud. "Assuming the ones he saw wearing sunglasses were Black and Leroy, one of the two women must have been the owner of the car. If he can identify who's who, maybe he can remember something that can help us figure out whether she's working with them. Call your guys and have them bring some photos down to the 6th District so that officer can have a look at them."

"Yes, sir."

"I also want another five teams out on the streets looking for these suspects."

"We're going to be stretching our resources kind of thin, sir."

"I know," Nelson said. "That's why you're going to call the state police and have them get some additional state units within the city limits. Get some of our units to set up communications with them so everybody knows what everyone else is doing.

"In the meantime, I want the communications for this thing moved from J band to M band. And I don't want any information—descriptions or anything else of interest to the media—to be put out over the air. The only broadcasts I want to hear are requests for phone calls and meets. Also, I want to hear from your guys about anything that goes on between now and the time this thing is officially declared a homicide."

"Yes, sir."

"Let's get the ball rolling," Nelson said, looking out the window at the sun burning orange against the Philadelphia skyline. "Because time is running out."

"I know," Sheldon said absently. "Time is running out."

Nelson didn't respond.

"I'm going to run down to headquarters to brief my guys in person, sir," Sheldon said, grabbing his jacket from a chair. "I'll make the phone calls on the way."

Sheldon rushed out the door, juggling his car keys and a cell phone. He was dialing the first of several numbers before he made it to the car.

But not all of his calls concerned police business.

The phone at Internal Affairs rang hollow, echoing through the dark room like an alarm. Usually, the office was empty at that hour. But Lieutenant Darren Morgan had been there since five A.M., and he was clearly relieved that the call came before the other officers arrived at the office.

He snatched the phone off the hook before it could ring twice.

"Hello."

"Meet me in the parking lot. I'll be outside in ten minutes."

"Okay," Morgan said, and hung up the phone.

Lieutenant Morgan was used to those types of conversations. It was all part of the game. Very often, the network of political connections he and Sheldon had built over the last year depended on four-word phone calls and meetings in public places. At least twice a day, someone would call, name a place and time, then hang up. They did it that way because they didn't have time to talk. They didn't have time to play, either. But after the stroke of luck that had removed Johnny Podres from the picture, Morgan was in a jovial mood. He almost felt like, well, playing.

Boarding the elevator for the trip down to the first floor of the Roundhouse—Philadelphia's police headquarters—Morgan began to reflect on his perfect life. He had enough time to do what he wanted. He had enough money to do what he wanted. Now, with Podres gone, it was just a matter of packing up and disappearing.

After he got off the elevator and walked past the officer who was posted at the desk, Morgan strolled through the glass doors leading to the parking lot. As he did so, he tried to put an exact figure on the stolen money he'd pocketed over the last few years. As always, the figure eluded him. Not that it mattered. He knew that it was enough to keep him from ever having to count.

The scheme, after all, was perfect. An Internal Affairs lieutenant and a divisional supervisor riding plainclothes through select police districts would shake down drug dealers, numbers runners, fences, and anyone else who was bringing in large amounts of illicit cash. They never used the same car, never used names, and never hit the same place more than once in a ninety-day period. It was easy money. Keeping it hidden was the hard part. But they even had a way to do that.

Morgan and Sheldon laundered the money by making campaign contributions to a select group of politicians through political action committees with phony membership lists. The politicians would take a little off the top, then donate the remainder to a phony nonprofit organization with a post office box for an address. At the end of the year, the nonprofit would fold, having donated all the money to worthy causes—namely Morgan and Sheldon.

Politicians who needed more money for one reason or another were given "advances" through the bogus political action committees. In return, they would pretty much stay mum on whatever happened to be the police scandal of the moment.

As he checked his watch and looked around for Sheldon, Morgan thought of how untouchable they were. After all, who was going to check out an Internal Affairs supervisor like Morgan? If anything, other cops tried to stay away from him. And Sheldon? No one could touch him as long as Morgan was there to protect him from Internal Affairs investigations.

Every base was covered and the scam ran like clockwork. But that wasn't always the case. Two years before, when a watchdog agency called the Police Civilian Review Board was founded, the clock almost ground to a halt.

The push for the creation of the board began after a college student was mistaken for a drug dealer and shot in the back by police. That case brought attention to instances of other young black men who had died in police custody. And though few people could disagree that it had to stop, the position of the police was simple. They were outmanned and outgunned by criminals. So even as the protests became more vocal, the shootings and beatings continued.

From the outset, the mayor and the Fraternal Order of Police—a police union of sorts—were against the board's creation. They claimed that it would impede the department's ability to perform. But as the pressure mounted, the issue became a political hot potato. Anyone who came down against it would look antiblack. And in a city whose electorate is largely African-American, that's not a good stance to take.

Eventually, several city council members forged a compromise. They created the board as a lame duck, thanks in large part to Sheldon's influence in city council. But as luck would have it, the one council member who was virtually incorruptible was selected to run the board. That member was Councilman Johnny Podres.

Initially, they tried to win him over with hefty campaign contributions. But money didn't work. In fact, Podres became more obstinate than ever. The board became his personal power base, and the police department became his whipping boy.

He held hearings on all manner of police corruption—from favoritism in hiring and promotion to negligence in police shootings. In some cases, the board even succeeded in having criminal charges filed against police officers. That worried Sheldon and Morgan. Even members of city council—the ones who had come to depend on the benefits they reaped from participating in the laundering scheme—could see that Podres had to be stopped.

And so, after two years of watching the board grow increasingly powerful, Sheldon and Morgan came up with a plan. It was based on a brilliantly simple, time-honored method of bringing men to their knees: seduction.

They knew they needed to find just the right woman to make a solid family man like Podres stray from a happy twenty-five-year marriage. After an extensive search of juvenile criminal records for females in the Philadelphia region, they chose Antonia Vargas. She was a seventeen-year-old Hispanic call girl who resembled a young version of Podres's wife. The only difference was, Miss Vargas had a simmering sexuality that even leaped off the page in her mug shots.

Sheldon contacted the call girl, met with her to set up payment arrangements, then set up a tricky psychological game. They knew from watching Podres that he attended morning Mass every day at six A.M. It was the only place he went, other than work, where he was away from his wife for any length of time. And it was the same place that the councilman had met his wife twenty-five years before. Sheldon and Morgan, hoping that the sight of a woman resembling his wife would stir up something, paid the call girl to start attending the service on a regular basis.

They gave her specific instructions: Always maintain close proximity to the councilman; wear tasteful yet revealing clothing; approach the councilman like someone in need of a shoulder to cry on (Podres, after all, had a soft spot for people with problems); and, above all, act innocent.

For two weeks, Podres all but ignored Antonia—a young woman who, by most people's standards, was the perfect combination of sex and vulnerability. With Podres acting like she wasn't even there, the girl began to question her own abilities. Even Morgan, who followed them every day with camera in tow, began to wonder if they should have gotten a young man to seduce Podres instead of Antonia. It was so bad that Sheldon, normally an atheist, was beginning to whisper a few prayers of his own.

But then, out of nowhere, Podres asked the young woman to lunch. That first lunch date led to other lunch dates, and eventually he started meeting her for late suppers. Within two weeks Podres was bedding Antonia in motels at lunchtime, in locked rooms at city hall, even at the church.

By the time the affair was in full swing, Sheldon and Morgan had paid Antonia more than fifteen thousand dollars for her services. And it was well worth it. The credit card receipts from the lunchtime motel rendezvous, the pictures from the church, and the sworn affidavits they obtained from motel clerks and the church janitor were more than enough to suit their purposes.

With the evidence in hand, they sent a letter to the councilman asking him to meet with their political action committee. When he refused, they had a manila envelope hand-delivered to Podres's office. It contained evidence of the affair and a check for five thousand dollars. The note they enclosed was simple.

It said, "Ease up."

Podres looked at the package and immediately absorbed it all: the pictures of him and the girl together; the extensive criminal record listing everything about her; the affidavits and credit card receipts. And then he looked at the check, which was drawn on the account of a political action committee that he'd refused to meet with on several occasions. It was called Safer Philadelphians.

The note, which he read only after looking through everything else, brought the entire scheme into perspective. Safer Philadelphians must represent some police organization, or even some individual officers who might have to come before the board. If he eased up, none of the information in the envelope would come out. But if he didn't . . .

His marriage, of course, would be under significant strain. His career would come to an abrupt and tumultuous end. His reputation would be ruined. There were all kinds of negative possibilities. That is, unless he eased up.

Podres thought about it for two days and decided to ignore the package. He couldn't, and wouldn't, be bought. And he did everything he could to make it clear that he intended to continue doing business as usual. He didn't cash the five-thousand-dollar check. He went on a talk show and said he intended to head an investigation into a ticket-fixing scam. The board, in three consecutive hearings, secured the suspensions of five more officers who were involved in a drug ring.

The headlines were heralding Podres as a possible mayoral candidate in the upcoming election. The councilman was flying high. That is, until Morgan—claiming to be a representative of the political action committee—called Podres at home and told him to go down to the phone booth at the end of the block.

The councilman told his wife that he'd be right back and walked to the corner. When he got there, the phone was already ringing. Without a word, Podres picked it up. Before Podres could say anything, Morgan proceeded to lay out the details of the money-laundering network. He told the councilman that if he refused to participate, the photos and affidavits would be delivered to every major media outlet in Philadelphia within twenty-four hours. Morgan even challenged Podres to go to the police, knowing that the councilman had made so many enemies in the department that they would never help him. When Podres remained silent, Morgan hung up.

The next afternoon, when Podres left City Hall, he went to the bank, cashed the check from Safer Philadelphians, and put the five thousand dollars in his sock. He didn't know what he ought to do next and he really didn't care. All he knew was that someone was intent on ruining him. His options? He could turn the matter over to the same police department he'd been purging for the last two years and hope that they would help him. Or he could play their game, launder their money, and hope that he didn't get caught. Either way, Podres knew that he could never respect himself again, even if he survived politically. And nothing was worth that.

So Podres decided to pack his gun, get drunk, go home, and wait for them to call again. When they did, he would ask for a meeting. Then he would blow the bastard's head off, leave the money on the body, and walk away with his dignity intact. He knew he would be caught, but he didn't care. At least he wouldn't have to live the rest of his life under someone's thumb. And in the councilman's mind, the death of his tormentor was a fair trade-off for political ruin. The plan would at least enable him to maintain a portion of his self-respect.

But it didn't work that way, because someone had anticipated Podres's lack of cooperation. The end was a foregone conclusion. Only, Podres didn't know it.

His plan started out the way he had envisioned. Podres managed to make it into a bar, and after several hours, he stumbled out to his car, thinking to himself how everything was going according to plan. His gun was packed, he was drunk, and he was on his way home to wait for the call. But then he saw a light-skinned black girl with long brown hair and hazel eyes walking up Broad Street.

He pulled over in his city-issued black Mercury and waited for her to walk up to the car. When she did, he asked her to get in. The girl smiled sweetly and introduced herself. And then, as if it were the most natural thing in the world, she pulled out a glass tube and offered him a hit of crack.

Podres had never smoked anything stronger than a cigarette, let alone crack. But when the girl offered him the straight shooter, he looked at it. Then he looked at the girl. To his inebriated mind, she was an angel. And what she was offering was a slice of her own private heaven. It had to be better than the hell he'd lived in for the past two days. So Podres took it. And then he followed Pookie to a place where all his troubles would finally end. Because the man with the gold bracelet had decided that it was over.

He knew that Podres would never cooperate, knew that the politician was backed into a corner, knew that there was only one way for it to end. And so he followed him. Watched him pick up the girl. Waited for him to go in the house. And when the pipers took Podres's gun and blew out the candles, the rest was easy. He just slipped in, fired a single shot, and slipped out.

Only one of them had seen him.

And that little problem would be eliminated soon enough.

"Morgan," Sheldon hissed, trying to catch his attention.

Morgan ignored the captain, dragged absently on his third cigarette, and stared straight ahead.

"Morgan!" Sheldon repeated.

Morgan walked over to the car.

"What's wrong with you?" Sheldon said as he got out of the car.

"I was just thinking about Podres," Morgan said wistfully. "And wondering why you were taking so long."

"I got caught up with something back at the scene."

"So what's the big emergency? Podres is gone, the payments are on schedule . . ."

"We got lucky last night when those pipers shot Podres. But we've still got a few loose ends."

"Such as?"

"We don't have a witness who actually saw Leroy or Black

shoot Podres, and neither of them has ever been arrested for anything involving a gun."

Morgan grunted. "First time for everything."

"Sure there is. But Accident Investigations found the probable murder weapon—Podres's own gun, mind you—in the getaway car."

"Leroy could've left it in the car."

Morgan wasn't getting it quickly enough for Sheldon. So he just told him straight-out. "You want to know what I think? I think the guy who died in that crash is probably the one who really shot Podres."

"So what. Wouldn't you rather it was him? That way the investigation's over quickly and nobody looks too deep into what was going on with Podres before he died."

"No, I wouldn't rather it was him," Sheldon said. "You think the Ricans are going to stand for a quick little investigation that pins this shooting on a dead guy? First thing they'll scream is racism."

"Even if the dead guy we pin it on is the guy who really did it?"

"Look, Morgan. You've still got people out there saying the mob teamed up with the Russians to kill JFK. You've got people saying they saw Elvis last Tuesday buying snakeskin belts out at Roosevelt Mall. Hoffa's been dead since the sixties and people are still writing books about where the body's really buried."

"And?"

"And," Sheldon said sarcastically, "people need closure. They need someone to blame when their hero dies. They need to know exactly what happened and how. They're not going to accept that Podres just happened to be in a crack house and the guy who killed him died in a car crash. No. They need someone they can look at and hate. Somebody they can look at and say, 'Let's give that son of a bitch the death penalty.' "

Sheldon could see Morgan coming around. His wrinkled brow was slowly unfolding and a grin was playing on his lips.

"Somebody like Black and Leroy," Morgan said as comprehension crept across his face.

"Exactly," Sheldon said. And then his words began tumbling out in a rush. "Pookie, too. I figure we let the nurse go. Say she was held against her will. People don't really want to see nurses go to jail anyway. They'd rather blame everything on crack heads. Quick investigation. Quick arrests. The whole thing dies down. Case closed."

"We hope," Morgan said, his voice filled with uncertainty.

"No, we don't hope. We make damn sure of it. We send a couple of packages to the press just like the ones we sent to Podres, so everybody knows what tremendous pressure he was under. We let the press make it look like he was smoking crack all along. Then we plant a story saying that Safer Philadelphians is run by Colombian drug lords or something. I don't know, whatever.

"In the meantime, we do everything we can to help his family through this time of crisis. We take up collections. We send flowers to his wife. We make the funeral arrangements if we have to. And the most important thing is, we make sure that the guys we're looking for take the fall for this thing."

"That should be easy enough," Morgan said.

"It will be, as long as we make sure that no one raises any doubts about Leroy being the shooter. And as far as I can tell, there's only one person who can raise those kinds of doubts."

"Who's that?"

"The guy who survived that crash in the getaway car. They finally identified him. His name is Darnell Thomas. They call him Butter."

"But that guy's up at Abbottsford in critical condition," Morgan said, his tone betraying his exasperation at Sheldon's paranoia. "He's probably going to die before the night is out. And even if he doesn't, he's going to wake up and say whatever the D.A. wants him to say, right? Aren't we going to offer him a deal?"

"Sure we're going to offer him a deal. But there's no guarantee he'll take the deal. And we don't need him saying he saw anyone but Leroy with that murder weapon. That raises doubts. And once you raise doubts about one thing, you raise doubts about everything. Before you know it, people are tracing the blackmail thing to us, and suddenly we're murder suspects."

Morgan just looked at Sheldon, unsure what he was leading up to.

"I need you to make sure that no one from the media gets anywhere near this guy Butter until we get a chance to speak with him."

"That it?"

"That's it. We'll talk to him later on today."

"You think he'll be a problem?"

Sheldon chuckled. "Not after we lay his options out for him."

"Okay. I'll take care of it."

"I'm sure you will," Sheldon said, getting back into the car. "I've got to get back up to Park Avenue and make a few more calls, but I'll beep you later on to make sure you've taken care of everything."

"Talk to you then," Morgan said, thinking that he'd better get over to the hospital quickly.

Not that it mattered. The media had already beaten him to Butter.

Chapter 11

Freelance reporter Henry Moore sat in the visitors' area of Abbottsford Hospital's intensive care unit and watched as Latoya Thomas sat stone-faced, determined not to grieve for her twin brother.

Moore couldn't have known that her grim expression came from too many years of watching her brother destroy his life. Nor could he have known that she would have given anything to have had her brother attend her college graduation, or witness her rise to junior partner at her law firm, or give her away at her wedding.

The only thing Moore could tell by watching her was that she wasn't the type to go for a scam. But she was his key to getting an interview with the only man who had actually witnessed what happened in that crack house. So Moore took a deep breath and struck up the conversation that he hoped would get him an exclusive interview with Butter.

"My daughter's supposed to be transferred from intensive

care sometime today," Moore said nervously as he stared straight ahead in mock grief.

Butter's sister looked over at him and picked up a magazine, dismissing his attempt at conversation.

"I wish I could go in there and sit with her," Moore continued. "But the truth is, I can't stand to see her that way. It's like she's . . . They've got all these tubes attached to her and she just lies there."

He broke off, placing his face in his hands as he tried to act overwhelmed.

Butter's sister lowered the magazine. "I'm sorry to hear about your daughter," she said, her words coming out in a clipped monotone.

Moore extended his hand and introduced himself as she raised the magazine again. "My name's Henry Moore."

She peered over the top of the magazine at his outstretched hand, then turned the page and adjusted herself in the seat. "Charmed, I'm sure."

Moore lowered his hand.

"Do you have a name?" he asked hopefully.

"Yes, I do," she said, and turned another page.

He was starting to get angry now. But he held his attitude in check and forced it out as mild sarcasm. "I'm sorry. I just thought that since we're both obviously waiting for word on our loved ones, maybe we could talk to pass the time."

"I'd much rather read, but thank you just the same."

Moore had to give it to her. She was cool. Even if he didn't get the interview, he could amuse himself by trying to break through that cool while he waited for the detectives to come and interrogate her brother.

"Do you have a relative here?" Moore asked.

"You're asking a lot of questions, Mr. Moore."

"I'm sorry. I really don't mean to pry, Ms. . . ."

She didn't fill in the blank with her name. Instead, she lowered the magazine and looked at his eyes. She peered into them and through them, staring so intently that Moore could have sworn she could see what was going on behind him.

When she spoke, it was in a creamy voice. But her words were pointed and deliberate. "Whatever it is you want, Mr. Moore, I wish you'd get to the point. But please, don't insult my intelligence with clumsy lies. I don't have the time or the patience for that."

She looked at him and waited for him to respond. And for the first time since Moore could remember, he was speechless. She gave him a few minutes before she put down the magazine and got up from the chair.

"Now, if you'll excuse me," she said, "my brother is dying."

Moore watched her walk over to the nurses' station to ask if there'd been any change in her brother's condition. The nurse said the doctors were with him, and that they would know in a few minutes. Moore walked over to her with his hands in his pockets.

"I'm sorry," he said in a voice that only she could hear.

She turned around, and he could tell that she was willing to listen, but not willing to talk.

"My name really is Henry Moore. And if I'm not mistaken, Darnell Thomas is your brother."

She gave no indication that he was right.

"I'm a reporter. I'm here to find out what really happened last night in that crack house, and your brother is probably one of the only people who knows."

"Well, I'm not interested in talking to any reporters, Mr.

Moore," she said, and walked back over to her chair and sat down.

"That's okay," he said, following her and standing up beside her seat. "Because I was hoping that I could talk to your brother."

She looked at him, and for the first time, her eyes flashed anger. "My brother is burned over ninety percent of his body, Mr. Moore. And in case you didn't know, he's been unconscious since he got here, so I don't see how you're going to talk to him. As far as finding out what happened in that house, I don't see any reporters banging down any doors to write stories about those houses any other time. And I think it takes a lot of nerve for you to come in here to ask my brother questions about it now, when he's this close to dying."

"You're right," Moore said. "It takes a lot of nerve. But if I don't ask him, the truth might never come out."

"Oh really? Who made you the keeper of the truth?"

"Look, I'm not saying I can write a story that will make any of this go away. I'm not even saying that it'll say exactly what you or your brother think it should. But wouldn't you rather take your chances with a black reporter than with someone else?"

Latoya shook her head in disbelief. "Please spare me the black man routine. My father was a black man. I've never seen him a day in my life. My husband was a black man. He ran around with every woman in a fifty-mile radius. My brother's a black man. He's a drug addict and probably an accessory to murder. Do I have to go on?"

Moore could tell that there was more to her attitude than her brother's condition. No matter what angle he tried to take, she was going to shoot him down. So he decided to tell her the truth.

"No, you don't have to go on," he said as he sat down next to her. "But this is what's going to happen to your brother, whether he talks to me or not. Some detective is going to ask him to tell him what he saw in that house. If what he says doesn't jibe with what the D.A. wants to hear, they're going to tell him what to say. If your brother lives, he's going to repeat what they told him to say in a court of law when he testifies against the piper of their choice. And no matter what, he's still going to get some jail time out of the deal. If he doesn't die here, in this hospital, he'll probably die there. Because nobody likes a snitch."

As a lawyer, she knew he was right. The first thing they would do would be to offer him a deal in exchange for testimony. But as Darnell's sister, she knew that the deal would probably be his only chance at survival. Because if he didn't deal, he would probably get the death penalty along with everyone else involved.

"So what do you think you can do about it, Mr. Moore?"

"I can give him a chance to say what really happened. I can give him a chance to go against the system that's swallowing up so many of us, before they come and feed him into the system, too."

"Spare me the idealism," she said cynically. "You want to get the story, or make up the story—whichever is more expedient—before the rest of the media get a chance to do it."

He looked down at his hands and then back up at Latoya. "Do you know who died in that house last night?"

"Yes. It was that city councilman. Johnny Podres."

"Yes, it was Johnny Podres. It was a guy who came up the hard way in the Badlands, right around 5th and Glenwood. Put himself through college washing dishes down at Bookbinders. Got a full scholarship to Wharton and graduated near the top of his class with an MBA. He was a guy who could've written his own ticket, but he never left the neighborhood. He stayed and spent most of his life fighting the cops."

Latoya looked like she was starting to listen, so Moore shifted into high gear.

"He fought against the brutality under Rizzo, then the shakedowns and payoffs that came later. He won some, he lost some, and nobody paid too much attention. But when he got elected to city council and became chairman of the Police Civilian Review Board, people started to notice. It wasn't just Podres testifying for a good kid who'd been arrested, or Podres fighting for a foot patrol in his neighborhood. It was Podres breaking up drug rings in the department and getting cops indicted. The man had powerful enemies in the department and even in city council. And I know in my gut that those enemies had more to do with his death than your brother or anyone else in that house. I just need to talk to your brother to prove it."

Latoya looked into Moore's eyes again, that same piercing look that she had given him just a few minutes before. But this time the look softened. She was just about to speak when a doctor walked over to where they sat.

"Miss Thomas. I'm Dr. Roberts. Your brother is awake and he's asking for you. He's still very weak, but you can talk to him for ten minutes. And I think I should let you know that some detectives are on the way here to speak with him, too."

"Thank God he's awake," Latoya said, then turned and buried her head in Moore's chest.

Unsure what to do, Moore hesitantly placed his arms around her. She looked at him and smiled a hint of a grin. And then Latoya surprised even herself with what she said next.

"This is my husband, Henry. I'd like to take him with me to speak to my brother. The two of them are very close."

Moore's mouth nearly dropped to the floor. But he recovered quickly and began fumbling in his pocket for his tape recorder.

"Okay," the doctor said, oblivious to what had just occurred. "But only for a few minutes."

Latoya took Moore over to the nurses' station and the two of them signed the visitors' list that was mandatory for prisoners. Then Moore tugged at her arm.

"I want you to take this," he said, and slipped his tape recorder into her open purse. "If the detectives come, they're going to ask me to leave while they question him. If you stay in the room, you can tape what he says to them."

Just then, homicide detective Reds Hillman got off the elevator with another detective. When Latoya and Moore walked inside, identifying themselves for the policeman guarding the door as Darnell's sister and brother-in-law, Hillman and the other detective flashed their badges and walked in behind them.

Latoya had barely managed to speak to her brother before Hillman got down to police business. "My name is Detective Hillman. I work Homicide."

"I'm Darnell's sister, Latoya Thomas. And this is Henry."

"I'm sorry to have to ask this," Hillman said with disarming sincerity. "But it's very important that we speak with Mr. Thomas about what happened last night. I'm going to ask everyone to leave. We'll make it as brief as possible so you can come back and visit with your brother."

The officer who was stationed inside the room got up and walked outside the door. Moore also left. But Latoya didn't move.

"I'm a lawyer, and I'm representing my brother in this matter," she said.

"The way he's looking right now, I don't think he'll know the difference," Hillman said.

They all looked down at Butter, who was fading in and out of consciousness.

"I'm going to the john," said the other detective. "I'll be right back."

Hillman nodded as the detective walked out the door. Then he looked at Latoya and shifted uncomfortably.

"You were going to advise my brother of his right to counsel, weren't you?"

When Hillman didn't answer, Latoya reached into her purse and turned on the tape recorder. As she saw her brother's eyes flicker open, she began to speak.

"Darnell, this man is a detective. He's going to ask you some questions."

She felt a tear forming in the corner of her eye as she reached down and touched her brother's bandages. Her voice cracked as she tried and failed to maintain a professional demeanor. "It's my duty to inform you that you don't have to answer anything that you feel may incriminate you."

Butter heard his sister's voice as his mind struggled back toward reality. But he couldn't see her. His vision was filled with the detective's face. And his mind was hazy, still caught in a space between the gunshots at the house and the twisting, fiery wreck on Roberts Avenue. His skin felt tight across his bones, like it was stretched to the breaking point.

When he tried to move, white-hot needles shot through his body, and the one image that wouldn't leave his mind came crashing through the pain until he couldn't help blurting it out.

"He had on a bracelet," Butter said.

Hillman and Latoya leaned in to listen closer.

"Who had on a bracelet?" Hillman said as he scribbled on a notepad.

"It was a white man with a big gold bracelet. A link bracelet."

Latoya was beginning to think that her brother was delirious. But Butter went on, raising his voice as his mind traveled back to the shooting.

"Rock took the gun and tried to shoot him, but he missed. The white man pulled back the curtain and . . ."

For the first time, Butter realized what he had seen. It was clear now, and as the image came into focus, an overwhelming fear consumed him. Because he knew that no one else had seen it, and that the shooting was a lot more than just a robbery.

But somewhere beyond the fear, there was a need for him to come out and tell what he had seen. There was a need for him, just once, to give his sister a reason to be proud of him.

"It was the white man."

"What was the white man?" Hillman said, now thoroughly confused.

"Don't say anything else, Darnell," Latoya said. "Save it for the preliminary hearing."

But he was determined to get it out. She could tell by the way he struggled to pronounce each word.

"He had on a white shirt and black pants," Butter said. "He was tall, with blond hair and blue eyes. And he had on this big link bracelet."

"And what did the white man do?" Hillman said as he feverishly scribbled notes.

"He shot the Puerto Rican. He reached out from behind that curtain and shot the Puerto Rican."

Hillman stopped scribbling. He couldn't believe what he was hearing. But then again, he could believe it. It was like he'd felt it somewhere in the back of his mind all along, known that the suspects were just a little too convenient. He was so convinced that he was hearing the truth for the first time that he almost dropped his notepad. And then Butter was speaking again, picking up steam as the vision came to him full-on, the bits and pieces assembling themselves into a complete picture.

"It was dark," Butter said, " 'cause I blew out the candles after the Puerto Rican pulled out his gun. We was gon' rob him, but we couldn't really get the gun away from him. And when Rock finally got it and tried to shoot him, he missed. But the white man didn't. He aimed straight at his head and slumped him. Then he ran out the back door."

"Where was Leroy?" Hillman asked.

"I heard Leroy, but I ain't see him. I think he was just comin' in when everything jumped off."

"What about Black?"

"I ain't see him, either."

At that, Butter arched his back against a pain that pulsed across his chest and the nurse who was stationed at the heart monitor came running into the room. The other detective followed close behind her, rubbing his hands on a paper towel as he returned from the bathroom.

"That's enough for now," the nurse said. "All of you are going to have to leave."

Latoya walked Hillman to the door, knowing that her brother was telling the truth and wondering if it would matter. "Here's my card, Detective. I'll be in touch."

"So will we."

As Hillman and the other detective got on the elevator, Latoya walked outside the room, slipped Moore's tape recorder into his jacket pocket, and whispered in his ear. "Write your story," she said.

"But what . . ."

She put her finger to her lips. "This information is my brother's only chance. I need you to get it out there. Otherwise, they're going to twist it and say that he's lying."

"Well, what does it—"

"Just trust me. Your story's here. Now promise me you'll write it."

Moore looked into Latoya's eyes. "Cross my heart and hope to die," he said.

Lieutenant Darren Morgan sat in the waiting room and watched as the detectives came out of Thomas's room. Then he watched a woman come out and give something to a man who had been waiting outside the room. The man, who looked vaguely familiar, spoke to the woman briefly, then walked quickly to the elevator, clutching his jacket pocket like he was protecting his most prized possession.

"Excuse me, Nurse," Morgan said, flashing his badge at the nurses' station. "Was that man in Darnell Thomas's room before the detectives went in?"

"Yes."

"Could you tell me his name, please?"

The nurse perused the list and found his name. "Henry Moore."

"Thank you."

Morgan recognized the name from a smear story the reporter had written a month before, outlining a perceived pattern of corruption in the police department. That's why the face was familiar. The story was published in a local magazine and picked up by a few television stations. Moore made some appearances on local talk shows. He probably was going to try to do the same thing with the Podres story.

Too late, Morgan tried to break for the elevator doors. When they closed, he ran to the stairs, skipping every other step as he bolted down three flights, caught sight of Moore in the lobby, and followed the reporter to the parking lot.

He watched and listened as an anxious Moore pulled the tape recorder from his jacket and rewound it a little. When he hit play, he heard the exchange between Butter and Detective Hillman.

"He had on a white shirt and black pants. He was tall, with blond hair and blue eyes. And he had on this big link bracelet."

"And what did the white man do?"

"He shot the Puerto Rican. He reached out from behind that curtain and shot the Puerto Rican."

Moore shut off the tape and muttered a strangled "Yes!"

As he fumbled in his pockets for his car keys, Morgan walked up behind the reporter, causing him to jump.

"Henry Moore?" Morgan said, pulling out his badge. "Darren Morgan. Philadelphia police, Internal Affairs."

"Man, you scared me," Moore said, looking down at his keys as he found the one that fit the door. "What's up?"

"Mr. Moore, I'm going to have to ask you for the tape."

"What tape?" Moore said, opening the door and getting into the car.

"The one you obtained illegally from the interview with Darnell Thomas."

"You don't have a warrant, you don't have probable cause, I don't have a tape," Moore said as he got in his car and tried to close the door.

Morgan held the door open. "I'm going to ask you once more for the tape, Mr. Moore."

"Don't bother. Because I'm not giving you any tape. Now, let go of my door so I can go home."

"Sure."

Moore closed the door, rolled up his window, and put his key in his ignition. When he looked up, the barrel of Morgan's gun was pointed at his head.

"Hey," Moore said, in a voice that was muffled inside the car. "Hey, what are you . . ."

The window shattered. The first bullet lodged in Moore's eye, splattering blood against the dashboard and the windshield. Morgan reached into the car and unlocked the door. Then he shot the reporter again, this time punching a hole through his chest that blew out the back of the driver's seat.

While Moore sat dying, Morgan calmly removed the tape recorder from his pocket, then went into the reporter's back pocket and removed his wallet. For good measure, he took Moore's watch, too, then dropped an empty cap on the floor between the reporter's legs.

As Morgan walked away from Moore's car and got into his own, a security guard came running out of the hospital yelling something into his walkie-talkie. Morgan ignored him, thinking to himself about how Homicide would have at least one more murder to pin on a piper.

He opened his car door, got in, and rewound the tape to the beginning. He looked down at the reporter's bloodstained watch and saw that it was seven A.M. That meant he had a half hour to get to work.

Morgan started his car, pushed play, and drove back to the Roundhouse listening to what turned out to be a very interesting conversation. He knew after listening to Butter's first few words that he needed to call Sheldon. Because if what Morgan was hearing on the tape was right, Sheldon needed to hear it, too.

• • •

Detective Reds Hillman was just leaving Abbottsford Hospital when he heard the shots in the parking lot. The other detective was already gone, and by the time Hillman circled his car around, Henry Moore was dead. Hillman called it in, and in a few minutes, the guys from Northwest Detectives arrived. He told them he'd just seen Moore in Butter's room, then waited around in case they had questions.

As he watched them stretch yellow crime-scene tape around the perimeter, Hillman wondered who would have wanted to kill Moore. He wasn't exactly an important guy.

In fact, Moore was a nobody. So much so that if Hillman had known that Latoya Thomas had smuggled a reporter into her brother's room, it wouldn't have been a big deal. He had expected to see reporters around the people associated with the Podres case. He'd expected them to try every trick in the book to get whatever information they could get before the competition. He'd half expected to see the entire floor filled with reporters when he got off the elevator to go see Butter. And when they hadn't been there, he'd shrugged it off, thinking that they'd probably already been there and left.

But none of that was important. What everyone needed to know now was why Moore had eaten two bullets once he'd left the hospital.

From what they could gather from the hospital security guard who had discovered the body, there were two shots fired in the vicinity of Moore's car. A brown-haired white man with a bushy mustache had walked away from Moore's car shortly after the shots were fired. He was wearing a gray blazer and black pants. And his car was one of the box-shaped Chryslers that police use. The security guard had even gotten the last three numbers on the license plate—342.

It didn't make sense to Hillman. If a cop was going to rob someone, it would be someone like a drug dealer: someone he wouldn't have to kill; someone with enough money to make it worthwhile; someone who wouldn't talk. He wouldn't rob someone like Moore unless it was about more than a robbery.

Hillman walked over to the edge of the yellow crime-scene tape, where he noticed steel nine-millimeter shell casings circled with yellow chalk. As he bent down for a closer look, he felt someone standing behind him.

He looked up and saw Latoya Thomas, her face blank, staring straight ahead as her eyes glazed over with hopelessness.

"Tell me that's not Henry Moore," she said.

Hillman was about to answer her when a detective called him over to the car.

"Hey, Reds. Take a look at this."

Latoya followed Hillman to the opposite side of the yellow tape and turned away as the bloody scene came into full view.

"The crime-lab guys just removed a tape recorder from the victim's pocket," the detective said. "But there was no tape."

"What do you mean there's no tape?" Latoya said, her words tumbling from her mouth as her cool exterior began to crack. "There must be a tape."

The detectives looked at each other, then rested their eyes on Latoya.

"How do you know there must be a tape?" Hillman said, though he already knew the answer.

She thought of her brother in the hospital bed, his body burned and his life slipping away, and she knew that there was nothing that anyone could do to her that was worse than watching him die.

"I taped the interrogation," she said, turning to look up into

Hillman's face. "I gave the tape to Moore and told him to write a story about it, because I knew that my brother would never have a chance if the truth didn't come out somehow."

A single tear formed in her eye. "I'm a lawyer, Detective. I've seen too many innocent brothers go to jail on trumped-up charges. I wasn't about to let it happen to mine."

Hillman couldn't argue. She was right. And from the description that the hospital security guard had given, the people who were hiding the truth about her brother and the other suspects were police officers.

"Whoever killed Moore must have taken the tape," Hillman said.

"Do you know who killed him?" Latoya Thomas said.

Hillman looked at the other detective, then at Latoya. And before he knew what he was saying, the truth was falling from his lips like dead leaves fall from trees in autumn.

"It was a cop," he said, grasping Latoya Thomas's hand as he looked into her eyes. "And I'm going to find him."

Hillman turned and walked away from the scene. If there had been any doubt in his mind before, it had just been erased. Podres's killer was a tall white man with blond hair, blue eyes, and a link bracelet. He was a cop. He was working with another cop—one with brown hair and a bushy mustache.

But the descriptions were just a start. Hillman knew where he had to go to get the rest of the information he needed.

When the lieutenant in command of the Radio Room looked up and saw a detective strolling toward his desk with a folder in his hand, he immediately stiffened. He knew that detectives thought they were too important to waste their time in Radio. But the lieutenant knew better. And he was going to make sure that this red-haired bozo knew it, too.

"How ya doin', Lieutenant?" Hillman said as he walked toward the desk. "I'm Reds Hillman, Homicide."

"And I'm busy," the lieutenant said, looking down and shuffling papers at his desk. "Things are pretty crazy with this Podres shooting, and we're shorthanded. So whatever it is, make it quick."

Hillman knew what the attitude was about. So he just smiled, looked at the lieutenant's name tag, and made small talk.

"Jervey, huh? I worked in the 23rd District with a Sergeant Charles Jervey back in '63. He was a hell of a cop."

The lieutenant relaxed at the mention of the sergeant. "He was my father."

"I knew you looked familiar," Hillman said, his smile broadening. "Your father used to get that same look on his face when somebody came to the district trying to act like a big shot."

Both men laughed.

"Lieutenant Jervey, I—"

"Call me Charles," the lieutenant said. "And I'm sorry about before. I guess I'm just stressed-out."

"Don't mention it," Hillman said. "Charles, I need to look at the printouts from every job in the 25th and 39th districts that came in between eleven P.M. and twelve-thirty A.M. last night. I also need to look at the unit histories for every car in East and Northwest divisions, and any 25-48s you might have."

"You want the calls that came in, the cars that responded, and police reports," he repeated, jotting down the request on a piece of paper. "I'll have everything for you in five minutes."

"Thanks a lot, Charles."

While Hillman waited, he opened up the folder he was carrying and looked at the suspects' criminal records. From what he could see, they all had clear patterns. Leroy did thefts, Black did burglaries, and Pookie did prostitution. Leroy and Black had been arrested together three times in the last two months. But none of them had ever done anything violent.

"Here's your printout, Detective," the lieutenant said, dropping a computer-generated sheaf of papers in front of Hillman. "I'll be right over here if you need me."

"Thanks."

As Hillman paged through the printouts, he saw the usual disorderly crowds and theft reports that always came in on Sunday nights. Then he ran across something interesting. It was a call for a theft in progress in front of the church at Broad and Butler.

A priest had called and said that someone was trying to take the tires off his car. Since it was the only thing Hillman had to go on, he called the church and asked the priest for a description of the person who'd tampered with his tires. The priest described Leroy. After the police had come and gone, the priest said, Leroy walked across the street to the barbecue place on Germantown Avenue in the opposite direction of the house on Park Avenue. The time was 11:45 P.M. The priest knew because he'd checked his watch to see if the news was still on.

Hillman wondered how Leroy could have doubled back and committed the crime when he was walking away from the scene of the shooting at 11:45 P.M. That is, unless the councilman was already dead by the time Leroy got to the house. And if Leroy had walked in on the tail end of the shooting and escaped in a car with the girl and the other two guys, where had his supposed accomplice been?

Hillman went through the printouts again, and it wasn't long before he found the answer to that question. Someone had called the police around midnight to report a burglary in progress after seeing a thin, dark-complexioned black male coming out of the alley that ran behind the bars and stores on Germantown Avenue. But the police hadn't responded to the call.

When Hillman looked at the unit histories for the cars in the 39th, 25th, and 5th districts, he immediately saw the reason why. All of them had responded to the assist that was broadcast over J band when the rookie's car flipped over on Roberts Avenue. The time for the assist was the same as the burglary in progress—midnight. And Hillman was willing to bet his life that Black was the burglar in the alley.

He had found what he needed. But he knew it wouldn't be easy to convince Ramirez or anyone else that he was right. Still, he had to try.

As Hillman rushed from the Radio Room and headed back to the crime scene to find the lieutenant, he knew that the suspects would never be safe until the killers were found. He only hoped that the four of them could remain alive long enough for the true story to be told.

Chapter 12

Black and his companions had smoked so much crack that they couldn't do anything but sit there with their mouths hanging open. In the part of their minds that hadn't been vaporized along with the crack they'd burned in their straight shooters, they were all asking themselves the same question: How are we going to get out of this alive?

For Clarisse, the question was different. She was asking herself what she was doing there.

While Pookie sat in one corner of the room rocking back and forth, Leroy sat in the opposite corner staring into space.

They were all caught up in one of those awkward silences that sometimes falls over a crack house, only they were in a hotel room. But the effect was the same. It was the kind of moment when stark tragedy and pain are etched into the faces of everyone there.

Black stood by the window and absorbed the moment, afraid to turn around for fear someone would ask what he planned to do to get them out. He stood there and he waited, knowing that if the question was asked, he couldn't provide the first clue as to what they had to do. Because as the radio droned on in the background, giving out their names and descriptions at what seemed like one-minute intervals, Black was becoming more and more afraid of what might happen next.

Images of police barreling into the room with guns blazing dominated his thoughts. He could actually feel the hot, stabbing sensation of the bullets and see the blood spattering the walls as they raised their hands in surrender. He could picture the serious look on the reporter's face as he delivered his lines on the evening news, repeating the official police explanation as he told the world that the suspects had resisted arrest.

Black could even see some fat white guy in Northeast Philadelphia sitting at home and hollering into the kitchen for another beer as he told his wife, "Hey, Marge, they finally shot those niggers that killed the spick from city council!"

The more Black thought about it, the uglier the images became, so he tried not to think of anything. But just as he managed to clear his mind, the questions began.

"Black," Leroy said quietly.

Black turned around and looked at him, but didn't answer.

"Yo, man, how we gon' get outta here?" he said.

Black hesitated, then turned to Clarisse, who sat on the bed and continued to scrape her straight shooter, seemingly oblivious to it all.

"We damn sure can't use her car," he said.

"Well, you might as well let me go, then," Clarisse said, still scraping.

"For what? If we let you go, they'll pick you up in five minutes. And by the time they get finished with you, you'll say whatever they tell you to."

"Why would I tell them anything about something I don't know about?"

" 'Cause they'll kick yo' ass if you don't," Leroy said.

"They might not even have to do that," Black said. "They might just scare her into sayin' she saw us do it."

"They can't scare me into doing anything," Clarisse said.

"They can if they start sayin' you the one pulled the trigger," Black said.

"Well, they could never say that because they know I didn't."

"They probably know me and Leroy ain't do it, either. You think that's gon' stop them from puttin' it on us? Matter fact, what's stoppin' them from sayin' you had somethin' to do with it? First thing they probably say, 'Yeah, well, you know we're going to have to charge you as an accomplice, Miss Williams.' They'll probably have you down there signin' all kind o' stuff."

"No they won't."

"Yeah right," Pookie said, speaking from the corner as she continued to rock back and forth. "What makes you so much better than everybody else?"

"What?" Clarisse said. "I know you're not talking—"

"You don't know shit," Pookie said. "You ain't gon' sit there and tell me that if they gave you the choice between going to jail for life and snitchin', you would be like, 'Oh no, I could never tell on someone. It's unethical.' "

Black laughed at Pookie's imitation of Clarisse.

"That's her problem," Pookie said. "She think she the only one ever had somethin'. Lookin' at us like we ain't nothin'. You know what I was before I started smokin'? I was a management trainee at Bell. Not sayin' that's a whole lot, but it's better than this."

"Look, Pookie," Black said. "Wasn't nobody even talkin' to you."

"So what?" she said, standing up and coming over by the window to stand beside him. "You another one, Black. Swear you so smart. Swear you know everything. Well, if you know so much, why we ain't gone yet? Why you standin' there lookin' out the window when you know they could come runnin' up in here any minute and knock all of us off?"

"Leroy, come get your woman," Black said, turning his back on Pookie so she couldn't see the truth of her words reflected on his face.

"Leroy can't do nothin' to me! He ain't my man. If he was my man, if he was a man at all, if he cared anything about me or hisself, we wouldn't be sittin' here waitin' for you to figure a way outta this. If Leroy could take the time to be a man, maybe try to get hisself together for a minute, he could get all this."

She swept her hand up and down her body in case they couldn't see clearly enough what Leroy could get.

"Hold up," Leroy said. "I could get all what? What I want with you? You everybody woman."

"Now, that's where you wrong," she said. "How many men you seen me do somethin' with since I been out here?"

Leroy opened his mouth to speak, but he was too slow.

"Let me give you the answer to that 'fore you blow up the damn room tryin' to think. None. Zero. I don't do nothin' out here, but you too stupid to see that. The only one that has ever done more than touch me in the last year and a half I been out here is you, Leroy. You know why? 'Cause I thought I could feel somethin' for a ninety-nine-cent rice-and-gravy-eatin' nigger like you. But I guess I was wrong again."

"Keep talkin', you gon' be a whole lot more than wrong," Leroy said.

"Man, that don't move me," Pookie said. "You can't do nothin' to me I ain't already do to myself. I lost everything it is to lose 'fore I even got out here like this. So if I lose some blood, if I lose a couple of teeth, if I lose my life out here, it don't even matter."

"Pookie," Black said, "why don't you sit down?"

By then it was too late to stop her. She ignored Black, ignored Leroy, and focused her venom on Clarisse, who had stopped scraping her straight shooter and was looking at Pookie as if she were an evangelist preaching the gospel.

"I had a house," she said, looking at Clarisse with contempt. "Right up there in Mount Airy. Four bedrooms, two bathrooms, wall-to-wall carpet. Shit was nice. I had a car. I had a boyfriend. I had all that. I had clothes and jewelry and a bank account. I had a family."

Pookie's tough exterior crumbled slightly as she paused to swipe at her eyes.

"I had a life!" she said, raising her voice to a high-pitched, broken squeal.

They were all caught up in the passion of her words, reflecting on what they meant to each of them. Pookie swiped at her eyes again. And when she realized that there were no tears, she looked at her fingers in wonderment, then went on as if she had never stopped.

"That wasn't enough, though. I had to have more than everybody else. My man wasn't the richest guy in the world. But he gave me everything he could with what he had. He gave me jewelry every now and then, paid the bills. We was even savin' up to buy another house.

"But I knew I could get a whole lot more than that if I played a little bit, so that's what I did. And it was cool for a while. You know, I'd go meet my little boyfriends, get what I could get from 'em, and come on home. It wasn't about fallin' in love or nothin'.

It was strictly about gettin' mine. It wasn't about what I wasn't gettin' from my man, either, 'cause like I said, he was givin' me everything I needed.

"But after a while it was like, I ain't want to come home no more, 'cause I couldn't stand lookin' in his face knowin' what I was doin'. I guess I thought he might o' knew or whatever. When I think about it now, though, I know he didn't know. 'Cause the more I would stay out late, the more I told him, 'Not tonight,' the more I pulled away from him, the harder he tried. He loved me like that, but I ain't care.

"It was like, I was gettin' the clothes and the jewelry and the money—all the things I said I wanted—and I was still feelin' like shit. That ain't stop me, though. I kept duckin' and I kept dodgin'. I kept slippin' and I kept dippin'. And if you asked me now what I was lookin' for when I was doin' all that, I couldn't even tell you."

They all looked at Pookie, then at one another, comparing her story to their own. Black stood by the window and wondered how long it had been since she had talked. And he wondered even more how long it had been since anyone had listened.

He wanted to say something to console her. He wanted to tell her that he knew what she was going through, because he was going through it himself. But by the time he fixed his lips to say something, Pookie began to speak again.

"So one day this guy beeps me," she said, her hands moving to the rhythm of her words. "Old nigger with plenty cash. I'm talkin' 'bout this nigger was paid, you hear me?"

She stopped long enough to allow them to imagine how paid he was.

"He beeped me, and I had to call him up a couple o' times before I caught up with him. When I finally got him, he asked me to meet him at this jazz club downtown. Not that I expected him to say anything different, 'cause that's all he used to want to do—just be seen with me at the jazz shows.

" 'Just smile and look pretty, baby.' That's what he used to tell me—'just smile and look pretty.' So that's what I did. I smiled and hung on his arm like his old ugly-ass was Denzel or somebody. I just figured it wasn't no thing, you know. Nigger was givin' up five hundred dollars just to take me to a show, so I was smilin' my ass off. Wasn't like we was screwin', right?"

They didn't respond, knowing that it was futile to offer an opinion. She waited half a second, in case one of them tried to challenge her, and then she went on.

"Well, on this particular night, somethin' just ain't feel right," Pookie said. "It was like somethin' was out of place, like somethin' was gettin' ready to happen. But the longer the show went on, the more I felt like I was bein' silly to think that.

"The music was corny, as usual. The drinks was watered down, as usual. The waitress rolled her eyes at me all night long, as usual. And the owner of the club tried to crack on me when I went to the bathroom, as usual.

"At the end of the night, when he pulled up at the corner of my block, dude handed me an envelope like he always did, and I put it in my pocketbook, like I always did, and kissed him on the cheek. But when I got ready to get out of the car, he said he had forgot to give me somethin'."

Pookie smiled when she said that.

"Now ya know I wasn't goin' nowhere when he said that, right?" she said, smiling even harder. " 'Cause Trish wasn't leavin' nothin' behind that was free, you know what I'm sayin'?"

"Trish?" Leroy said, making it sound like an alien word. "Who Trish?"

"Who you think?" Pookie said. "My name ain't no damn Pookie. I made that up so I ain't have to tell nobody out here my real name. But that's messed up now, too, ain't it? Y'all got my name on the radio like it's number three on the countdown.

"Patricia Oaks! Patricia Oaks! They mess around and throw a beat behind it and have niggers dancin' to it."

"Ain't nobody get your name on the radio but you," Black said. " 'Cause if you wouldn't o' never got the man shot in the first place, none o' this wouldn't be happenin'."

"Whatever," Pookie said. "I ain't even gon' argue with you."

Pookie went back to the corner, put her head between her knees, folded her arms around her legs, and began to rock again. Black looked out the window and began to think of where they would go and how they would get there, wondering but not really caring what the end of Pookie's story would have been if she had finished it.

It wasn't like he needed to hear the end anyway. He already knew the story's end, because he knew his own. And knowing his own tragedy was enough. He didn't want to have to listen to it, too. He didn't want to hear much of anything. All he wanted to hear was that everything they had gone through was nothing more than a pipe dream: something that would go away in a few minutes, like the ghostly puffs of crack smoke that shrouded their broken lives in tattered cloaks of fantasy.

It wasn't that easy, though. Because the more Black tried to push Pookie's story to the back of his mind, the more it tried to push itself to the surface. It was like someone who was fighting to keep from drowning. It would go down, then suddenly bound back to the surface, hands flailing wildly against the water.

After all, Black was just like Pookie. But he hadn't sold his smile, or his beauty. No, he had sold something far more valuable than that—his future. And he had sold it for far less than the five hundred dollars she got for a night of cloying smiles and watered-down liquor. He had sold it for a hit.

But they'd all sold their futures, Black thought. Weren't they selling themselves even now, giving up their lives in exchange for a high that wasn't legal tender anywhere except their minds? Or had they been sold, shipped across the airwaves like their ancestors had been shipped across the ocean; sold to the highest bidder like Kunta Kinte; sold to a judicial system eager to gorge itself on their misery . . .

"Patricia," Clarisse said, snatching Black's mind from its free fall.

Pookie stopped rocking and raised her head from her knees.

"Is that where you got your first hit?" Clarisse asked timidly.

"What?" Pookie said, sounding irritated.

"The old man," Clarisse said. "Is that who turned you out?"

Pookie laughed. It was a hearty sound that Black had never heard her make before.

"Giiirrrrl," Pookie said between fits of laughter, "you been watchin' too many *Mod Squad* reruns, 'cause I swear to God, I ain't heard nobody say 'turned out' since like 1975."

They all joined in her laughter. Even Clarisse began to chuckle, falling down on the bed and allowing herself the first good laugh she'd had since she'd let them into her home the night before. For a full minute, they shared a piece of humanity that was never present when crack was involved. For that minute, they weren't pipers. They were just regular people, relaxing and enjoying one of those laughs that lift the weight of the world from one's shoulders.

Pookie was the first to stop laughing. She sat there in the corner, with her arms wrapped around her legs, and looked at Clarisse. While the last vestiges of laughter seeped slowly from the room, Pookie's look became a stare, as if for the first time she could see the resemblance between the two of them. Somewhere down deep, they were sisters.

They had come from the same mold and traveled many of the same paths. They had lived many of the same experiences and seen many of the same things. They had both fallen somewhere along the way, and they had both ended up in the same trap. Now, amid the strains of laughter that enveloped the room, they both tried to fight through the haze that was their lives to come to an understanding of it all. By the time the laughter stopped, Pookie was ready to begin.

"Why you ask me that?" she said to Clarisse.

Clarisse, who had just stopped laughing, was momentarily confused.

"Why did I ask you what?" she said, then suddenly remembered the reason she had started laughing in the first place. "Oh, you mean why did I ask you *that.* I was just curious."

"You was more than curious," Pookie said. "You knew. I mean, it ain't like you was wrong or nothin', but if you know all that before I even tell you, you must know it from experience."

"That's why y'all keep tryin' to kill each other," Black said. "Y'all just alike."

Nobody bothered to offer a conflicting opinion.

"So are you going to answer the question or not?" Clarisse said.

"What question?" Pookie said, teasing.

"What happened when the guy told you he'd forgotten to give you something?"

Pookie stood up and walked across the room to where Clarisse sat on the bed. She sat down beside her. And then, with a deep sigh, she continued her story.

"It ain't like it's a whole lot to tell," Pookie said. "He played me. After he told me he forgot to give me something, I closed the car door and we rode to his house. I'd say he lived about ten blocks from us, in one of those big mansions up there on Stenton Avenue, so it only took like two minutes to get there. But in those two minutes, I musta asked him at least ten times what he had for me. You know how little kids act when you get something for 'em and you won't tell 'em what it is? Well, that's how I was."

Pookie shook her head, thinking of how gullible she'd been. Then she slapped her hands against her thighs and continued.

"So when we got to his house, he hit a remote control and these big black gates opened. Now, I'm sittin' there like, drugged, 'cause I ain't never seen this before, right? But I'm tryin' to play it off like I'm used to bein' in big mansions with big black gates and driveways that's a block long. And he just drivin' along, actin' like he don't notice me over there lookin' happier than a faggot in Boys Town. But every time I think about it, I know that he knew right then that he had me.

"I can't imagine how I musta looked, just sittin' there, lookin' stupid, wonderin' what was on the other side of those big oak doors with the brass handles that I saw comin' up at the end of the driveway. I guess y'all can probably imagine how I musta looked, too."

Black couldn't imagine how Pookie must have looked. And he couldn't imagine her being stupid about anything, either. He guessed that she must have been a different person before. Maybe she had the luxury of being able to show her feelings, or the luxury of being able to make stupid mistakes. But the streets had taken that away from her. They had taken that away from all of them. Because showing your feelings or making mistakes in the streets can be fatal. And with so many other lethal things in such close proximity, feelings and mistakes become unattainable luxuries.

They all knew that, and Pookie did, too. But she needed to finish, to purge herself. The rest of them needed to listen. So when she started talking again, Black turned from the window, looked in her face, and did just that.

"When we got in his house," Pookie said hesitantly, as if she were struggling to remember the details, "we walked through this big hallway. I guess you would call it a foyer, 'cause it was way too big to be a vestibule. He told me to sit down while he went upstairs to get my gift. So I'm sittin' there, chillin', and he hollers downstairs and tells this guy to bring me some cognac, right? It ain't click till like the next day that dude was the butler, but that's a whole 'nother story.

"So anyway, I take the cognac. I'm sittin' there sippin', tryin' not to just scream out loud 'bout how phat dude's crib is, right? Then he came downstairs and asked me to come in the next room.

"When I went in there, I almost fell out. Dude had a Jacuzzi in the middle of the floor, six-foot speakers in every corner of the room, a bar on one wall, and a fish tank, no, not a fish tank—an aquarium that ran around the other three walls of the room. He told me to sit down. But I think I was too busy tryin' to drag my bottom lip off the carpet. It was like somethin' on *Lifestyles of the Rich and Famous*.

"Well, it took me a minute, but when I finally got myself together to the point where I could sit down, dude reached behind one of the speakers and pulled out this little box and handed it to me. So I looked at it, and it was too big to be a ring, and too small to be a necklace. He told me to open it. But I was so nervous, thinkin' it was gon' be one o' them big diamonds with a platinum chain attached to it, I couldn't even get my hands to work together long enough to take the ribbon off.

"He saw what I was goin' through, so he laughed a little bit, then he took the box and opened it for me. When I looked inside, it was a gold key on a gold link chain. He took it out the box, put it around my neck, and pointed to a cabinet over by the bar. When I walked over to the cabinet, I noticed it had a big lock in the middle of it. I looked over at him, and he pointed to the key around my neck. When I opened it . . ."

Pookie stopped and reminisced for a moment, thinking about what she saw in the cabinet.

"When I opened it," she said, quieting her voice to dramatize the moment, "it was a coke rock in there that was so big, it scared me. I looked at dude like: What is this? He just smiled and came over to the cabinet. He took out two pipes, two little blowtorches, broke off a piece of the rock, and lit it up.

"I swear to God, y'all. Soon as I seen him light that pipe, I was ready to leave. Somethin' in my mind kept tellin' me to go get my little pocketbook and walk out the front door. But the more I tried to walk away, the more my body wouldn't let me move. It had me curious, man.

"It was like, I had seen pipers before, and I knew by watchin' them, I ain't want to go out like that. But then here was dude, livin' in the phattest house I ever seen in my life, drivin' a brand-new Lexus, givin' out five hundred dollars like it wasn't nothin', callin' the butler and tellin' him to go get me a drink. So I guess anything dude did, in my eyes, it was cool. 'Cause he had all the things I was tryin' to get, and if smokin' was part o' how he got there, or if that was part o' the life once you got there, then that's what I wanted."

Pookie stopped again and put her face in her hands. She looked like she wanted to cry, but there wouldn't be any tears. Because the crack had dehydrated her body so badly that her eyes couldn't produce enough moisture to make tears. So whatever she felt at that moment, she was stuck with it.

"I watched you last night, Clarisse," Pookie said after she'd gathered herself. "I watched you when you took that blast, and it scared me, you know why? 'Cause it reminded me of the first time I took a blast. But I wasn't lucky as you. It didn't take me a while to get that first good one. I got it from the door. That's why I'm out here like this now. 'Cause I'm still tryin' to find another blast like that first one.

"I still remember it. Dude lit that thing up, and the smoke swirled around in his bowl like a storm cloud. It ain't turn gray, though. The whole thing turned this clear, shiny white. He sucked like half the smoke out of the bowl and sat it down on the bar. Then he held it in for like half a minute and blew it out real slow through his nose.

"When he handed me the other pipe, I ain't know if that's what I really wanted to do. But he looked so happy—not that old bug-eyed, scary look you get when you smoke this garbage we be smokin'. I'm talkin' 'bout dude looked straight-up happy. So, lookin' at him, I ain't think it would hurt me. I relaxed a little bit and watched him take off a big chunk of that rock he had sittin' in the cabinet. He put it in my stem, told me to hold the pipe to my lips, and next thing I know, he was holdin' that little torch next to the rock and telling me to pull the smoke in slow.

"I saw the same cloud rollin' around in my bowl that I saw in his, and I remember thinkin' to myself how pretty it was. Then I heard his voice in my ear tellin' me not to swallow the smoke. He was like tellin' me to hold it in and blow it out slow through my nose.

"After that, it was like everything was caught up in this wind. But the wind wasn't a wind. It was a sound. And the sound was like this bell that just rang through me and made me all wet and sticky inside. I closed my eyes and got lost in it for a long time. It felt like it was a hundred tongues just lickin' me, fingers just touchin' me. I think I mighta even came. And when I opened my eyes and looked up at this ugly man, I swear to God, he was Denzel. And I was in the hot tub, jumpin' up and down on him all night long while the fish swam around his aquarium and watched us.

"I stayed there for four days. That's how long it took to smoke up the rock he had in that cabinet. When I came home, my clothes was in trash bags with a note on top that said: *Don't be here when I get home.*

"I ripped up the note and started hangin' my clothes back up in the closet, like I really thought my man was just a little upset and everything was cool. While I was hangin' my stuff up, I rewound the answering machine. It was a message on there from my job sayin' I was terminated for going AWOL. It was another message on there from my mom askin' where I was at. It was another one on there from my best friend askin' where I was at. And you know what I did? I ain't call my job. I ain't call my mom. I ain't call my girlfriend. I called dude, and I asked him how much coke I could get for five hundred dollars. He told me to come on over.

"I stayed with that man for a month after that. He bought me a brand-new wardrobe, fed me, bought me brand-new jewelry. Nigger was tellin' me not to worry 'bout my job or my man or none o' that. He was gon' take care o' me. But I was smokin' too much. Sneakin' out and drivin' his Lexus down the way to buy dope, callin' up niggers, havin' 'em bring packages to the house, wakin' up and goin' to sleep with the pipe in my mouth.

"It was cool for a minute, but after a while he wasn't goin' for that no more. He came home one day, dragged me in the bathroom, took off my clothes, and made me look at myself. I had lost like forty pounds in a month. After I got a good, long look, he gave me a hundred dollars and told me I had to go.

"I tried stayin' with my mom for a minute, but I stole some stuff outta her house and she told me I had to roll. It took me two weeks to get kicked out o' four different houses. When the last one kicked me out, I ended up in the street, down Broad and Erie, settin' niggers up for forty or fifty dollars at a time.

"And now look what it got me," Pookie said, looking slowly around the room at all of them. "Everything I got away with, or thought I got away with, and they lookin' for me for killin' somebody I ain't even touch."

Chapter 13

By the time Hillman got back to the crime scene, Ramirez had already received a copy of Podres's death certificate from the medical examiner and was on his way to the bail commissioner's office to pick up the warrants.

As Ramirez was getting into his car, Hillman pulled up, jumped out of his car, and jogged over to him. He had to stop to catch his breath before he started talking.

Ramirez chuckled. "You look like you're about to keel over. You only ran, what, twenty feet?"

"I'm an old man, remember? Anyway, I'm glad I caught you."

"Unless you're going to tell me that you've apprehended the suspects, I don't have time to talk. I'm on my way to pick up warrants."

"Okay, I'll ride with you."

When Hillman got in the car, he got straight to the point. "I think we're looking for the wrong people."

"What are you talking about?" Ramirez said, stopping the car. "I don't have time for this, Hillman."

"Listen to me, Lieutenant. I just finished going through the radio calls from last night and I've got a priest in a church at Broad and Butler who says Leroy was crossing Broad Street heading toward Germantown Avenue maybe three minutes before the shooting took place. I've also got a burglary that happened right around the time of the shooting. It was probably committed by Black."

"Did you talk to a complainant on the burglary?"

"No, but I talked to Black's mother and she told me something that I already knew: that the Samuel she knows would not have killed anyone."

"She's his mother!" Ramirez yelled. "What do you expect her to say?"

Hillman was silent for a moment. When he spoke, it was with a quiet anger.

"Every mother isn't blind to her children's faults," he said evenly. "Especially not his. But you wouldn't know that, because you've never taken the time to learn anything about these suspects that's not written down on some sheet of paper."

Ramirez pulled off, thinking of how the normally aloof Hillman had managed to connect with the people in the community. Ramirez admired that. But Hillman's connection was starting to cloud his judgment. And Ramirez couldn't allow it to cloud his own.

"Look, Hillman," Ramirez said. "I know you don't think these suspects are capable of something like this. I heard what Leroy's friend said about his past and the gang wars and everything. But we've all got a past. And I learned a long time ago never to put anything past a drug addict."

"But, Ramirez—"

"We've still got Mrs. Green on Park Avenue saying she saw Leroy go in the house right before the shots were fired," Ramirez said. "She heard his voice, recognized it, and knew what he was wearing when he went in. She's a good, solid witness."

"Come on, you don't believe that any more than I do," Hillman said. "In her statement, Mrs. Green said that the shooting started five seconds after Leroy went in. Think about it. How does Leroy ambush the councilman, wrestle away his gun, and get off four shots in five seconds? And not only that, how does he rifle the councilman's pockets and get away from the scene before the police arrive at the house at eleven-fifty? Mind you, the priest at Broad and Butler says that Leroy was walking *away* from the house at eleven-forty-five."

"Okay," Ramirez said, turning onto the expressway. "Suppose you're right. Suppose Leroy didn't have enough time to come in and rob Podres, and Black was around the corner committing a burglary that no one's reported. Suppose all of that is true and they didn't do it? Who did?"

"Let me tell you a little story," Hillman said. "I was over at Abbottsford Hospital about an hour and a half ago, talking to Darnell Thomas—our only eyewitness. Granted, he's a piper, and he'll probably say anything to save his ass at this point. But he swears that a blond-haired white man wearing a white shirt, black pants, and a gold link bracelet killed Podres."

"Yeah, right," Ramirez said.

"That's the same thing I said. But his sister was in the room when we interrogated him. She taped the interrogation and passed the tape off to some reporter. Five minutes later, the reporter's dead in the parking lot, the tape is gone, and witnesses are saying that a cop in an unmarked car is the shooter."

Ramirez's attitude began to change. He looked like he was beginning to take Hillman seriously. "Was there a description?"

"The hospital security guard said he had brown hair and a bushy mustache, and that he was wearing black pants and a gray blazer."

Ramirez was silent.

"Lieutenant," Hillman said earnestly, "I know it sounds crazy. But when you put it all together . . ."

"When you put it all together what? Are you saying that a cop had something to do with Podres's murder?"

"Who had more to gain from Podres's death than corrupt cops?" Hillman said.

Ramirez knew that Hillman was right. There were plenty of cops who would have liked nothing more than to see Podres dead. Ramirez had seen them operate: robbing criminals, planting evidence, taking bribes. There was nothing in the world worse than a dirty cop.

Still, there was the unwritten rule: You never rat on another cop, no matter what. If he does something to someone on the street, you look the other way. If he does something to you personally, you take care of it man-to-man. But you don't rat. You never, ever do that.

Ramirez hated the rule. But he followed it anyway. Of course, Ramirez had never run across a cop who was killing people, especially people who were involved in the biggest murder investigation to hit Philadelphia since the Ira Einhorn case.

"Did anybody get the tag on the unmarked car?" Ramirez said.

"They got the last three numbers," Hillman said, flipping through his notebook. "It was . . . 342."

"If we assume that the first three are UJV or UNV, like the prefixes the narcs use, can't we call Fleet Management and find out what unit the car's assigned to?"

"You're talking about a city agency knowing where its equipment is located," Hillman said, his voice laced with sarcasm.

"I think it's worth a shot," Ramirez said, handing Hillman his phone. "If there's a car with that plate number assigned to any of our units, you may be right. And God help us if you are."

"So what do we do now?" Hillman said, dialing the number to the office that handled police vehicles.

"We get the warrants because that's what we've been ordered to do," Ramirez said. "But after we get them, we go back and have a talk with the commissioner and Sheldon. Then we hope that nobody else has to die before we find out what's going on."

Jeanette Deveraux knew that there was more to the Podres investigation than what appeared on the surface. And since nobody was talking, she went back to basics and started checking details. She knew that if she did that, she'd eventually uncover something.

She'd spent the better part of the night trying to find out who lived in the house on Dell Street and had finally ended up at the deeds office in city hall. She hadn't slept at all, and the hour-and-a-half wait was a little more than she was willing to bear. To make matters worse, people who recognized her as a reporter kept trying to hold conversations with her because they felt as if they knew her from seeing her on television.

She had a standard response for all of them.

"It tears my heart in two to report the news sometimes," she would say, looking into their eyes with the same grave sincerity she used on the nightly newscasts. "But I feel that people need to know what goes on in the world around them. Now, if you'll excuse me."

At that point, she would go into a mock conference with her

cameraman, discussing some contrived vital fact for the next story. She was in one of those miniconferences—not knowing how many more she could bear—when the clerk emerged from the back room, called Deveraux's number, and handed her a copy of the deed to 3934 Dell Street.

The deed said the property belonged to Clarisse Williams.

"Where to now?" the cameraman asked when they got out into the hallway.

"I'm just going to make a couple of phone calls," Deveraux said as she sat down and pulled out a cell phone.

Her cameraman sat down and watched her while she dialed the number.

"Robin?" she said when her contact at the Roundhouse answered the phone. "I've got a big favor to ask you. . . . What? Oh, sure, you can call me right back."

Deveraux's phone rang a minute later.

"Hello?" Deveraux said, listening as the woman apologized. "No, that's all right. I know they tape the calls in the office. Could you do me a big favor? Could you run the license tag CWRN, and let me know if it comes back on a Honda to a Clarisse Williams?"

Her source asked if it had anything to do with the Podres case.

"Yes, that's the tag they're looking for in the Podres shooting," Deveraux said.

She listened with mounting panic as her source said she couldn't help her with anything having to do with the Podres case because she'd risk losing her job.

"Is Podres that much of a priority?" Deveraux asked, removing a notepad from her purse and jotting down her source's response as her cameraman edged closer to listen to the conversation.

"And how long have supervisors been threatening disciplinary action for anyone releasing information on the Podres case?" she added, glancing at her cameraman as she wrote down the source's answer.

"Look, whatever you tell me, it'll never get traced back to you," Deveraux said earnestly. "Have I ever let anything get traced back to you before?"

The source agreed to run the license plate and took about five minutes to come back on the line and confirm that the tag belonged on a 1991 Accord owned by Clarisse Williams of 3934 Dell Street.

"Thanks so much, Robin. I owe you one. Could you do me another favor? Could you tell me where the call came from for 3934 Dell Street last night?"

Her source said something Deveraux hadn't expected.

"What?" the reporter said, flabbergasted.

Her source repeated the demand.

"Hold on," she said, placing her hand over the phone and speaking to her cameraman. "Mike, could you give me a minute?"

Reluctantly, he got up and walked down to the end of the hallway. When he was out of earshot, Deveraux resumed the conversation.

"I can't give you eight hundred dollars," she hissed into the phone. "We don't pay for stories, and even if we did . . ."

Her source said she couldn't help her for free. Then she said she had to get back to work and got ready to hang up.

"Okay, okay, wait," Deveraux said, looking up and down the hallway self-consciously and cupping her hand over the phone. "I'll meet you outside the Roundhouse in ten minutes. I can't give you eight hundred. But if you have the information, I'll give you five."

The source agreed to the meet, and Deveraux disconnected the call, feeling dirty. As she walked down the hallway toward her cameraman, she shivered and scratched her arm feverishly, wishing that the low-down feeling that gripped her would go away.

"You ready?" he asked as she walked up to him.

"Yeah, Mike," she said, her voice nonchalant. "Just let me go over to Market Street and tap the cash machine."

"And then?"

"And then I want to make a run down to the Roundhouse," she said, trying hard not to look in his eyes for fear that he might see the truth.

After all, even Jeanette Deveraux had a conscience.

The source came out of police headquarters and walked past the throng of reporters who were standing around listening to another staged police press briefing.

"Mike, I've got to talk to this woman for a minute," Deveraux said to her cameraman. "Would you be a doll and wait for me over there?"

He looked at her like he wanted to say something, then he thought better of it and went over to stand next to one of the thirty or so unmarked police cars that occupied the Roundhouse parking lot.

"Hey, Jeanette," the woman said, walking up to her and hugging her warmly as if they were old friends.

"Hi, Robin," Deveraux said, wondering when the woman would loosen her bear hug.

"I hope you put the money in an envelope," the source whispered in Deveraux's ear.

"I did. It's in my pocketbook."

"Good. When I let you go, we'll exchange envelopes."

The woman disengaged her embrace and Deveraux handed her the envelope. Then the source passed her an envelope containing the Scotts' address and phone number. Without a word, the source turned and walked quickly back toward the Roundhouse. Deveraux turned slowly and walked over to her cameraman, pulling out her cell phone and dialing the number.

"What'd you give her?" the cameraman asked her.

Deveraux didn't answer.

"Hi," she said to Eldridge Scott, turning on the charm as the man answered the telephone. "I'm calling from Homicide, Mr. Scott. We need to ask you a few more questions concerning last night's incident at Miss Williams's house."

Deveraux listened intently as the neighbor asked her if the police had found Clarisse.

"No, we haven't, Mr. Scott. That's why we want to ask you a few more questions. Perhaps you can help us determine where she might be."

Eldridge hesitated slightly, then asked her why he couldn't just talk to the officers who were posted outside Clarisse's house.

Deveraux thought frantically. She should have known that there were police posted outside because they would want to protect whatever evidence was in the house. But that presented another problem: how to get past them to talk to Eldridge Scott.

"Well," she said, stalling and hoping that what she was about to say would sound authentic. "They're not handling the case, Mr. Scott. They're just there to keep the property secure until we can get back there with a search warrant."

As Deveraux bit her bottom lip, hoping that Scott wouldn't detect that she was a phony, the old man said something that caused her mouth to drop completely open. He asked why they needed a search warrant when they'd already searched Clarisse's house the night before.

"Are you sure about that, Mr. Scott?" she asked, trying not to sound excited.

He said that he and his wife had watched the officers break into the house almost immediately after they got there.

"Okay," she said, pausing in a way that she thought would let him know how serious her next question was. "I want you to think about this, Mr. Scott, because we need to double-check this. Was Miss Williams, or anybody else, there when the officers searched her home?"

Scott, sounding suspicious, told her that she should already know the answer to that.

"We're just double-checking the information that was given to us by the officers on the scene," Deveraux said quickly.

Scott ignored her explanation and asked why she was calling instead of Lieutenant Ramirez.

"Well, Mr. Scott," she said, trying to come up with a commonsense answer. "Almost the entire Homicide Unit is working on this case, including myself. My job, to put it simply, is to check behind the other officers."

Scott didn't say anything.

"Are you there, Mr. Scott?"

When he said yes, she went into her pitch.

"I want you to listen very carefully, Mr. Scott, because this is extremely important. We're going to need you to answer a few questions about what you saw last night. So what I want you to do is to come down to the Roundhouse as soon as possible. Do you know where it is?"

Eldridge said there wasn't a black man in Philadelphia who didn't know the location of the Roundhouse.

Deveraux smiled. She was beginning to appreciate the old man's wit.

"I'll meet you in the parking lot," she said. "And we'll go up to my office from there."

Eldridge said he didn't own a car.

"Catch a cab, Mr. Scott. We'll pay for it. And do me a favor. Don't discuss this with anyone until you talk to me. My name is Officer Deveraux, and I'll be here in the parking lot in one of our undercover vehicles. It's a black GMC Jimmy truck."

Eldridge said he'd have to wait for his wife to get dressed, but that he'd be there as soon as possible. He made sure to add that he was only cooperating because he thought it might help Clarisse.

"Oh, any additional information you can give to us will definitely help Clarisse, Mr. Scott," Deveraux said. "It'll be of invaluable assistance to her."

Deveraux disconnected the call, smiling ear to ear.

"What're you cheesing about?" her cameraman said.

"The police broke into Clarisse Williams's house and searched it without a warrant."

"That's an illegal search."

"I know," Deveraux said. "Now all we have to do is get this guy and his wife to say they saw them do it."

"What are you gonna do when they get down here and see that you're not a cop?" the cameraman said.

"You're going to point the camera at them, I'm going to identify myself as a reporter, and then I'm going to ask them to name the officers they saw go into Clarisse Williams's house to conduct the search," she said.

Deveraux looked over at Sergeant Harris, who stood by the door of the Roundhouse reading yet another meaningless statement to an unenthusiastic media corps.

"Then we'll get the little spokesperson to comment," she said. "At least that'll give her something to think about other than those bullshit statements she's been reading all morning."

With a self-satisfied smirk, Deveraux walked over to their news truck to wait for the Scotts to arrive.

As she did so, Lieutenant Darren Morgan left his office window, where he had watched Deveraux hand the envelope to the woman from Reports Control. He sat down at his desk and beeped Sheldon. When he called back, Morgan told him about the reporter.

"I just saw one of the girls from Reports Control talking to Jeanette Deveraux," Morgan said, talking quickly. "Deveraux handed the girl an envelope and the girl handed her something back. I'm not sure what it was. But Deveraux made a call and now she's down in the parking lot waiting for somebody."

"Is she alone?"

"No, she's got a cameraman with her."

A bead of sweat made its way from Sheldon's hairline to the corner of his mouth, and the questions that floated on the edge of his consciousness began to filter into his mind: What if the envelope contained a document that could bring their entire operation crashing to the ground? What if Deveraux was cooperating with a politician who was going to turn state's evidence against them?

Sheldon closed his eyes and tried to force the ugly images from his mind. When his thoughts slowed to a normal pace, he managed to ask a question. "Has she done anything unusual?"

Morgan got up from his desk, walked over to the window, and watched as Deveraux sat in her truck with the cameraman. She hadn't moved from that spot since she'd talked to the woman from Reports Control.

"She's the only reporter who isn't talking to the sergeant from Community Relations," Morgan said, walking back to his desk. "I'm guessing she knows something the rest of them don't."

Sheldon ran his hands through his hair. "Look. I don't know what Deveraux knows, but whatever it is, we can't afford to have it become public knowledge. We want a nice, smooth little investigation and quick arrests in this thing, and I think we both know that isn't going to happen if Deveraux gets any inside information. So I want you to handle it."

"Okay," Morgan said, trying to rush off the phone before Sheldon asked any more questions. "I'll handle it."

"Before you go, what happened with the guy at the hospital?"

Morgan hesitated. He didn't know if it was the right time to talk to Sheldon about Moore. And truthfully, he didn't know if it would ever be the right time. Because what he'd heard on the tape was gnawing at him. And the more he talked with Sheldon, the more he became convinced that his feeling about the tape was right.

"Morgan, you there?"

"Yeah, I was just . . . Look, I ran into something at the hospital. There was a reporter named Henry Moore. He had a tape of a detective interrogating the Thomas guy."

"So what did you do?" Sheldon said, hoping that Morgan hadn't gone too far.

"I killed him."

"You did *what*?" Sheldon said, looking around the Command Center self-consciously when he realized how loudly he was speaking.

"Look," Morgan said. "It had to be done. He was going to publish a story with Darnell Thomas saying the shooter was a white man."

"Yeah, but . . ." Sheldon stopped in his tracks and hoped that he was hearing Morgan wrong. "What did you say?"

"Darnell Thomas told Detective Hillman that the shooter was a tall white man with blond hair and blue eyes, wearing a white shirt, black pants, and a gold link bracelet. Somehow, Moore got a tape of the interrogation. And to make a long story short, he was going to write a story saying that we're pursuing the wrong suspects for the Podres shooting."

Sheldon tried to speak, but his voice would no longer come out of his mouth. Instead, it streamed from his pores in a cold sweat, screaming out like it was awakening from Sheldon's worst nightmare. It shook in his hands, trembling against the cold truth. Sheldon was afraid. So he did what he hoped was the right thing. He tried to make light of Butter's accusation.

"That's the most ridiculous thing I've ever heard," he said, his uncertain voice trembling along with his hands. "A white man in a crack house killing Podres is a real stretch. Even if Moore did write the story, nobody would've believed it. That's why I don't understand why you had to kill him."

"Look," Morgan said. "I took his wallet and his watch and everything. I even dropped a couple of empty caps in the car. They'll call it a robbery, blame it on a piper, and go on to the next case."

"You're right. Maybe they will blame a piper. Or maybe they'll start wondering why the only reporter to get close to the only suspect we have in custody is suddenly dead. That was sloppy, Morgan. And it was stupid."

Morgan had taken all that he could from Sheldon. And he was growing tired of the charade. So he just came out and said it. "It wasn't as stupid as killing Podres."

Before the words had even left Morgan's mouth, the tremors in Sheldon's hands became violent shudders. The cold sweat ran hot over his skin. Then the heat and the trembling converged in a blanket of fear that smothered him and took his breath away.

"Are you there?" Morgan said. "Hello?"

"I'm here," Sheldon said, squeezing his words between short, panting breaths. "I just dropped the phone."

"I see," Morgan said, picturing Sheldon sweating on the other end. "You know, it's funny how descriptions make us think of the people we know. I mean, a tall white man with blond hair and blue eyes could be anybody. But when you throw in the white shirt, that could be a captain's uniform shirt. Black pants could be part of the uniform, too. And even though I've never seen you in a gold link bracelet, who knows what you've got in your little jewelry box."

Sheldon was starting to hyperventilate. With each word Morgan spoke, his head felt as if it were growing heavier. He just knew that if Morgan said one more word, his head was going to explode.

"Look, Irv, I just wish you would've told me what you were going to do before you went out and killed Podres."

"No, *you* look. I don't care what some crack head on his deathbed told Hillman. Leroy and Black killed Podres. Not a white man. And especially not a white man who looks like me. Now, if you meant that *they* were stupid to kill him, you're right. They were. And Darnell Thomas was stupid to be a part of it. So now he's making up some phony description that could be anybody. But it's not going to work, is it, Morgan? Because Darnell Thomas, and Leroy, and Black are going to have to pay the consequences for their actions, right? They're going to have to pay."

In that moment, everything that they'd done in the last few years seemed to flash in front of Morgan. All the shakedowns, all the schemes, all the bribes. All of it ran across the screen that was his mind and he knew that it was over. And now it was just a matter of cleaning up the loose ends.

"Yeah, I guess you're right," he finally said. "They do have to pay the consequences for their actions. We all do."

Sheldon didn't respond. But he knew what Morgan meant. It was over. They would both have to try to get out while they could. It was every man for himself now. But neither of them could say it. And so they continued their conversation as if things could remain the same after that, knowing deep inside that things would never be the same again.

As he put the phone back in its cradle, Irv Sheldon did the only thing he could do. He took off the heavy gold link bracelet and slipped it into his pocket, along with the rest of his memories of the late Johnny Podres.

He didn't think he'd have to worry about Hillman doing anything with the description. He would do what he was told, just like he'd always done. But Jeanette Deveraux was a different story. Sheldon wondered how much she really knew. And he wondered if she had shared that knowledge with whomever she had called from the parking lot of police headquarters.

Mildred Scott woke to the sound of her husband holding a stilted telephone conversation with someone he obviously didn't feel very comfortable talking to. After he hung up, she turned to him, hoping that he had received some good news about Clarisse.

"Who was that on the phone, Eldridge?" she said, her voice laced with worry.

"Some woman talkin' 'bout she from Homicide."

"They ain't ask you enough questions last night?"

"That's the same thing I was thinkin'," Eldridge said. "All

them questions they asked me last night and then somebody gon' call with some more? Make it so bad, the woman ain't even sound right."

"What you mean she ain't sound right?" Mildred said. "How she supposed to sound?"

"She supposed to at least know what she talkin' about," Eldridge said. "And she didn't. Now, I don't know if she think I'm stupid 'cause I'm old or 'cause I'm black or whatever. But seem to me like the woman was just tryin' to get me to tell her about what happened over there last night."

"What she ask you?"

"A whole bunch o' questions about whether the police went in Clarisse house, and was anybody home when they went in there, and what cops went in there, and all kind o' foolishness.

"Then she had the nerve to say, 'Get in a cab and meet me in the parkin' lot down the Roundhouse, and don't discuss this with anybody till you talk to me.' "

"What?" Mildred said in disbelief.

"Yeah, like I'm supposed to believe that nonsense," Eldridge said. "I must either sound like the biggest fool Jesus ever died for, or she is the biggest fool. 'Cause ain't no way in the world I'm gon' meet somebody in the parkin' lot o' the Roundhouse talkin' about they a cop when I know they ain't."

"What was the woman's name?" Mildred asked.

"She said her name was Deveraux."

Mildred paused for a moment.

"It's a woman on the news named Deveraux-somethin'-or-other," she said thoughtfully.

"You think that's who it was?" Eldridge said.

"I don't know. But you need to call that detective that was here last night and ask him if somebody named Deveraux works with them. If he say it's all right, I don't see no harm in goin' down there and talkin' to her."

"That woman wasn't bit more the police than the man in the moon," Eldridge said.

"Well, it won't hurt to check, will it, Eldridge?"

The way she said his name—in that singsong way that always tended to calm him—made Eldridge think of Clarisse. She was so sweet once; a little girl whose big, sparkling eyes could melt away the most sour disposition.

But now she was gone. She had probably been gone for a long time. It was just hard to tell because she was there physically. There was no hiding it now, though. Whatever lifestyle Clarisse was trying to shield in darkness had come roaring into the light. And as Eldridge Scott dialed Ramirez, hoping that the detective could tell him something about the sweet little girl he once knew, he couldn't help wondering how it all started, and how it was going to end.

Chapter 14

Clarisse sat on the bed and thought of how similar Pookie's story was to her own. The way she had started off in control of everything in her life, and the way she had watched it all unravel until her life was as thin as the clouds of white smoke that had ruined it all. The way she had put all her faith in men, and then in crack, and then in nothing, until all that remained of her spirit was a shadow of what had once been a tower of strength.

She thought about how Pookie was exactly like her. And then she looked at what Pookie had become. She dared not ask herself how long it would take her to end up the same way. Just thinking about it was frightening.

She was trying to avoid that thought when she felt the bed start to shake, as if something were trying to wriggle out from beneath the covers. The motion tore her from her private thoughts and when she looked around, she realized that what she felt was

Pookie, still sitting next to her, wrapped in an eerie silence. She was trembling.

Hesitantly, Clarisse wrapped her arm around Pookie and began to rock her back and forth. And with that small gesture, the two of them seemed to become friends. No, they seemed to become sisters.

Black watched them, and the resemblance between them was striking. It was more than their outward appearance. The similarity burrowed down into their very souls—to that place inside where spirits are born.

That's when it came to him. He knew how they were going to get out of there. It was risky, but then so was staying there, waiting like sitting ducks for the police to burst into the room and kill them all. Of course, their capture probably wouldn't be half as dramatic as all that. Black figured that the only one who could've gotten a good look at any of them was the desk clerk. And odds were, he had finished his shift, gone home to sleep, and wouldn't wake up until well into the afternoon. By the time he realized that he had checked the most-wanted people in Philadelphia into the hotel, they'd be long gone.

"Pookie," Black said. "I need you to do somethin' for me."

Pookie ignored him and snuggled closer to Clarisse.

"Patricia," he said. "Or whatever your name is."

"You ain't been callin' me Patricia, so don't start now," Pookie said without looking up.

"Oh, but it's all right for Clarisse to call you Patricia?" he said, his voice laced with irritation.

"Why can't you just respect that she doesn't want you to call her Patricia?" Clarisse said. "Why does everything always have to be a constant battle with you?"

"Look, I can respect all that, but—"

"No, you know what I think your problem is?" Clarisse said. "I think you just don't have any respect for women. I think you look at every woman as a bitch or a ho, something to have, to possess, like . . . like a toy or something."

Black hoped his face didn't betray what he thought. He hoped that he was standing there wearing the same expression he'd worn every day for the last six months, ever since the day he'd walked away from his life. He hoped that the contempt he felt for Clarisse didn't show through, as he wondered how she could possibly try to pass judgment on him. And then, somewhere in the recesses of his mind, he heard a small voice tell him that she was right.

She'd said it so calmly, in a voice that was like a lullaby. And she'd said it in a way that left little room for question. She'd said, in so many words, that he hated all women; hated them for not being the woman he'd left behind, and for being the woman he'd left behind, and for being—period. He hated them and he hated himself for hating them, and for loving them, and for wanting them, and for needing them.

So he told himself that they were nothing. And he told himself that he would never let them hurt him again. Perhaps that's why he could never let them be important to him. And it was obviously apparent to Clarisse. Because she had looked right through him and seen it.

"Don't stand there and act like you don't hear me, Everett," Clarisse said, stirring him from his reverie.

Black gave her a blank stare in response.

"You're just like the rest of them," she said.

"Just like the rest of who?"

"Just like every man I know," Clarisse said, looking at Pookie, who was asleep in her lap. "You feel threatened by women. You know you can't control us because we don't need you. And to tell you the truth, you probably wouldn't know how to bring home the bacon if somebody sliced it up and put it in a bag for you. So you try to make us into nothing. You try to tell us we're nobody. You try to act like we can't make it without you, when you know for a fact that you can't make it without us.

"And then you want us to respect you," she said, spitting the words as if they left a foul taste in her mouth. "Respect you for what? You don't even respect yourself. If you respected yourself, if you respected anybody, you wouldn't be out here doin' what you're doin'."

"Oh, so you better than me?" Black said, becoming angry. "You don't need no man and you don't need nobody to help you do nothin', right? All you need is that pipe to make it all right, huh, Clarisse?

"Well, dig this here. It ain't all right. 'Cause you know what's gon' happen if you keep smokin' that dope? After a while you gon' run outta caps, and the only thing you gon' have left to put in that straight shooter is your life. And once you put that in there, everything goes up in smoke and disappears. Just like it was never there."

Clarisse looked down at Pookie and continued to rock back and forth as if she couldn't hear him. But he knew she could, so he went on.

"If you wanna blame men for everything that ever went wrong in your life, that's on you. But I think you need to look at yourself, too. 'Cause you got yourself out here smokin'. Not me. I ain't do nothin' to you."

She looked up with rage and hurt pouring from her eyes. "You call getting me mixed up in a murder nothing? You call holding me here against my will nothing?"

"Look . . . ," Black said.

"No, you look. I'm tired of people screwing me around and

then telling me it's nothing. Do you know what that feels like, Everett?"

Clarisse got up, carefully moving Pookie's head from her lap to the bed. Black moved from his spot by the window and sat on the desk, but said nothing.

"Can you answer me, Everett?"

He didn't respond.

"Oh yeah," she said, making the words sound like something slimy. "You can't answer anything like that, because somebody might find out you actually have feelings, right? No, don't tell me. You really don't have feelings. Feelings are for suckers, right? In the place where everybody else has feelings, you have nothing."

She swept one hand through the air and placed the other hand on her hip in an utterly female gesture.

"Well, I'm tired of nothing, Everett. I'm tired of people offering me the moon and stars and leaving me with nothing. I'm tired of looking at men like they're the knights in shining armor Mommy told me about and then finding out that they're nothing. I'm tired of waiting for something and then finding out that it's nothing. I'm just tired."

"Well, shut up, then," Leroy said from the seat in the corner that he hadn't left for the last hour. "I ain't tryin' to hear that *One Life to Live* shit anyway."

Clarisse looked over at him and twisted her lips into a look of disgust.

"I just want to leave here," she said. "It's not fun anymore."

Black looked her in the eye and asked a question that he had always contemplated, but never answered.

"When was it ever fun?"

Clarisse couldn't think back that far, so she changed the subject.

"You know what the strangest part of all this is for me?" she said. "The strangest part is knowing that nobody's going to miss me anyway. I mean, I'm a private-duty nurse, and I was just going to start with a new patient today. So it's not like I have a supervisor or coworkers who'll be like, 'Where's Clarisse?'

"I don't have any friends. So nobody's going to wonder why I didn't show up for lunch or dinner tonight. I don't have any family. Not unless you count Mr. and Mrs. Scott, the people next door."

Clarisse stopped, like something had just struck her. "Come to think of it, they're probably the ones who told the police about my car."

She paused again.

"They might have even seen us leave," she said, her face a portrait of anxiety.

Leroy smiled a mirthless grin and said, "Or maybe they just two old nosy-ass niggers that's all up in your business like that."

"You know what?" Clarisse said. "Why can't you just have a little bit of respect for somebody? Damn! Those people have never done anything to you."

"Why should I respect them?" Leroy said, as if the idea of respecting his elders were impossibly far-fetched. "What they ever done for me? I ain't never seen none o' the old people in my family come around and do nothin' for me, let alone say, 'Here, Leroy, here go a toy for Christmas,' or, 'Here, Leroy, this how you throw a baseball.' You know what I got from old people when I was comin' up? I got my ass beat. I got my arm twisted. I got my head smacked. I got told I wasn't gon' be shit so many times I started believin' it myself. That's what old people did for me."

"Well," Clarisse said, building a head of steam, "those same old people marched the soles off their shoes so you could have a voice, and got sprayed with fire hoses so you could walk with your head up."

"I ain't tryin' to hear that old 'We Shall Overcome' bullshit, either," Leroy said. "That was thirty years ago. What they doin' now?"

"They're waiting for you to stop trying to blame your problems on people whose only crime was loving you before there even was a you."

"Whatever," Leroy said, pulling out his straight shooter and dumping a cap inside.

He pulled two matches from a matchbook and lit the crack, the hiss and sizzle of the rocks echoing across the room like so many dreams exhaling for the last time.

"So that's the answer to everything, right, Leroy?" Clarisse said. "Is that supposed to make everything go away?"

Leroy exhaled slowly through his nostrils.

"Bitch," he said, his jaw moving side to side as he forced his words out between the smoke. "You must think it's the answer to everything, too, 'cause you smokin' it just like I am."

Clarisse fell silent as her thoughts traveled backward.

"I used to think it was the answer to everything," she said. "I guess I still do. Especially when those lonely nights roll around, when I'm sitting there wondering what happened to my life."

She walked across the room and sat on the floor next to Leroy, looking toward the ceiling as if she could find the answers there.

"I guess that's when I want to take a blast and just . . ." Clarisse leaned against the wall, looking wistfully at the ceiling as she drew little shapes in the air. "Just float up to nowhere and wonder if I'll ever come back down."

Black watched her and thought of what a waste it was to chase after the cloud. Clarisse, he knew, realized that it was a waste, too. But she would keep chasing it anyway, like a dog that runs in circles, chasing its tail. And perhaps she would eventually catch it, even if catching it meant spending the rest of her life nursing the wounds.

Black looked at her and imagined the cost of it all. He imagined it and a sadness fell over him, the kind of sadness that comes with watching a loved one hurt and knowing that only they themselves can stop the pain. His imagination was cut short by Clarisse's, though. And his sadness was replaced by one that was infinitely deeper.

"I wonder sometimes," Clarisse said thoughtfully. "I sit back and I wonder what would have happened if my parents would've lived. I mean, I've seen all the psychiatrists on the talk shows, and they always try to make you believe that everything that happens to you when you grow up is your parents' fault. I used to believe that, too. Maybe that's why I hated my parents for so long after they died.

"But I don't believe it anymore. Now I just think your parents do the best they can, and then you make your own choices after that."

"So why did you hate them in the first place?" Black said, realizing that he was the only one listening to her.

"I hated them because they died," she said. "To me, when they died it was like they'd abandoned me."

She chuckled at the absurdity of her reasoning.

"Can you imagine that? Can you imagine hating someone because they die? Like it's their fault they got killed in a car accident, right? Or like it's their fault that the only thing they had to leave me was a little bit of money and a house. Like it's their fault I didn't have any other family to take care of me except the two old people who lived next door.

"But you know what?" she said haltingly. "I hated them anyway. And I guess I hated them for so long that I started hating myself, if that makes any sense. It's like, when you start to hate yourself, you do stupid things. You put yourself through things that you wouldn't put yourself through if you cared anything about yourself. You let people walk all over you because you think you're not worth anything anyway. You know what I mean?"

Black knew exactly what she meant. He had been hating himself for a lifetime, walking through a haze of feelings that he didn't know he had and trying to find a way out of the cloud, only to end up trapped inside.

"That's why I don't have any friends now," Clarisse said, shaking him from his thoughts. "Because I'm afraid to allow anyone into my life again."

She looked up at the ceiling again, but this time there was no fantasy in her eyes. There was only hurt.

"Every time I let someone in," she said, pausing to look away from him, "they either abandon me, like my parents did when they died, or they hurt me so bad I wish they would just leave.

"Like the last man I was seeing. The one whose clothes were in my closet."

Clarisse sighed and shook her head, as if even the memory were too much to bear.

"He was a doctor over at Jefferson when I worked there," she said, looking at her hands. "Dr. Carl Bancroft was one of the few young black doctors I'd ever met. It wasn't like he was so fine or anything like that. But with me just graduating nursing school and him doing his residency over at Jefferson, we were naturally attracted to each other, I guess. I think it was more fear and nerves at being two of the few young blacks on the job than a sexual attraction. But eventually, it turned into more than that. I thought we might even end up getting married."

Leroy lit another cap and released the smoke through his nose. As it wafted past Clarisse, it gave her face an almost surreal glow, lending a ghostly backdrop to her words.

"I didn't have a lot of friends even then," she said, squinting against the smoke. "I guess it was because I was shy or whatever. But the one friend I did have was like everything to me. As a matter of fact, I think she came to Franklin right after you transferred to Dobbins, Everett. That was around tenth grade, right?"

Black nodded.

"Well, by the time me and my one little friend, Nicole, grew up and got jobs and everything," she said, "we were more like sisters than friends. We laughed together, we cried together, we talked about everything under the sun together, from periods to pregnancy.

"When my parents died, she was the one who helped me get through it. She was over at my house every day when all I could do was cry and wish I was dead, too. She made me eat when I didn't want to. She made me bathe when I didn't want to. She was with me when I finally got to the point where I could come outside again, and she walked me through getting back into everyday life when I couldn't make it through by myself.

"When she got married, I was the maid of honor. When she and her husband had a baby, I was the godmother. We had keys to each other's houses and keys to each other's cars. She was like everything I needed in a friend.

"She knew the Scotts, I knew her parents. I knew her husband. And she knew all my boyfriends—all two of them—the one I had in high school and Carl.

"When Carl and I started getting serious, we started hanging out with Nicole and her husband. We would meet each other for plays or dinner or football games or whatever. You know, I wanted Carl to know Nicole and I wanted Nicole to know him because they were both important to me.

"So anyway, about a year after we met, Carl had a shift change, so I was working twelve to eight and he was working eight to four. We didn't get to see each other as much as we used to, but we still made time for each other whenever we could. It was good for our relationship, in a way, because we weren't together enough to get on each other's nerves. At least that's what I thought."

Clarisse sighed deeply before continuing.

"Everything was working out," she said, the pain evident in her voice. "We were starting to get kind of serious, and I was really happy about it. I used to call Nicole every night and tell her how I thought it was only a matter of time before he popped the question, and she seemed to be just as excited about it as I was. She used to tell me that I really deserved to be happy because I'd been through so much. And she was right. Nobody deserved happiness more than me. I mean, you couldn't have told me that what Carl and I had wasn't the best thing to ever happen to me. Well, I guess it wouldn't have mattered what you told me, because I was just head over heels, nose wide open, whatever you want to call it. I loved that man.

"So everything's just flowing and I'm up on cloud nine until one day, when he was getting off and I was coming in, Carl told me he had something to ask me. So I'm all excited and I get on the phone and I call Nicole and I'm like: 'Girrrl, Carl is getting ready to pop the question!'

"You should've seen me in that nurses' lounge. I'm jumping up and down screaming and she's on the other end screaming and I'm just acting like a pure fool. Everybody was looking at me like I was crazy, but I didn't care. Because it was like, I felt like I was finally going to get something I wanted out of life instead of the leftovers life kept giving me.

"So when I got off the phone with Nicole, I started calling around trying to see if I could get somebody to come in and pick up the rest of my shift. Because there was no way I could stay there and give people needles and check I.V.'s and whatnot. As hyped up and nervous as I was, I probably would've messed around and killed somebody doing that mess."

Black imagined Clarisse repeatedly trying to jab a needle into someone's arm—accidentally at first, and then in a deliberate stabbing motion. He grinned, thinking of how silly the whole thing would look, and then she was talking again, the story pouring out of her like so much water.

"I wanted to go home," she said. "I wanted to take a shower and put on something sexy. You can't just be looking any kind of way when people are trying to propose to you, right?"

Black shrugged.

"Well, that's what I was thinking," she said. "So anyway, I kept calling people, going down the list of the nurses who were on call, telling them that I had an emergency at home and I needed someone to relieve me so I could go. All of them saw right through that, though, and I didn't get anyone to come in until I broke down and told this girl Lynn the truth about why I wanted to go home. That was around three o'clock in the morning.

"So I get myself together to go home, and when I get there the first thing I notice is that my bedroom light is on. Now, I knew I always kept my living room light on, because I didn't want anybody to think the house was empty. But I never kept my bedroom light on, because I didn't want to waste electricity like that. So when I saw the light like that, the first thing I'm thinking is somebody's in my house robbing me blind. But then I was thinking that Carl might've been waiting for me there, because he had a key to my house, too. That didn't make sense, though, because if he wanted me to meet him at his house in the morning, why would he be waiting for me at my house?

"Now, all this is going through my mind, and I'm like reaching into my glove compartment to get my gun."

Black looked at her with what must have been total surprise because he just couldn't imagine Clarisse with a gun. She noticed the look on his face and stopped to explain herself.

"Honey," she said. "Being a woman and working at night when you live in North Philly, you'd better have a gun or something, because you never know who's waiting for you to leave your house at eleven-thirty. So what was I saying? Oh, I crept in the house and pulled my gun out of my pocketbook, and I heard music and voices coming from upstairs. It sounded like somebody was arguing or fighting at first, but by the time I got to the bottom of the steps, it sounded like . . . it sounded like . . ."

She put her face in her hands and shook her head violently from side to side, as if she were trying to make the image disappear. Then she looked up and stared into the past, and the rest of the story almost seemed to come alive.

"I got to the top of the steps and stood outside my bedroom door with the gun in my hand," she said, her voice breaking with emotion. "I stood there and imagined what it would feel like to kill somebody. I stood there and ran my hand along the door, rubbed against the door, edged closer to the door. And then I just pushed it open."

Black looked away, feeling like an intruder in Clarisse's private hell. He was ashamed to listen to her, embarrassed for her. Yet he wanted her to continue. He wanted her to finish it.

"They didn't even notice me at first," she said, the bitterness in her voice strangling the words. "They just kept fucking, like two dogs."

Clarisse laughed, a humorless, dry sound that died as soon as it left her lips.

"So I blew a hole in the stereo," she said, a sort of madness playing in her eyes. "And a hole in the television, and a hole in the mirror, and a hole in the nightstand, and a hole in the dresser. And I kept shooting until I shot every bullet in that gun."

Clarisse's chest heaved up and down as if she might hyperventilate. But in a few seconds she calmed herself enough to continue.

"By the time I finished," she said, her nostrils flaring, "Carl and Nicole, my man and my best friend, the people I had trusted with my life, both of them were balled up on my bed like babies, crying and shaking and probably wondering if they were still alive."

Clarisse sighed and looked across the room at Black. "I didn't have to wonder whether I was still alive. I knew the answer to that as soon as I walked in that room. I knew I had died more times than anybody deserves to. I just hadn't stopped breathing yet.

"I guess that's when I stopped caring. I started drinking at first. Then I started stealing painkillers from the job. When they stopped working, I started stealing morphine. That lasted for about a year, until they found out I was stealing medication and told me to either leave voluntarily or go to jail. Well you know what my choice was, right?

"For a while, I didn't even want to work anymore. I just stayed in the house listening to old Billie Holiday records and drinking. I did a little private-duty nursing now and then, but I mostly just stayed in the house and waited for . . . well, I don't know what I was waiting for. But by the time I ran into you last month, it was like: Okay, so Everett's smoking crack and he's not dead yet, so I might as well try it, too.

"So here I am," she said, looking around her as if she were just accepting what was happening to her. "Stuck between wanting to live and wanting to die."

Black looked down at the traffic that passed by on I-95. Since it was after rush hour, everything was running smoothly. The only unusual thing he saw was a helicopter hovering over the highway. If they were looking for them that way, he thought as he turned to face Clarisse, they would have an awfully long search. Because they weren't going to see Clarisse's car for a while.

"Everett?" Clarisse said, sounding like a frightened little girl.

"What?"

"We're not going to make it out of this alive, are we?"

The question took him by surprise. He opened his mouth to say something, then remembered the images of police bursting into the room that had crowded his thoughts earlier.

"Yeah. We'll make it."

"Even if I leave?" she said.

Black walked over to the corner of the room where she and Leroy sat and looked down at her.

"Where you goin' if I let you leave?" he asked harshly. "Where would you go? What would you do? You don't have no friends. You don't have no family. Far as I know, don't nobody care if you live or die. Not even you."

She stood up slowly—her body flowing up from the floor like steam—and looked him in the eye.

"Including you, too?" she asked, her voice a sultry whisper. "Do you care if I live or die?"

"I care about me," he said. "I care if Black live or die. I don't have time to be worried about nothin' else, or nobody else."

She began to lick behind his ear.

"A-and I . . . if you wanna make it out th-this . . ."

She walked around him and began to kiss the back of his neck.

"I'm s-s-sayin' . . ."

"Damn, Black," Leroy said as he pulled out another cap to dump into his straight shooter. "You startin' to sound like me."

Black grinned. "She keep lickin' my neck."

"Don't act like you don't like it," Leroy said, pulling two matches from the matchbook and taking a blast.

"Look," Black said, hunching his shoulders and turning around as she began to make circles on his neck with her tongue. "I care about you. That's what you wanna hear?"

"Yeah, that's what she wanna hear," Leroy said, his jaw moving rhythmically from side to side as he went through his ritual of searching for rocks in the carpet.

"It look like I'm talkin' to you, rug man?" Black said.

"Least I ain't all in love," Leroy said, relighting his straight and pulling out the remainder of the smoke.

Black didn't respond because he recognized the truth in Leroy's words. Clarisse had become real to him. He couldn't lump her in with other women, because now she had thoughts, and wants, and a past, and a life. And although she didn't realize it, she'd chipped his shell just enough to allow a shaft of light to creep inside. She'd chipped it just enough to allow him to feel.

"You need to be tryin' to figure out how we gon' get outta here," Leroy said, speaking so quickly that Black had to take a moment to replay the words in his head.

Black turned around and looked at Clarisse, then traced a

vein in her neck with his forefinger. She shuddered slightly, and he pretended not to notice.

"I already know how we gettin' outta here," he said.

"How?" Clarisse said, looking at him with an expression of amused puzzlement.

"You havin' a baby."

Pookie looked up from the bed and Leroy stopped digging in the carpet. And for the first time since they'd left Clarisse's house the night before, Black felt like he was in control.

"You ready?" Leroy said, puffing impatiently as Clarisse slipped a trench coat over a stomach that was artificially swelled by a rolled-up blanket.

"Why is he rushing me?" she said to Pookie.

" 'Cause that's what ignorant asses like him do."

"Why I gotta be all that?" Leroy said.

"I don't know," Pookie said. "I was hopin' you could tell me."

"Look," Black said, trying to stop another petty argument before it began. "A cab is on the way and we ain't got a whole lotta time for all this. So could y'all just stop arguin' for once so we can get outta this damn hotel?"

Everyone looked at one another like little kids who'd been caught with their hands in the cookie jar.

"I still don't know what it is I'm supposed to be doing," Clarisse said, breaking the silence.

"You supposed to be pregnant," Black said. "What's so hard about that?"

"I mean, if I'm going to act, don't I need some motivation for the role or something?"

"Your motivation is keepin' my foot out yo' ass."

"That's excellent," Clarisse said. "You're obviously directing this in the John Singleton, *Boyz N the Hood* tradition."

"Why you messin' with me?"

"Because you're there."

"You're forgettin' your motivation," Black said.

"Oh yes, keeping your foot out of my ass."

"Right."

"Man, y'all trippin'," Leroy said. "Can we just get outta here?"

He was right, of course. They had been in the same spot for too long. And if they hoped to ever make it out of that place alive, the time to move was then.

The plan was solid enough. Clarisse would get off the elevator with the rest of them, acting really loud and crazy, and they would all pile into the cab like she was going to have the baby any minute. Then they would do whatever they had to do to get the cabbie to drive them to 30th Street Station, where they would split up and catch trains to wherever. Black figured it was safer than trying to go to the airport, and faster than trying to go to the bus station. Of course there was the matter of the Amtrak police. But the Amtrak police probably wouldn't be able to recognize them from the previous night's descriptions. Leroy and Black weren't wearing church hats and sunglasses anymore. They were going to go out there in suits and ties. And Clarisse would be the only one wearing a trench coat, since she was playing the role of the pregnant woman.

"You ready?" Black said, picking up the suit jacket he had draped over the chair in the corner of the room.

"I don't even know what I'm supposed to do," Pookie said.

Black sighed, genuinely frustrated that someone who spent so much time conning people couldn't run game when it really counted.

"I told you. Act like you Clarisse sister. Hold her hand and push people out the way. Cuss out the clerk and the cabdriver. Stir up somethin'."

"Oh," she said. "The same thing I do all the time."

Clarisse opened the door and pale light flooded in from the hallway. Without a backward glance, she affected the wobbly walk of the expectant mother she was supposed to be, and started toward the elevator. Black followed Clarisse, then looked over at Leroy, who seemed the most hesitant of them all. Pookie came next, walking quickly toward Clarisse and reaching for her arm like the dutiful sister.

"You talked all that shit," she said to Leroy, looking back at him as they waited for the elevator. "Let's go."

"I'm comin'," he said, and walked out of the room like a baby taking its first steps toward its mother.

"You was supposed to say, 'I'm comin' *honey,*' Black said. "Tryin' to front like that ain't your woman."

"Yeah, all right," Leroy said, trying to dismiss Black's words.

Black looked over at Leroy and saw that he'd accomplished what he wanted. Leroy didn't look as tense as he had a few seconds before. Not that Black could blame him. None of them, not even Black, had as much to lose as Leroy. If the cops rolled up on them, they would concentrate the most energy on Leroy. He might not even make it to jail. Instead, he might become really clumsy all of a sudden and suffer one of those falls in the back of the police van: the kind of fall that results in multiple contusions about the face and head; the kind of fall that Rodney King took, only worse; the kind where the victim never gets up.

As far as Black could tell, the best way to keep Leroy—or any of them—from taking that type of fall was to be relaxed, because people think better when they're relaxed. And thinking better than the police was the best, if not the only, chance they had. They needed every chance they could get, too, because every rent-a-cop, Robocop, wanna-be-cop, used-to-be-cop, and never-been-cop in the city would be looking for them.

"You okay, Black?" Leroy said, pulling him from his thoughts.

"Yeah, I'm cool. I was just thinkin' about somethin'."

"You better think about what we gon' do when we get outta here."

The bell rang and the doors opened on the first floor. Leroy and Black just stood there, spellbound. But Pookie and Clarisse went right into their act, as if they had been practicing it for years.

"Get out the way!" Pookie screamed to no one in particular, then spoke to Clarisse in a comforting whisper. "You can make it, baby. You'll be there soon."

Clarisse clutched Pookie's arm and looked at her with an expression of pain mixed with fear. Black walked off the elevator and approached the man behind the desk, who looked as if he were asking himself why something like this had to happen on his shift.

"Where's the cab?" Black said calmly.

"What cab?"

"What cab!" Pookie repeated the question loudly. "What the hell you mean, what cab? My sister 'bout to have a baby and you talkin' 'bout what cab! We called down here ten minutes ago for a cab and you mean to tell me it ain't here yet?"

"Call 'em again," Black said. "Call 'em and tell 'em it's an emergency."

"But, sir—"

"But nothin'," Leroy said, slamming his hand against the counter. "Just do it."

Clarisse let go a wail that seemed to echo off the walls of the lobby. The clerk craned his neck to look around Black and see what was the matter with her.

"Don't be lookin' at her," Leroy said. "You just call the cab."

"He ain't call the cab yet?" Pookie said, leaving Clarisse's side and running toward the desk like she was about to jump over it and attack the clerk.

Black grabbed her just as she reached the desk.

"If somethin' happens to my pregnant wife . . . ," he said in low, threatening tones.

Clarisse wailed again. Leroy and Pookie both launched a tirade at the clerk, who picked up the phone and dialed feverishly just as the cab pulled up in front of the door. Black went over to Clarisse and got the room key from her, then placed it on the desk and walked quickly toward the door. He signaled to Pookie that the cab had arrived, and she went over to help Clarisse. Leroy yelled at the clerk for a second more, and in a flash they were gone, piled into the cab and yelling at the driver the same way they had yelled at the confused and nervous clerk.

"Where to?" the cabdriver asked, an accent thickening his words.

Clarisse screamed in response. For someone with no children, she had it down pat, right down to the sweat beading up on her forehead.

"What?" the driver said.

"Hahnemann Hospital," Black said.

"Where is that?"

"Dig this, man," Leroy said. "All that actin' like you don't know where nothin' at is gon' cease right now."

"Take my sister to the hospital!" Pookie shouted, raising her voice to a shrill scream.

Clarisse started to whimper, and Leroy, who was sitting in the front seat, inched closer to the driver.

"Pull off," he said in a menacing voice. "Now."

The tires of the cab screeched against the white driveway of the hotel, leaving two sweeping black marks in their wake. They were going back to the very city that they were supposed to be running away from, and Black couldn't help wondering exactly where they would end up. Everything that Black had done in his life—the good and the bad—had come down to that question.

As the cab rolled down I-95, an announcer on KYW said the name he'd come to despise: Johnny Podres. When he got to the part of the story that included the suspects' descriptions, the cabbie turned to Leroy and laughed.

"Can you imagine the whole police department not being able to find four people just because they dressed up in trench coats and ladies' hats?" he said, shaking his head in disbelief. "It's ridiculous."

Leroy turned his head and the cabbie said nothing more. But the radio announcer went on.

"In other news, freelance reporter Henry Moore was shot to death this morning in an apparent robbery in the parking lot of Abbottsford Hospital. Police have no suspects in that shooting."

When Black heard that, he couldn't help thinking that the police would find suitable suspects in the Moore shooting, just like they'd found them. It wouldn't surprise him. In fact, nothing about the police surprised him. He'd seen too much of what they could do to people, and felt too much of what they'd done to him. Maybe someone who'd never seen them beat a man unconscious or plant a gun on an unarmed man would have been shocked.

But not Black. The only thing that shocked him was that he wasn't dead yet.

Chapter 15

Ramirez and Hillman left the bail commissioner's office with the arrest warrants. The papers said that Samuel Jackson, Leroy Johnson, and Patricia Oaks would be charged with the murder of city councilman Johnny Podres, criminal conspiracy, violations of the Uniform Firearms Act, aggravated assault, armed robbery, possession of an instrument of crime, theft by unlawful taking, and a variety of other offenses.

If convicted, they could get the death penalty, or they could get life in prison. But with a "high-quality" victim like Podres, and predatory defendants like drug addicts, the odds always skewed toward capital punishment—something that always seemed to stir up the public's blood lust.

Ramirez and Hillman knew that. And as they left the bail commissioner's office and walked out into the Roundhouse parking lot, they realized that the media knew it, too.

Ramirez tried to hide behind Hillman so he could slide past

the throng of reporters who stood around waiting for the next briefing on the shooting. As soon as the reporters recognized him, though, they descended upon him like locusts.

"Lieutenant Ramirez, has there been any progress in the investigation?"

"Lieutenant Ramirez, do you have any leads on the whereabouts of the suspects?"

"Lieutenant Ramirez, have the suspects been spotted outside Philadelphia?"

It was all he could do to fight his way through the crowd muttering a few halfhearted "No comments."

As they made their way to the car, Ramirez noticed Jeanette Deveraux sitting in a news truck in the parking lot. That struck him as odd. Normally, she was the most aggressive reporter in the crowd. Yet there she was, allowing him to walk by without asking a single question.

"What's that all about?" Ramirez said, gesturing toward Deveraux as they got into the car.

"She is awfully quiet, isn't she?" Hillman said.

"Too quiet."

As they were leaving, a brown-haired man came out of the Roundhouse, walked up to her truck, and stuck his head in the window. Hillman caught a glimpse of him in the rearview mirror when Ramirez turned out of the parking lot.

"Do me a favor," Hillman said. "Come back around and ride past Deveraux's truck again."

"Why?"

"I just saw a cop who matches the description of the man who shot Henry Moore at the hospital."

"Where?"

"He just came out of the Roundhouse to talk to Deveraux."

Ramirez stopped the car and threw it into reverse. But he

couldn't back up because there was a line of cars behind him. He put it back in drive, flipped on his dome lights, and went around the block.

By the time they got back to the parking lot, Deveraux and Morgan were gone. Hillman jumped out of the car and looked around for the reporter, and Ramirez ran into the building and shouted through the glass at the officer standing guard at the desk.

"Did you see an officer with brown hair and a bushy mustache wearing black pants and a gray blazer?"

"Sure, he just left," the officer said.

"Who is he?"

"That's Lieutenant Morgan from Internal Affairs. He should be . . ."

Ramirez was out the door before the officer could finish. He didn't hear the reporters yelling after him. He didn't see the officers walking in and out of the building. He didn't even see Hillman when he jumped back into the car. All he saw was the truth, forming itself from bits and pieces in his mind, like a mosaic.

"Did you see her?" Ramirez asked.

"No. Did you see the cop?"

"No. But I found out who he is. His name is Lieutenant Morgan, Internal Affairs."

Ramirez gunned the car and skidded out of the parking lot, wheels spinning against asphalt as he drove toward the Command Center.

Before they were two blocks from the Roundhouse, his phone rang.

"Lieutenant Ramirez, please."

"This is Ramirez."

"Lieutenant Ramirez, this is Eldridge Scott. A woman just called me and said she was from Homicide."

"Okay," Ramirez said.

"Well, I don't know whether it was okay or not," Eldridge said. "I'll leave that up to you, since you supposed to be the professional."

Ramirez held his tongue and prayed for patience.

"Now, I know y'all got female detectives and everything," Eldridge said. "And I don't mean to sound like some kind o' male chauvinist just because it was a woman callin', but somethin' about her just wasn't right."

"Something like what?" Ramirez said, his head bouncing toward the roof of the car as they hit a deep pothole.

"First of all, she was askin' me about things I know I already talked to you about," Eldridge said.

"Sometimes we ask the same questions over and over again, Mr. Scott, because people forget things sometimes, and the more you ask, the more details you get."

"All right, well, since you so sure about it . . ."

"No, Mr. Scott, it's not that at all," Ramirez said, trying not to get on the old man's bad side. "I'm trying to understand what you're trying to tell me, that's all."

"I just didn't think the woman was right," Scott said. "Now, it's one thing to ask the same questions over and over again. But she was tellin' me not to discuss our conversation with anybody, and then she asked me to come down and meet her in the parking lot of the Roundhouse. Now, if the woman was from Homicide, would she be tellin' me to keep our conversation secret, like she was hidin' somethin', and then tell me to meet her outside someplace, instead o' in her office?"

The old man made sense. Quickly, Ramirez ran through the names of the people who worked day shift, because he knew there weren't any female detectives in his squad. Of the twenty-six detectives in the other two squads, he could only think of one female.

"Mr. Scott?" Ramirez said. "Did the woman give you a name?"

"She said her name was Deveraux."

Ramirez held the phone away from his ear as another piece of the mosaic pushed itself down into the mortar of his mind. It all made sense. Jeannete Deveraux had been waiting in the parking lot for Eldridge Scott. She was going to try to trick him into coming to the Roundhouse and then push a camera in his face. But Morgan had somehow convinced her to leave with him.

"Thank you, Mr. Scott."

"Wait a minute," Eldridge said before Ramirez could disconnect the call. "Was I right? Was the woman from Homicide?"

"Well, no, she wasn't."

Eldridge let loose a self-satisfied laugh. "Learn to listen to your elders, boy. We ain't lived all this time by bein' fools."

"Yes, sir," Ramirez said, disconnecting the call.

"Deveraux was waiting for the guy who lives next door to Clarisse Williams," he said to Hillman.

"Morgan must have told her that he had a better story," Hillman said. "Hopefully, it's not the same type of story he fed to Henry Moore."

Ramirez didn't respond. He knew that Hillman was right. He had been right from the very beginning. Now people were dying because Ramirez had refused to listen to him. It was just like Eldridge Scott had told him: Listen to your elders, because fools don't usually live that long.

Lieutenant Darren Morgan looked in his rearview mirror as he turned onto I-76 East and headed for the airport. He half expected to see Jeanette Deveraux and her cameraman take the next exit ramp and go back to the Roundhouse, but when they passed the Gray's Ferry Avenue exit and switched into the left lane to keep pace with him, he knew he had them. The only problem was figuring out a way to get rid of their news van when he was done.

It had been pretty easy to convince the reporter that the information he had was better than anything she was going to get standing around in the Roundhouse parking lot waiting on whomever. All he had to do was mention the words "police conspiracy." From there, it was a piece of cake. He told her that if she promised not to contact anyone at the television station before she had the evidence in hand, he would provide her with the paperwork and photos to prove that the Podres shooting was the result of a wide-ranging police cover-up involving at least two ranking officers. What he didn't tell her was that he was one of the officers, and the paperwork was nowhere to be found.

Morgan turned onto the bridge that led to the airport and looked in his rearview mirror again. Then he smiled to himself and wondered what Deveraux and the cameraman were thinking about as they followed him.

"Do you think it's safe to come out here with this guy?" Jeanette Deveraux's cameraman said after they followed Morgan into the airport, through A, B, C, D, and E terminals, around the entire international terminal, and through a hole in the gate at Philadelphia International Airport.

Deveraux didn't answer. She was too busy wondering what the cop was going to tell them about the Podres shooting and hoping that whatever information he had was worth disregarding the interview with the couple who lived next door to Clarisse Williams. After all, the illegal search thing would've been pretty strong. But if this guy could give names and dates and link the whole thing to the police department, that would be like someone giving Deveraux her own world someplace, to pillage and plunder to her heart's content.

The only catch was, there was no way to be sure about the cop. This little excursion could be anything from a delay tactic to some kind of public-relations ploy. Who knew?

Maybe that's what was bothering her about this thing. She didn't know. She'd always pretty much stuck with the "bird in the hand is worth two in the bush" philosophy because it helped her keep things really simple. But when it came to this, probably the biggest story she'd ever covered, she was willing to risk doing something different. She was willing to toss the dice and risk losing the sure story for the bigger story that she wasn't so sure about. That's what Morgan was offering her—something infinitely bigger than anything she'd ever covered. And he hadn't even asked for anything in return.

Deveraux watched as Morgan stopped his car a few feet from the high grass at the edge of the airport. But she wasn't really seeing him, or his car, or the grim expression he wore as he got out and closed his door. She was only seeing a Barbara Walters–like rise to one-woman shows and hour-long specials.

"Jeanette?" the cameraman said as he got out of the van and pulled his camera from the backseat. "You coming?"

"Oh yeah," she said, snapping out of her reverie. "Just let me get my microphone."

Deveraux got out and leaned over the backseat just as Morgan walked back toward the news van. She had to rummage through some stuff to get to the microphone, because the wire had tangled on something.

"Mike," she said, still looking down at the floor. "Could you come over here and help me get this wire untangled?"

The cameraman didn't say anything.

"Mike, I need you over here now," she said.

When he still didn't answer, Jeanette Deveraux felt something cold run through her. It was like everything she had ever done up until that moment came together and pressed against reality until it burst through the other side. She felt it all over, that something had just happened that would change her whole existence. It was like ice water pouring over her body, but it was something much colder. It was mind-numbing, all-consuming fear.

Without raising her head, she glanced over at the other side of the van and saw Mike's hand draped loosely over the camera handle. A smear of blood soiled his sleeve. The rest of his body wasn't visible, she assumed because it was on the ground next to the van. Jeanette Deveraux's eyes began to dart wildly from side to side, trying to find where the cop had gone. When she didn't see him, she clasped her hand over her mouth and willed herself not to scream. That's when everything came into focus for her.

The whole thing had been a ruse by this cop to get her out to the airport and kill her. That could only mean one thing—that he was smack-dab in the middle of whatever conspiracy had caused Podres's death, and he was willing to do anything to keep that conspiracy under wraps.

"Oh my God," she whispered, forcing herself to continue rummaging through the backseat until she could think of what she was going to do next.

She couldn't hear anything, because the sound of the planes flying overhead drowned out everything, including the gunshot that had killed Mike. She couldn't see anything, either, because she didn't dare look up and let the cop know that she saw her cameraman crumpled in a bloodstained heap next to the van. There was only one chance for her, and she was going to take it.

"I got it, Mike," Deveraux said as loudly as she could, the tears squeezing out from between her eyelids. "I got the microphone."

Before she had even finished saying the words, Jeanette Deveraux turned around and ran away from the van, tumbling toward the hole in the fence that they had driven through a few minutes before. Morgan darted from the other side of the van and ran after her, cursing himself for allowing a woman to get the jump on him.

Deveraux tripped, put out her hands to steady herself, half crawled, half fell through the opening in the fence, and ran toward an expanse of grass that led to the nearest runway. Morgan ran through the hole after her, gaining momentum as he took aim and squeezed off a shot that missed badly. Deveraux started zigzagging, hoping to make herself a more difficult target. Morgan squeezed off another shot, barely missed, then tripped on a rock and fell down in the grass. When he looked up, Deveraux was about twenty yards away, still running toward the runway.

Morgan lay there in prone position, calmly took aim, and shot Jeanette Deveraux in the small of her back. When he saw her fall, he looked at his gun, realized that he had squeezed off the last round, and began fumbling in his pockets for another magazine as he got up and walked over to her. Deveraux was still trying to crawl toward the runway when he got there, though she could no longer move her legs.

"Go to hell," she said as he came to stand over her.

Morgan grinned as he watched her writhe back and forth in a sickening pain dance that looked almost like some kind of ritual.

"I never heard you say anything like that on the news," Morgan said, panting as he struggled to catch his breath. "Do they let you say stuff like that on the news?"

Deveraux looked up at him and tried to maintain her defiant demeanor. But the look on his face was too evil to defy. She began to cry uncontrollably, her body bouncing up and down on the patches of weather-beaten grass like a doll on the string of some cruel puppeteer.

"Shut up," Morgan said, digging into the inside pocket of his jacket after failing to find an extra magazine in the outside pockets.

"Please," Deveraux said, sobbing and crawling backward in the grass. "I don't know anything. I really don't know anything."

Morgan found a magazine and took it out of his pocket.

"Sure you know something," Morgan said, slapping the magazine into the gun and chambering the first round. "You know you're good at your job."

His face crinkled into a self-satisfied smile as he continued to tease her.

"And I know I'm good at mine," he said. "Now, I don't know what was in that envelope that woman handed to you back at the Roundhouse, but—"

"Nothing," Deveraux said, frantically shaking her head and dragging herself away from him. "There wasn't anything in the envelope. . . ."

Morgan kicked Deveraux in the side and she screamed out in pain.

"Now, what was I saying before I was so rudely interrupted?" Morgan said. "Oh yeah. I remember now. I was asking you what was in the envelope back at the Roundhouse."

"A number," Deveraux said, choking on her words as she struggled to hold back the sobs.

"Whose number?" Morgan said.

"The Scotts," she said. "But they're harmless. They're old. They don't know anything about—"

Morgan bent down and slapped her across the head with the barrel of the gun. She winced and let out a strangled sob as a trickle of blood oozed from beneath her hairline.

"Where's the envelope?" he said.

Deveraux coughed and choked on the blood that was starting to well up in her mouth.

"Where's the envelope!" Morgan screamed, his eyes bulging as he reared back to pistol-whip her again.

"It's in my purse," she said, clutching at the cut on her forehead. "It's in . . ."

Deveraux lost consciousness and fell against the ground. Morgan looked at her for a moment, contemplated leaving her there, then aimed the gun at her head and fired three times. When the reporter's face was no longer recognizable, he walked back to Deveraux's GMC Jimmy and found her purse.

As he looked over at the cameraman, still slumped between his camera and the ground, Morgan's options became clear to him. Quite simply, he didn't have any. The only thing he could do was take the money he'd made from the laundering scheme and leave town.

It should be simple enough to do that. After all, he had anticipated having to leave quickly one day, and he had squirreled away some of the money in a locker at 30th Street Station.

He didn't even know how much it was. And he didn't care. He was sure it would be enough to get him someplace where he could get started. He'd get the rest of the money later, when things cooled down some.

Sheldon was the one who had killed Podres, so he'd have to take care of the rest of his problems on his own. And if things went sour, Morgan knew that he could always cut a deal to help land the bigger fish.

But Morgan didn't plan to let it come to that. Because there was only one thing in Philadelphia that he planned to catch—a train.

Captain Sheldon sat in the Command Center and thought about Morgan. He had proved to be Sheldon's biggest asset and his biggest liability. His intercepting the tape from

Moore had kept the truth hidden. But Morgan was a loose cannon who knew too much. And if Morgan had figured out that Sheldon was Podres's killer, how much longer could Sheldon keep the truth hidden from the rest of the world?

The unpredictability of it went against Sheldon's methodical nature. In everything he had ever done, Sheldon had always considered every possibility and made backup plans. But this thing had spun completely out of his control. There were too many intangibles, too many people digging for the truth, too many possibilities to consider, too many mistakes to cover up.

The longer the suspects remained at large, the more time people had to theorize. Sheldon knew that it was only a matter of time before the conspiracy theory became a serious consideration. And once the truth began to come out, Morgan would turn on him. That is, if he hadn't done so already.

Sheldon looked over at Nelson and knew that there was no other way. He would have to leave, because the situation was rapidly collapsing into bedlam. He couldn't stand by and watch it all come tumbling down on him. He had gone through too much to let that happen.

"Commissioner Nelson," he said, standing up and grabbing his jacket from the back of his chair, "I'm going to get something to eat."

"Why don't you send somebody to get it for you? I need you here."

"Sir, if I don't get out of here and get some sunlight, I'm going to turn into a vampire," Sheldon said, shifting nervously from one foot to the other. "I'm only going across the street. Do you want anything?"

"No, not right now. But hurry back. Ramirez and Hillman will be here in a few minutes to report on the progress of the investigation."

"I'll only be a minute, sir."

As Sheldon walked across the street and climbed into his car—looking back at the Command Center for the last time—he knew that he had to turn on Morgan before Morgan had a chance to turn on him.

Once he had taken care of that problem, he could go over to Abbottsford Hospital and eliminate the final loose end.

When Ramirez and Hillman walked into the Command Center on Park Avenue, it was like walking into a monastery where everyone had taken a vow of silence. The commissioner sat draped over a computer, his eyes glued to the monitor as if the answer to it all were going to jump off the screen. And Ramirez and Hillman stood awkwardly, looking and feeling very out of place.

"Commissioner," Ramirez said quietly.

Nelson waited a few minutes before he responded. "Good morning, Lieutenant," he said, still looking at the monitor. "I guess you have the warrants."

"Yes, sir."

"Do you have any new leads?"

"No, sir."

"Then why are you here?"

"Sir, we believe we're looking for the wrong suspects in this shooting."

Nelson leaned back and formed his hands into a church steeple. "Do you have evidence to prove that someone else committed this crime?"

"We've got a priest who says that Leroy was going away from the shooting right before it happened," Ramirez said. "Which would make it nearly impossible for him to have committed this crime within the time frame we're looking at. We believe that

Black was committing a burglary at the time of the shooting, and Hillman has a witness who says that Black wasn't with Leroy when Leroy left the scene of the shooting."

Nelson stared at Ramirez and said nothing.

"Sir," Hillman said, filling in the empty space, "there's also the matter of the only eyewitness to the shooting—Darnell Thomas."

"What about him?"

"I interrogated him this morning. He says that a tall white man with blond hair and blue eyes shot Podres."

"Was that the extent of the description he gave?" Nelson asked.

Hillman flipped through his notes. "He said the shooter was tall, with blond hair and blue eyes, and that he was wearing a white shirt and black pants."

"That could be anybody!" Nelson said, throwing up his hands and walking over to the door.

Hillman continued to flip through his notes. "There was something else," he said. "I'll find it in a minute."

"If you ask me," Ramirez said, "that description almost fits the captain."

"If that's supposed to be some kind of joke, Lieutenant, I fail to see the humor in it," Nelson said, turning to face Ramirez.

"Where is the captain anyway, sir?" Hillman said.

"He went to get something to eat. He'll be right back."

Ramirez and Hillman looked at each other.

"How long ago did he leave?" Ramirez said.

Nelson looked at Ramirez with an expression that bordered on contempt.

"You know, Ramirez, instead of standing here questioning me, you need to have your ass out there finding these suspects."

"Whether or not they shot Podres?" Ramirez said, his words drenched with sarcasm.

"It's not our job to determine guilt," Nelson said. "Our job is to gather enough evidence to allow the district attorney to try them."

"Commissioner," Ramirez said, "what real evidence do we have? Some lady saying she saw Leroy go in the house a few seconds before the shots were fired? Some paperwork on some theft cases that indicate Leroy and Black like to get arrested together?"

"I understand your concerns, Lieutenant," Nelson said, choosing his words carefully. "And your points are valid. But Leroy Johnson, Samuel Jackson, and Patricia Oaks are the best suspects we have right now, and you're the best detective we have right now. As far as Clarisse Williams, we're going to wait until at least this afternoon to call that a kidnapping, if we choose to go that route. But the long and short of it is this: We have to find these people and I need to know if you're committed to doing that."

"I don't know if I—"

"I need to know if you're committed to doing that, Lieutenant."

Ramirez thought of what would happen to Leroy and Black if someone else found them first. He thought of how cops treated suspects who were involved in police shootings or police assaults. He thought of how he would feel knowing that he had let innocent people die at the hands of cops who blamed them for something they didn't do. He thought of all those things, and the question he had been burning to ask came tumbling out before he could stop it.

"How many times have you watched innocent people go to jail?" Ramirez said, looking at Nelson with weary resignation.

Nelson gave him a long, hard look. Then he walked back

over to his chair and sat down, staring into his terminal with the faraway gaze of a man staring into his past.

"Never," Nelson said. "I've never watched an innocent person go to jail, Lieutenant. You know why? Because it doesn't matter whether someone is guilty of committing a crime. What matters is that we make an arrest, gather enough evidence to make it stick, and let the district attorney prove that person's guilt in a court of law. If the district attorney can't do that, the suspect's innocent and he walks."

Nelson's face took on the hard lines of a man who had long ago stopped believing in the very system he was sworn to uphold. Ramirez thought he saw something between those lines. Sadness, maybe. But he couldn't be sure.

"What matters is that the system works. Not whether some piper pulled the trigger. Now, I need to know if you're still with us on this investigation, Lieutenant. Because if you're not, I'm going to have to find someone to take your place."

Ramirez didn't answer. So Hillman spoke for the both of them.

"Commissioner, I'm going to be straight with you," he said. "I've been around this department as long as you have, and I've seen all the things you're talking about, more times than I care to recall. I know that I've helped send innocent people to jail. We all have. But I can't stand here and watch it happen this time. I just can't."

"And what makes this time so special, Detective?"

"Do you know what happened after I talked with Darnell Thomas this morning?" Hillman said, his eyes drilling into Nelson's. "A reporter got a tape of the interrogation and he was killed in the parking lot by a police officer. He was murdered, Commissioner, by Lieutenant Darren Morgan of Internal Affairs."

Nelson returned Hillman's stare. "If you can prove that,

Hillman, we can go out and bring him in right now. But if you can't, I don't want to hear it."

"What's the difference, sir?" Ramirez said. "How come we can bring in Black and Leroy on next to nothing, but we have to have irrefutable proof that Morgan killed the reporter?"

"You know why."

"Let me guess," Hillman said. "Because we take care of our own? Because we're supposed to look the other way when an officer breaks the law? Commissioner, Morgan and someone in this department conspired to kill Podres, and now they're killing anyone who gets too close to the truth."

"Hillman, you're making all these allegations without a shred of proof," Nelson said. "The two of you come marching in here like the gestapo, and I'm supposed to just take your word for it that police officers are going around killing people?"

"We've got an eyewitness at the hospital who saw Morgan leaving the scene of the shooting this morning," Hillman said. "He gave us a partial license plate of 342. I checked. The only operational city vehicle with the numbers 342 is assigned to Internal Affairs.

"You don't have to take our word for it, sir. But the longer we wait, the worse it's going to get. We just saw Morgan leave the Roundhouse with another reporter. And I believe that she's going to wind up dead, too."

Nelson turned his head, as if to say he was no longer listening.

"Don't you see?" Hillman said, his voice filled with exasperation. "They're covering their tracks."

"You keep saying *they,* like you know for sure that this other person is someone from within the department," Nelson said. "But you don't know that."

Hillman flipped through his notes again. "You're right, sir. I don't know. But I do know this. Morgan killed Henry Moore over a tape containing this description: a tall white man with blond hair and blue eyes, wearing black pants, a white shirt, and . . ."

Hillman flipped through his notes some more. "Here it is . . . a heavy gold link bracelet."

Nelson's mouth dropped open. "What did you say?"

"I said a white man with—"

"No," Nelson said. "Repeat the last part."

"A heavy gold link bracelet."

"Oh my God," Nelson said.

"What?" Ramirez said. "What is it, sir?"

"That's Sheldon."

Nelson agreed to allow Ramirez and Hillman to search for Sheldon and Morgan, but he stopped short of calling off the search for the original suspects. If they were completely innocent of the charges, he reasoned, they would never have fled in the first place.

Ramirez and Hillman tried to convince Nelson that fear, not guilt, motivated the suspects' flight. But Nelson would not be moved. So Hillman and Ramirez set out to find the suspects, knowing that if someone else found them first, the results would be catastrophic.

As they rode away from the Command Center, Ramirez fought against the cloud of disillusionment that formed in his mind, and wondered if he'd ever look at the department the same way again.

Nelson's words haunted him: What matters is that the system works. Not whether some piper pulled the trigger.

"Thinking about Nelson?" Hillman said, rousing Ramirez from his thoughts.

Ramirez pursed his lips angrily. "Do you believe that guy?"

"I've been on the force almost as long as you've been alive," Hillman said. "There's not much I can't believe. But I learned a long time ago that you've got to go along to get along."

Ramirez looked at him sharply.

"Not that I always go along," Hillman added quickly, sensing that Ramirez misunderstood what he was trying to say. "I guess what I'm saying is, when the job goes against what I believe—and there have been a few times over the years—I do what I have to do. But I do it quietly."

"Well, you didn't do it quietly in there," Ramirez said.

"I've only got six months to go," Hillman said. "I don't have a whole lot to lose now. But Nelson does, and I think he knows it."

"What do you mean?"

"You've got to put yourself in Nelson's shoes," Hillman said. "If you're him, you've been presiding over a corrupt department for the last two or three years. It's impossible that all the corruption has gone on without your knowledge. You know it, and everybody else knows it.

"So after a while, you get nervous and you try to distance yourself from it. You stop letting things go on as much and you stop turning the other way as much. You even crack down a little bit. But then the Police Civilian Review Board starts to get a little too powerful. With each investigation it conducts, they get closer to the top of the department. And now, if you're Nelson, you're really scared, because you know you were right in the thick of things about six months ago, even if you're not doing anything now. Then the head of the board gets smoked.

"At first, you're happy. I mean, you're really happy. And then the news coverage starts, and you're even more scared than you were before, because you know how it looks. So what do you do? You close ranks. You get everybody in the department in lockstep. You latch on to a suspect or two you can convict, conduct a quick investigation, get a quick trial date, and you do it all knowing that if this thing doesn't go over just right, it's your ass.

"So if anybody stands in your way, you remove them. Because as long as it's the little guys getting caught with their hands in the cookie jar, it's okay. They're supposed to get caught. But not you. You'd rather die than get caught."

"So what does arresting the wrong people have to do with them getting caught?" Ramirez said.

"A quick investigation means less media coverage. Less media coverage means less scrutiny. Less scrutiny means less chance of their little extracurricular activities coming out."

"Maybe it's more than that," Ramirez said. "Maybe Nelson is the one who set Podres up to be murdered in the first place."

"I doubt it," Hillman said. "Nelson's one of those guys who'll cut your throat politically, but he's not a killer. Whatever Sheldon and Morgan were doing, Nelson wasn't getting a piece of it. If he was, this whole thing would have went down a whole lot smoother than it did."

Ramirez was silent as he considered the truth in Hillman's words.

"Can I tell you something?" Ramirez said.

"Sure."

"I never pegged you to be the type of guy to stand up to Nelson. To tell you the truth, I've never known quite how to take you."

"Join the crowd," Hillman said.

"I mean, you give off this vibe like you just want to be left alone."

Hillman took a moment to think about what Ramirez had said.

"When you've been around as long as I have," Hillman said, "your life is full of memories. And memories are like diamonds:

Each one is precious in its own way. Some of them are round and brilliant, and you can look at them all day long and never get tired of them. But some of them are ugly and damaged, and you can't stand the sight of them, because you know that you made bad investments when you bought them."

Ramirez glanced over at him.

"I guess I've spent too many years trying not to look at the bad memories," Hillman said.

"You can't live in the past," Ramirez said.

"I'm getting old now," Hillman said. "I've got a lot more past than future. The future belongs to guys like you, Ramirez. If you just learn to listen, I think you'll probably be all right."

Ramirez smiled. Then the radio crackled to life.

"Dan 25, take the airport, outside the international terminal," the dispatcher said. "Meet Southwest Detectives for a founded job. Use caution, an officer may be involved."

"Dan 25, okay."

"Sounds like one of our friends made an appearance at the airport," Ramirez said as he placed the handset back in its cradle.

"If you're going to check that, why don't you drop me off at the 39th?" Hillman said.

"For what?"

"I'm going to get a vehicle and take a ride up to the hospital. I've got a hunch that Sheldon might show up there."

Ramirez turned on Hunting Park Avenue and drove toward the 39th District. As he dropped Hillman off and watched him walk into the building, his mind drifted back to the suspects.

If they were still in Philadelphia, it would be that much harder for them to escape from the city with their lives.

Chapter 16

When the cab got down to the Center City exit, which would have taken them to the Broad Street exit and Hahnemann Hospital, Leroy told the cabbie to double back and take I-76 East, which would take them to 30th Street Station. The driver started to protest, but Leroy gave him one of his looks and the driver just turned it around and took them where they wanted to go.

Clarisse toned down the moaning just enough to convince the cabbie that it wasn't quite as urgent as before, and Pookie and Black sat on either side of her, patting her hand and making soothing sounds. The whole thing looked like something from a movie set. But it was more convincing.

When they pulled Clarisse out of the cab, she pushed against her lower back and arched it like she was carrying a baby that weighed at least ten pounds. It looked so genuine that Black almost dropped her hand and started clapping at her performance.

It was all he could do to maintain his composure until they got into the station and walked past the information booth.

"What now?" Pookie said, whispering under her breath as they walked Clarisse past a group of Amtrak police.

Black had to think about it for a minute, because he hadn't planned that far ahead.

"To the souvenir shop?" he said, making it more a question than a statement.

"To the *souvenir* shop?" Clarisse repeated, making the idea sound really stupid.

"Yeah, we tourists now," he said, trying hard not to look at the police officers. "And you not in labor no more. You just real pregnant and you havin' a hard time walkin' up and down in this big train station. So we just helpin' you 'cause we love you so much."

"Yeah, well, you're going to have to love me enough to let me go to the bathroom right about now."

"You need to do *somethin'*," Leroy said. " 'Cause that blanket look like it's just about to fall out from underneath that coat."

They all looked down and saw the bulge beneath her coat dropping lower and lower, as if she were going to have the baby any minute.

"Come on," Clarisse said, pulling Pookie toward the ladies' room.

In an instant, Leroy and Black were left standing there, alone and exposed. Leroy looked after Pookie and Clarisse like he expected them to run away. After all, there was really no reason for them to stay.

"They comin' back," Black said, reading Leroy's thoughts and trying to sound reassuring.

"How you know?" he said, looking at Black with skepticism.

"I don't."

"Well, shut up then."

Black was too tired and too wrong to argue his point. Because the truth was, he didn't have a point. All he had was the money Leroy had given him and a vision of the four of them getting on the train. But he didn't have what he really needed at that point. He didn't have any faith.

"We might as well go 'head over here and sit down," Black said.

"Man, I ain't sittin' nowhere waitin' for five-o to walk up on me."

"We in a big-ass train station," Black said. "Ain't nobody just gon' instantly recognize you in here with a suit on. You look just like everybody else that's goin' outta town."

"We need to be goin' over there tryin' to buy some train tickets," Leroy said.

"In a minute," Black said, walking toward the bench in the corner where most of the people were milling back and forth.

It took Leroy about half a minute to decide that it was probably best for him to follow. When Black heard Leroy's footsteps behind him, he let out a sigh of relief. Because nothing would get them caught faster than standing there in the middle of 30th Street Station looking like they didn't know where they wanted to go or what they wanted to do. It was better for them to fade into the crowd and sit down. At least that way they could have a few minutes of relative safety to make a good decision. That's what Black was going to tell Leroy when he came over to the bench to sit down with him. But by the time Black turned around, Leroy had disappeared.

When Black realized that Leroy was no longer there, his head started to swim. But he sat down anyway and tried not to panic. He looked around casually and forced himself not to get up. Then he thought about where Leroy could have gone. When he couldn't come up with an answer, he began to narrow down his choices and came up with two. He could either go and get his own ticket and go wherever, by himself, or he could sit there and wait for Leroy.

Black realized after a few minutes that he really couldn't decide what to do. The decision shouldn't have been that hard. They would have to split up in a few minutes anyway, because it just made sense to do that. But he was afraid. They all were. Black could see it in the way Clarisse looked when she left them to go to the bathroom; in the way Pookie walked away with her without uttering a word; in the way Leroy looked when Black told him they needed to go over to the bench and sit down.

It wasn't a game anymore. Not that it ever was. But it was almost over. And they all faced the end with both fear and anticipation, wondering when someone would walk up behind them and end it for them. Their lives had been down so much more than they were up that they expected to fail.

Black shuddered and let out a long sigh, then looked over at the ladies' room and saw a white woman go inside. He was tempted to go over to her and ask her to see if Pookie and Clarisse were in there. But then he thought about the way they'd been saying their names on television and on the radio all night long. He could imagine how the scene would play out.

"Excuse me, white woman, can you tell Pookie and Clarisse that Samuel Everett Jackson, aka Black, is waiting for them outside? Thank you."

Her face would crinkle into the classic Jamie Lee Curtis expression of horror, like he was the black reincarnation of Michael Myers, and then she would scream and point. No, she wouldn't even scream. She would make that sound they made in *Invasion of the Body Snatchers* whenever the aliens walked up on a real person: a real bloodcurdling-type scream.

Black smiled to himself at the thought, and just as he looked up again, he felt someone walk up behind him and tap him on the shoulder. All at once, everything became a jumbled mess. The fear, the excitement, and the anticipation joined and became something else, something indescribable. He had visions of guns pointed at the back of his head and police waiting for him to move so they could decorate the bench with his brain. There was nothing for him to do but sit there and wait for them to decide what they were going to do, so that's what he did.

"Turn around slowly," a familiar, muffled voice said.

When Black turned around, Leroy was standing there, smiling and holding train tickets in his hand.

"Remind me to hurt you."

"Remind yourself to get up from there and come on," Leroy said. "We ain't got time to be sittin' around waitin'."

Black looked over at the bathroom again, and Pookie and Clarisse were just coming out the door, walking toward them. Clarisse had taken off the coat and removed the blanket, and Pookie had on sunglasses.

"Come on, man," Leroy said. "The trains supposed to leave in like a half hour."

"Trains?"

"Yeah, trains," he said. "What you think we all can get on the same train and roll out like that?"

"I think we need to roll out of Philly together, then go wherever we gon' go when we get to the next stop."

"Why?"

" 'Cause that way, if somebody get caught once we get past the first stop, they can't snitch, 'cause they don't know where everybody else went."

"Don't nobody know now," he said.

"You know."

"I ain't gon' tell."

"I don't know that."

Leroy looked at Black like he wanted to say something more, but Clarisse and Pookie walked over before he could put it into words.

"Why y'all sittin' here talkin'?" Pookie said, looking around nervously. "Let's go."

Black looked up at Clarisse, who stood there looking down at the floor. Her expression was difficult to read, and so were her actions. She'd walked away and come back. She'd had the chance to just keep going, but she hadn't, and that confused Black. After they'd taken her car and parked it in a hotel parking lot, caused her to lose a brand-new job, and made the world think that she'd been kidnapped by murderers, she was standing there waiting for them to tell her what to do, like she was one of them.

Then again, Black thought, she was one of them. Not like Patty Hearst when they kidnapped her and had her robbing banks. No. Clarisse was one of them before she even came with them. She just didn't know it. She probably still didn't know. Even though she had one foot on the path they'd all traveled and was waiting for the other foot to fall, even though she was suffering from the same rejection, anger, and disappointment they'd all gone through, even though she had no idea where her life was going and had probably lost the ability to care, she still wasn't certain that she was one of them.

"Why are you looking at me, Everett?" she said loudly. "Come on!"

"Why don't you just tell everybody my name?"

"Sorry."

"From now on," Black said, "we ain't got no names."

Everyone nodded their agreement.

"Now," Black said, getting up from the bench and walking slowly toward the gift shop, "the first thing we gotta do is go get some little corny Philadelphia baseball caps and some little cheap travel bags from the gift shop, so we look like tourists. 'Cause if we gettin' on the trains with nothin', people gon' be lookin' at us like: Where they goin' with no luggage?"

"I told you we ain't got time for all that," Leroy said, reluctantly following Black with Pookie and Clarisse. "The trains roll out in twenty minutes."

"You got time to spend the rest o' your life on lockdown?"

"Look," Pookie said impatiently, "I don't care what we do. Just do somethin'."

Black tapped Leroy on the shoulder. "I hope you got tickets for the sleeper compartment so we don't have to sit around everybody else and wait for five-o to walk up on us."

"I ain't know they had a sleeper compartment."

"All right, that's problem number one. We gotta find a way to get in the sleeper compartment."

"What's problem number two?" Clarisse said as they walked into the gift shop.

"Figurin' out why you still here."

Everyone looked at her, waiting for her answer.

"I guess," Clarisse said, pausing as she walked up the first aisle and took two garment bags from the shelf, "I guess it's because I really don't have anywhere else to go."

"Girl, you know that ain't the only reason," Pookie said. "So you need to go 'head and stop frontin'."

Clarisse looked at Pookie with an irritation that bordered on hostility, but said nothing. Leroy and Black ignored their little display and walked over to the souvenir shirts and hats, pretending that they weren't with them. When Clarisse and Pookie paid for their bags and walked out of the store, Leroy and Black walked up to the counter and paid for theirs. Then they all met outside the store.

"What now?" Pookie said.

"Now we get on the train," Black said.

"What train?" Clarisse said.

Black looked at Leroy, waiting for him to tell them which trains they were going to catch.

"The twelve-fifteen to Atlanta," Leroy said.

"I thought you said it was two different trains," Black said.

"I thought you said you was gon' get us outta Philly," Leroy said.

"What it look like I'm doin'?"

"Look like you standin' there runnin' your mouth. And this damn sure still look like Philly to me."

"Dig this," Black said, walking toward the steps that led down to the train platforms at 30th Street Station. "We can talk about all that once we get up outta here. But right now, what you need to do is give everybody they tickets so we can get on the train. 'Cause all this standin' around together ain't even cool."

Leroy puffed up, angry that Black had ignored his remarks. But he handed out the tickets anyway.

"Come on," Black said, grabbing Clarisse by the hand and pulling her behind him.

"Hold up," Leroy said.

Black stopped and turned around.

He looked down and shuffled his feet uncomfortably, then sighed and looked around him before looking Black in the eye.

"Be safe," he said.

Black looked at Pookie, who stood silently behind him. Then he looked at Leroy and wondered if he'd ever see him again. Black was used to him, and not having him around would mean that things had changed. Black didn't like change. He liked for things to stay the same as much as possible. That's why he went to such lengths to keep smoking crack, even though he hated it. He was afraid to try to go back to the life he'd had before. He knew it would be different. He knew there would be change.

"Be safe," he said to Leroy.

But even as the words left his mouth, Black wondered how safe they could be in a world where the police could say or do just about anything and never worry about being questioned.

Commissioner Nelson turned on the television in the Command Center and hoped that he wouldn't see anything about Sheldon or Morgan. But as soon as the picture came into focus, Nelson knew that he had hoped for too much.

Anchorman Mike Hansen was wiping tears from his eyes and apologizing to the viewers for his outburst. Coanchor Lorraine Anderson was patting his shoulder and fighting past tears of her own.

"Ladies and gentlemen," she said, pausing to take a deep breath. "Channel Ten reporter Jeanette Deveraux and cameraman Michael Yates have been found in a field at Philadelphia International Airport. Both were pronounced dead at the scene with gunshot wounds to the head. Details are sketchy, but . . ."

As the reporter spoke, the phone at the Command Center rang. A detective answered it and listened to the supervisor on the scene of the Deveraux shooting. After a few minutes, he picked up a pencil and started to jot down some information.

"Thank you, Lieutenant," he said, placing the pencil carefully on the table. "I'll consult the commissioner about that and get right back to you."

"What is it?" Nelson said.

"They've got a suspect in the Deveraux shooting. He's a cop. A fuel-truck driver at the airport saw him leave the scene of the shooting."

"Is there a description?" Nelson asked. But he knew before the detective even responded that it had to be one of two people.

The detective looked down at his notes. "He's a white male, driving a black unmarked Chrysler with a license tag of UJV-342. His name is Lieutenant Darren Morgan from Internal Affairs. Do you want to put his description out over the air, sir?"

"I think it would probably be better to keep this within the department," Nelson said, the color draining from his face. "I've already got one team looking for him. Have each district assign two teams each to join the search."

As the detective picked up the phone to call in the commissioner's orders, the news anchor looked into the camera and started to speak.

". . . may be related to the murder of freelance reporter Henry Moore, who was found shot to death this morning in what was thought to be a drug-related robbery at Abbottsford Hospital. We take you now to Philadelphia International Airport, where Channel Ten reporter Myung Kim is standing by with information from a police commander who is closely linked to the Podres investigation."

"Oh no," Nelson said, placing his head in his hands.

"Thanks, Mike," the reporter said. "I received a call a few minutes ago from a highly placed police commander who claims to have proof that the late Police Civilian Review Board chief Johnny Podres was having an illicit affair with an unnamed woman shortly before his death. The commander also says that Podres was receiving threats from a pro-police political action committee called Safer Philadelphians, whose members were obviously aware of the affair."

The reporter paused to allow the anchorman to ask an obvious question.

"So, Myung, what is the significance of this information and where does it come from?"

"Apparently, Mike, Safer Philadelphians was blackmailing Podres with this information, and the group may eventually be implicated in the councilman's death, according to the police commander, who spoke on condition of anonymity."

"Has this commander given us any definitive information on Jeanette?" Hansen said.

"Well, Mike, the commander said, and I quote: 'I wouldn't be surprised if the deaths of Miss Deveraux, Mr. Yates, and Mr. Moore are all linked to the Podres shooting.' He wouldn't elaborate, but he did say that an Internal Affairs officer may have been involved in the shootings."

"As a suspect?"

"That's right, Mike. The commander confirmed several minutes ago that an Internal Affairs officer may be implicated in the shootings, and that he has hard evidence to prove that the officer was involved. We are working to find out the identity of the Internal Affairs officer."

"Get back to us if you get anything further, Myung."

"Sure, Mike. And let me take this opportunity to express my heartfelt sympathy to the families of Jeanette Deveraux and Michael Yates. They will be sorely missed."

As Nelson got up and turned off the television, his mind was racing. He knew that the highly placed police source was Sheldon. He just didn't know how to find him.

"Call Radio and have them try to raise Lieutenant Darren

Morgan on the air," Nelson said, switching into high gear. "If he doesn't respond within five minutes, put together a GRM saying that he's wanted for investigation at this time."

"So now we're not keeping it in the department, sir?" the detective said.

"We don't have time for that. I'd rather let the world know what's going on than have his name and description broadcast on television first."

"Yes, sir."

"I also want you to call Homicide," Nelson said, pressing his lips firmly together in a look of pure rage. "Not that Sheldon's going to be there. But when you call, and when he fails to answer, try to raise him on the air, then page him. When he doesn't respond to that, put out a GRM on him, too."

"Yes, sir," the detective said, picking up the phone as it rang.

"One more thing," Nelson said. "Find Ramirez and Hillman, and get them over to the airport as soon as possible."

"There won't be any need to do that," the detective said, hanging up the phone. "That was Ramirez. He's already there."

"What about Hillman?"

"Ramirez said that Hillman was on his way back to the hospital to check on the witness."

"Raise Ramirez on the air and tell him to call here immediately if he finds any new information," Nelson said.

"Yes, sir. Anything else?"

"Yeah. Pray to God we can find Sheldon before he does any more damage."

But Nelson knew that it was probably too late for that.

The policeman guarding Butter's door looked at his watch and wondered when he would be relieved. He had already been there for twelve hours, and the overtime was beginning to look less and less attractive. The only thing he wanted to do was go home, kiss his wife, and lie down for a few minutes.

Getting overtime on a prisoner detail was great, but he needed sleep, too. And at the rate he was going, he wasn't going to get any because he would have to leave the detail and go straight to the district to work his regular shift.

So when the captain walked up and told him that his relief was on the way, he looked up and thanked God.

"I know you're tired, son," Sheldon said. "And I need to talk to Mr. Thomas anyway. So I'll tell you what. I'll take over the detail for you so you can knock off a few minutes early."

"I couldn't let you do that, sir," the officer said, praying that the captain would insist.

"Don't worry. I'm sure a half hour or so won't kill me."

"Are you sure, sir?"

"I'm positive. Go home and get some rest."

"Thank you, sir."

When the officer got on the elevator, Sheldon opened the door and walked into Butter's room. "You've been relieved," he said to the second officer on the detail. "You can go."

The officer didn't have to be told twice. He got up and hustled toward the door. When he left the room, Sheldon locked the door behind him and smiled at the sleeping Butter.

"You've been a bad boy," Sheldon said as he removed his bracelet from his pocket and fastened it around his wrist.

Butter struggled to wake himself as the sound of the strange voice drifted into his consciousness. There was something in the voice that prodded his sleep-numbed mind and told him that he should be afraid. But before he could open his eyes, the voice was there again.

"I know we all do things that we shouldn't," Sheldon said as he walked over to the bed, twisting a silencer onto the end of his gun. "But you broke the rules."

When Butter finally opened his eyes, he had to squint against the sparkle of the heavy gold link bracelet hanging from Sheldon's wrist. When he was able to focus, the blond hair was like a yellow blur framing the cold gray steel of the gun.

Butter had known the number-one rule: You never tell. And even as he had broken it, hoping that he could somehow make his sister proud, Butter knew that he would soon have to pay the price. So when he saw the gun and realized that it was time, he closed his eyes and waited patiently for the bullets to strike his skull. And somewhere, deep down inside, he hoped that his only sister could forgive him for a lifetime of pain.

Sheldon looked down at Butter one last time and calmly pumped two bullets into his bandaged head. Then, as Butter's blood soaked into the pillow, he crept out of the room.

When Reds Hillman walked into the hospital lobby, he could feel that something wasn't right. Everyone there seemed to stare at him, as if they were looking for some untold truth to be revealed. Patients rolled by him in wheelchairs, their faces fixed with blank stares that foretold of things to come. The air, usually antiseptic, was thick with the smell of death.

Yet Hillman knew that this hospital was where he belonged. There was something there that he had to do. He just didn't know what it was.

As he got on the elevator, he felt something pulling him closer to itself, comforting him and filling him with reassurance. And when he got off the elevator at Butter's floor, he knew that he would need all of the strength he gained from that feeling in order to deal with what he saw.

Sheldon was backing out of Butter's room with his back to the elevator, glancing nervously to his left and right. When he turned around, he was face-to-face with Hillman.

Sheldon stood perfectly still, watching for an outward sign of the detective's intentions. Hillman's eyes bored into him, and the whole truth seemed to crawl out from beneath Sheldon's uniform and stand defiantly in the space between them.

Hillman could see the money changing hands, the deals being made, the promises being broken. He could see drugs and expensive cars and political connections. He could see entire communities laid bare before the insatiable greed that fueled Sheldon's entire operation. And he could see himself, fighting a useless battle against corruption.

Hillman reached for his gun. Sheldon pushed him into a gurney. An orderly who had stepped into the hallway was caught between Hillman and the wall, and as Hillman fought to untangle himself, Sheldon disappeared into the stairwell.

Hillman got up, his breath already shortened by the exertion, and drew his gun. Several nurses ducked behind their half-moon-shaped enclosure, and two doctors who had watched the confusion erupt stood with their backs against the wall, pointing to the stairway where Sheldon had run.

Hillman saw the stairwell door closing on its hydraulic hinge. In a matter of seconds, Sheldon would be gone. But Hillman refused to let him walk away without a fight.

As Hillman stepped into the stairwell, a pale, fluorescent light washed over him and gave his face the same surreal, flat texture that it gave to everything else.

He looked up and down the stairs, trying to find some sign of Sheldon. But he didn't hear anything. He didn't see anything, either: only the gray concrete walls and the dark metal of the railings that led from one flight to another.

Something clicked on the stairwell. From the sound of it, the noise had come from one flight below. Hillman crept toward the sound, the soles of his shoes scraping against the rough cement stairs as he descended them. He slipped and grabbed hold of the railing to keep his body from banging against the rock-hard steps, nearly dropping his gun in the process.

When he regained his footing, Hillman gripped his gun in both hands and held it out in front of him, pointing it as if it were some sort of beacon, leading him through the darkness of the moment. His breath came faster, pushing out of his chest like a baby emerging from the womb. He began to sweat, and his clothes clung to his body, restraining him, warning him, pulling him back from the next step.

Hillman peeped around the edge of the railing and something smacked into the bridge of his nose, knocking him backward. His gun flew from his hands, tumbling into the space between the railing and falling four stories to the basement. Instinctively, he swung in the direction of the blow, hitting Sheldon in the groin and knocking his head into the railing.

Sheldon wrapped his arms around Hillman's knees, pulled them together, and wrestled him to the ground. Then he reached into the small of his back and pulled a gun. By the time Hillman made it to his feet, Sheldon had chambered a round.

The last thing Hillman saw was a bright flash of light, exploding in his face like a thousand suns looming over the horizon. And then the feeling washed over him again, pulling him into its bosom, enclosing him in its warmth. He gave himself over to the sensation. He had done all that he could.

He had kept the promise he'd made to himself, to Latoya Thomas, to his badge. He had found Podres's killer. And now, after thirty years and countless nights of sloe gin, sad songs, and dreams, Reds Hillman could finally rest.

Sheldon walked back up the stairs and looked into the faces of the terrified hospital staff. As he made his way to the nurses' station, people backed away from him, their faces twisted into fear-filled grimaces.

"It's all right," he said. "I'm a police officer. Get a doctor down to the stairwell and call 911. Tell them there's an officer down."

As the confused nurses followed his orders, Sheldon went down to the hospital lobby. He took an envelope out of his inside pocket and dropped it into the hospital's mail slot. Inside, there was a detailed explanation of the money-laundering scheme and a contrived plot implicating Morgan as Podres's killer.

When Sheldon was done, he walked out into the parking lot, climbed into a rental car, and set off for somewhere—anywhere except Philadelphia.

Chapter 17

Black and Clarisse boarded the train like they owned it. They had to act that way, because they were running for their lives. If they didn't at least look like they knew what they were doing, the two of them would end up dead.

So when the conductor asked them what section they were looking for, Black jumped right in and told him they were looking for the sleeper compartment. The conductor didn't glance at them twice. He just told them that the sleeper compartment was three cars down.

"What time should we expect the train to leave?" Clarisse asked.

"Well, we're having a little engine trouble, ma'am," the conductor said. "We've got mechanics checking into it now, but we should be under way shortly."

"Thank you," she said, and they moved past him unhurriedly, walking toward the sleeper car as if they belonged there, like their lives had been nothing more than a prelude to that moment.

Clarisse strode in front of Black, leading him to whatever it was that awaited them in that compartment. A trap? Maybe. Freedom? Perhaps. Black couldn't concentrate on that anymore.

Walking through the cars, pulling back the sliding doors, and feeling the dank, cold air brushing against him like cold autumn kisses, he could think of nothing but Clarisse. He watched her walking in front of him, her gait a slight bounce that swayed provocatively, like a pendulum keeping time. He realized for the first time in a long time that something, someone, was beautiful. He watched her and admired her, and the only thing he could think about was how quickly the crack would suck the life from her body. For once, for the first time since he'd been out there, he allowed himself to think of someone else, and that someone was Clarisse.

"Are you okay, Everett?" she asked as she walked into one of the compartments.

"Huh?"

Black looked up and saw that she was sitting on a bunk, watching him with a worried sort of curiosity. He was so absorbed in his thoughts of her that he hadn't even noticed that they weren't in the aisle of the train anymore.

"I asked if you were okay."

"Yeah, I'm cool. I was just thinkin'."

"About what?"

"About you."

"You need to be thinking about something other than me right now."

"Is that what you do?" Black said, staring down at her as he walked over to the bunk.

"What do you mean is that what I do?"

"I mean is that how you deal with all this—by thinkin' about somethin' else?"

"No."

"How do you deal with it then?"

"By thinking about you."

Black looked down at her and he knew that she was telling the truth. There was no reason for her to be there with him. It couldn't have been the money, because there wasn't much left. It couldn't have been the dope. That was almost gone, and they weren't going to get any more until they reached their destination. So there was really only one reason for her to be there. She had to be there for him.

"What you thinkin' about me for?" Black said, a slight smile playing on his lips as he sat down next to her on the bunk.

"Remember what you said in the shower about the first time I walked in Miss Shaw's class wearing that yellow sundress and those black Mary Janes?"

"You mean the first day of school in sixth grade?" Black said, touching her face. "You was the finest thing in there."

She smiled and her eyes lit up, the same way they used to light up when she was a little girl.

"I've been trying to remember if I even saw you that day," she said.

"You had to see me. I had on some Sergios and a sweat-suit jacket with a pair of shell-top Adidas, and—"

"And you were sitting in the back of the class, trying real hard to be a part of that clique."

"What clique?"

"The back-of-the-room clique. The ones who could hardly read and didn't care that they could hardly read. The ones that picked on anybody who answered a math problem."

"Norman and them."

"Why did you want to be like them?"

Black thought back to his childhood, and all of it came rushing back to him, like he was still sitting there in the back of the room, trying desperately to be accepted. He remembered how important it was to be cool, to be down, to be smart, to be a little bit of everything and everybody except himself.

He wasn't a nerd. But he wasn't one of the cool ones, either. He couldn't play sports—not well, anyway. He didn't fight all the time—the truth was, he hated to fight. He wasn't a mack daddy—didn't even know girls had different parts than boys until about the fourth grade. He was just a regular little boy. He liked school, though. He learned pretty early that it wasn't a good idea to tell anybody that. He went to church on Sunday with his family, and in some ways he even liked that, but liking church wasn't something to brag about, either.

Every now and then he would get a girlfriend, but he really didn't know what to do with a girlfriend. So he just coasted along, pretending to know millions of things that he didn't have a clue about.

"I don't know why I wanted to be like them," he finally said, turning away so she wouldn't read the lie in his eyes.

"I remember when you answered that question that nobody else could answer. Remember? Miss Shaw asked if anybody knew the value of pi."

"And I said 3.14. She asked me how I knew that and I said I had read it somewhere."

"She used to always call on you after that."

"And Norm and them stopped hangin' with me after that. They started callin' me brainiac."

"You were."

"I was what?"

"You were probably the smartest kid in the class."

"Yeah, well, look where bein' smart got me."

"Being smart got you me."

"Crack got me you."

Before he knew it, she was swinging at him.

"Why do you always have to try to hurt me, Everett?" she said, punching him in the chest and arms as the tears streamed down her cheeks. "Why can't you just take it for what it's worth?"

Black grabbed her hands and held them together, but not before she had smacked him hard across the face.

"Take what for what it's worth?"

"Take me!" she said. "I'm trying to tell you that I want to be with you. I'm trying to tell you that I know you didn't do anything wrong."

"How you know? For all you know I could be ready to cut your throat right now."

He was angry and he didn't even know why. It was like something inside of him was jumping up and down, demanding that he push her away, although that was the last thing he wanted to do.

"But you're not going to cut my throat," she said. "Not if you're the same little boy who knew the value of pi when nobody else in the class had the slightest idea what the teacher was even talking about."

"That's the problem. I'm not the same little boy. I'm a big boy now. I'm a big boy who's been through more than any boy should ever have to go through."

"Is that why you keep running away from me?"

"No," Black said, sighing impatiently. "I ain't runnin' away from you."

"What are you doing then?"

"I'm tryin' to get you to run away from me. I'm tryin' to help you."

"I don't need your help."

"You need somebody's help! You damn sure ain't tryin' to help yourself."

"I know you're not talking," she said, rolling her eyes. "Look at you."

"That's what I'm trying to tell you, Clarisse! Look at me. Take a good, long look at me and tell me what you see."

She opened her mouth to respond but closed it again after a few seconds and looked down at the edge of the bunk.

"I'll tell you what you see, Clarisse," he said, taking her face in his hands and turning it toward him. "You see a man who walked away from everything because he was too scared to live—a man who refused to love anybody or anything as much as he loved this."

He reached into his pocket and pulled out a cap. Then he pulled the top off of it and poured its contents on the floor.

"You see that?" he said, raising his voice, then lowering it in case someone was listening. "I'll probably be crawlin' for that in a little while. Diggin' in corners like a rat lookin' for crumbs. That's my life now, Clarisse. And I just don't want it to be yours. I hurt enough people already.

"You think I want to be out here like this? You think I like smokin' this shit, hidin' in alleys and sleepin' in abandoned houses just so I can keep on killin' myself? Well, I don't. I stopped likin' it the day I started back."

She looked at him oddly, but said nothing.

"Yeah, I used to do it before," he said, answering the unasked question. "Ended up damn near the same way I am now. No place to live, no job, no money, no life, no hope. No nothin'. But I stopped. I just got tired of it.

"It wasn't like it was no big miracle or anything. I just went through a rehab and stayed clean for a little while. Started goin' to them meetings they be havin', got me a little piece o' job, started stackin' a little bit o' dough, met a girl, and got married."

Her eyes opened wide and she gave him a look that said: Why didn't you tell me? Black just ignored that and kept on talking.

"For a while things was workin' out all right. We had a few arguments here and there, just like anybody else, but we told ourselves everything was cool. When we looked around, it looked like everything was goin' the way it was supposed to. We had a car, a house, we was both workin' and savin' up. But somethin' was missing.

"She didn't want to do the things I wanted her to do for me, and I didn't want to do the things she wanted me to do for her. At first, it was just little things. She didn't want to cook one night or I didn't want to talk one night. But then the little things started gettin' bigger. She didn't want to sleep with me for weeks at a time. I would leave out for work and I wouldn't come home until two days later.

"I'm not sayin' it was all her fault, and I'm not sayin' it was all my fault. I think we was just too different. She wanted to be with me and I just wanted to party. But I always put her first. And I wanted her to do the same thing for me."

Black looked at Clarisse to see her reaction, and she just kept looking over at the corner of the bunk. He knew by the blank look on her face that the things he was saying were hurting her, but he couldn't stop. He had to get it out.

"I always put her first," he said, looking down because he couldn't stand to look at Clarisse. "In everything, even in my thoughts. It wasn't like that for her, though. Not after a while."

Black sighed and tried not to think too hard about the way things were, but it didn't work.

"We stopped talking to each other for a long time before it all ended," he said, the sadness creeping over him as his past came roaring into focus. "We really talked at each other. It was like, when you hit somebody—the way you swing and try to hurt them. That's the way we talked to each other.

"I would call her the worst thing I could think of. Then she would call me the worst thing she could think of. Then I would bring up somethin' from two years ago. Then she would bring up somethin' from three years ago. Then I would say I was leavin'. Then she would cry.

"We'd go through that like every three days, until one day, I told her I was leavin' and she just looked at me. She didn't yell. She didn't cry. She just looked at me real cold and said, 'Go 'head and leave, 'cause I got somebody else anyway.'

"Everything stopped for me when she said that. I didn't know what to say. I didn't know what to do. I just stood there for the longest time, feelin' like I ain't have no reason to live. I wanted to hit her, to just slap her and keep slappin' her until I couldn't anymore. But my hands wouldn't move. My lips wouldn't move. The only thing that moved was my mind.

"I thought of all the nights she wouldn't let me touch her. I thought of all the times she told me she was goin' out with her girlfriends and didn't come home until four in the mornin'. I thought of somebody else touchin' my wife, and somethin' inside me died."

Black was about to say something else, but the words got stuck in his throat. He leaned against Clarisse's shoulder and fought against the pain he felt welling up inside.

"Maybe I deserved that," he said. "I don't know. It ain't like I wasn't cheatin'. But I think it's different for men. We can't forgive like y'all can. We don't look at it like: My woman laid up with the next man. We look at it like somebody took somethin' from us that was ours."

He sat up quickly, pretending he had never lost his composure.

"It was never the same after that," he said. "Even though I told her I forgave her and tried to act like everything was okay, even though she stopped going out with her girlfriends and I stopped staying out all night, it wasn't the same. We slept together, we ate together, we talked to each other, but not about nothin' real. We talked about the weather or the news, or somethin' on television, but never about us.

"We didn't share nothin'. Not dreams, not hopes, nothin'. We just stood around tellin' each other, 'I love you,' knowin' it was a lie. I was so miserable I decided to leave, to start over again with somebody else.

"But the day I came home to tell her that I was leavin', she said she was pregnant. So I kept it to myself, hopin' that ugly feelin' I got every time I thought about her with somebody else would just go away.

"It didn't, though. It got worse. I would look at her sometimes and wonder if the baby was even mine. Jealousy had me crazy. But it wasn't like I could talk to anybody about it. How do you tell somebody you think your woman might be pregnant by somebody else? You don't. You hold it in, and it eats at you. 'Cause it ain't no two ways about it. Either you stay with her and act like it ain't nothin' wrong or you leave.

"So I thought about it for a long time. Sometimes I would sit up all night just thinkin' about it. But you know what? It wasn't never really a question of what I was gon' do. Just like it wasn't never really no question o' whether the baby was mine. I knew that was my baby. But all that other stuff had me messed up. Livin' in a house with somebody you don't trust have you like that. You don't see nothin', so you start makin' up stuff. Then after a while the things you make up start lookin' real. Sometimes it *is* real."

Clarisse looked up from the corner of the bed and stared across the cabin toward the door.

"So was it real?" she asked, interrupting him for the first time.

"The only thing that was real for me was that baby—if that makes any sense to you. So I stayed and I worked and I smiled and I played the happy father until my son was born. And that's when everything fell apart for me. I had stopped goin' to meetings a while back, and the same things that used to keep me up nights before started keepin' me up even more, until one night I just went out to get a blast and I never came back. Two weeks later, my wife filed for divorce."

Clarisse looked at Black. He chuckled. But there was no humor in the laugh, only pain.

"That was six months ago," he said sadly. "The messed-up part about it was, I knew what would happen if I went out to get that blast. I knew I wasn't gon' be able to stop. I knew that, Clarisse. But you know what? I did it anyway. I did it anyway and it ain't a day that goes by when I don't think about it. I wonder what my son looks like now, what his first words were, if he's walking yet. I wonder if he remembers what I look like. I wonder if he'll hate me when he grows up. Some days it eat me up so bad I just wanna go 'head and take myself up outta here."

He climbed down off the bunk and reached across the floor to pick up some of the rocks he had dropped there a few minutes ago. Then he took out his straight shooter and placed the rocks carefully in the stem.

"And the only thing that keep me from doin' it," he said, pulling out a matchbook and desperately tearing off two matches, "is this."

Black lit the crack and pulled the smoke into his lungs, holding it there and looking at Clarisse. Then he released the smoke and watched it swirl in the space between them before it disappeared.

"You don't want me, Clarisse," he said as she watched him with something that looked almost like pity. "My mother don't even want me. She tells everybody I'm dead."

Black uncorked another cap with an intensity born of the desire to forget.

"I might as well be dead," he said, pulling on the straight shooter and blowing more smoke into the air. " 'Cause I'm about as real as that smoke. And I disappear just as fast."

Chapter 18

The sergeant in charge of the dispatcher's section of the Radio Room wasn't one to buck authority. But when he received the call from the Park Avenue Mobile Command Center instructing him to put out a general radio message on two ranking police officers, he had to question it, because he'd never in his five years as a Radio Room supervisor been asked to do such a thing. And if he was going to do something that would ruin his career, he wanted to hear it from the top.

That's what he was trying to explain to the detective on the other end of the line, but the message didn't seem to be getting through.

"Look," he told the detective. "I'm not trying to give you a hard time. I just need to get verification before I do something like that."

"What do you mean you need verification? This is a direct order from the commissioner."

"I just need to talk to the commissioner if he's there."

"Sounds to me like you're refusing an order."

"No disrespect to you, buddy. But I have no idea who you are, you've never been in the Radio Room, and I just need to hear this from Commissioner Nelson."

"Hold on," the detective said, grudgingly handing the phone to the commissioner.

"Nelson here."

The sergeant hesitated when he heard the commissioner's voice, hoping that he wouldn't be disciplined for questioning the order.

"Sir, I understand you want us to put out a GRM indicating that Lieutenant Darren Morgan and Captain Irv Sheldon are wanted for investigation."

"That's correct, Sergeant."

"Sir, I'm sure you understand my hesitation in doing something like that."

"Hesitation?" Nelson said, making the word sound like something foreign. "Sergeant, haven't you been trying to raise both of them on all bands for the last ten minutes?"

"Yes, sir."

"And have either of them responded?"

"No, sir."

"You've also sent cars to deliver messages to both their houses. Is that correct?"

"Yes, sir."

"Did they respond?"

"No, sir."

"Well, Sergeant, I've got some news for you. We have reason to believe that Lieutenant Morgan was involved in three shootings today. We also have reason to believe that Captain Sheldon may have conspired with Lieutenant Morgan and several other people to cause the death of city councilman Johnny Podres."

Nelson stopped long enough to allow his words to sink in.

"Sergeant," Nelson continued, "I want you to know that heads are going to roll when the Podres investigation is over, and I'm sure you don't want to be on the list of people who are heading to the chopping block. Correct?"

"That's correct, sir."

"Then carry out my orders, Sergeant. Don't question them. Don't add or detract from them. Just carry them out. Can you do that, or do I need to personally come down there and see to it that you do?"

"That won't be necessary, sir."

"You have the GRM prepared?"

"Yes, sir."

"Well, read it over the air, Sergeant. And keep reading it every five minutes until we find those two officers. Is that understood?"

"Yes, sir."

"Do you need any more verification, Sergeant?"

"No, sir."

Nelson hung up the phone and the sergeant walked over to the J band console and handed a sheaf of papers to the dispatcher.

"Read this over every band every five minutes until further notice," he said, and walked back to his desk.

The dispatcher read over the GRM and looked at the sergeant, the shock etched on his face like the ridges on a relief map.

"Every five minutes starting when?" the dispatcher said, the puzzlement obvious in his voice.

"Starting now."

The dispatcher hesitated. Then he flipped the switches that would allow the message to go out to every division, pulled down the lever that made the alert tone, and proceeded to read.

Ramirez stood over the body of the slain cameraman, drifting toward his own separate reality, his eyes glazed over as his mind lost itself between the dried rivulets of blood that ran along the man's face. Ramirez thought that if he looked hard enough, the answer to it all would curl out from the bloodstained cheek and touch him. It would whisper in his ear and tell him why Podres had died. And then, somewhere beyond the blood of murdered reporters and the wisdom of old detectives and the deathbed claims of addicts, there would be peace.

The alert tone came over the radio and interrupted Ramirez's thoughts. As the dispatcher began reading the GRM, Ramirez looked up from the cameraman's bloody face and saw a detective from Southwest Division watching him. Their eyes locked, and the two of them exchanged a look that said they wanted the truth to be a lie.

". . . wanted for investigation in connection with three founded shootings at Abbottsford Hospital and Philadelphia International Airport—two males. Number-one male, Lieutenant Darren Morgan, Philadelphia police, Internal Affairs, is a white male, thirty-seven years, six feet tall, 215 pounds, brown hair, brown eyes, bushy mustache. He is wearing a black blazer, a tie, and gray slacks. He is driving an unmarked black Chrysler with a license tag of UJV-342. Number-two male, Captain Irv Sheldon, Philadelphia police, Homicide, is a white male, forty-eight years, five-eleven, 190 pounds, blond hair, blue eyes, clean-shaven. He was last seen wearing a Philadelphia police captain's uniform, but may have changed clothes. Both males should be considered armed and dangerous. Please use extreme caution. This is KGF-587. The time is now 12:45 P.M."

For almost thirty seconds, there was complete silence. But after the silence, the facts poured through Ramirez's mind like floodwater bursting through a ruptured dam of hope. And when it was over, he was shocked, and hurt, and angry. But finally, he was free to face the truth. The career he'd taken so seriously, the police department that he'd loved so much, was peppered with murderous leeches like Sheldon and Morgan.

It hadn't been clear to him before, even as he and Hillman had stood before the commissioner and argued their case. But there it was: the department admitting its guilt, casting the net to catch two of its own, destroying the carefully built illusion of justice for all.

Ramirez didn't speak. Instead, he retreated back into his private crystal ball—the one that lay between the streams of dried blood on the cameraman's face. And as he stared at the dried and cracked maroon flow that had once run through the man's veins, he wondered how much more blood would be shed before it was over.

Just then, a 16th District officer came over the air, breaking the radio silence that had reigned for almost a minute.

"1611."

"1611, proceed," the dispatcher said.

"Could you repeat the tag on that vehicle?"

"Certainly, sir. It's UJV-342."

"Radio, I've got that vehicle, unoccupied, outside 30th Street Station."

"16A," the sergeant chimed in, his siren wailing in the background. "I'm en route. And please advise Amtrak police that Morgan might be at that location."

"Okay, sir."

"I've got to go," Ramirez said, then looked back over at the other detective. "Are you going to handle the scene here?"

"Sure, I can do that."

As Ramirez jumped into his car and drove around the labyrinth that was the airport, he thought of Hillman. He knew that the old man would want him to bring Morgan to justice. And he was going to try to do just that. One way or the other.

Lieutenant Darren Morgan walked into 30th Street Station and headed straight for the locker where he had left his garment bag. When he got to the locker, he started searching through his pockets for the key, grinning to himself because the whole thing reminded him of the way he'd searched his pockets before he shot Jeanette Deveraux.

It wasn't that Morgan thought shooting the reporter was some kind of joke. He didn't really like to kill people. But starting a new life with a couple million after spending fifteen years scratching and clawing in the Philadelphia Police Department was enough to make almost anything funny. At least that's the way Morgan looked at it.

He was still smiling when he found the key. But the smile faded when he realized that someone was standing behind him.

"Excuse me," a female voice said.

Morgan almost pulled his gun. But he was able to regain his composure and turn around with what he hoped was a relaxed look on his face.

"Yes?"

"Can you tell me where the B platform is?"

Morgan took a deep breath and exhaled slowly.

"I don't know, ma'am," he said, the relief showing through in his voice. "But the information desk is right over there. You should ask that gentleman."

“Thank you,” the woman said, and ambled slowly away.

When the woman left, Morgan turned around and leaned against the locker until his heartbeat slowed to its normal pace. Then he opened the locker, pulled out the garment bag, and walked down the steps to the trains.

When he stepped onto the platform, Morgan got on the first train he saw. He thought the sign said ATLANTA, but he couldn’t be sure. Not that it mattered. The train could be going anywhere, as long as it was leaving Philadelphia. He only wished he could catch a plane. There was no need to dwell on that, though, because the bodies of Deveraux and the cameraman weren’t even cold yet, and Morgan needed to avoid the airport at all costs.

“Can I help you, sir?” the conductor said, startling him.

“Huh?”

“Can I help you?” the conductor repeated. “You look kind of lost.”

“Oh,” Morgan said, flipping his badge. “I’m sorry. I’m a police officer on official business and I was just . . . is this the train to Atlanta?”

“Yes, sir, it is.”

“What time does it leave?”

“We were supposed to leave about a half hour ago, but we had some engine trouble,” the conductor said. “Fortunately, the mechanics were able to find the problem and we should be leaving in about ten minutes.”

Morgan looked across the platform at the other track.

“Are there any trains leaving sooner?” he said.

“Not to Atlanta.”

“How about someplace else?”

“No, sir. The next train doesn’t leave for a half hour, and that’s going to—”

"Thank you," Morgan said, cutting him off. "I'll just stay on this one."

The conductor looked at him strangely, then shrugged and walked away. Morgan sat down and tried very hard to relax, but he couldn't. The money in the garment bag wouldn't let him. To make matters worse, there were some kids sitting across the aisle from him throwing cookies and screaming. Their mother was just sitting there, wearing the overwhelmed expression of a parent who has spent too much time in a closed-in area with her children.

Morgan knew that expression. He had worn it for the last fifteen years. It was the look of a prisoner, trapped in the closed-in cell of a dead-end life.

He watched the woman and the children for a few minutes more, then clutched absently at the garment bag, and hoped that money was enough to buy freedom.

Leroy and Pookie lay in the sleeper compartment, draped in the heavy rumble of Leroy's breathing and the noisy whir of the train engines coming to life. Somewhere between those two sounds, Pookie's mind was racing.

She thought of the car crash the night before, and how Leroy had held himself together long enough to get them out of it. She thought of the way his self-assurance had helped to quiet her fears. She thought of the way she'd told herself that she would be willing to follow him anywhere after that, and how right it had felt to make that promise.

But that was then. She wasn't so sure about that promise anymore. Not with the two of them running for their lives, with no idea where they were going or what they would do once they got there. Not with the police chasing them, probably with every intention of settling the case their way, before it ever reached a courtroom.

She couldn't be sure about promises or anything else. But then she looked at Leroy, lying there with his eyes closed, looking so very innocent, like a baby untouched by the world. Looking at him, she could be sure of one thing. She could be sure that she loved him. After all, it felt right when she wrapped herself around him, allowing him to take all that he wanted and giving back all that she could. It felt right when he held her, or when he stood up for her, or when he protected her. There was even something right about the way he scolded her. Of course, it didn't feel as right as it felt when she cursed him out. But that would always feel better than listening to a man, she thought with a smile, no matter who the man happened to be.

For the most part, when she looked at Leroy, or thought of Leroy, she felt like everything was going to be all right. It wasn't like she could ever actually tell him she felt that way. But then, she didn't feel like she should have to tell him. He should have known. If it was right, he should have been able to feel everything that was going on inside her, just like she was able to feel everything that was going on inside him.

He should have been able to feel her uncertainty and her fear. He should have been able to feel how wrong she felt about running away from a murder she didn't commit. As far as Pookie was concerned, just luring Podres into the house didn't make her responsible for his murder. She had no way of knowing the man had a gun, and she had no way of knowing that somebody was going to be killed. All she knew was that the man had money. It hadn't worked out like she planned it, though. And she would just have to accept that.

Pookie dismissed the thought of Podres and allowed her

thoughts to wander, running unchecked until she heard Leroy grunt and mumble something in his sleep. She smiled and watched him turn over, and as she did so, everything Pookie had been thinking in the last five minutes disappeared from her mind like a puff of smoke. Because when Leroy turned over, his pants twisted around his waist and a wad of money rose up to the edge of his pocket. It was just sitting there, like a prize. All she had to do was reach out, and it would be hers.

Like clockwork, Pookie's mind began to click. The same thoughts she'd had before came back in a jumbled mess, twisted and mangled into a mix of rationalism and insanity. She remembered the way Leroy had stuck up for her, but then she remembered the way he had called her everybody's woman. She remembered that she was an accomplice to Podres's murder, but then she remembered that she hadn't actually pulled the trigger. She remembered that she loved Leroy, but then she remembered that he was trying really hard not to love her back. She remembered that she had nowhere to go, but then she remembered how money had always opened doors for her. She remembered how bad things always seemed to happen to her whenever she took somebody's money, but then she remembered her favorite saying and said it aloud.

"This time," she whispered, "it's gon' be different."

With those words reverberating in her mind, Pookie touched Leroy's hair, then ran her hand along the side of his face, then down the center of his torso until she reached the top of his pants. She worked her hand around his waist and with a gentle tug on the edges of about three of the bills, extracted the money from his pocket.

And then she was in the aisle of the train, walking quickly to the next car, whispering to herself that this time, it was going to be different.

• • •

By the time the first 16th District officer walked inside 30th Street Station, Amtrak police had already ceased train operations, radioed Morgan's description to the conductors, and posted every available officer inside the station. SEPTA—the local transit authority that runs trains in and out of 30th Street—sent over a large contingent of police and replaced its trains with buses. The postal police got word of the situation and blocked off the entrance to the main post office across the street.

The result was something just short of bedlam.

Amtrak police were running up and down the steps, trying hard to look like nothing was wrong. SEPTA police were filtering into the station, walking back and forth in groups of three or four. The postal police were changing into riot gear at the main post office across the street. And to make matters worse, Philadelphia police were gathering outside the station like they were preparing to lay siege to the entire block.

To the casual observer, the whole scene probably looked like just what it was—a disaster in the making. With so many police from so many different departments all gathered in one place, there were more than enough bodies to handle whatever resistance Morgan or anyone else was prepared to offer. The only problem was, no one had bothered to organize them under a single command. So everybody was doing the same thing as everybody else, and they just ended up in each other's way.

Amtrak officers asked baggage handlers and clerks and conductors if they had seen anyone matching Morgan's description. When they said no, SEPTA police came through and asked them the same question. When they said no too, Philadelphia police came through and asked the same question.

By the time the police got down to the platform where the

12:15 to Atlanta was waiting, even a fool could see that something was wrong. People gathered at the windows of the train, watching the officers walk back and forth on the platform. But when they asked the conductors what the problem was, they were told that someone had lost a child.

The conductors had been instructed to say that until the Amtrak police could figure out the safest way to evacuate the trains without risking Morgan's escape. But by the time they decided that the safest thing to do was to post officers in each car and evacuate the trains one car at a time, it was too late.

Morgan was up and running.

He spotted the police milling around on the platform and immediately began to move through the aisle of the train, hoping to lose himself in the crowd. His mind was racing, frantically searching for a way out. But every time he thought he had figured out something, reality crept in and told him in no uncertain terms that it could never work. Still, he kept moving.

He reached the end of the car and tried the door to the bathroom. It was locked. He walked through to the next car, willing his legs to move faster. They wouldn't. He pushed through the aisles and strained to keep from knocking people over. Then he clutched his garment bag and stood behind a group of people who were gathered at the window of the train.

As Morgan stood there, he removed his jacket and laid it on the seat in front of him, hoping that the absence of the jacket would throw everyone off just enough to allow him to walk out of the car and the station unchallenged. He leisurely removed his shirt from his pants to cover the gun he had tucked in the small of his back. Then he took a deep breath, backed away from the crowd, and started toward the end of the car, angling for the bathroom door. When he tried the door, it was locked.

Morgan held back the curses he felt rising in his throat, then reached for the door to walk through to the next car. The door opened before he could turn the handle. When he looked up, he was staring into the eyes of the same man he had talked to earlier—the conductor who had told him there wouldn't be anything leaving for the next half hour.

For a moment, their eyes locked. Morgan didn't see anything there. Not fear, not recognition, just an irritated look that told him the conductor wanted to get by.

"I thought you said we'd be leaving in a few minutes," Morgan said, checking to see if the other man remembered him.

"Excuse me?" the conductor said, trying to sound confused.

"Didn't you . . . never mind. I'll just get out of your way."

Morgan walked through to the next car just as an Amtrak policeman was walking through the door at the far end. The conductor, praying that the man he knew to be wanted by the police wouldn't open fire, turned around at the last second and pointed at Morgan. Too late, the Amtrak officer reached for his gun.

Morgan released his garment bag, dropped to one knee, pulled the gun from the small of his back, and squeezed off a round, hitting the officer in the shoulder and knocking the gun from his hand. As Morgan picked up his garment bag and ran toward the end of the train, Pookie came through the same door as the Amtrak policeman, walking toward Morgan.

She looked down and saw the policeman on the floor. Then she looked up and saw Morgan's gun. The first thing she thought about was the money. She couldn't let the man with the gun get the money because this time, it was going to be different. This time, she was going to make a better life for herself. She was going to stop living the way she had been living for the past year and a half. She was going to get herself together. She was going to start all over. And the only thing that was going to allow her to do that was the money.

She took a step backward and reached into her pocket to make sure the money was still there. Morgan thought she was reaching for a gun. She saw him taking aim and started to yell something. But before Pookie could take another step or say another word, Morgan squeezed off two rounds, hitting her square in the chest with each shot.

The impact of the bullets lifted Pookie's feet from the floor and tossed her backward like a rag doll. When she landed, the breath rushed from her mouth in a great *whoosh,* like the sound of a bat being swung mightily at the air. Her head bounced against the floor of the train and her eyes lost their focus. The only thing she saw was the blur that was Morgan stepping over her on his way to the next car.

As Pookie lay bleeding, the life ebbing from her body in a slow and steady stream, she tried to tighten her grip around the money, holding on to it like some strange talisman. And then she mouthed Leroy's name. It was the one word that she knew could bring her peace.

Leroy thought he was dreaming when he heard the gunshots. He was at the back door of the house again, and Rock and Butter were struggling with Podres. There was the first shot, then three more shots. And then, as often happens in dreams, everything split into fragments.

People running down the steps and out the back door. Butter and Rock scuffling to remove the money and drugs from the dead man's pockets. Pookie crying. Leroy hiding. Then something that hadn't been there before—the sound of Pookie calling his name.

Leroy's eyes flew open. He looked around him and saw that Pookie was gone. Then, as an afterthought, he felt his pocket and saw that the money was gone. Enraged, he looked out into the aisle of the train.

A woman was screaming from the next car, repeating over and over again, "He shot her! Oh God, he shot her!"

Others followed the woman, running toward the back of the train and trying to squeeze out from between the cars. Leroy wondered why they didn't just use the doors. And when he looked at the doors in the sleeper car he saw why. They were closed.

Dazed, he started to walk toward the car the people were running from, the eerie sound of Pookie calling his name repeating itself in his mind like a forbidden chant. He didn't know what he was walking to, but he did know what he was walking to. He didn't know why he was going there, but he did know why he was going there. It was the strangest feeling he'd ever had. He was like a ghost, passing through the world of the living on his journey to the world of the dead.

"Go back," a man warned him. "He's got a gun up there."

Leroy kept going, pulled toward his destiny by an unseen force, drawn to it like waves are drawn to moonbeams. He kept going and he knew before he got there what he would see. But knowing wasn't enough. He had to see her, to feel her. Leroy opened the door, and his legs almost gave out at the sight of her.

"Pooookie!" he screamed.

She looked up at him, but she couldn't see his face. In fact, she couldn't see anything. She could only hear a voice, the same sweet voice she had come to know so well, the voice that she would follow to the ends of the earth.

"Leroy," she said, her weak voice fading with each breath.

"Ssshhh." Leroy reached down to pick her up. "Don't talk, baby. I got you."

The injured Amtrak officer lay a few feet away, taking in the exchange and inching toward the gun that had been knocked from his hand by the impact of Morgan's bullet.

"It's gon' be different this time?" Pookie said, the blood staining Leroy's arms as he lifted her.

"Yeah, baby," Leroy said, a single tear rolling down his cheek as he watched her life pour out in a crimson rush. "It'll be different."

Pookie pulled Leroy's face down to hers, and with lips that grew colder with each passing second, she kissed him. The kiss said everything she couldn't. It was an apology, and a promise, and a symbol, and a gift. It was all she had left to give.

"I love you, Leroy," she said softly.

And then she was gone.

"I love you, too," he said, another tear rolling slowly behind the first.

Leroy placed her in a seat and took the money from her hand. He looked at her once more, then started to walk toward the other end of the car.

"Leroy Johnson!" a voice called.

Leroy turned around and saw the injured Amtrak police officer aiming a gun at him. Then he looked at the end of the car and saw a group of policemen gathering at the door, walking through the opening slowly as if they were expecting him to make a sudden move.

"Give it up, Leroy!" an officer shouted.

For a moment, Leroy thought of doing just that. But then he looked at Pookie, lying there wrapped in a strange sort of peace he'd never seen before.

"Turn around slowly and put your hands in the air!" another officer called out.

Leroy heard the voice, but he didn't hear it. He could only think of Pookie. He could only hear her dying voice whispering, "I love you." He could only feel her lips clinging to his. He could only see her peace.

He looked at her again, and he knew what he had to do.

"It's gon' be different this time, Pookie," he mumbled.

"Stop!" an officer screamed from behind him.

Leroy ignored him and ran toward the Amtrak officer who lay on the floor. The officer shot once, missing badly. He shot again, and hit Leroy in the groin. He fired once more, and the top of Leroy's head seemed to explode.

When Leroy finally stumbled and fell, he landed right in front of the officer. And the final sensation he felt before drifting away in death was something he'd never felt in life. Peace.

Black had never seen Clarisse cry before, not even as a child. But she was crying then, each tear punctuating the sound of the gunshots and the screams of the people running by in a panic.

She cried because they both knew what those sounds meant. Neither she nor Black had to say it aloud. Leroy, or Pookie, or both, had been caught. And now the police were looking for the two of them.

Black looked out into the aisle of the train and saw police combing the cars, looking at each person, opening the door to each compartment, searching as if they knew what they were looking for. When they got closer to the sleeper compartment, Black slipped back behind the door and tried to think. Clarisse sat down on the bunk behind him and cried.

"Look, Clarisse," he said. "You gotta stop cryin'. We ain't got time for that."

She cried harder. Black looked out the window and saw police crowding the platform. Then he heard them coming closer to their compartment and he almost started crying, too.

"I gotta go," Clarisse said, lunging for the door.

Black reached out and tried to grab her, but she was out of the compartment and into the aisle before he could stop her. The next thing he heard was a man calling out to Clarisse and footsteps running past their compartment. From the sound of it, she had panicked and run away.

It was all the diversion Black needed.

He came out of the door and started to walk the other way, hoping they wouldn't hurt her and trying hard not to care. He reached the end of the car and was about to climb out from between the space leading to the next car before he heard a gunshot and the sound of Clarisse screaming for someone to stop. When he heard her voice, something inside of him clicked. It may have been the beginnings of a conscience, but he couldn't really say for sure. All he knew at that moment was that he could never go on knowing that he had let something happen to Clarisse because of him.

He stared at the end of the platform, toward the sound of Clarisse's voice. It didn't take long to spot her. A white man with brown hair was holding her by the neck and walking backward toward the steps that led to ground level, above the train platforms. The man was carrying a bag and favoring his right leg. He looked like he might have been shot.

"I'll kill her," he said, sounding desperate. "If I don't make it outta here, she dies."

Black started toward the man who was dragging Clarisse, then stopped and looked around, trying not to look as confused as he felt. Not that there was any question as to what he should have done. He should have turned his back and walked away from it all. He should have closed his ears to the sound of Clarisse's cries and opened his eyes to reality. He should have run away. But he couldn't.

Police were starting to gather on the platform across from the one where he stood, and others were coming off the train. Black couldn't see them, but he knew there had to be some police sharpshooters crouching somewhere, waiting for just the right shot at the man with the bag. For all Black knew, they could've been crouching and waiting for just the right shot at him.

"I'll kill her," the man said, swinging Clarisse from one side of his body to the other, making himself a more difficult target.

"Put the gun down, Morgan," a cop with a megaphone said from somewhere on the platform. "Let the woman go and we can talk."

The man with the gun laughed—a squealing, strangled sound that was probably more from pain than from amusement. The cop with the megaphone said something else and the man laughed again. But even as he laughed, he kept moving toward the steps at the end of the platform, dragging Clarisse along with him.

The closer they came to Black, the more muddled his thoughts became. He stood there, unable to move, and waited for something, for anything.

"Black," a voice said from behind him.

He looked up and saw a Puerto Rican detective he hadn't seen before. The detective was looking at a picture and comparing it to Black's clean-shaven face. When he saw that it was him, the detective started to walk slowly down the steps and reached into his pocket.

"Black, I don't want you to run," he said, holding his hands up in a gesture almost like surrender. "I know you didn't shoot Podres."

Black almost believed him.

Before the detective could make it down the steps, Black started to back away from him. The detective started to walk faster. That was all Black needed to see.

Black ran toward the other end of the platform, listening as the detective shouted something that he couldn't quite make out. He ran and he watched as signs and lights and benches and people shot past him in an unending spectrum of color and sound. He almost ran into a pole, then weaved toward the edge of the platform, nearly falling down onto the track. He hopped on one foot, darting back toward the center of the platform. Then he straightened out his path and ran, faster still, toward an impossible escape.

Everyone, it seemed, was watching him. The police who had been focusing on the man holding Clarisse were now focused on Black. The people who had been rushing toward the steps slowed down to watch the chase. The people who were still on the Atlanta train crowded against the windows, scuffling to get a view of the platform. And the detective ran relentlessly behind him, yelling for Black to do something he must have known he would never do.

"Stop!" the detective shouted.

Black ignored the detective like he was his mother, telling him to stop hanging with the guys on the corner.

"Stop, Black!" he said, his voice fading as his footsteps trailed in the distance.

Black pretended not to hear him, like he was his teacher, telling him to stop talking in class. Or his wife, begging him to stop neglecting her. Or his father, telling him to stop wasting his life. Or his son, begging him to stop ignoring him.

Black couldn't stop. He clung to the illusion of escape like a freezing man clings to the fading embers of a dying fire. He clung to it because he knew it would destroy him. And somewhere down deep, he wanted to be destroyed. Black clung to it because it was the easy way out. Because it was the only way out. He clung to it and prayed that there would be no more swirling clouds and crackling illusions on the other side.

Black turned his head in midstride to see if anyone else had joined the chase. They hadn't. Everyone was just watching, standing there waiting for the inevitable. When he turned back around, he saw why.

The man who was holding Clarisse was still backing up, angling toward the middle of the platform, and Black was running toward him on a collision course. By the time Black tried to swerve, it was too late. He had already run into him.

From that point on, nothing felt real.

Black saw the man's mouth open wide and watched his eyes squeeze shut as he crumpled to the ground grasping helplessly at his leg. He saw the man's bag hit the ground and fall open, and watched as stacks of money tumbled out onto the platform. Black saw Clarisse's eyes focus on someone behind him as she raised her hands to her mouth and turned away. He saw the police at the end of the platform raise their weapons and take aim. He saw the light from the midday sun, creeping in from the open end of the train shed and reflecting brilliantly off the man's gun as it skidded toward the edge of the platform.

With all Black saw, that was the only sound he heard: the gun clattering against the cold concrete, its echoes ringing hollow like church bells on a Sunday afternoon. He couldn't hear the man scuffling his way across the platform as he got up and hobbled toward the gun. He couldn't hear the detective running toward them and yelling for the police to hold their fire. He couldn't hear Clarisse crying and begging for him to get down. He only heard the gun skipping across the platform.

Black hesitated, and then reached for the gun. He didn't know what he thought he was going to do. He didn't know what he thought, period. His mind was in another place, filled with writhing, snakelike images that swirled through his head like the cream-colored cloud he'd seen so many times against the glass. There was no today, no yesterday, no tomorrow. There was just the same cloud he had always chased: the one that made something inside of him kneel down and surrender. Only this time, he thought, there would be no surrender. Because this time, he was going to fight against it. If only he could reach the gun.

The man suddenly lunged. Shots rang out. Blood splattered from the man's arm, from his chest, and from his face. He fell down and Black made a final, desperate grab. As he did so, he felt searing heat burning violently against his leg, then a sharp, cutting pain in the middle of his back. And then nothing.

Black fell down, unable to move, and looked into the dead man's face, his eyes lingering on the blood that ran against the man's cheek. The man somehow reminded him of Podres, though Black had never seen Podres before. And then, in the crack-depleted cauldron that was Black's mind, the man became Podres, and this was Black's final chance to explain.

Black strained his eyes and willed them to focus, but they wouldn't. He tried again, but his eyesight was fading like the puffs of creamy smoke that had brought him to that place.

"I didn't kill you," Black said, the words rushing out in a single breath.

But somehow, he knew that wasn't enough. He knew that it would never be enough.

Chapter 19

When Black finished telling his story, he sat there, handcuffed, looking across the table at his lawyer and waiting for him to say something. But as the lawyer turned off the tape recorder and stumped his last cigarette, they both knew that there was nothing left to say.

The whole thing seemed like something from another life. The train station didn't seem real anymore. Neither did Pookie or Leroy. Neither did Black, for that matter. The bullet in his back had taken reality away and left him an empty shell, slouched against the plastic and metal confines of a prison within a prison—rolling up and down like a shrunken ghost.

Black had spent the past year in the prison library, reading anything and everything he could get his hands on concerning his case. And nobody ever bothered him, because they all felt sorry for the brother in the wheelchair.

But none of that mattered when the case went to trial. The district attorney knew that Black was the Commonwealth's last chance to secure a conviction in the murder of Johnny Podres. So she used the only thing she could to link him to the crime—the seven hundred dollars the police found in the suit jacket he was wearing when they arrested him at the train station.

The prosecutor set the tone for the trial in her opening statement, when she held up a plastic bag filled with the money and drugs Black had had in his possession at the time of his arrest.

"Johnny Podres was not killed as the result of some wild conspiracy," she said, twisting the bag so everyone in the room could see it. "No. Johnny Podres—a man who spent twenty years speaking out for all of us against drugs, crime, and corruption—was killed for this."

She emptied the contents of the bag onto a table and paused to look into the face of each juror as she picked up a cap that had fallen to the floor.

"Whatever conspiracy caused Johnny Podres to be murdered was as small as the rocks of crack cocaine that Mr. Jackson bought with the councilman's blood," she said, holding the cap at eye level. "It was a conspiracy fueled by the addiction that whispered in the defendant's ear; a conspiracy that convinced Mr. Jackson to join Leroy Johnson and Patricia Oaks to destroy a twenty-year legacy of hope."

She walked toward Black with the cap in her hand, drilling her eyes into his face as she spoke.

"While Mr. Johnson and Miss Oaks aren't here with us to be tried for their crime, Samuel Jackson is. And so is his coconspirator."

She slammed the cap onto the table in front of Black.

"They're both guilty of murder in the first degree."

When the district attorney took her seat, Black's lawyer looked at him with a troubled expression, then got up and recounted the story Black had told him just two days before. He was nervous, he was stumbling, he was constantly referring to his notes. And he was well on his way to losing the contest before it even began. When he sat down, exhausted and covered with a thin layer of sweat, the prosecution called its first witness.

Eldridge Scott hobbled to the stand, shuffling his feet behind an aluminum walker. It had only been a year since the murder. But Eldridge Scott had aged a lifetime.

His frail body was small and withered. His hands looked like the gnarled branches of an oak tree. And his watery eyes were hidden behind the forgotten tears of years gone by.

"Mr. Scott," the prosecutor said, after she'd given the jury ample time to develop compassion for the sickly old man. "Do you know the defendant?"

"I used to see him visiting our neighbor—well, more like our adopted granddaughter—Clarisse Williams."

"And did she ever introduce you to the defendant?"

"No."

"Was that unusual?"

"If we was just neighbors it wouldn't be unusual. But we practically raised Clarisse. She was pretty young when her parents died, and we watched out for her, tried to make sure she didn't get mixed up in a bunch of foolishness. We even helped with her tuition when she went to nursin' school."

"Mr. Scott, did Miss Williams change when she began to spend time with Mr. Jackson?"

"Objection," the defense lawyer said. "Changes in Miss Williams's behavior are irrelevant."

"Your honor," the prosecutor said, "the changes in Miss Williams's behavior speak to motive, which in this case is the defendant's addiction."

"I'll allow it. Please answer the question, Mr. Scott."

Eldridge Scott turned to face Black, his hand shaking violently as he extended an accusatory finger toward the defense table.

"He dragged Clarisse down. It was like he sucked the life right out of her; sucked her dry just as sure as he sucked the smoke outta that pipe."

The old man lowered his trembling finger and slowly shook his head, as if the memory were too much to bear.

"It wasn't just the way her body wasted away," he said. "It was the way her spirit died. He killed Clarisse's spirit."

One by one, the jurors began to look at Black. He tried not to show any emotion, but it was hard for him not to feel a sense of loss when he thought of Clarisse. He had been her example. He had shown her how to smoke crack. He had watched as she had changed from a proud black queen to a frightened and hopeless addict. And he hadn't tried to stop it.

He sat there wishing that he hadn't dragged her down the same path that had destroyed him. If only he could see her again, he thought, things would be different. He shut his eyes and tried to visualize her. But before her image could form itself in his mind, the prosecutor asked the next question.

"Did you see Miss Williams with the defendant on the night of the shooting?" she said.

"No," Eldridge Scott said. "But I heard him in her house. He was tellin' her to shut up. Then I heard a lot of banging and Clarisse yelled, 'Oh my God!' I called the police and, sure 'nuff, him and them other two was in there with her. But they left before the police came."

"And what happened after the police discovered that the suspects had been at Clarisse's house?"

"They called me and I gave them a description of Clarisse's car. Next thing I know, all these people was dead and Clarisse was on the news and they was sayin' she had been kidnapped and she wasn't gon' be charged."

"Have you heard from Miss Williams since the night of the shooting?"

"We waited for her to come home," Eldridge said. "When she didn't, we thought she might call us. But she never did. She just disappeared. So we started spendin' our days tryin' not to talk about how much we missed her. But after while, my wife couldn't live like that no more. She couldn't live not knowin' what happened to Clarisse."

Black couldn't bear to look at the hurt in the old man's eyes anymore, so he turned away.

"I buried my wife two weeks ago," Eldridge Scott said as silence enveloped the room. "Now I don't have nobody. Not Clarisse. Not my wife. I guess I'll be gone pretty soon, too. But I promised myself I wouldn't die until I got a chance to see this boy pay for what he done to my family."

Scott turned back to the defense table and began to lift himself up from the witness stand.

"If Clarisse don't turn up alive," he said, struggling to stand up, "I'm gon' see you in hell, boy. One way or another, I'm gon' see you in hell."

The defense attorney didn't cross-examine Eldridge Scott. It was better to get him off the stand and away from the jury as soon as possible.

But the Commonwealth's next witness had nearly the same effect on the twelve people who had assembled to decide his client's fate. She made them hate him.

Viola Green was the neighbor who said she'd seen Leroy going into the house seconds before the shots were fired. She later amended the statement to say that she'd seen both

Black and Leroy going into the house. When the district attorney asked her why she hadn't mentioned Black in her first statement, Mrs. Green took a deep breath and explained.

"When you've lived in a home for fifty years, paid for it with the sweat of your brow just so you could have something to pass on to your grandchildren, a little piece of you dies when you watch the neighborhood fade away."

"Objection, Your Honor," the defense lawyer said. "Irrelevant."

"Your Honor," the prosecutor said, "this testimony goes to the state of mind of the witness at the time of the shooting."

The judge's answer was immediate. "I'll allow it. Please continue, Mrs. Green."

"Well, like I was saying, when your neighbors die, nobody buys the house because the neighbors that died the year before couldn't sell their house. And before you know it, the property taxes pile up and the house is fallin' down, and nobody wants to pay what it takes to fix it. Not in that neighborhood, they don't.

"So instead of children playin', you got drug addicts runnin' in and out of every abandoned house on the block. And then they in the house next door. And you go to sleep every night prayin' and askin' Jesus to keep you out of harm's way just one more time. So when somethin' like this happens, you just so afraid that sometimes it takes a minute to get it together. Now, I know I didn't say it the first time, because I guess I was just in shock. But that boy was there that night. I know he was there because I saw him."

"Thank you, Mrs. Green," the prosecutor said. "Your witness."

When Black looked at the jurors, they were all glaring at him, like he was solely responsible for destroying the dreams of people like Mrs. Green. But when his lawyer got up to cross-examine, he began with a very simple question.

"How old are you, Mrs. Green?"

"I'm seventy years old."

"I see. And do you wear your glasses all the time?" he said, indicating the thick bifocals that framed her eyes.

"Yes, I do."

"Were you wearing them the night that you believe you saw my client outside the house?"

"No. I was sleep and I got out my bed and looked out the window, because they was makin' more noise than they usually do on Sunday."

"Mrs. Green," the lawyer said, "how far is it from your window to that house?"

"About forty or fifty feet."

"Would you agree that the jury box is about twenty feet away from where you're sitting?"

"Yes."

"Please take off your glasses."

She pulled her glasses from her face and let them dangle from the chain around her neck.

"Thank you, ma'am. Now, would you please describe the fifth juror from the right in the second row. What is that person wearing and what do they look like?"

Mrs. Green stumbled through a description. She got more than one detail wrong, and even described the juror, who was a woman, as a man.

"Let the record reflect that Mrs. Green has identified a female juror wearing a gray dress as a male juror wearing a blue suit. Thank you, Mrs. Green. You've been most helpful."

That was the brightest moment for the defense.

Over the next day, the prosecutor brought in several crack addicts who swore that they had seen Black at the scene of the shooting. None of them came across as credible.

She also brought in the detectives who'd answered the call at Clarisse's house. They testified that they had seen the suspects leaving the block in Clarisse's car, dressed as women.

The Commonwealth's final witness—the 6th District officer who'd given the suspects directions to I-76—corroborated the detectives' testimony. He said that the suspects had intentionally and convincingly disguised themselves as women in an effort to elude the police.

On cross-examination, Black's lawyer asked the officer if he'd ever known people to act out strange sexual fantasies while using drugs.

"I don't know anything about what people do when they use drugs," the officer said. "I'm not in Narcotics."

"Of course you're not in Narcotics," the lawyer said. "Forgive me for that oversight. But is it a fact, or an assumption on your part, that my client dressed as a woman on the night of Podres's murder solely to avoid the police?"

"It's an assumption, but—"

"If they were trying to elude police, why didn't they run away from you when you approached them?"

The officer thought about it before he answered. "I don't know."

"Thank you. No further questions."

The prosecution rested its case without calling any of the witnesses they knew would mention Captain Sheldon. After all, Sheldon was long gone, disappeared with an estimated $5 million in stolen money. And if it was at all possible, the district attorney wanted to keep Sheldon's and Morgan's names off the minds of the jurors.

Black's lawyer knew that. So he began his case by calling Latoya Thomas to the stand.

"Miss Thomas, what were you doing on the morning of September 24, 1992?"

"I was at Abbottsford Hospital, visiting my brother, Darnell Thomas, who had been burned in a car accident the night before. My brother is—was—a crack addict who was in the house when Mr. Podres was murdered."

"And what happened during this visit?"

"Detective Hillman came to the hospital to interrogate my brother," she said. "I informed him that I would be representing my brother and I taped the interrogation."

"What did your brother say during this interrogation?"

"He said that a white man killed Johnny Podres—a tall white man with blond hair, blue eyes, wearing a white shirt, black pants, and a heavy gold link bracelet."

The spectators began to murmur as her words floated up from the witness stand and burst like a bubble against the ceiling.

"Did he name a person who might have matched that description?"

"No. But the person he was referring to was Captain Irv—"

"Objection," the prosecutor said. "Conjecture."

"Sustained."

The defense lawyer immediately asked his next question.

"What happened to the tape of the interrogation, Miss Thomas?"

"I gave it to a reporter named Henry Moore right after the interrogation, and Mr. Moore was killed. My brother was—"

"Objection. Mr. Moore's death is not germane to these proceedings."

"Sustained. Please answer the question, Miss Thomas. What happened to the tape?"

She paused and looked over at Black with an apology lingering in her eyes. "I gave it to Henry Moore. I don't know what happened after that."

"Thank you," the lawyer said, ending his questioning before it did any further damage. "Your witness."

The district attorney walked up to the witness stand and said what everyone else must have thought.

"I'm sure you're aware that Detective Hillman is dead, Miss Thomas."

"Yes, I know that."

"Was there another detective present for this interrogation? Someone who could corroborate your story?"

"There was, but he left the room right before Darnell started talking. And by the time he came back, the nurse was telling us that we had to leave."

"So, you're telling this court that the only two people to hear your brother make these claims were you and Detective Hillman."

"Yes."

"And there was a tape of this interrogation with your brother, who—and I mean no offense by this—was not a very credible witness to begin with. But you don't have the tape and you haven't seen the tape since you gave it to Mr. Moore."

"That's correct, but—"

"How convenient. And how utterly believable. No further questions."

As Latoya Thomas stepped down, the judge called a recess and said that the trial would resume at one P.M. that afternoon.

Black sat in his wheelchair, watching the jury file out and wondering if they would ever hear the entire truth.

Lieutenant Jorge Ramirez was the best hope for the defense. The Commonwealth hadn't sought his testimony because everyone knew that he blamed Sheldon for the councilman's death.

When Black's lawyer called Ramirez to the stand, he asked a question that would allow him to convey that sense of blame to the jury.

"If you would, Lieutenant, please tell us who headed the Homicide Division during the investigation into the death of city councilman Johnny Podres."

"Captain Irv Sheldon. He was commanding officer at the time."

"Did Captain Sheldon carry out his duties effectively during that investigation?"

"Objection, Your Honor," the prosecutor said. "Calls for an opinion."

"Your Honor, I'm merely trying to establish whether there was a thorough investigation into the shooting. Lieutenant Ramirez was the lead investigator. Who better to establish that fact than him?"

"I'm going to allow it. Answer the question, Lieutenant."

"No, Captain Sheldon didn't carry out his duties effectively, because he was very singular in his approach to the Podres shooting," Ramirez said. "He told me that the suspects were our best chance for a conviction in this case, as if he were saying that we needed to bring them in whether or not they were guilty of the crime."

"Objection," the prosecutor said. "Conjecture."

"Sustained."

"What, if anything, did the captain do that was detrimental to the progress of the investigation?" the defense lawyer said.

Ramirez took a few seconds to think about his answer.

"Captain Sheldon urged me to hide the fact that we'd conducted what turned out to be an illegal search. He was also very adamant about not pursuing a kidnapping charge against the suspects because he didn't want the FBI to become involved in the investigation. Then, after Detective Hillman spoke with an eyewitness who described Podres's killer as a man fitting the captain's description—"

"Objection," the prosecutor said, jumping out of her seat. "Captain Sheldon is not on trial here."

"Your Honor," Black's lawyer said, "Lieutenant Ramirez is merely recounting the events as they occurred. I believe he will testify that Captain Sheldon was fixated on my client as a suspect, because the captain believed that—"

"Your honor, the defense is putting words in the mouth of the witness!" the prosecutor said.

As Ramirez listened to the attorneys, he was reminded of the way Sheldon had dressed his deceptions as truth. He thought of the people who had paid with their lives so that Sheldon and Morgan could break the very laws they were sworn to uphold. He thought of how Reds Hillman had stood for the truth, only to be struck down for a lie.

Ramirez took it all in and mourned the illusions that had been shattered, the realities that had been unearthed, the never-ending game that would always protect the Sheldons of the world. He took it in and was consumed by a fiery anger that filled him to overflowing.

As the judge overruled the prosecutor's objection and the defense lawyer approached the witness stand and repeated his question, Ramirez knew that he couldn't leave the courtroom without revealing the truth he'd come there to tell.

"Lieutenant Ramirez?"

Ramirez's eyes snapped forward as the lawyer's voice pulled him from his reverie.

"I ask again, Lieutenant, what, if anything, did Captain Sheldon do that was detrimental to the investigation?"

Ramirez took a moment to gather himself, then answered the question.

"Captain Sheldon went AWOL and disappeared from the Command Center."

"And was Captain Sheldon seen or heard from again?"

"Five witnesses at Abbottsford Hospital said they saw a man fitting the captain's description go into Darnell Thomas's room, then come out of that room and struggle with Detective Hillman. When officers came to investigate, they found that the witness and Detective Hillman were both dead, with gunshot wounds to the head."

"Objection," the prosecutor said, jumping from her seat.

"On what grounds?" the judge said.

"I withdraw the question and I have nothing further for this witness," the defense attorney said before the prosecutor could explain her objection.

But Ramirez couldn't hear the lawyers anymore. The only thing he heard was the truth ringing in his ears. So he kept talking.

"Captain Sheldon killed Johnny Podres because the councilman wouldn't give in to his attempt to blackmail him."

The judge banged his gavel. "That's enough, Lieutenant! You may step down!"

But even as the sound of the gavel reverberated throughout the courtroom, Ramirez's voice kept getting louder.

"Sheldon tried to pin the murder on Mr. Jackson and the others because he believed they would be easy to convict," he said.

"Lieutenant, I'm going to hold you in contempt if you don't stop this right now!" the judge warned, banging his gavel again.

Ramirez began to yell. "Captain Irv Sheldon murdered Johnny Podres—not the man on trial here!"

The judge stood up and called out to the bailiff and the sheriff's deputies who stood in the back of the room. "Remove him from my courtroom!"

The deputies approached Ramirez and gestured for him to step down. He looked at both of them, then looked up at the judge, and he knew that he had probably done more harm than good. But it was off of him. The truth had been told and they could do with it what they liked.

"I'm holding this witness in contempt," the judge said, continuing to bang his gavel as the courtroom collapsed into a den of confusion.

The deputies escorted a struggling Lieutenant Ramirez from the witness stand.

"Take him to the holding cell!" the judge yelled over the growing din.

Some of the courtroom spectators rose from their seats to get a better look as the deputies led Ramirez away.

The judge kept banging the gavel in an effort to restore order, but it was useless.

As Ramirez walked out of the room, he could hear the judge's decree: "The jury will disregard Lieutenant Ramirez's comments and his entire testimony will be stricken from the record. This court is in recess until eight A.M. tomorrow morning."

But Ramirez knew, even as he was forced into the holding

cell, that no judge on earth could ever kill truth, because truth always found a way to resurrect itself.

The next morning, when the judge called a five-minute recess and a few people walked out into the hall to stretch their legs, Black's lawyer turned to him and looked him in the eye.

"I've done the best I can for you, Samuel," he said. "I hope you know that."

Black couldn't deny that the lawyer had exceeded his expectations. Usually, court-appointed lawyers provided shoddy representation. But this lawyer had done all that he could to represent his client well.

"I know you tried," Black said. "I appreciate that."

"I didn't want Lieutenant Ramirez to lose control up there," the lawyer said, shaking his head. "And frankly, I don't know how the jury's going to take that. But the bottom line is, you might have about a fifty-fifty chance at acquittal, if that."

He paused to give Black a chance to weigh that statement.

"This is the time in a trial when the defense has two choices," the lawyer said. "Either we put you on the stand and take the chance of having the prosecutor portray you as a career criminal, or we rest our case and hope that somewhere along the way we created enough doubt to convince the jury of your innocence."

"But I *am* innocent," Black said. "It don't matter how the district attorney tries to make me look. That don't turn a lie into the truth."

"Oh, but it does matter. Because truth is what those twelve people say it is. It's not about what you did or didn't do, Samuel. It's about what they believe. And I don't want to see you risk your life to try to change that."

Black was quiet for a moment, reflecting on his lawyer's words. When he spoke, it was with a finality that belied his uncertainty.

"I spent a lotta years riskin' my life," he said slowly. "Livin' in the street, smokin' crack, takin' things from people. I risked my life for next to nothin'. But now I'm riskin' it for a lot more than that. And this time, I think it's worth the risk."

The lawyer was silent, knowing that his client was right, but wishing that there was another option.

"I'm testifyin'," Black said. "I don't have a choice."

The lawyer nodded. Then he shook his client's hand and looked into his eyes like he was seeing him for the last time.

As the lawyer took his seat at the defense table, Black felt something inside of himself come alive. It felt like a loving touch, stroking his hair, whispering in his ear, singing him sweet lullabies, and protecting him from harm. Black closed his eyes and relished the familiarity of the feeling. And as realization burst onto the landscape of his mind, he quickly turned around in his chair.

Black feverishly scanned the spectators' seats, looking for the face he knew must be there. And when he saw her, the peace that engulfed him was indescribable. His mother's head was bowed. Her lips moved ever so slightly. He saw her lips form the word "amen." And when she looked up, their eyes met.

She smiled, and in that moment they both knew that God had brought him back from the dead. No matter what happened, he was alive again. They both mouthed the words "I love you." But before Ruth Jackson could make her way toward the defense table, the judge reentered the courtroom.

Everyone stood, and it seemed that the judge's flowing robes shed a black pall over the entire room. Everything about the day became darker as he took his seat. Perhaps it was because Black knew that he was about to expose his entire life to the scrutiny of the twelve people in the jury box. Or perhaps it was the knowledge that he would be tried on the events of a lifetime, and not just the events of that night. Whatever it was, Black was suddenly stricken with an uncontrollable fear.

As his body shook against the seat of his wheelchair, he hoped that no one noticed the salty streams of moisture that popped from his forehead and rolled quickly down his face.

Black reached for a tissue to wipe away the sweat, and there was a rustling sound at the back of the courtroom.

"Your Honor, the defense would like to call another witness to the stand."

As the lawyer spoke, the judge's eyes shifted to the back of the room. The rustling grew louder as a young woman squeezed past the two sheriff's deputies who were guarding the door.

"The defense would like to call . . ."

The lawyer stopped as he sensed, along with everyone else, that there was a presence in the room that hadn't been there before.

The jurors' eyes went to the back of the courtroom. Black saw recognition dawn on some of their faces. It was her, they seemed to say to themselves. It was the young woman whom no one had seen since she was released from police custody following the shooting at the train station.

It was the old man's missing granddaughter; the missing link between the reality of Podres's murder and the fantasy of a drug-fueled escape from a world of conspiracy and intrigue.

The sound of voices followed her path to the front of the room, growing from a soft murmur to a steady hum as the sound of her name blew in behind her like a wind urging her forward.

They whispered it, almost in unison, until the sound of it reached Black's ears and snatched him from the grips of his life's most frightening moment.

"Clarisse."

The sound of it settled into his ears again and again.

"Clarisse."

The defense attorney turned around and looked at her as she walked regally down the aisle, slowly pressing toward the defense table with a swaying gait that seemed to tick away the seconds as they all waited to hear the only story left to tell.

Black turned around, and in an instant, his mind and his heart joined hands and carried him back to the train station. It was like he was there again, filled with all the hope he'd held for their future. And free of all the pain he'd shared from his past. He was there again, draped in the love that propelled him back to her when she was taken by Morgan. All of the memories converged and brushed softly against him, like the whispers that carried her name across the room.

As the sweat that dripped from his forehead leaped into his eyes and turned to tears, he was filled to overflowing, until her name burst from his lips.

"Clarisse," he said aloud, and the evidence of his love for her spilled over from his eyes and trickled down the sides of his face.

She smiled almost imperceptibly as she stood in the middle of the aisle and waited for what they all knew must come next.

"The defense would like to call . . ."

Black's lawyer looked at him and Black nodded his approval.

"The defense would like to call Clarisse Williams."

Clarisse walked through the wooden swinging gate in front of the courtroom and made her way to the witness stand. She stated her name, then looked at Black and breathed deeply as the lawyer asked her the question that was burning in everyone's mind.

"Where have you been, Miss Williams?"

"I . . ." She paused for a moment and composed herself. "After the police told me that I wouldn't be charged in the shooting and released me, I went to work as a live-in nurse for a man in Delaware. He died about a month ago and I came back to Philadelphia. But I didn't want to come forward too quickly. I knew I had to wait for the right time."

She looked at Black for a split second and her eyes were like mirrors, reflecting the love he felt for her. He saw it looking out at him, absorbing him. And he knew in that moment that she loved him, too.

"I wouldn't be alive today if it wasn't for Everett," she said. "He could've walked away from me in that train station. He could've turned his back and left me there to die with Morgan. He could have gotten away from this."

She swept her hand through the air, indicating the courtroom.

"But he turned around. He came back for me. The only other people who've ever done that were the Scotts."

She looked toward the back of the room at Eldridge Scott, who'd attended every day of the trial since he'd testified. Her eyes offered him an apology. He nodded his acceptance. No words ever passed between them. There was no need for words.

"And why are you here today, Miss Williams?" the lawyer said, prompting her.

Clarisse fixed her gaze on the lawyer. "I came back to fight for him. I'm not going to let anyone hurt him again."

Her breath came in gasps and her chest heaved up and down like she'd been saving up those words for the past year. Then she looked at Black, and a single tear rolled down her cheek. "Nobody is ever going to hurt you again."

"Objection, Your Honor," the prosecutor said, jumping up from her seat. "This testimony is irrelevant."

The judge glared at her. The prosecutor looked up at the judge, and then at the jurors, and she knew that everyone in the room was caught up in the emotion that ran between Clarisse and Black. So she took her seat and hoped that irrelevance was the only thing Clarisse had to offer.

"Objection overruled," the judge said slowly, pronouncing each syllable in a deep resonating voice that was as much a warning as anything else.

Then he turned to the defense attorney. "I'm going to need this witness to get to the point of her testimony, Counselor. But you may proceed with your questioning."

"Thank you, Your Honor," the lawyer said, looking over his shoulder at Black and hoping that Clarisse had something other than passionate words to defend him.

"Miss Williams, you said earlier that you were waiting for the right time. Waiting for the right time for what?"

Clarisse pulled a cassette tape from the folds of her dress. "I was waiting for the right time to come forward with this tape," she said. "This is a tape of Darnell Thomas speaking with Detective Hillman about the Podres shooting."

There was a flurry of voices as the spectators and the jury realized that Latoya Thomas's tape was indeed real. The judge had to bang his gavel to quiet the room.

Black's lawyer allowed for a dramatic pause, then asked a question whose answer was obvious. "Why didn't you come forward earlier with this tape?"

"I was afraid," Clarisse said emphatically. "People have died over this tape."

"And how did you get the tape, Miss Williams?"

"Lieutenant Morgan had this tape in his pocket at the train station. When he was shot, the tape fell out of his pocket, slid across the platform, and landed right in front of me. I picked it up. I don't know why. Something just said take it. I didn't know at the time what was on it. But once I found out, I kept it to myself because I was afraid."

She lowered her eyes and turned the tape over in her hands.

"But I can't be afraid anymore," she said, looking over at the jury. "Everett is sitting there paralyzed, waiting to be sentenced to death because he couldn't leave me behind. The least I can do now is stand up with the truth and hope that it's enough to save his life."

The lawyer looked at the judge. "With your permission, Your Honor, I'd like to have this tape admitted as defense exhibit A and play it for the jury."

The judge paused. "This is an unusual request. But I'm going to allow it since this tape was mentioned in earlier testimony."

The judge directed the bailiff to find a cassette player and plug it into the sound system. When he did, Clarisse passed the tape to the bailiff, and he played it.

Latoya Thomas's voice blared over the speakers.

"Darnell, this man is a detective. He's going to ask you some questions. It's my duty to inform you that you don't have to answer anything that you feel may incriminate you."

Her voice was followed by the haunting sound of Butter speaking out from beyond the grave. "He had on a bracelet."

Detective Hillman's voice was next. "Who had on a bracelet?"

"It was a white man with a big gold bracelet. A link bracelet. Rock took the gun and tried to shoot him, but he missed.

The white man pulled back the curtain and . . . It was the white man."

"What was the white man?"

Then Latoya's voice.

"Don't say anything else, Darnell. Save it for the preliminary hearing."

Butter spoke again, apparently ignoring his sister's advice.

"He had on a white shirt and black pants. He was tall, with blond hair and blue eyes. And he had on this big link bracelet."

"And what did the white man do?"

"He shot the Puerto Rican. He reached out from behind that curtain and shot the Puerto Rican. It was dark. 'Cause I blew out the candles after the Puerto Rican pulled out his gun. We was gon' rob him, but we couldn't really get the gun away from him. And when Rock finally got it and tried to shoot him, he missed. But the white man didn't. He aimed straight at his head and slumped him. Then he ran out the back door."

"Where was Leroy?"

"I heard Leroy, but I ain't see him. I think he was just comin' in when everything jumped off."

"How about Black?"

"I ain't see him, either."

The sound of a door opening, and then another voice, apparently a nurse, came over the speakers.

"That's enough for now. All of you are going to have to leave."

There was a clicking sound as the tape was stopped, and then a three-second hiss, then nothing.

When the tape finished playing, the jurors exchanged glances. Some of them looked down at the floor. But their eyes all eventually rested on Black. He returned their stares full-on, knowing that they were looking into his eyes to find the guilt that they would never see.

Clarisse sat up in her chair and looked across the room, across space and time, and into a place deep inside of Black that no one else could touch. She looked down into his soul and brought forth the hope he had never dreamed of and the love he had never felt.

And there he was, exposed for all the world to see, his humanity pouring out in an endless stream of tears, cleansing him of all his fear and hatred, preparing him to love her for more than just a lifetime.

Black went through the rest of the proceedings in a daze. When the jury went to deliberations, he didn't see them. When they came back, he didn't hear them. And when the "not guilty" verdict was read, he was oblivious.

The only thing he could feel—the only thing he wanted to feel—was Clarisse. As she took the handles of his chair and rolled him out into the bright sunshine, she settled down into the place he had reserved for her in his heart, filling in the final piece of his puzzle.

"I love you," she whispered, and the words echoed in his mind for what seemed like an eternity.

Black felt his dead loins grow warm as the sound of her voice poured down through his ears like syrup, replacing the hard clank of the prison doors he'd come to know so well. And as he looked up to the clouds that swirled against the expanse of the midday sky, he knew that he would never again indulge the cloud that danced provocatively through the hollow glass tube.

Because Clarisse had finally set him free from his pipe dream.

About the Author

SOLOMON JONES is a staff writer for the *Philadelphia Weekly*. He is a native of Philadelphia, where he lives with his wife. He is currently working on his next novel. For more information, visit www.solomonjones.com.